THROUGH
DARKEST
ZYMURGIA!

Also by
William H. Duquette

Vikings at Dino's

Very Truly Run After
(forthcoming)

Praise for
Vikings at Dino's

THROUGH DARKEST ZYMURGIA!

⌣∴⌣

A Ripping Yarn

by William H. Duquette

ZYMURGIA
HOUSE

Glendale, California
ZymurgiaHouse.com

ZYMURGIA
HOUSE

Glendale, California
ZymurgiaHouse.com

Printed in the United States of America

First Printing, 2017

ISBN 978-0-69285-383-2

Cover illustration:
Jason Bach, jasonbachcartoons.com

Cover and interior design:
Julie Davis, General Glyphics, Dallas, Texas

To Jane

AN EXPEDITION TO ZYMURGIA

by Leon Thintwhistle III, DMg.

꒓∴꒑

Being a narrative of the expedition
undertaken in the year 680
by Dr. Thintwhistle and his colleagues
Thomas Carbuncle and Dr. Thaddeus Philpott,
all of Glastonbury University,
of their explorations in the remote land of Zymurgia,
and of the divers incidents which occurred
on the journey there and back again.

TABLE OF CONTENTS

᠁

AUTHOR'S PREFACE

ᴗ∶ᴗ

READERS FAMILIAR with my accounts of my earlier travels with Thomas Carbuncle will recall that Mr. Carbuncle and I made a short foray into Zymurgia some years ago. Due to a lack of supplies and the onset of inclement weather, we spent fewer days there than we would have wished, but returned to our base in Seros, and thence ultimately home again. Happily, we were able to rectify matters on our most recent journey, an account of which the reader now has before him.

We present this volume in the hope that, by reading it, our audience will be as entertained and edified as we were by the experiences related herein.

Leon Thintwhistle III, DMg.
3 Oratory 682,
Glastonbury University

CHAPTER 1

◡⃪∶◠

The expedition is planned. ᖚ Dr. Philpott joins us.
A change of plans. ᖚ We set sail from Pelham Pond.

GLASTONBURY UNIVERSITY is filled with blessed peace for three months of each year, three months usually known as the summer hiatus. The students, whether industrious or indolent, disperse to their homes after Spring Exams and are not seen in quadrangle or classroom until the first lecture of Fall at the very earliest. Summer hiatus is therefore a sterling opportunity for weary academics to rest, relax, and pursue their scholarly interests—elsewhere.

For many years, my colleague Thomas Carbuncle and I have had the pleasant habit of traveling together during the months of the hiatus. Our journeys have been a fruitful source of raw material for our scholarly papers in mythogeography and applied phantastics, respectively, as well as for less formal but more lucrative accounts such as this one. As 680 began, and winter grew into spring, Carbuncle and I were therefore deeply involved in planning our summer outing.

On the afternoon I have in mind, Carbuncle and I had cancelled our afternoon lectures and were seated before the fire in his University lodgings, sipping sherry. Drizzle shrouded the quadrangle outside Carbuncle's window (the statue of "Woody" Grenville was barely visible through the mist), and we congratulated ourselves on escaping the clammy interiors of Sambridge and Nortingon Halls.

We were in deep contention over our destination. I favored the south shore of the Lyricum Peninsula, while Carbuncle preferred the mountain lakes of High Bastille. A compromise was visible in the distance, perhaps a glass of sherry or so away, when the speaking orb whistled. Carbuncle hastened to answer it. I sipped placidly until his return.

"Leon, have you ever heard of a Dr. Thaddeus Philpott? Apparently he's in the vestibule and would like to come up and see us."

"Never have I heard the name," I said. "Does he claim acquaintance?" Carbuncle returned to the orb, and after a muttered discussion with the porter said, "Only with our work. He seems quite complimentary."

"Then bring him on, Thomas, bring him on," I said, for the sherry and the fire had put me in an expansive mood.

The porter knocked gently a few moments later, and Dr. Philpott entered; he was a tall, tweedy sort of fellow, with spectacles. Carbuncle got him a sherry, and I showed him to a fine chair by the fire, indicating the plate of biscuits. He thanked us most graciously, and when we all were settled comfortably Carbuncle asked, "And so, Dr. Philpott, to what do we owe the pleasure of your visit?"

"Why, any scholar, such as myself, could not help but wish to meet the famed Thintwhistle and Carbuncle!" I glanced quizzically at Carbuncle. This was not an attitude widely shared by the faculty at Glastonbury, nor, perhaps, by the students. "I am on sabbatical, visiting Glastonbury University, and I wished to acquaint myself with you as soon as possible. The things you have done for the study of ethnomonotony are simply indescribable." Philpott beamed at us.

"Ethnomonotony, you say?" I frowned slightly. "I fail to see the connection."

"Ah, but the ethnomonotonist's work begins where the mythogeographer's ends. Without men such as yourself exploring far-off countries and bringing them into the realm of the day-to-day, ethnomonotony would soon become a dull field. We would be reduced to writing footnotes, and squabbling over trivialities. Thanks to you, however, there are ever new fields of endeavor." I lifted my glass to him, and Carbuncle hastened to refill it.

"As for phantastics," Philpott continued, "classification of a country's phantasmagoria is one of the ethnomonotonist's primary tasks—an easy one where men such as you have passed, Mr. Carbuncle." Carbuncle smiled, and wagged his head. Like many phantasticists, he is more comfortable with phantasms than with people, and compliments embarrass him. "I still remember your analysis of the phantasmagoria needed to build the monuments and temples of Seros. Superb!" I raised my eyebrows, and he hastened to add, "Assuming, of course, that they ever were built, as such, Dr. Thintwhistle. I'm well aware that this is still a matter of some controversy among mythogeographers." I nodded, pleased.

"It's very kind of you to say these things, Dr. Philpott," I said, "and I am glad to make your acquaintance." At this, Carbuncle nodded. "Is there anything I or Carbuncle can do to make your stay at Glastonbury more pleasant?"

His eyes shone (or perhaps it was the fire on his spectacles), and then he looked down for a moment. He hesitated, and then said, "Summer is fast approaching, Dr. Thintwhistle, and I will have no teaching duties until fall. I understand that it is your custom to undertake an expedition each summer, and I have greatly hoped that I might be permitted to come along. I have a tidy income, and would be glad to contribute to the costs."

"What a capital idea," I said, filled with a glow of warmth for humanity, "simply capital. Why, Carbuncle and I were just discussing our plans when you arrived. We'd be glad to hear your views."

"And where are you planning to go this year?" he asked, moving to the edge of his overstuffed chair. "Seros? Anselms? Or perhaps the long overdue return to Zymurgia?"

"Actually, we were contemplating staying closer to home this year," I said. "I'm in favor of the Lyricum Peninsula, but Carbuncle's plumping for High Bastille."

"Lyricum?" said Philpott, owlish in his surprise. "I'd have thought that Lyricum would have little to offer a mythogeographer by this time."

"You'd be surprised," I said. "There must be hundreds of streets and avenues—"

"—and taverns and inns!" interrupted Carbuncle.

"Yes, and taverns and inns we have not yet explored. As a scientist, it is my duty to leave no corner unturned. And in addition, the Grand Opera of Lyricum is performing the entire *Rigatoni Cycle* this year. It's an event not to be missed."

"Ah, I see," said Philpott, who plainly didn't. "And High Bastille? No one lives there but sheep and rockhounds. What possible interest can it have to a phantasticist?"

"Sheep, and rockhounds, yes," relied Carbuncle, "but you've forgotten the snapping trout. If you don't consider angling for snapping trout with nothing but a few yards of thin line, some colored thread, and a barbed hook to be an exercise in applied phantastics, I'm afraid you don't truly understand the subject."

"Oh, yes, of course, I see your point," said Philpott, and perhaps this time he did.

"We were approaching a compromise when you arrived," I said. "If we were to spend just the first six weeks of the hiatus in High Bastille, we could reach Lyricum Town in time for the performance of Rotini's masterpiece, *La Profiterole*. I'm told it's sure to be delightful."

"What's your view, Dr. Philpott?" asked Carbuncle. "Perhaps you'd rather spend the whole summer exploring the brooks and trout streams of High Bastille?"

"On the other hand, the sublime pleasures of Lyricum's south shore in the month of Melee are not to be discounted," I said.

"I regret to say that neither is what I had expected," he said, downcast. "Are you sure Zymurgia is out of the question? Even a trip to Seros would hold great interest."

"I am afraid not, Dr. Philpott. I am no longer as young as I once was, and I fear my taste for adventure has decreased. You are still quite welcome to join us, however."

Shortly after this, Philpott glanced at the artificial sun dial on the mantel, and, exclaiming at the time, left us, pleading a dinner engagement. "A pity," said Carbuncle, "A likable fellow, I thought, if imperfectly well acquainted with phantastics."

"But quite sound on MG," I said. "And the extra funds would have been useful."

I thought no more of Philpott until the next morning, when I received a summons to see the Dean of Faculty at his earliest possible convenience. Entering the Dean's antechamber, I was surprised to see that Carbuncle had preceded me. "Old Nufty sent for you, too, eh?" I said, ignoring the secretary's disapproving glance. "I wonder what's in the wind?" Carbuncle shrugged as the secretary said, "Dr. Nuftison will see you now."

Nufty scowled at us as we entered his dark-paneled sanctum. The dean is a large man, and his desk, chair, and office were built to a similar scale. The effect was calculated to convert any casual visitor into a cringing supplicant in a few seconds.

"Gentlemen," he said, "I am shocked to discover that you have been neglecting your teaching duties for the sake of planning a pleasure trip."

"Pleasure trip? What nonsense is this, Eddie?" (He hates to be called Eddie.)

"This nonsense of Lyricum and High Bastille!"

"Nonsense?" I exclaimed. "There remains much to be done in Lyricum. Why, there must be hundreds of streets and avenues—"

"And taverns and inns!" interrupted Carbuncle, and Nufty and I both stopped to glare at him.

"As for High Bastille," I said, "the scope for phantastics experiments is simply amazing." I eased Carbuncle off of my foot as I continued, "I'm afraid that anyone who doesn't consider angling for snapping trout with nothing but a few yards of thin line, some colored thread, and a barbed hook to be an exercise in applied phantastics, doesn't truly understand the subject." Nufty and Carbuncle both glared at me, and too late I remembered that, prior to his exaltation, Old Nufty had been head of the Theoretical Phantastics department.

"It surely would be amazing to one as ignorant as I, Dr. Thintwhistle. I would gladly be enlightened. And yet I have seen no papers on the topic from Mr. Carbuncle, nor any from you on the mythogeography of Lyricum."

"Well, of course not, Eddie, our research is hardly complete!"

"But didn't the two of you visit Lyricum and High Bastille last summer?" I admitted we had.

"And wasn't it Lyricum and High Bastille the year before that?"

"Actually, it was High Bastille and Lyricum that year," said Carbuncle, helpfully.

"And didn't you write your seminal papers on Anselms and Seros after a mere three months of investigation?"

"Oh, indeed we did, Eddie, indeed we did. But Lyricum is a much older, more complex, more settled place than Anselms or Seros, you know. Why, there must be hundreds of streets—"

"Hundreds of streets which perhaps are adequately explored each year by hundreds of Anglish visitors?" Nufty raised an eyebrow.

"Rank amateurs, Eddie, rank amateurs." I scoffed in derision.

"And wasn't the annual meeting of the Royal Mythogeographic Society held in Lyricum last spring, thus giving ample opportunity to seasoned professionals?" Having no useful response, I held my peace.

"I am forced to conclude, Gentlemen," he said, glaring at each of us in turn, "that you have been planning yet another pleasure trip at the expense of your duties. This is unacceptable. Tenure was designed to protect freedom of thought, gentlemen, not freedom from work. Push it too far, and you will see how far it stretches."

This was very bad. An academic of my standing, being threatened with loss of tenure! I asked Nufty what he proposed.

"I am sure you have completed sufficient research on Lyricum and High Bastille for your preliminary findings, at least, to be of interest. Consequently, I feel you should remain here at the university during the hiatus, and get them into shape for publication this fall." Carbuncle and I looked at each other. This was worse than I had feared. Summer in University! But Nufty continued.

"Of course, I would be willing to see these papers postponed if you were to undertake a more serious expedition this summer...to Zymurgia, perhaps. I had the pleasure of dining with the youngest son of the Earl of Luton yesterday evening; he expressed great interest in such an undertaking. I gather his father would foot the bill. Under such circumstances, the papers describing your Lyrican and Bastillian investigations might be postponed indefinitely." The dean smiled at us sardonically.

"This earling of yours," I hazarded, "Would he happen to rejoice in the name of Thaddeus Philpott?"

"Indeed, young Thaddeus told me he had made your acquaintance yesterday afternoon. His father is an old school friend of mine, and would be very grateful to the University if you could bring Thaddeus along. I am sure you understand."

When threatened in one meeting with loss of tenure and the dark necessities of university finance, it is wise to capitulate graciously. "I have, of course, been longing to return to Zymurgia," I said. "I know Carbuncle feels the same." Carbuncle nodded on cue. "We would have returned sooner, but for the difficulty and expense of putting together a first-rate expedition."

"I am sure that funds will be no constraint," said Nufty. "I am so glad we were able to come to an understanding." He cocked a warning eye as we rose and slipped towards the door. "Well, don't let me keep you any longer, as I know you have afternoon lectures to prepare for."

And so it was that on the Fifteenth of Scone our belongings, our supplies, and ourselves, with Philpott in tow, were assembled on the wharf at Pelham Pond, ready to embark on a voyage to darkest Zymurgia.

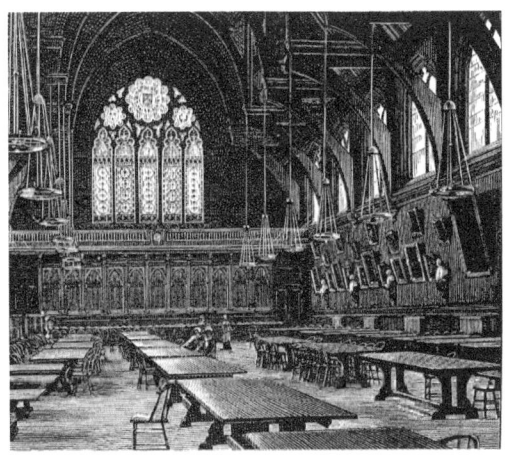

CHAPTER 2

⌒∶∽

The Sea-Spaniel. ?♥ Philpott's sincerity.
Equipment and supplies. ?♥ Life at sea.

WE EMBARKED at once, and wafted down the slow-moving Lees River from Pelham Pond to the Sea of Dogs. I should spend a few moments describing our craft, as the aptly-named *Sea-Spaniel* was to be our home and good friend for most of our journey. The *Spaniel*, as we called her, was a new craft, large, well-appointed, and designed with the most modern techniques of Anglish phantasmagoria. She was equipped with two masts, and several suits of gossamer sails that allowed her to ride the ur-winds like the sailing ships of older days, but more usually she was driven over the water on a cushion of foam by powerful strokes of her phantail. This represented a great advance, and no sooner had we left the dock than Carbuncle had gone below to talk to the ship's phantasts, babbling about power ratios and ley-lines.

Meanwhile, Philpott and myself explored the upper decks. The staterooms were large and spacious, with running water and speaking orbs, and the central lounge was surprisingly luxurious. It was quite a vessel for a scholarly expedition, and I wondered how it had been paid for. The Earl of Luton's secretary had handled most of the arrangements, and it was in my mind that perhaps the *Spaniel* was the Earl's personal yacht. If so, Philpott gave no sign of it, exclaiming over each new discovery as eagerly as myself, and indeed never so much as mentioned his father's rank during the whole of the summer. He had shown nothing but surprise and delight at our change in plans, and Carbuncle and I were eventually forced to conclude that he knew nothing of his father's dealings with Dean Nuftison.

After settling into our quarters, we descended into the hold to take stock of the expedition's supplies. The earl, while careful to avoid any unwarranted expenditure, had nevertheless been open-handed, and we had everything important that we had asked for. To begin with, there was the *Spaniel* herself. She would be our

home and conveyance from Angland to the upper reaches of the
river Aram, which flows through the antique land of Seros. Even
then we would not leave her for long, making short forays into
Zymurgia, and then returning to the river to write up our notes.
In addition we had all the tools of the mythogeographer's trade:
pencils, paper, a number of transit compasses, and my especial
darling, a Hansen's geometer.

This invaluable device had been invented not many years
before, and in this short time had completely replaced all other
methods of determining position at sea and in strange lands...at
least, for those who could afford it. Gone are the days of naviga-
tion by the height of the moon and the transit of the sun! A few
minutes with the Hansen's geometer suffices to determine both
the direction and distance to the Observatory in Pelham to within
a few seconds of arc and a few yards of distance. This, combined
with a transit compass, is all the skilled mythogeographer needs
to construct accurate maps; and mapping, after all, is the heart
and soul of mythogeography. Fortunately, I had Carbuncle along
to operate the device; the use of any but the simplest kind of
phantasm is utterly beyond me, and I had already promised never
to touch the geometer, or the phantasmic equipment, or indeed,
even to pass the door of the Carbuncle's work room in his absence. I have been known to stop phantasms by my mere presence, and Carbuncle was taking no chances.

In addition to the scientific supplies and equipment, we of
course had sufficient food and drink for explorers and crew for
the expected duration of the sea-voyage, plus sufficient funds to
purchase anything we should run out of. I shall not often have to
speak of such things, save to say that Carbuncle and I had provided several dozen cases of the finest sherry and other dainties out
of our own pockets—pockets, of course, that did not have to foot
the bill for any of the rest of the trip. We projected that the sherry
would last at least a month and a half; after that, it appeared that
the *Spaniel* had a well-stocked wine-locker. Carbuncle judged the
locker's lock to be of no great consequence.

At first glance it may seem odd to bring an applied phantasticist along on a mythogeographic expedition, but I trust that the
practicality of such a choice has been made plain. An expedition
lives on its equipment, and Carbuncle it was that kept the various

phantasms in working order. Carbuncle, though an academician, is a man of his hands, and he relishes the chance to muck about with phantasms where his colleagues in the Theoretical Phantastics department can't see. But beyond this, there is a deeper rationale; after all, a mere phantast could be hired for the maintenance work, and on many expeditions would be.

Phantasmagoria vary from country to country, and indeed from town to town, even in the Known World. The phantasmagoria of a hitherto undiscovered culture can be strange indeed. Should we find such in Zymurgia, it would be up to Carbuncle to figure it out; and moreover how to use it and bring the techniques back to Angland. If the defining question of Theoretical Phantastics is, "Why ever did it do that?", that of Applied Phantastics is, "How can I make it do that again?" Carbuncle is an applied phantasticist in the best sense. His skills have been life-and-death on previous expeditions, and would be so again.

Shipboard life has a rhythm of its own, and we had settled comfortably into our daily routine before the *Spaniel* reached the mouth of the Lees. Carbuncle's days were occupied with the expedition's equipment, of course, and Philpott's were spent cramming cartography. Carbuncle and I had managed many previous outings without an ethnomonotonist, and though I know less of ethnomonotony than I do of phantastics it was hard to see how it could be useful to us. The expedition might be of great interest to Philpott in that capacity, but I saw no reason why he should not contribute more centrally. As a result, I had set him to studying the more basic texts on mythocartography: Carmichael's *Projective Dysplasia*, Eucalypt's *Geometry of Plains and Mountains*, and especially *A Short Course in Surveying*, by Petronius—still one of the best, despite its age. For variety, he also had available to him our past publications and notes on Seros and Zymurgia.

For my part, I spent the days walking the deck, conversing with Captain Halvorsen and his crew, watching the coast glide by, and, as I recall, napping a great deal.

In the evenings we would gather in the lounge after dinner for sherry and conversation. Philpott had (and has) a distressing tendency to talk shop on such occasions, but as he was, after all, in training, and as he played a skilled game of backgammon we forgave him this foible. On one particular evening, early in the voyage, he had been reading about position-fixing.

"It seems such a difficult task," he said, "that I'm surprised that maps get made at all. The height of the moon isn't so bad, at least at night and in clear weather, but how does one measure in the daytime? And even with good measurements, the results seem approximate at best."

"Ah," I said, "I had forgotten. The texts I've given you are the best on the subject, but they all predate the invention of the Hansen's geometer!" I was about to explain the uses of the geometer when Carbuncle interrupted me.

"Speaking of which, Leon," he said, "someone let it out of its box. I went below this morning, and found it scampering about the hold. It was greatly distressed, of course, but more than that, the fumble-fingered idiot who released it had gotten it completely out of adjustment. It took me the better part of the day to get it soothed and retuned." He eyed me as he spoke. "You will speak to the Captain again, won't you, and remind him that our equipment must not be disturbed?"

"Of course I will, Thomas, when next I see him." I privately resolved to check the latch more carefully in future, and changed the subject. "But surely, Philpott—"

"Thaddeus, please."

"Very well, Thaddeus, surely—"

"And actually, my friends call me Thad."

"Thad, then. And you may call me Leon. Now, surely, you haven't spent all day with Eucalypt and Petronius? Fundamental, but rather dry, don't you think?"

"But fascinating, sir,—"

"Leon," I said. Childish, I suppose.

"But fascinating, Leon. However, I spent most of the afternoon renewing my acquaintance with your own mythogeography text. Cartography is all very well, but I want to understand what I'm mapping."

"Laudable, indeed," I said, pleased. "Have you any questions I could help you with? Oh, and Thomas, the bottle stands by you." Philpott was silent as Carbuncle refilled our glasses and I set up the backgammon board, and he did not speak again until Carbuncle had beaten me three times running. I sometimes think that Thomas has an arrangement with the dice, though of course I would never say such a thing.

Finally Philpott pursed his lips, and said, slowly, "I'm afraid, Leon, that I still don't understand your previous plans for an expedition to the Lyricum Peninsula. It seemed to me then, and your own writing confirms it, that Lyricum is too well-visited to be an appropriate region of study. But perhaps I'm missing something."

"Only the joke, young Thaddeus," said Carbuncle. "Leon and I were contemplating a pleasure-trip, no more, this season."

"Then the hundreds of streets and avenues—"

"—And inns and taverns," winked Carbuncle.

"—are adequately well-explored by hundreds of Anglish visitors," I finished, "as Dean Nuftison was so quick to remind me. No, Lyricum is very much a part of the Known World, and its character and identity firmly fixed in place. Thousands of people visit it each year, and the glory of Lyrican wines and Lyrican opera are a byword from Pelham to Plum Street. It offers no interest to the serious mythogeographer."

"But then, why go?"

"One can't always be a serious mythogeographer, Thad. Those hundreds of streets and avenues, yes, and inns and taverns, Thomas, have been adequately explored, but not by me. And then, of course, there is the Grand Opera of Lyricum. Tell me, Thad, have you ever been to the opera?" I glanced at him quizzically.

"Why, no. This is my first trip away from England."

"Well, then," I said. "I understand that we will be stopping at Lyricum Town in a few days to restock and take on phantail fodder. The Captain had planned to remain only a few hours, but I see no harm in making a full day of it. The weather has been so fine that we are ahead of schedule, and as the Dean was kind enough to cancel our fall classes, we are in no great hurry."

"But shouldn't we use our good fortune to get to Zymurgia that much earlier?"

"Oh, no one will begrudge a short layover in Lyricum Town. Think of it as an opportunity for some fieldwork. Lyricum may be a closed book to me, professionally, but it's a ripe field for the ethnomonotonist. The opera, alone, is a remarkable phenomenon. I happen to know that Rotini's *Chianti* will be performed during our visit; perhaps you'd care to join me? It's your best opportunity to see the Lyricans in their natural habitat." That persuaded him, as I knew it would. Fieldwork and pleasure seldom mix, but when they do the result is irresistible even to the most disciplined researcher. Philpott, having never before left Angland, was, as they say, a pushover.

And so it was settled: we would spend a day and a night in Lyricum Town. It would be our last taste of high culture for many months, and I, at least, intended to enjoy it fully.

CHAPTER 3

⤜⋅⤏

Lunch at La Mortadella ⁊ A day in Lyricum Town.
We recruit a new member.

LYRICUM TOWN sits at the extreme southern tip of the Lyricum Peninsula, as it has done for thousands of years. Its position on the shore of the sheltered Bay of Biscotti makes it a natural harbor, secure from the winter storm surge; its position at the center of the Sea of Dogs makes it a natural center of trade. A fishing village at the rise of the Paloman Empire, it soon became the chief port of entry for Serosan grain, and the prop of the Imperium. The Palomans had little use for the sea, however, and it was over a thousand years before Lyricum Town, now in truth a wealthy and prosperous city, became the commercial and political capital of all Lyricum.

It is a distinctive city, perhaps because it is built in no one style. Classical temples with their vaults and fluted porticoes sit by Orthic cathedrals from the time of the Regeneration. Palatine villas are cheek-by-jowl with Neo-Orthic hotels and civic buildings. The harbor district has the finest collections of Grottic warehouses in the Known World, lined up in ranks along the wharf.

That line of warehouses shone under a fine yellow sun as we entered the Bay of Biscotti. It was midmorning on the 22nd of Scone, and the Bay was filled with shipping. More kinds of craft than I can name lined the long wooden docks or sat at moorings out in the bay. We floated at the point of entry for some time as we waited for the harbor pilot. I was resigned to a distant mooring and a long pull in the ship's boat to the wharf, but Captain Halvorsen told me not to worry. He had a few quiet words with the pilot, and somehow dock-space was found for us near the center of the row of docks, just a hundred yards from the mouth of the Dolce Vita. Again I was led to wonder about the connection between the *Spaniel* and the Earl of Luton.

The work of Lyricum Town is done on the docks and in the warehouses, but its life is lived in the neighborhoods surrounding the Promenade, which is the square where the Dolce Vita intersects the Via Palazzo. Upon reaching dock, accordingly, I gathered up Carbuncle and Philpott and hailed a caleza. Soon we were skimming down the broad, tree-lined avenue which runs, straight as an Anglish ruler, from the harbor to the sleepy village of Paloma, a hundred miles to the north. As it was nearing midday I proposed that we should lunch at La Mortadella, a splendid restaurant on the Promenade, and then wander through the stalls and barrows of the Market district. In the meantime, I settled back into the caleza's leather upholstery to enjoy the sights and sounds of a summer's day in Lyricum Town.

Presently I noticed that young Philpott seemed in the grip of some kind of intermittent seizure. He would bob his head up, turning in his seat at as he stared at a wagon of freshly caught fish or a dockworker in pantaloons and rope sandals, and then he would huddle down over something in his lap for a few moments. The process repeated every few seconds.

"Philpott," I shouted, for the rush of air made conversation difficult, "What in the name of Prudentius are you doing?"

"Taking notes, sir," he shouted back, without ceasing his activity. "I don't want to forget anything."

"Well, I do wish you'd stop, you're giving me the twitch." Clearly, Philpott was taking his fieldwork too seriously.

In due course, however, we reached the Promenade, with its cafes and Pineapple Fountain. The caleza driver brought his beasts to a halt directly in front of La Mortadella. Had we more time, I would gladly have explored a few more of those hundred streets and avenues and taverns and inns, but under the circumstances I was inclined to be choosy. La Mortadella's offerings exceed anything to be found anywhere in Angland.

As the others were shown to a table, I sought and was granted the use of the restaurant's speaking orb. My arrangements were quickly made, and I soon joined them for an excellent lunch of monteverdi alfredo. We finished with a capital bottle of Don Giovanni; the vineyards of the Lyricum Peninsula are justly famous. I should perhaps be more precise, as befits a scholar; Carbuncle and I finished with a capital bottle of Don Giovanni. Philpott lunched with a good appetite, but then resumed his bobbing and scribbling.

"What, young Thaddeus," said Carbuncle, "You're not having any wine with us?"

"Hmmm? Oh, no, not today."

"The Don Giovanni doesn't suit your fancy?" I asked. "How about some Vivaldi, then?"

"What? Oh, no, thank you," said Philpott. "I mustn't."

"Mustn't? And why not, young Thaddeus?" asked Carbuncle.

"It's all right for the two of you," said Philpott. "This is just a pleasant excursion for you. But this is my first chance at some real fieldwork. Drinking wine could only erode my scholarly detachment."

"Well, it's a pity, so it is," said Carbuncle. "You'll not taste a wine like this until we pass this way again on the homeward voyage."

After lunch we parted. Carbuncle went off to visit an old friend of his, a maker of precision phantasms. "They'd call him a work-a-day phantast back at the University, but he's the finest craftsman I know," he said. "I want to try out some ideas on him. I'll see you both back at the *Spaniel* tonight."

"You won't be joining us for the opera?" asked Philpott.

"Ask him," Carbuncle replied as he sauntered off, smiling. "He'll never have gotten a seat for me." And it was true; I hadn't. Nor does Carbuncle require that I catch, clean and cook snapping trout when we visit High Bastille, though I'm quick enough to eat them.

As Philpott and I strolled across the Promenade, I pointed out the Grand Opera House, the Hall of Merchants, and other prominent buildings. Philpott had found it hard to take notes standing up, and was now bobbing and kneeling every few steps.

"Philpott, please, do stop that. It hurts me just to watch you. And anyway, people are staring."

He stopped, one knee on the tiles, pencil in hand, and gazed at me owlishly through his spectacles. "But I don't want to miss anything."

"Miss anything? You've hardly seen anything! How many blocks of warehouses did we pass on the Dolce Vita?"

"Um...seven?"

"Three. How many triumphal arches did we drive under?"

"Two?"

"Four. What was the color of our waiter's mustache?"

"Brown?" he asked, biting his lip.

"What an unkind thing to say! Our waitress was no beauty, but she had no trace of a mustache either," I said, pulling him to his feet. "Now close your notebook and open your eyes. And keep one hand on your wallet, if you wish to keep it," I added, for we had reached the mouth of the Market district.

Lyricum Town is a center of trade, and the goods that are stored in bales in the warehouses and sold in shiploads in the Hall of Merchants are available in smaller quantities in the Market district. Carpets and coffee from Seljurkia, inlaid boxes and blankets from Eporus, spices from the no-longer-so-fabulous lands of the east, and household phantasms from my own Anglish homeland; all were available, along with wines, breads, fresh fruits and vegetables, and were we so inclined, less pardonable things.

Persuading Philpott to close his notebook was a mixed blessing. On the one hand, he was no longer a source of eye-and-neck strain; on the other, he now had the leisure to make his observations verbally. I suppose I was fortunate that, knowing no Lyrican, he was forced to speak Anglish.

"Look at how friendly everyone is," he said, smiling at each stallholder in turn, "All smiling and waving at us."

I took his arm, not accidentally stepping on the foot of a small boy with light, experienced fingers. "Of course they are smiling at us, it's good for business."

"Oh," he said, "I'm sure it's more than that. Look at that one, waving at us to come and sit down with him."

"He's a tea seller," I said, not letting go. "One doesn't sit down unless one is willing to taste his wares, and ultimately to buy a pound or so. He's friendly, all right, at least until you try to get up without paying."

"Really? How mercenary!"

"This is the Market district, after all. What did you expect?"

In this way we passed the afternoon. I bought a few bags of oranges and other treats, and Philpott bought a large dog while my back was turned. I'm not entirely sure how it happened, and Philpott's explanation was unenlightening. I gather he saw the dog, a handsome black retriever, and knelt down to scratch it behind the ears. A man smiled at him, and said something in Lyrican, and

Philpott smiled back, and said "What a fine dog," or something of the kind, and the man smiled more broadly, and asked a question in Lyrican, and Philpott said, "Yes, what a fine dog indeed," nodding, I suppose, and the man held out his hand, and Philpott stood, and shook it, and then turned to go. Or so I gather. The first I knew of it was a high-pitched "Dr. Thintwhistle!" When I turned, a burly stallholder had Philpott backed against the wall; the stallholder held the dog's leash in one hand and was rubbing the first two fingers of the other against his thumb. He must have looked quite fierce to young Philpott.

"What seems to be the trouble, my friend," I inquired in Lyrican.

"This man is the trouble," the stall holder said in the same language. "Two-hundred fiacres he owes me for this fine hunting dog."

"I'm sure it's just a misunderstanding, my friend. Philpott here doesn't speak Lyrican, you know."

"Misunderstanding, bah! He understood enough to make a deal with me. We shook hands on it."

"Oh, dear," I said in Anglish, and turned to Philpott. "Did you shake hands with him."

"Yes," he said, looking from me to the stallholder and back again, "Yes, I did."

"I'm afraid there's no help for it then, Thad. You owe the man two-hundred fiacres."

"For what?" He still looked puzzled.

"For the dog, of course."

"But I don't want a dog!"

"Evidently you do, or you wouldn't have shaken hands with this gentleman. Get out your wallet."

It was gone, of course. I paid the man myself, and stopped him as he was removing the dog's collar. "Just a moment, my friend," I said. "Two-hundred fiacres is an absurd price for a dog, no matter how fine it is."

"We shook hands on it," he replied.

"And so you did, and so you have your two-hundred fiacres. And so we have our dog, and his collar, and his leash."

"Twenty fiacres for the collar and leash,"

"Come now, my friend…I am sure the Hall of Merchants takes a poor view of fleecing foreign visitors quite so flagrantly. Were I not teaching my young friend here an important lesson in ethnomonotony, I'd still have my two-hundred fiacres, and you'd still have your dog."

"Very well." He glowered at me as he handed me the end of the leash.

"I'm sure the dog is healthy; nevertheless, what is your name," I asked, "In case I should need to find you tomorrow?"

"Bruno," he answered, scowling—a scowl that would last only, I was sure, until we were out of sight.

"Well, now," I said, in Anglish, to Philpott. "Let's take Bruno here back to the *Spaniel*. Captain Halvorsen can't very well complain about sailing with a dog on a dog on the Sea of Dogs, now can he?"

"I guess not," said Philpott, taking the leash and scratching Bruno behind the ears once more. "He's a fine dog, after all. A retriever like this is hard to find. I wonder where that man got him."

"He stole him, of course. Some rich man's kennels are a dog short today," I said, as we turned toward the harbor. Bruno fell into step beside Philpott.

"Shouldn't we try to return him, then?"

"After paying two-hundred fiacres for him? Surely you jest."

We hailed a caleza after regaining the Promenade and spun back along the Dolce Vita to the *Spaniel*. Bruno stretched out his head, as dogs will, and let his tongue flap in the breeze of our passage, barking at the other calezas. It was only fair play, as I'm sure the passengers of the other calezas were commenting equally on the two Anglish madmen with their dog.

CHAPTER 4

꒦:꒷

A night at the Opera.

O N REACHING the *Spaniel* I quickly handed Bruno into the care of the steward, an excellent and most unflappable man, and we hurried to dress for the opera. My first act on reaching La Mortadella had been to call my old school chum, Sir John Bertram, now serving as Her Majesty's Ambassador to Lyricum. He was immediately able to procure an excellent box at the Grand Opera, on the understanding, I think, that I wouldn't visit him at the embassy to reminisce about old times. I suppose Ambassador Sir John Bertram has little to say to Johnnie "Pig's Knee" Bertram at that.

After an excellent ship-board dinner, the steward having also visited the Market district that afternoon, we boarded a gilt coach-and-four sent by Sir John, and returned to the Promenade. I must say, I had never conducted an expedition in such style; not least of the *Spaniel's* luxuries was sufficient space for such fripperies as proper evening dress. On the way, Philpott asked me what to expect.

"Your first impression," I said, "will be of a gaudy over-decorated hall, rather like a magnified version of this coach. Your second will be of hundreds of over-dressed people, each striving to out do the other, and utterly failing to out do the hall itself. On one side is the stage, which will be hidden by a scarlet curtain. On the other three sides are many elegant boxes, each with its own group of overdressed people. On the floor are the stalls, where sit those who actually want to see the opera."

"Then what do the people in the boxes want?"

"To be seen by each other, of course," I said, as we reached the Grand Opera House. A footman rushed to open the coach and place a stool below the doorway. Another rushed to open the opera house door as we swept up the red carpet. A third, for a reasonable gratuity, undertook to escort us to our box. It was on the right hand side of the stage, about halfway back, on the second level, with a good view of the entire hall.

My description had, if anything, been understated. I had forgotten the gilt chandeliers, sparkling with thousands of glowing phantasms, the ornate gilt carvings (in the Bizarre style) which adorned the front of each box, and the careful lighting, so that the occupants of each box were clearly visible.

"My word," said Philpott, gazing into a box directly across from us, "Is that...is she...I say, Dr. Thintwhistle, is that legal?"

"That's just the style here, young Thaddeus," I said. "Her gown, while scandalous by Anglish standards, is not nearly as revealing as it looks from here, nor is it particularly outlandish by Lyrican standards. It's nothing compared to, say, the costume worn by that lovely lady in the box to the left."

"I'm afraid I don't see any difference, sir."

"Ah, but the gown worn by the lady on the left is considered quite daring, for it *is* as revealing as it looks."

"How can you tell?", Philpott asked, rising in his seat and craning his neck.

"Sit down, Philpott, everyone can see you gaping. Granted, they are here to be seen, but it's not considered polite to be seen looking. I can tell because the one on the left is Signorina Rosalina, and the one on the right is Signorina Lucia. If the lovely Lucia appeared in a cape and velvet slippers, Rosalina would forego the cape just to outdo her."

"Who are they that they can act so shamelessly, Dr. Thintwhistle?"

"Is it not obvious? They are ladies of negotiable affection."

"Ah, I see. Forgive me, sir, it did not occur to me. Prostitution is an accepted part of Lyrican culture, then?"

Once again I was glad that Philpott spoke no Lyrican, though from the raised eyebrows in the nearby boxes I fear some of our fellow opera goers spoke Anglish. "It's somewhat more complicated than that, Philpott."

"Is it?" He gazed into space for a moment, lips pursed. "If I were to walk around to their boxes, do you suppose they would talk to me for a few minutes?"

"Philpott, I am shocked at the very idea," I said, lightly. He blushed, but rallied.

"Dr. Thintwhistle, I have no intention of 'negotiating their affections,' as you so discreetly put it."

"Ah. Be that as it may, they won't see you."

"You think not? All I want is a few minutes of their time," he said.

"I know not. To a lady in their profession, time is affection. You must negotiate the one to gain the other. But that is irrelevant. Do you see the large man with silver hair, seated beside Signorina Rosalina?"

"The one dressed in russet and gold, into whose ear she is whispering?"

"Indeed. He sits at the head of the Council of Merchants. He is extremely wealthy, and doubtless that affected the negotiations. He will not wish to share his investment with an Anglish academic. I've no doubt his bodyguard is just on the other side of the box door. But this also is irrelevant. She would not speak to you anyway."

"Why not?"

"She has a contract with someone else at present. It would be unprofessional."

Philpott sat in silence for a time. He might have been studying the ceiling (gilt, with a variety of bizarre excrescences), but I knew better. Eventually, he came out with it.

"Dr. Thintwhistle, do you know, how would one enter into negotiations with such a professional? I presume the Signorinas would not object to selling their attention, rather than their affection."

"Philpott, have you ever been to the jewelry department at Eton's?" As he began to nod, I continued, "Never mind, of course you have. Do you know what they say about the prices there?" He shook his head. "Ah. They say, 'If you have to ask, you can't afford it.' Now hush, the music is beginning. Though we sit in a box rather than in the stalls, I really would like to hear the opera."

For the sake of those who do not remember the story of Rotini's *Chianti*, I offer this summary. It is considered a flawed masterpiece, for reasons which, I believe, will become clear as I continue; nevertheless, as the first opera of Rotini's renowned *Rigatoni Cycle*, it is an essential foundation.

In Act 1, we find Alberto Chianti poling his barge down a Lyrican canal toward the Bay of Biscotti. It is raining, and the arpeggios of rain are a poignant counterpoint to his glissandos of despondency and despair. He is a poor man, and unable to support his new wife; in desperation he has undertaken to bring the barge to harbor for a few pennies. The barge stops at a lock, and as Alberto waits for the lock to fill so that he can continue his journey he spies a glint of gold in the murky waters of the canal. Diving in at great hazard to his health, he retrieves a golden ring, which he places on his finger. Rising remarkably unsoiled from the dirty water, Alberto sings at great length about his changing luck and good fortune.

In Act 2, Alberto is hailed by a young woman on the bank of the canal. She is Sophia Rigatoni, the lock keeper's daughter, and she claims the ring as her own. If he will return it, she will marry him and be his always. Alberto calls to her leap aboard the barge, and she does so. They consummate their union (lyrically speaking) in a duet of great beauty and passion, and she claims the ring. Strangely loath to release it (and well-aware of his previous marriage), he refuses, and they struggle. At last he smothers her under a bale of cotton. Alberto hides Sophia's body under the bales of goods on the barge as he sings of his great love for the ring.

In Act 3, Alberto is hailed by Lucia Rigatoni, the lock keeper's second daughter. She claims the ring as her own, and says she will marry him and be his always. No wiser than Sophia, she comes aboard at his bidding, the union is consummated in song, and all is serene until she tries to take the ring from his finger as he sleeps. In the ensuing duet Alberto pushes Lucia over the side, and she is crushed between the bank and the barge. He pulls her from the water, singing of his ring, and hides her body beside her sister Sophia's.

These things run in threes, of course, and in Act 4 appears Antonia Rigatoni, the lock keeper's youngest daughter. She makes the same claim, and the same offer, she hops aboard, and so forth. She is somewhat brighter than her sisters and has brought a knife with her; it does her no good. Alberto stabs her with it, and hides her beside her two sisters.

The lock is finally full at the beginning of Act 5, and Old Rigatoni himself appears out of the lock keeper's hut. At first he hails Alberto as an honest bargeman, and they drink together, singing of the pleasures of wine, woman, and song. Worse for drink, Alberto sings that he is not just a bargeman but a collector of things of great beauty; has he not three treasures aboard his barge? Has he not this fine ring? Old Rigatoni questions Alberto about the ring, and Alberto lies, saying that it has been his always. At this the three slain women rise from the graves on the barge and denounce him. Old Rigatoni attacks Alberto at their urging, but is no match for the young man. Alberto throws him into the lock, and he is crushed by the water gate, and dies, but not before he curses Alberto (at great length) with eternal restlessness. He will feel at home nowhere, and everyone's hand will be turned against him so long as he retains the ring of the Rigatonis.

In Act 6, Alberto abandons the barge and returns home by the speediest route, yet finds that the spirits of the three slain women have preceded him. His wife is not best pleased. She curses him, though not so completely as old Rigatoni, and he is forced to kill her before she shouts and summons her father and brothers to do away with him.

In Act 7, Alberto comes to his senses for the first time in the entire opera, and reasons that eternal restlessness is no reason to eschew comparative safety. Fleeing his crimes, Alberto seeks out a remote valley in the Lundt mountains. Here he builds himself a fortress, vast and impenetrable, and wanders, day and night, to and fro, fondling the ring of the Rigatonis, and cursing any who would take it from him, as the spirits of those he has murdered fly about him and accuse him in shrieks and wails.

Critics of the *Chianti* feel that its greatest flaw is the introduction of logical thinking in the last act, especially after so promising a beginning. Nevertheless, the opera establishes the premise for all that comes after, and is therefore indispensable.

If the plot is flawed, the music is delightful—if repetitious. Who can forget the glissandos of Alberto's despair as he poles his barge down the canal; his duets with Sophia, Lucia, and Antonia, rising now in elegant glissandos of passion, counterpointed with the arpeggios of the rising water in the lock, lowering now in ugly violence as his lover is smothered, stabbed, or crushed; the boisterous glissandos of play and good fellowship Alberto sings with Old Rigatoni; or the threatening, wailing glissandos of the slain counterpointed by the arpeggios of rain on Alberto's fortress? Rotini was a young composer when he wrote the *Chianti;*

it is utterly amazing that one so young could do so much with glissandos and arpeggios. In his later years, even Rotini would not have attempted it.

The evening thus passed quickly and pleasantly. Philpott divided his time between watching the singers on the stage, asking me what was going on, and gazing thoughtfully at the Signorinas Rosalina and Lucia across the way. I foresaw potential complications on our return trip.

During the interval between acts four and five I saw a surprising sight; below us in the stalls was a man that I was sure I had seen swabbing decks on the *Spaniel*. He was neatly, if cheaply, dressed, and had a sailor's tan. I observed him periodically throughout the rest of the evening, and each time I looked he was on the edge of his seat, elbows on his knees, completely taken up by the opera.

At the opera's end, Philpott and I made our way down the stairs, out to the coach, and back to the *Spaniel*. I gave Captain Halvorsen orders to put to sea as soon as he deemed prudent, and retired to my cabin a happy man. No matter what happened in Zymurgia, the summer would not be a total loss. The *Chianti* was not *La Profiterole*, but it was opera, done in the grand Lyrican style. I settled into my bunk, expecting to awaken in a bright new morning, far out in the Sea of Dogs.

CHAPTER 5

⌣∶∾

Glissandos in the dark. ᷉ *A morning in jail.*

EARLY THE next morning, indeed, shortly after I retired, a banging on my cabin door woke me from a dream in which ghosts were shrieking and howling and harrying me from one end of the Known World to the other. The dream ended; the howling did not, as the steward was quick to point out when I stumbled to the cabin door. That excellent and most unflappable man was on the edge of being seriously flapped.

"It's the dog, Dr. Thintwhistle. He won't stop howling. The ship's kennels are empty except for him, and I suppose he's lonely."

"My goodness! The ship has kennels?"

"Why, of course, doctor. But I fear they are next to the crew's quarters. I'm afraid some of my less well-bred shipmates are in favor of throwing the poor beast overboard. Is there anything you can do?" He looked me in earnest.

I stifled a yawn. "He's Philpott's dog, I suppose. Why don't you run him up to Philpott's cabin? The two of them can bunk together."

The steward's eyes widened. "Oh, but Doctor...I couldn't do that."

"Why ever not? Would you rather ask Philpott to bunk in the kennels?"

"Very good, doctor. Thank you for your help." He set his teeth, adjusted the fit of his coat, and strode off, the picture of dismayed determination. I closed the door, and returned to bed.

The howling ending shortly after, and did not resume, though I believe I did hear, on the edge of sleep, a shriek of surprise.

Some time after dawn I was awakened by the orange light of dawn coming through my porthole. Usually I remember to draw the blinds before retiring, but it had been a long day and a longer evening. I arose and peered out of the port, fully expecting to see long swells and the coast in the far distance. To my surprise, we were still at the dock. I dressed in my shore-going clothes, to be safe, and went to find Captain Halvorsen.

I found him on the dock at the foot of the gangplank, conferring with a Town Messenger. Communications are as essential to
the merchant as to the general, and the Lyricum Town messenger
service was as good as that in Pelham. The messenger, instantly
recognizable in black cape and scarlet tights, bowed slightly and
withdrew a few steps as I approached.

"Ah, Dr. Thintwhistle. One of my men didn't return last
night; it appears he was arrested for brawling. Shall we retrieve
the sorry fellow now, or on our return trip?"

I judged from our presence at the dock that it had better be
now, and I so indicated. "Which man is it, Captain?"

"Hodgins," he said, "one of our deckhands."

"Tall?" I asked, "Sandy hair? Broken nose?"

"Yes, that's Hodgins." The captain turned back to the messenger. "Return to the Hall of Merchants and tell the magistrate
that I'll be along shortly." The messenger bowed and ran off
at speed.

"If it would not inconvenience you, Captain, I believe I would
like to accompany you." I had some inkling of what had happened, and it promised to be amusing. Accordingly the Captain
hailed a caleza, and we spun off along the Dolce Vita to the Promenade. The Dolce Vita perhaps deserves a better description than
I have given it so far.

The Dolce Vita is Lyricum Town in miniature. Perhaps one-
hundred yards in width, lined with palm trees on both side, it
runs through every part of the city, from the warehouses near the
harbor, through the tenements of the poorer districts and pala-
zzos and villas of the wealthier, to the civic center around the
Promenade. Traveling north from the Promenade, which we did
not do on this visit, is like taking the same trip in reverse, with
the cattle yards substituting for the harbor and the open country
and farmland substituting for the Bay of Biscotti. And indeed, the
same road, built originally by the conquerors of the Known World
for their legions, runs on in a straight line through fields, villages,
and lesser towns to the village of Paloma, drowsing amid its ruins
and its dreams of past grandeur. As one drives down it one sees
all of the inhabitants of Lyricum Town: the beggars in their rags,
the fisherman, the merchants in their gaudy robes and gaudier
coaches, the pretty girls in their gowns. It is a daily carnival, a

pageant of color and comedy, of the graceful and the grotesque. Yet today there was a hush over the boulevard, a sullen refusal to smile or to meet our eyes as we spun past.

An orange sun was high in the sky when we reached the Hall of Merchants. This surprisingly modern building (the previous hall had been destroyed by fire in 662) is the seat of Lyrican government, and includes in its vast bulk the law courts and the jails. We gave our names to the receptionist in the marble-paved lobby, and were soon met by the magistrate himself, Luigi Marconi. The might of Angland is a great help in foreign countries; I rather doubt a Lyrican captain would have received the same courtesy.

"Captain Halvorsen, Dr. Thintwhistle," said that worthy as he conducted us down the wide stone stairs to the cells, "You are both well known here in Lyricum Town, as in all the Known World. The Council of Merchants has no wish to make trouble for your expedition. But I am bound by my position and by my responsibility to the people of Lyricum Town to say that this is a serious matter, a very serious matter."

"A serious matter?" I asked. "I thought it was a simple tavern brawl. Hodgins is a sailor, after all, I'd have thought brawling was commonplace. Or have I missed something?"

Marconi drew himself to his full height, which left him still some inches below sea-level. "Dr. Thintwhistle, as a known lover of the arts I had thought you might understand. Insulting the great Rotini, especially at the beginning of the Summer Festival—it is nearly unforgivable."

I raised my eyebrows at this. "Insulted Rotini did he? Yet I saw him at the Grand Opera House last night." Now Captain Halvorsen raised his own eyebrows.

"As you say, Dr. Thintwhistle, the man has no excuse," said Marconi. "We will release him as a sign of our friendship with Angland, but he must return directly to your vessel, and must not leave it before your departure. Should the crowds discover who he is, there may be a riot. We should not wish to rebuild the Hall of Merchants so soon."

As we reached Hodgin's cell, Marconi gestured to the attending guard, who unlocked the door. Before Captain Halvorsen could speak, I caught his arm. "Allow me, Captain, if you will." He nodded his agreement.

"Come out, Hodgins, come out." The sailor rose from the bunk, and walked gingerly out of the cell. His neat shore-going togs were torn and bloody; I could smell beer and other less pleasant substances.

"You know who I am, Hodgins?" I asked.

"Yes, sir, you're Dr. Thintwhistle." Hodgins spoke with effort and a scowl.

"They tell me you insulted the Great Rotini, Hodgins. I saw you at the opera last night; what happened?"

"I stopped at a tavern near the wharf, sir. The *Chianti* is a long piece, as you know, sir, and I couldn't afford the prices at the opera house. It took most of my savings just to get in the door."

"I see, Hodgins; and then what."

"Well, sir, the tavern was filled with Lyrican sailors. I speak Lyrican fluently, sir, having been taught by my father, and I was quite surprised to find that they were all discussing the opera."

"Yes, they take opera quite seriously in Lyricum; I'm surprised your father didn't teach you that, too....wait a moment, a moment," I said. "Your father—not Theophilus Hodgins?"

Hodgins' shoulders slumped. "Yes, sir."

"What in the name of Prudentius is the son of the Regius Professor of Classics of Glastonbury University doing working as a common deckhand?"

"I ran away from home, sir. He wanted me to follow in his footsteps, but I had no heart for the Classics, sir. I had to follow my own muse, and the call of the sea was stronger, sir." He looked sheepish at being found out.

"Ah. Well, Hodgins, what happened in the tavern?"

"I thought I'd join the conversation, as the Lyrican sailors seemed friendly enough. At first they were glad to hear from me; apparently Anglish sailors with a taste for opera are as much of a rarity to them as they are to me. They bought me drinks, and hung on my every word."

"And then what?"

"I'm not sure, sir. I must have said something wrong, because one man dashed the glass of Salieri from my hand, and another pulled my chair out from under me. After that, it got rather confused." He rubbed at a lump on his head, and winced.

"Think, Hodgins. What did you say?"

"I think, sir, I think I had just mentioned another opera I had seen on a previous visit. The *Valpolicella*, it was, by Fusilli. I liked the *Chianti* well enough, sir, but I thought that the *Valpolicella* was better.

"You see?" exclaimed Marconi, who had been listening intently. "He says it again! He is convicted out of his own mouth!"

"Hodgins," I began gently, "you walked into a dockside tavern in Lyricum Town, and said that Fusilli was better than Rotini? During the Summer Festival?"

"No, I didn't, sir, I said that the *Valpolicella* was better than the *Chianti*."

I waved the objection away. "It matters not. Just as it matters not that Fusilli, clearly a second-rate composer, was at the height of his powers when he wrote the *Valpolicella*. Just as it matters not that the Great Rotini, composer of the most sublime operas in the Known World, was but an untried youth when he wrote the *Chianti*." Marconi shifted uneasily at this. "Even at his height, Fusilli could never match the excesses of the young Rotini. How you can possibly compare the utter absurdity of Fusilli's plot with the fractured reality of Rotini's, or the lack of resolve in Fusilli's use of many different compositional structures with Rotini's determined focus on the arpeggio and glissando is beyond me." Marconi looked happier for a moment, and then puzzled, as did Hodgins. "The fact remains that you spoke ill of Rotini in his home city, at the beginning of the festival held in his honor, and of the opera which begins his majestic *Rigatoni Cycle*. Believe me, Hodgins, you're luck to be alive, and your shipmates are lucky that the brawl didn't spread to the docks."

At this, Hodgins hung his head, but he scowled at me from under his lowered brows.

"I must take a serious view of this, Hodgins. You've endangered the entire expedition with your frivolous ways. You shall be severely disciplined. With your captain's permission, I shall see to it myself."

Captain Halvorsen bowed. He had a puzzled look as well, but there was a twinkle in his eye.

"Starting tomorrow, Hodgins, you'll no longer be able to spend your days frivolously sunning yourself on the deck and singing with your crewmates. I want you to report to me personally, promptly after breakfast. Ahhh, that would be my breakfast, not yours. Say nine o'clock. I'll have you doing such work that you'll wish you were back in Glastonbury." I turned to the rotund little magistrate. "Does this meet with your approval, Signor Marconi?"

"As you know, Dr. Thintwhistle, Lyricum Town is not in a position to demand any action at all," he said, smiling. "I am glad that I had not underestimated you. You are a man of great understanding and culture." He gestured for us to return the way we had come. "I will have a coach meet you at the rear entrance to the Hall. Get this man into the coach quickly, and do not let him be seen. I rely on your discretion." We thanked him sincerely, and took our leave.

"By your leave, sir," said Hodgins as we rode back to the *Spaniel,* "thank you for clearing things up with the magistrate."

"You are quite welcome, Hodgins," I replied.

"Were you serious, sir? Shall I really report to you in the morning?" He looked from me to the captain, and back again. The captain himself looked at me quizzically.

"Indeed you shall, Hodgins. I brought no secretary with me on this trip, and frankly, any sailor who knows the names of Fusilli and Rotini, let alone one who can see the inferiority of the *Chianti,* is utterly wasted as a deck hand." I smiled at the look of dismay on the sailor's face.

"Don't worry, lad," I said. "It won't be much worse than learning Lyrican under your father's tutelage. You'll see." Hodgins settled back with a nearly inaudible groan, winced, and settled in a more comfortable position. The captain chuckled.

"I like your way of doing things, Dr. Thintwhistle. I had tried every means I could think of to get him off of the deck and into a position of responsibility, but I had never considered bailing him out of jail. I wish you luck of your prize!"

"And my thanks for your support, Captain," I said. In truth, I was well-pleased at the morning's work despite the delay, and was in high good spirits when we reached the *Spaniel* at last. The small crowd gathered at the *Spaniel's* dockside parted before the coach-and-four, and we were able to step directly from the compartment to the gangplank. We made it aboard without altercation, and in minutes were out in the Bay of Biscotti, heading for open sea.

CHAPTER 6

᠊᠊

A missed communique. ᠊᠊ Bruno settles in. ᠊᠊ Shipboard routine.
A flight of dolphins.

WHILE WE were gaining Hodgin's freedom, another Town Messenger had appeared at the *Spaniel* with a communique for me. We had hardly left the dock before the steward was at my elbow.

"This arrived for you while you were gone, Dr. Thintwhistle. Also, I am concerned about Dr. Philpott, sir. He is still in his cabin."

"Had a rough night, did he?" I murmured, looking at the addresses on the communique. It was from Dean Nuftison.

"I believe so, sir."

Now, why would Nuftison go to the expense of sending me a communique? On the whole, I judged it best not to read it. If it contained good news, it would keep; if bad, it could only disrupt the expedition. As the steward looked on in surprise, I tore it to shreds, and let the headwind blow them away.

"A great pity, wasn't it, Baxter, that the communique blew away before I could read it? My fault, of course, it slipped out of my fingers in this wind. I should never have opened it on deck."

"Indeed, sir, it was most unwise," said the steward, resolutely ignoring the light breeze.

"I knew I could count on you, Baxter. Now, I suppose I should go pay a visit on young Philpott."

I mention this occurrence, which after all hardly reflects well upon me, only because it was to have significant consequences later on.

I seldom resemble an Angel of Mercy, and yet that is how I felt as I went below and along the passage to Philpott's cabin. I listened at the door for a moment, heard nothing, and knocked softly. There was a soft woof in return, but no other sound. I scratched my chin, reflected for a moment, and tried the latch. Ordinarily I would never invade a colleague's privacy, of course, but stern measures seemed indicated.

Bruno woofed softly again, in greeting, as I entered the cabin. He was sprawled comfortably on the bunk, from which all of the bedclothes had been stripped, leaving a bare mattress; evidently, he had been passing the time gazing out of the porthole. He licked his chops companionably, and panted happily at me.

Were this a novel, rather than a serious travelogue, I'd no doubt say that my first thought was on the lines of, "Oh, no! The beast has devoured Philpott, and his bedclothes!" This was not, in fact, the case. My first thought was more on the lines of, "My, doesn't he look comfortable." Though Bruno was (and is) a large dog, he is far too small to devour an entire professor, even an untenured one.

I had not far to look. Glancing about, I soon saw a kind of cocoon on the floor, lying half under the desk. While I saw no exposed Philpott whatsoever, the soft resonant snores convinced me that I had found the missing academic. I saw no reason to wake him, for I was sure his slumber had been dearly bought. Instead, I took Bruno's leash, and led him to the steward's cubby, closing Philpott's cabin door quietly behind me.

The steward was behind his tiny desk, fiddling with bits of paper; accounts, no doubt. He looked from me to the dog, and turned a shade paler, but asked what he could do for me pleasantly enough. "Baxter," I said, "can you please locate Hodgins for me?" I explained the situation. "The captain has assigned him to me, and I need him. He can find me on the sundeck." Baxter brightened immediately, and undertook to do so.

Bruno and I ascended to the sundeck, where Bruno took immediate possession of a deck chair. My respect for the dog rose a notch; he had his priorities in order. I have always felt it wrong to abuse a sea voyage by working during the day; there is too much to see. And of course, one must be sociable in the evening. It is a formula which has stood me in good stead for many, many years. In token of my respect, I took possession of the adjacent chair, and joined him. So it was that Hodgins found us, shortly thereafter.

I gestured at the open chair on my right. "Sit down, Hodgins, I need to speak with you. I was going to wait until tomorrow morning, but something has come up."

"I can't sit there, sir. I'm on duty. It's not allowed." Hodgins looked shocked.

"The captain has assigned you to me now, Hodgins. It's your present duty to sit in that chair. Hop to it!" I waved my hand at the chair languidly. He sat down gingerly, not reclining properly, like Bruno and I, but at right angles to the length of the chair, facing me.

"Well enough, Hodgins," I said, "Though I don't think you've quite got the spirit of this, yet."

Hodgins didn't reply, but looked at me uncomfortably, so I continued.

"You speak Lyrican fluently, Hodgins, as I well know; I assume you can also read and write it?"

"Yes, sir, I can."

"Very good. And I believe I can safely assume that you can read and write Anglish as well?"

"Indeed, sir."

"Legibly?"

"I do my best, sir."

"Well, that's all one can do, I suppose." I paused, and studied the distant coastline for a moment. "Can you speak any other languages, Hodgins?"

"The classical languages, sir. My father taught me those even before he taught me Lyrican."

"No other modern languages?" I asked.

"No, sir. Father claimed there was no literature worth the name in any of them." I raised my eyebrows. "Truly, sir. I didn't learn to read and write Anglish until my father sent me off to school. He claimed it was for tradesmen and shopkeepers."

"Indeed, it would be difficult to talk to the grocer without it," I mused. "Well, Hodgins, I've arranged for you to have the cabin next to Philpott's. It's well-lighted, and has a desk, which you'll need."

"A cabin of my own, sir?" He brightened at the thought. "What will I need the desk for?"

"Translations, Hodgins, of writings on Zymurgia. No other Anglishmen have ever been there but Carbuncle and I, but the place is right next to Seros, after all, and that's been part of the Known World for thousands of years. Zymurgia had few visitors in all that time, but of course the Serosans had stories, and many of those have been recorded. The best are in Ancient Serosan, but there are several in the classical tongues, and the latest and most interesting are in Lyrican. I'd like Philpott to read them, but the poor soul only speaks Anglish. Your first task will be to read them yourself, and translate the relevant passages into Anglish. Think you can do it?"

"I expect so, sir. My father had me construing reams of Flautinus and Sophisticos before breakfast every day when I was child. I'm not sure how quick I'll be, though, sir. It's been quite a long while."

"I'm sure you'll do fine, Hodgins, just fine." I clasped my hands behind my head, and stretched in the warm breeze. "This is quite nice, Hodgins, you must learn to relax. Well, that's all for today. The steward will give you the key to the cabin; you'll no doubt want to move your gear immediately. Come to me tomorrow at nine, as I said before, and I'll give you the materials you'll need."

"Oh, and Hodgins," I said, as Hodgins rose from the deck chair, "You'll probably want to rig a hammock in your cabin."

"A hammock? Whatever for, sir? There's only one of me."

"One of your other duties will be attending to Bruno, here, especially at night. He gets lonely in the kennels, poor beast. He bunked with Philpott last night, and the poor soul nearly perished. We can't have that, so Bruno will have to bunk with you. I doubt he'll want to share the bed." I stretched again; the sea air was invigorating. "Run along, now, Hodgins; Bruno is fine for now, and I have some thinking to do." As Hodgins' footfalls receded, I leaned over and scratched Bruno behind the ears. He leaned his head into my fingers, but otherwise did not stir.

"What an admirable beast you are, Bruno," I said to him, "and a sterling example to us all." And with that, I shifted my position slightly, lowered my hat over my eyes, and settled down for some serious morning thought.

The following day set the pattern for the next week or so. Hodgins reported at nine as requested, and I got him started with Gambinus' classic work on Seros. Gambinus never got any further south than Philippi at the mouth of the Aram, and so most of what he recorded was hearsay, which of course loses him points with the Serosan scholars. Zymurgia, however, was (and is) almost completely fabulous, which is to say that hearsay is the best information available. That being the case, who is to say that one writer's hearsay is worse than another's? Every story would add to our expectations as we ventured on towards that little-known, seldom-visited land of fable.

Philpott was pathetically grateful that I had taken Bruno off of his hands, the more so as he could not afford to repay my two-hundred fiacres. He had intended to discount a note with a banker in Lyricum Town the morning of our departure, but had not awakened until long after we had left the dock. During the night they had spent together, he had conceived a great dislike for poor Bruno, a sentiment I am glad to say that noble beast never reciprocated. Many is the time I have seen Bruno raise his head from his deckchair at Philpott's approach, and greet him with a soft woof! Be that as it may, Philpott continued with his studies, and began to practice his cartography. With time and experience, I felt he would become a fair draftsman.

We saw little of Carbuncle during this period. He spent his days, and frequently his evenings, down in his workroom with some device, or devices, he had acquired from his friend in Lyricum Town. He was cheerful and talkative at mealtimes, but no word would he speak about his current project. "What you don't know about, Leon, you can't jinx," he'd say to my questions. "You'll thank me for it eventually, that you will."

In truth, there was little in our passage to Cuprios to distract him. It rained for two solid days, which were particularly hard for Bruno. We passed few other ships, and those few far to the north or south. Still, it was not all mindless tedium. A flight of dolphins spent most of a day playing off our bow, easily keeping up with the *Spaniel;* occasionally, one would dive deeply and then leap from the water, flying completely over the ship before disappearing again with never a splash. Toward the end of the day one young dolphin misjudged and came down hard on our foredeck, thrashing about and in danger of breaking its wingfins. The crew managed to get it over the side before it did any permanent damage to itself or to the ship...or to them, for that matter. A blow from a dolphin's wingfin can break a man's back. But the sailors revere the dolphins, calling them good luck, and so they got it back into the water alive. Killing it would have been rather safer, but on the whole I agreed with the sailors.

The other dolphins had formed a circle around the *Spaniel* as the young one thrashed and pounded on the deck. When the youngster regained the water, it joined the circle of dolphins, which proceeded to swim several times clockwise around the ship at great speed. Then, one by one as they reached a certain point to starboard, each dolphin dived and leaped in a great arc over the ship. For a brief time there was a veritable rainbow of fins and flukes hanging overhead. And with that, they were gone as suddenly as they had come.

The crew were agreed: they had none of them ever seen or heard of such a display, and they considered it an omen of the best possible sort. The *Spaniel's* was a happy crew, but they outdid themselves that night, dancing and singing on the foredeck. Philpott and I eschewed our regular evening in the lounge to sit with Bruno on the dark sundeck, listening to the singing and laughter far into the night. It would never have done to have joined them, of course.

CHAPTER 7

⋌⋊

An unexpected delay. ?⋫ A fish-dinner in Cuprios.

LANGUAGE IS an odd thing. This is a commonplace, I suppose, and absurd even to mention, yet it is true. I believe the culprit is untrammeled metaphor. During the course of this narrative, for example, I have referred to "phantail fodder"; I have spoken of Carbuncle's soothing the Hansen's geometer which had been scampering about the hold in distress; in general, I have spoken of phantasms as if they were alive, when they manifestly are not. Why do I do this? That's easily told: I picked it up from Carbuncle. But, more generally, why do we speak this way? True, phantasms do exhibit some of the symptoms of life. They frequently move on their own. Many consume some kind of stuff as fuel, which they use to perform some kind of work. Some phantasms are even capable of a kind of growth. And yet they lack other symptoms. They do not bring forth young according to their kind, but must be made; they have little independence of behavior; they certainly do not think! Nor do they build cities, drink sherry, or attend the opera.

I suppose the phantasts started it as a sort of misguided affection for their creations. Knowing full well that their little toys do not eat, they spoke of feeding them, and other phantasts understood. The phantast's motto is, "If it works, it works. Don't break it." The food metaphor worked for them: it was simple, descriptive and concise, even while being, in the strict sense, untrue. Other metaphors grew in similar ways. And those for whom phantastics is a closed book, like myself, came to speak the same way precisely because we did not understand. I know full well that the phantail doesn't eat...but please do not ask me to explain just what it does instead.

This reliance on metaphor rather than logic is one of the reasons why I find phantastics so dashed difficult to understand. My field is based, in part, on geometry, which is to say, on mathematics. You always know where you stand with mathematics. If you prove a theorem in one country, you know it holds good in the next country over. If a computation was correct yesterday, it will still be correct tomorrow. If a mountain is shown to be at a particular location relative to Pelham Observatory today, it is still there tomorrow—assuming the mountain itself didn't move in the meantime, as sometimes happens.

But I digress. It suffices to say that when I use such language I have no intent to mislead the reader; I simply have no better language to use.

On the 2nd of Melee, then, about a day's cruise out of Cuprios, Captain Halvorsen informed us that the phantail had sickened and could no longer work; moreover, we would need to stay in Cuprios Harbor for at least a week, to allow the phantail to recuperate in dry dock. He thought that perhaps it had picked up some kind of parasite and needed a thorough drying out. I discussed this with Carbuncle that evening in the lounge.

"It's nothing of the kind, you know," he said, shaking his head gently. "The captain is a fine man, but I suspect his phantasts are teasing him a bit. There's no beast in the sea that would have any kind of a taste for a phantail, or on land either. You might just as well dine on your silverware, rather than with it."

"Do you think the crew are just conniving at a week in Cuprios?" asked Philpott.

"Not likely, I'd say," replied Carbuncle. "The *Spaniel* is new enough that every phantast in His Majesty's naval yard will want a look at her phantasmagoria. Being a guest, and in need of their care, as it were, Captain Halvorsen can't very well refuse them. They'd soon notice any such mischief. And Halvorsen's phantasts are sound men, good at their work. Any problem with the phantail reflects poorly on them; they'd never make it sound worse than it is. No, if they told the captain a week, a week it will be."

The phantail's indisposition was not an unmixed blessing, however ruinous it was to our schedule. For the first time in this voyage the gossamer sails were unfurled on the *Spaniel's* two masts, giant glistening triangles and squares of material so fine it could scarcely be seen. A more glorious sight can scarcely be imagined than a tall ship sailed as it should be, the breath of the ur-winds swelling the gossamer yet never touching a hair of my head. It was a sight I had been anticipating for many days, and had so far been disappointed. Three days we had to watch it, three days of beautiful, perfect sailing—not one day, for the urwinds did not blow fast enough, or from the proper quarter. Thus, we reached Cuprios on the 5th of Melee, rather than on the 3rd as we had intended. Nor would we leave until the 12th.

Cuprios Harbor is a stirring sight. It is His Majesty's chief base in the eastern Sea of Dogs, guarding as it does the merchant shipping between Angland and the Bundi Nations, and therefore is home to naval vessels of all kinds. A few of the old, sail-powered frigates and line-of-battle ships remain there; the Admiral's flag officially flies over the aged *Dauntless*, though he is more usually to be found on land than at sea in these peaceful times. Cuprios also has a strong garrison of more modern phantail-powered warships, though none quite so modern as our own *Sea-Spaniel*.

There is an antipathy of long-standing between the Royal Navy and the merchant marine, and so I was rather surprised by the warmth of our reception. As we sailed into the harbor we were saluted by the castle that guards it, rising sheer from the water at the harbor's mouth, and also by the *Dauntless*. Sailors lined the yards of the sailing ships, and the decks of the modern vessels, and raised a lusty huzzah as we glided past. It was completely outside of my experience, and unspeakably delightful.

It was not until later (though fortunately before I remarked upon it in the wrong circles, and made a fool of myself) that Captain Halvorsen explained to me that they had not been honoring the *Spaniel* or her crew, but rather a certain small flag flying at our masthead. Evidently this small, striped piece of cloth proclaimed us His Majesty's courier, charged with the speedy delivery of dispatches of import to the Kingdom of Angland.

"And are we?" I inquired.

"Oh, indeed. Sir John at the embassy sent over a pouch while you were gallivanting around Lyricum Town. It's not that unusual a request, and of course it's always pleasant to have His Majesty's government owe one a favor."

"And that's why we received such a warm welcome, is it?"

"The seven sacks of mail we received with the pouch are evidently much anticipated," he expanded.

"Ah, I see. Anything of interest in the pouch?" I have always been inquisitive; that's why I am an explorer.

"Good god, man, it's a sealed pouch!" The captain snorted. "I haven't the faintest idea what's in it. Nor am I likely to find out, and glad I am to think so. An official dispatch that concerns me and mine is a thing to avoid." With that, I could only agree.

Whether it was because we were bearers of good news (if such we were), or whether we simply broke the tedium, the fact remains that we were treated warmly and generously for the whole of our stay. No sooner had we reached the dock than Carbuncle and I, and our suite, were invited to guest in the governor's palace for the duration of our stay. This was a great blessing, as no sooner had we disembarked with such belongings as we would need than the *Spaniel* was lovingly escorted to the dry dock, to receive the best care that His Majesty's phantasts (and her own) could give her.

In all, our party consisted of myself, Carbuncle, Philpott, and Bruno, with Hodgins and Baxter to attend to our needs. Captain Halvorsen was also invited to guest at the palace, and I do believe he slept there, but we seldom saw him. It is an old naval maxim that unwatched work is never finished, and so he divided his time between the dry dock and the chandlery, sparing no apparent expense to get the *Spaniel* back in top condition.

I have referred to the governor's palace, that being the term with which my readers will be most familiar, and yet that is not the building's name. Cuprios being controlled completely by the Royal Navy, and having no indigenous population, is administered as a ship, rather than as a colony. The palace is more properly called the Admiral's Great Cabin, and the coach which took us up the cobbled road from the docks to the hilltop is affectionately known as the Ship's Gig. But though it lacks an indigenous population, it has a sizable population of transplants and transients both. In practice, Admiral Jamison is understood to be the governor of Cuprios, and while he is on dry land the more usual names and practices are used. With a few exceptions, of course.

The admiral held a banquet for us on the evening of the day we arrived; we, in this case, consisted of myself, Carbuncle, Philpott, and Captain Halvorsen. Bruno, alas, was not invited, though I am sure he would have been willing to attend. Philpott himself was nearly excluded, until I pointed out that he was no mere secretary, but rather a scholar in his own right, and the youngest son of the Earl of Luton.

The company met at seven o'clock, and entered the dining room promptly at eight o'clock. Admiral Jamison declared that this was not a moment too soon; from long years at sea his appetite still kept naval hours, and had been waiting since four. It was a hearty meal, primarily of seafood. There is no pasturage on Cuprios, and the so-called meat course was a large white fish; some kind of halibut, I believe. A fish chowder arrived for the soup course, and the fish course proper was a delicate flurry of baby prawns. The wine, alas, was unexceptional.

The conversation was such as might be expected from such a gathering: Admiral Jamison himself, and his flag captain, Michael Wyburn; a smattering of other captains; and an old friend, Douglas Willoughby. Willoughby and I had met on my first expedition. He was second on a dingy old tub of a merchantman, and I was second to Ambrose Elliot, of unlamented memory. Willoughby and I became close friends on the strength of shared misery. He'd gone east and joined the Chartered Bundi Company, keeping the natives down and the profits up, and making an enormous pile with it. I, on the other hand, had remained in academia. I hadn't seen him in years.

Time had treated Willoughby well, time and patience and hard work. He was resplendent in white linen, with a monocle and a fine gold timepiece in his waistcoat pocket.

"Willoughby, old fellow, you're looking well," I exclaimed.

"And I'm better than I look, Thintwhistle, I'm better than I look. You should have come with me to the Bund while you had the chance." He smoothed his mustache, and struck a pose. "You wouldn't know it to look at me, Thintwhistle, but you are looking at Lord Willoughby of Bundiyal, His Majesty's latest peer of the realm."

"A peer, is it? His Majesty's reward for years spent helping the company build a paradise in a savage land?" He smiled, and agreed that it was so. "You're right, I should have come with you. It would have been more peaceful. But what brings you to Cuprios?"

"I'm just in port for a few days; I'm heading home for my formal investiture as peer before the House of Lords. And how are things in Angland?"

This led to a popular outcry for news of home from all sides. "Well, let me see," said Captain Halvorsen. "The Derbies are back in power again, I believe. Cranford is a Derby, isn't he?" There was general laughter.

"This year, Captain, I believe you are correct," said Admiral Jamison. "Of course, you've been away from home for several weeks. Perhaps he's a Topper by now."

Politics had the floor for a considerable time after, focussing, as I recall, on Government's failure to deal forcefully enough with Eporus. As this had been a familiar refrain for lo these many years, I paid little attention until I was hailed by the admiral himself.

"A glass with you, Dr. Thintwhistle," he said. I raised my glass in return, and as they were being refilled by a silent young fellow in brass buttons, he continued, "I am eager to hear of your latest expedition. Will it be Seros again?"

"In part, Admiral," I said. "We will be traveling through Seros, and I've no doubt we will observe many interesting things. Our ultimate destination, however, is Zymurgia."

"Zymurgia? Refresh an old sailor's memory, will you?"

"It is the country directly to the south of Seros. Carbuncle and I made a brief visit some years ago. Thanks to a generous grant made to the University, we are finally able to return and spend some real time there."

"What's it like? Sand and tombs and things, like Seros?" asked Wyburn.

"With luck, I'll be better able to answer that on our return trip. It's greener than Seros, and it is inhabited. There's a certain amount of trade between the Zymurgians and the Serosans, but beyond that little is known of them."

"Trade, really?" asked Willoughby. "I was under the impression that they discouraged visitors."

"That's one of the stories, but it's hard to say," said Carbuncle. "We had no trouble from the one Zymurgian we met on our previous trip."

"Zymurgia is on a plateau," I said. "There are few paths to the top. It's possible that the fabled reclusiveness of the Zymurgians simply reflects difficulty of access."

The admiral sat back in his chair. "What do you expect to find?" he asked.

"Beer," I said.

"Beer?" asked Wyburn, in surprise.

"Beer," I said. "That's what Zymurgia means, you know... the land of brewing. They've been selling beer to the Serosans for thousands of years. The trade is only carried on in a small way these days; just with the folk at the base of the plateau."

"It seems a long way to go to get a drink," said Wyburn.

"The ancient rulers of Seros might have agreed with you," I said, "but they apparently bought large quantities nevertheless."

"Beer," said Admiral Jamison. "The beer of the ancients. A remarkable thought, that, Dr. Thintwhistle. I wish you luck of your expedition. Now," he continued, "it is late, and time for the loyal toast. Perhaps you and your companions are unaware, Dr. Thintwhistle, that we follow naval custom here on His Majesty's Ship Cuprios, and drink the toast while seated. Gentlemen, the King!" We drained our glasses, and the banquet came to an end.

CHAPTER 8

⤳⤺

Life on Cuprios. ❧ Philpott investigates the natives.
A day in the country. ❧ A celebration. ❧ The hazards of chilling wine.

A WEEK ON Cuprios is much like a week on board ship. One has the same hours of restful tedium in a warm climate, with the occasional spark of light and interest; the same limited circle of acquaintance; the same lack of sufficient fresh water for bathing. The primary difference is that the scenery doesn't change, no matter how long you watch it. This latter circumstance is often considered Cuprios' greatest defect, but I for one would gladly swap the little scenery we had for a wider range of conversation. On some days we talked politics, lunched, talked hunting, dined, and talked politics. On other days politics were not discussed until after lunch, but the forenoon hours were spent discussing hunting. On the whole, it was an odd thing to spend so many hours on these topics, when Cuprios itself has little politics and less game. Those hours not devoted to hunting and politics were spent rehashing old sea-battles. Of course we must dine with the Admiral. Of course we must dine with his flag captain. Our social obligations were regrettably numerous and unavoidable.

Despite these dire pastimes, a few sparks of light stand out. The morning after our arrival, I arose late, broke my fast, and went looking for Philpott and Hodgins. I wanted to make sure that they had sufficient occupation for the day. After a certain amount of hallooing, I tracked down an elderly servant of the Admiral's who told me that all the other gentlemen had gone out. He was, however, able to track down our steward. I inquired after our missing scholars.

"Mr. Carbuncle has gone off to the dockyards, Dr. Thintwhistle. He said he was curious to know what was really wrong with the *Spaniel's* phantail."

"Ah, very good, though I was more concerned with Philpott."

"He went off first thing this morning, sir. He said he was going to observe the natives."

"What natives, Baxter? No one lives here but servants and sailors, and not a one of them was born here."

"Natives is what he said, sir. He said he wanted to study their folkways, sir."

"Baxter," I said, "do you honestly mean to tell me that Philpott is roaming all about the island looking for natives so that he can observe their folkways?"

"Yes, sir," he said, "Though I think he was planning on going to the area down near the docks, sir."

"Where there are bars and places of ill-repute," I said.

"Yes, sir."

"Filled with drunken sailors and their ladies, no doubt," I said.

"Yes, sir."

"Aggressive, uncouth men with a taste for brawling," I said.

"Yes, sir."

"And you let Philpott go down there to 'observe their folkways'? He'll come home in pieces!"

"It's all right, sir. I suggested he take Hodgins with him. To translate, sir." Baxter smiled.

"This is the same Hodgins who nearly started a riot at our last port of call?" I asked.

"But those were Lyricans, sir. These are just honest Anglish sailors. Dr. Philpott will come to no harm, sir."

And no more did he. I did not actually see him, or Hodgins, for some days, though I was occasionally awakened in the wee hours of the morning by bits of "The Raggle-Taggle Guppies" and other rustic ballads. I judged from this that young Thaddeus was enjoying his observations immensely, albeit with some loss of objectivity.

The third day of our visit, Carbuncle proposed an excursion "into the country", as he said, meaning a ramble to the Bay of Angels on the north side of the island. Baxter assembled a large luncheon hamper for us, and found a donkey to carry it and a lad to lead the donkey. We saw Willoughby as we were leaving, and called out to him, and the three of us (plus the lad, plus the donkey) set out on the dusty island road.

Willoughby and I fell to reminiscing, as old friends will. "Whatever happened to that old dictator, what was his name…"

"Ambrose Elliot," I said, "that was his name, the old scoundrel. Though I suppose I shouldn't speak ill of him; he was my mentor in mythogeography, after all. If I hadn't gone on that first expedition with him, I might never have gone on any."

"Yes, that old dictator Elliot. What ever happened to him?"

"I thought you knew. He got eaten."

"Eaten? You don't say."

"Indeed, it was on that same expedition. It was his own fault, of course," I said.

"How so?"

"He didn't bring a phantasticist with him," said Carbuncle. "It's a fatal mistake, leaving such things to amateurs."

"That's right," I said, "and he was a bloody arrogant fool as well. You remember, Willoughby, we were going to a small island in the South Bundi Sea. The natives were thoroughly delightful people—cannibals, of course, but polite with it. It would never do to eat a guest, you know." We crested a rise, and, catching sight of the bay below, stopped to catch our breath as well. "Well, the Pumbawis, as they called themselves, worshipped a kind of sacred flame. It burned in a valley at the center of their island, rain or shine, and was the source of all fires, whether for lighting, or, ah, cooking. It was sacred to them, you see, because it never went out."

"Remarkable. Some kind of naturally occurring phantasm, was it?"

"Indeed; or perhaps it was put there by some previous explorer in ages past. At any rate, it offended old Elliot no end, you see. He claimed it was impossible. 'A phantasm,' he said, 'must have some source of power. This flame cannot possibly be what they say it is.'" I paused, as Carbuncle muttered "Bloody idiot!" under his breath.

"But isn't that correct?" asked Willoughby. "It's what I've always been taught."

"Certainly. And yet, here was this flame that never went out, and it galled him. All might have been well, but Elliot made two mistakes."

"The first," said Carbuncle, who knows all of my stories as well as I do, "was to forget the primary maxim of Applied Phantastics: if it works, it works...don't break it."

"The second," I continued, "was to talk about it constantly...and worse, to talk about it with the Pumbawis. He sowed the seeds of doubt in their minds, you see, and phantasms are sensitive to that kind of thing. The next rainstorm put it out for good."

"Oh, dear."

"The Pumbawis were a tad disgruntled, naturally," I said, "and just as naturally, they blamed Elliot."

"As they should," said Carbuncle with unusual firmness.

"They required his presence at their next banquet, and that was that. It fell to me to lead the expedition afterwards, which I did with great distinction if I say so myself, and it made my career. So as I say, I shouldn't be too hard on old Elliot."

"Yes, you should." said Carbuncle. "Had the old fool kept his mouth shut and his mind open, that sacred flame might have had hundreds of thousands of cousins by now, and you'd be a wealthy man."

"That is so; and my first act on returning to the University was to find a first-rate phantasticist for my next expedition. Carbuncle and I have been together ever since. I've never since been faced with so potentially lucrative a discovery...but I've not been eaten, either."

"Good luck for you," said Willoughby, "but rather hard luck on old Elliot."

"Actually, I am convinced that some such unpleasantness was inevitable. He'd started being rude to the Dean."

"But Leon, you're rude to the Dean," objected Carbuncle. "You call him 'Eddie'."

"Yes," I said, "but never in public."

By this time we had reached the shore, and found a pleasant boulder, well shaded, on which to spread our lunch. It was to be a lavish meal indeed, and I exclaimed at its size.

"Nothing but the best for your birthday, Leon!" said Carbuncle.

"Why, so it is," I exclaimed, "The 8th of Melee as ever was."

"How old are you now, old friend?" asked Willoughby.

"Tenured," I said. "Remember, once a don gaineth tenure, he ageth not until he is forcibly put out to pasture. Thank you, Thomas. This is a delightful surprise."

"I daresay I can improve on it," he said. "No doubt you're thirsty after that long walk. Would you care for some chilled wine?"

"Get away," I said. "Chilled wine? There's no ice for hundreds of miles, Thomas!"

"Now who has the open mind, Leon? Would I offer you chilled wine if I had none?" And with that, Carbuncle pulled a reddish cylinder out of the hamper; I recognized it to be one of the devices he'd been tinkering with since we left Lyricum Town. He handed it to me. It was surprisingly warm. "There you go, Leon. A portable wine chiller. Happy birthday!"

On closer inspection the object proved to have a hole at one end, just large enough to allow a bottle of wine to be inserted— or removed, which I did posthaste. The wine was nicely chilled, as advertised.

"You've outdone yourself, Thomas." I sipped my wine with great pleasure. Not only was it chilled, I recognized it as one of the vintage Rigolettos from the *Spaniel's* wine locker.

"It chills whatever you put into it," he said. "The little beastie just sucks the heat out of the inside, and transfers it to the outside. That's why it feels so warm."

"Fascinating," said Willoughby. "How long does it take?" I could hear the money jingling in his head.

"About half-an-hour," said Carbuncle. "I can make it work faster, but the outside gets uncomfortably warm."

"Amazing," said Willoughby. "Have you considered the commercial possibilities?"

Carbuncle had, but was not averse to a bit of advice, and perhaps a bit of capital. After that it was all money and marketing for the rest of the bottle, and most of the next (also nicely chilled). My attention wandered.

At last we packed up the remains of the lunch and placed them on the donkey. On the way back Willoughby regaled us with tales of killings made in the Bundi trade, adding to the air of restful tedium I have already spoken of—until, just as we came within sight of the governor's mansion, there was a loud smashing sound from behind us, immediately followed by the braying of a donkey in fear for his life. Willoughby and I narrowly escaped being trampled, and poor Carbuncle was thrown into a rather muddy ditch alongside the road. The donkey vanished down the road to the harbor, hamper still on its back.

The lad we had hired to lead the donkey could hardly contain his laughter. He was quite sure that the noise had come from the hamper.

"Oh, dear." said Carbuncle. "Leon, did you put the bottle of champagne in the chiller?"

"I did," I said. "I expected that we would want it when we got back."

"It froze," he said. "It must have. The noise we heard was the bottle bursting." He stood and pondered for a moment, ooze dripping down the front of his white suit. "Yes, that was it. I suppose if I were to... Oh, dear, I hope the chiller is all right! Leon, Willoughby, perhaps I'll see you at dinner. Oh, dear!" And with that he was off, hot on the tracks of the donkey.

CHAPTER 9

༈

Another communique. ৯ *A distressing discovery. The fruits of Philpott's investigations.* ৯ *We continue our journey.*

THE REST of the week passed much as I have already indicated. Carbuncle tinkered with the chiller, which was rather distraught but not otherwise harmed. I napped when I could, and endured tedious conversation when I must. Philpott and Hodgins continued their revels among the lower classes, and Baxter continued as efficient as ever. The day before the *Sea-Spaniel* was to be ready for sea, he came to me with a communique.

"I gather it arrived about two weeks before we did, sir. It's been gathering dust in one of the admiral's secretary's pigeonholes."

I looked at the envelope with a mixture of curiosity and apprehension. It was, of course, from Dean Nuftison, and had clearly been sent at the same time as the one I had disposed of in the Bay of Biscotti. That, at least, was a good sign. It meant that he hadn't been sure of catching us in Lyricum Town. On the other hand, it was a bad sign. It meant that he wasn't simply urging me to get out of Lyricum and on with business. Moreover, it was a matter of some importance. I sighed.

"I suppose I'd better read this one, Baxter." I opened the envelope, and pulled out the folded communique form. I turned it over in my hands, still tempted to shred it unread. I will be everlastingly glad that I did not.

On the face of it, it was a baffling message: "LUTON BANK-RUPT. RETURN AT ONCE. NUFTISON." I supposed that "LUTON" was the Earl of Luton, which seemed rather hard luck on young Philpott. What I failed to see was how it affected the expedition. After all, it had already been paid for, hadn't it? I knew that the University would not let a bankruptcy come between it and funds legally donated. I certainly saw no reason for a return to England. It was puzzling.

"It's puzzling, Baxter," I said. "I can't see why Nuftison would send such a thing."

"I'm sure I can't say, sir," he replied.

That afternoon things became much clearer. I was reclining in a chaise on the terrace when Hodgins approached me. "Ah, Hodgins," I cried, "There you are. Where's young Thaddeus?"

"Dr. Philpott is still in the sailor's village, sir, with friends." said Hodgins.

"Friends, Hodgins? In the sailor's village?"

"Yes, sir. Dr. Philpott is a friendly gentleman, sir."

"Yes, he is that." I looked closer at Hodgins. He was looking at me uncertainly, shifting his weight from one foot to another. "What is it, Hodgins?"

"It may be nothing, sir." He frowned. "There's been a man asking after the *Spaniel* down in the village."

"What kind of a man, Hodgins?"

"A smarmy little fellow, sir. He arrived this morning on a merchantman, and immediately started asking about the *Spaniel*, and about Captain Halvorsen in particular. He seemed to be carrying a piece of parchment, sir."

"Parchment, is it?" Things began to drop into place. "Tell me, Hodgins, did he get to see Captain Halvorsen?"

"No, sir. The captain's been at the navy yard all day, getting the *Spaniel* ready for sea. The man tried to get in to see him, but the sentries saw to him. They didn't like his looks either." Hodgins smirked. "When he came into the bar where Thad and—where Dr. Philpott and I were seated, he was walking rather stiffly, sir, and I noticed he didn't sit down."

I waved Hodgins to a chair, and thought furiously. Could it be? Would it be worth it? I contemplated the palatial nature of the *Spaniel,* and concluded that it would be. At length I nodded, and said, "You say you and young Thaddeus have made friends in the village, Hodgins?"

"Yes, sir."

"Sporting lads, are they? Ready for an innocent bit of fun?"

"Oh, yes, sir."

"What I'd like you to do is this, Hodgins. I'd like the smarmy little fellow to make some new friends. I want him to drink his fill. And furthermore, I don't want him to see the light of day until after we've sailed tomorrow." Hodgins was smiling broadly at this.

"I think that would be easily done, sir, given sufficient funds. They aren't a well-off lot, down the village," he said.

"Very good, Hodgins." I pulled some silver from my pocket, and handed it to him. "Will that do?"

"I think it will suffice, sir."

"Very good. And Hodgins…" I looked at him intently. "I want that parchment burnt. If your friends would be so good as to make sure that he has no other copies, so much the better."

"Understood, sir, well understood."

"And after you've seen to that, Hodgins, hie yourself to the navy yard, and find Captain Halvorsen. Tell him, with my compliments, that he'd better sleep aboard the *Spaniel* tonight; I'll see that his belongings are brought on board tomorrow. Tell him to stay out of sight as much as possible."

Perhaps I was being over-cautious, but on the whole I thought not. Too many things were making sense.

Hodgins was as good as his word. When the "ship's gig" took us back down the hill to the docks the following morning, the *Spaniel* was there but Captain Halvorsen was nowhere to be seen. More to the point, a fierce-looking seamen was stationed at the foot of the gang-plank. I gathered that no strangers would be allowed to board.

Philpott and Hodgins had, as usual, been nowhere to be seen that morning, but their kits were packed and waiting in the hall, and had come along with us in the wagon. As I boarded, I fancied I heard, off in the distance, the heartfelt strains of "Ladies of Hades". Closer examination revealed the two slovenly singers as our two prodigals.

Philpott was indeed a sight. His shirt was torn and stained, his collar was a-fly, his trousers were most marvelously spattered, and the heel of his right boot had gone. His hands and face were cut and bruised, and one eye was almost swollen shut. His companion was similarly accoutred. They had their arms about each other's shoulders, and were staggering forward in time with their singing, pausing a moment and rising to their full heights each time they reached the chorus.

Oh-OH,
Those ladies of Hades are supple and sweet
And friendlier lassies you seldom will meet.
They'll dispose of your troubles, my friends, and what's
    MORE—
They'll empty your pockets and show you the door!

"Good God, Philpott, whatever have you been doing?" I was shocked.

"Brawling, Leon," he said happily. His speech was none too clear. "I'm greatly honored."

"Honored? Half-murdered, more like!" I cried, pulling him toward the sick-berth.

"Honored!" he shouted. "It wasn't my fight, y'see, but the natives let me help anyway. It's part of their folkways."

"Philpott, you're not well. Just settle down here, and we'll find you something to calm you down."

"Folkways, Leon! It's part of their culture. When somebody tries to steal your girl, you have to take steps."

"And did someone try to steal your girl, Thad?" I asked gently. I would have to speak harshly to Hodgins, I feared.

"Oh, not my girl...it was Throckmorton's girl. It was Throckmorton's girl, wasn't it, Bill?"

"That it was," said Hodgins, nodding.

Philpott settled down on the bunk, smiling, and then winced. He touched his swollen eye gently, and then smiled again. "When that smarmy little guy tried to get cozy with Throckmorton's girl, well, something had to be done. That's how their culture works, isn't it, Bill."

"That it is," said Hodgins. "And when the Admiral's men came to break it up, why, it was clear to everyone that the smarmy little guy was the cause of it. He's locked up right and proper, sir. Though I'm not sure he's aware of it yet. He was fairly horizontal when they carried him out."

By this time I'd gotten Philpott something to drink, with a little extra added, and he was curled up on the bunk, snoring.

"I see, Hodgins. And the parchment?"

"So many ashes, sir."

"Thank you, Hodgins, good work. But couldn't you have handled it less violently?"

"He so wanted to see a brawl, sir."

"I see, Hodgins. I see." I dismissed Hodgins to his hammock, and went to see the captain. I found him in his cabin.

"Dr. Thintwhistle," he said, looking up from the charts that covered his desk. "I have done what you asked. Now, perhaps you would be so kind as to explain." His voice was devoid of expression.

"I take it," I said, "That the *Sea-Spaniel* belongs to the Earl of Luton?"

"And if it does?" asked the captain stiffly.

I handed him the communique from Dean Nuftison. In other circumstances it might have been interesting to watch the color drain from his face. He looked at me in wild surmise.

"A man arrived on the island yesterday, Captain Halvorsen, asking about the *Spaniel* and for you in particular. Fortunately, the guards at the navy yard refused him entry, or we would of necessity be returning to Angland even now."

"What happened to him?"

"I gather—I wasn't involved, of course—that while waiting in one of the bars in the sailor's village he annoyed the wrong man. There was an altercation, and he's now in the admiral's lockup, sleeping it off." Halvorsen continued to stare at me without speaking, so I went on. "I have it on good authority that the parchment he was carrying has been destroyed." At that, Halvorsen relaxed and wiped his brow.

"I see. What do you expect me to do?"

"That all depends on you, captain, and on your loyalty to the Earl and his family. You are, if you wish, free to set course for Pelham, and deliver the *Spaniel* and her contents up to the Earl's creditors. That would no doubt be preferable to bringing her home at the word of a smarmy little writ-server. On the other hand, you have had no official notice of the Earl's plight."

"And so?"

"If we were to continue on the expedition, it is hard to say what interesting, and possibly lucrative discoveries we might find." At this point I related the story of Dr. Elliot and the Eternal Flame. "Young Thaddeus would, of course, come in for a share of any earnings. I won't mislead you—it's unlikely in the extreme, but it isn't impossible. If something like the Eternal Flame were discovered and brought home, though, Philpott, Carbuncle and I would all be wealthy men. Far better to return to Pelham as heroes, I'd say. Not to mention the loss to the scientific community if the expedition were to be cancelled."

The captain looked away for a few moments. He pursed his lips, and stared off into space, and then nodded his head. "I quite agree, Dr. Thintwhistle. The scientific importance of this mission is such that it must not be endangered on hearsay evidence. If I had had word from the Earl himself, you understand, my decision would be different."

"Capital," I said. "I knew I could rely on you, captain. Now, there remains the matter of Phillipi. It is entirely possible, and indeed likely, that we will find another writ-server waiting for us there."

"Do not worry yourself, doctor. I shall take every care to get us up the river to the plateau of Zymurgia."

I took my leave, and within minutes we had left Cuprios Harbor. As I watched the village and castle diminish in the distance, I wondered whether Philpott's friends had left the smarmy little fellow passage home, or whether he must needs become, as Philpott put it, a "native".

CHAPTER 10

⌣⋰⋱

The city of Phillipi. ֍ The many mouths of the Aram.
The mystery of Seros.

THE CITY of Phillipi has a history perhaps thousands of years longer than Lyricum Town, and comprises a correspondingly more exotic array of architectural styles. Sited in the Aram Delta, it has had the finest harbor on the south shore of the Sea of Dogs for all of recorded history. Under the name of Kairos it was the capital of several dynasties of Serosan rulers. In the 18th century B.U., Phillip of Chalcedon paused in his conquest of the Troasene world and made it his own capital. His empire collapsed upon his death, as such shoddy one-man empires are wont to do, and it has passed through many hands since. At present, it is nominally in the hands of the Seljurks; in practice, the Ophir of Phillipi is largely independent, and largely in debt to the bankers of the civilized nations of Arrastia.

From ancient times, the city has been divided into four quarters, not including the harbor district, which perhaps is oldest of all. To the northeast is the Quarter of the Seljurks, where the aristocrats and working people of the Seljurk majority live. To the northwest is the poorly named Quarter of the Hyksos; indeed, a sizable community of that ancient people dwell there, but so do most of the non-Seljurk minority. To the south-west is the Royal Quarter, wholly given over to the parks and palace of the Ophir, the offices of his ministers (mostly corrupt), and the barracks of his soldiers (mostly lazy). Finally, to the south-east is the University Quarter, where stands the oldest institute of higher learning in the Known World, and the great library of Phillipi. In the Royal and University Quarters the buildings are of carved marble, the avenues are wide, and the plants are lush and well tended. In the Quarter of the Hyksos, the buildings are of broken marble and eroding sandstone, the streets are narrow and crooked, the stench is remarkable, and the only vegetation is the algae that grows in the public fountains—non-Seljurks are heavily taxed, and therefore live in real or apparent poverty. The Quarter of the

Seljurks is mixed, ranging from elegant marble villas in the south to tenements and hovels in the north.

The scholars and travelers of Arrastia have been coming to Phillipi in increasing numbers since the beginning of the century. None but the most exalted have been able to stay in the Royal or University Quarters; none but the most hardy or heedless have been willing to stay in the Quarter of the Hyksos; and as none but Seljurks are welcome in the Quarter of the Seljurks, an Arrastian District has grown up on the west side of the city. Centered on Clark's Hotel, the most fashionable gathering place for Arrastians in all of Seros, the district has every convenience for the civilized traveller. Nor does it lack the color and charm of the other quarters, as the Phillippians, Seljurk and Hyksos alike, have turned their attentions to fleecing the visitor of every coin they possess, and thus are to be seen in great numbers wherever the visitor looks...and occasionally where he does not.

I have included this description of Phillipi in the hopes it will interest my readers, as despite all of our plans (and reservations at Clark's) we did not go there.

Captain Halvorsen had promised to get us up the Aram to Zymurgia in safety, and the captain was as good as his word. The voyage from Cuprios to the mouths of the Aram, normally a three-day journey, took us five days, because we proceeded almost entirely by sail. The captain had had the *Sea-Spaniel* well-stocked with phantail fodder and other supplies in Cuprios, and now used the gossamer sails to save the fodder for the trip up river. In this way we avoided the need to take on supplies in Phillipi. The Aram has many mouths; only those which serve Phillipi are dredged and therefore suitable for commercial shipping. A vessel like the *Spaniel*, however, which scuds along the surface of the water on a cushion of foam, is well-suited for river travel. Any mouth of the Aram would appear a broad highway compared to the upper reaches of the river, and so the Captain was able to avoid the city altogether. We slipped through at night, and by dawn were well past the delta and into the main channel of the river.

It had been my intention to spend several days in Phillipi buying supplies and getting the latest news about conditions to the south, and then to make a slow journey up the Aram, making numerous visits to the monuments, temples, and tombs which fill the desert on either side of the cultivated river bank. In light of what we had learned on Cuprios this would have been extremely unwise. We had to assume that a writ-server awaited us in Phillipi, and that he would head up-river as soon as he learned we had passed him by. Under the circumstances, any kind of slow, leisurely trip was out of the question. Our only hope was to get so far up the river so quickly that the knave would be discouraged and give up. Fortunately, there was only one article our expedition lacked: a Serosan who could speak the Zymurgian tongue and translate for us. As we would be most likely to find such an individual in the southernmost reaches of the country, our detour was only an annoyance rather than a catastrophe.

Although we passed them quickly by on our passage upriver, I find I am unable to pass lightly over the Serosan antiquities. On the one hand, Seros has been an established part of the Known World for thousands of years; on the other, the ongoing controversy over the nature of the Serosan antiquities strikes right at the heart of mythogeography.

In one sense, mythogeography is nothing more than the exploration and mapping of the lands of fable, those little known, storied realms at the edge of the Known World. As such a land is explored it becomes less and less fabulous, evolving with time to the merely phantastic. Eventually it joins the lands of the Known World. As the Bundi Nations were mythical only a few generations ago, so now they are inescapably Known, and the lands on their borders have ascended from the mythical to the fabulous.

The great question, the burning issue of mythogeography, is the nature of these new lands. Did they and their peoples exist before their neighboring lands were explored, charted, and civilized? Or did they spring into existence as their neighbors become Known?

At the heart of the controversy is the Law of Consensus: "What is, is what is agreed upon." Every aspect of any country is subject to this law. Although the magnitude of the law's effect is controversial, its existence is demonstrably true; every Anglishman over 50 years of age remembers the assassination of King Harold V. The self-image of the Anglish people was shaken, and the very earth was shaken with them, such a tumult as had not been felt in hundreds of years. Birds flew upside down, trees walked, dogs spoke with human voices. The assassin was swallowed by the earth, and Harold's Revenge, a mound made not by human hands, stands in memory over the assassin's grave.

The self-consciousness that made such an earthly vengeance inevitable is the hallmark of the lands of the Known World. Angland is what she is because of the consensus of her own people, and also of that of the people of the the other civilized nations. It may seem odd at first glance, but the inhabitants of the lands of fable rarely possess this self-consciousness. They do not reflect on the nature of their own land. Life is as it is, as it has always been. They do not agree, but merely expect. Some scholars claim that this is due to their previous isolation—a people cannot examine themselves without some other people as a mirror. Others claim that this is a sign of their very newness. These latter scholars believe that the lands of fable do not even exist when unobserved by outsiders; as they say, "If a country is inhabited, but is unvisited, does it have a culture?"

Whatever its cause (and I will not take a stand here), this lack of self-awareness leaves them subject to the whim and observation of the first explorer to happen along. He reports his observations and speculations, more or less precisely depending on his skill and honesty. Other explorers follow, expecting the same; or indeed, expecting the exact opposite. Before long, the country's past, present, and future nature are set. Consensus has been reached; the country and its people have become Known. Thus did the sage truly say, "The unexamined culture isn't worth a shaved penny."

There is a serious moral question here. If the people of a land of fable do not exist except when observed by outsiders, then the action of the Law of Consensus upon them is morally neutral. It is therefore reasonable for a party of explorers to expect wondrous, beautiful, and financially remunerative things of a new land, in hopes that they will make their fortunes. If, on the other hand, the land and its people are simply unsophisticated and unaware, then it is indeed an evil thing to try to manipulate their culture and country for personal gain. We may be comforted by the knowledge that the Anglish, an upright and moral race, are the foremost explorers and consensus builders of modern times.

It is difficult to measure the effects of the Law of Consensus on a land as it becomes Known, for one only knows what one has observed. One has no knowledge of how things have changed because of one's observation; indeed, many scholars would say that the question has no meaning. Certainly, the country's own recorded history is of no use, as it is subject to the Law of Consensus along with everything else. Seros provides an apt example.

It is unknown (and likely unknowable) which country first became sufficiently aware of itself to wield the sword of consensus against its neighbors. Many countries have written records extending far back into antiquity, and so claim the prize. Most reputable scholars, however, agree that it was the Troasenes. The first philosophers, the Troasenes spread from their homeland in what is now Seljurkia and colonized every shore of the Sea of Dogs. In ancient days they came to Seros, and being insufferably nosy went everywhere and wrote everything down.

Even at that time Seros was a country of extremes: a narrow ribbon of cultivated land on the banks of the Aram, contained in a vast ocean of sand. Even then Seros's days of greatness were past, signified only by crumbling monuments and decaying tombs. And this is the root of the controversy: were these monuments and tombs the relics of a great civilization and a mighty race? Or had the first Troasenes to visit Seros expected a far-off, drowsy, antique land? Were the obelisks and temples, and the mighty Pharynx itself, the product of Serosan engineering, and Serosan hands, or were they the product of Troasene romance and love for the exotic?

These questions challenge us down to the present day. Each year, researchers find new tombs and new monuments in the vast expanse of the Serosan desert. Have they been there, lost, for thousands of years? Or are we, in our great wisdom, literally creating a history for the Serosan people? Alas, it is impossible to say. I do, however, believe that the desert was smaller and the Aram shorter when the ancient kings of Seros imported beer from the brewmasters of Zymurgia. Always assuming, of course, that they existed.

The goal of the Serosist, of course, is to study the monuments and their inscriptions to learn more about the ancient inhabitants. The goal of the mythogeographer in Seros is simpler: has anything changed since one's previous visit? If so, why? There were several sites I was eager to review. It was not to be. Not for us the glories of Shebas; not for us the grandeur of Amenor. I spent the days of our trip upriver sitting by the rail, gazing wistfully at the shore as the antiquities passed inexorably by.

CHAPTER 11

༈

*The Lake of Saco. ﷯ We make camp. ﷯ An old friend.
Plans and preparations.*

THE JOURNEY up the Aram took us seven days, traveling in
daylight and mooring at night. The Aram is a wide, powerful
river, but without a skilled Aram pilot, which we lacked, even
the *Spaniel* could not safely run the river at night. We passed innumerable smaller boats, swamping one or two that got too close
to our cushion of foam, and I am afraid we did not stop to help
them. On the 24th of Melee, at long last, we reached the Lake
of Saco at the base of the Zymurgian plateau. Saco is several
miles in diameter, and surrounded on three sides by dense beds
of reeds. The cliffs of the Zymurgian plateau rise sheer from the
water on the fourth side, stark and gray, and tufted along the top
with dense greenery. In the middle of that side the cataract of
the Aram plunges from a deep notch in the side of the plateau,
thundering down into a cloud of mist. It is the only place in Seros
where the rainbow can regularly be seen.

The *Spaniel* anchored on the western shore of the lake, not
far from the base of the plateau. There is a small village nearby; the villagers keep the reeds cut back along a short stretch
of shoreline, and that is where we came to rest. To rest! A poor
word. After many days of peaceful inactivity, it was finally time
to get to work.

The first task was guaranteeing easy access to the shore.
Lumber was hauled laboriously from the hold, and under Captain
Halvorsen's direction the crew soon had pilings sunk deep into
the ooze of the lake bottom. Working neck deep in the water, or
from the ship's boat, cross pieces and decking were added, and
soon there was a simple but functional pier stretching from the
ship to the shore. The *Spaniel's* gangplank was lowered, and there
we were. As we would eat and sleep on-board, our basecamp
was complete.

The next step was to make contact with the locals, an easy
task as a large group of them had gathered along the shore to

watch the men build the pier. Most were standing and openly staring; a few took their ease on the ground. This task naturally fell to me, as the only fluent speaker of Serosan on the expedition, though I'd no doubt that one or two of the sailors could translate in a pinch. The people of Seros have largely adopted the Seljurk faith; the modern Serosan tongue is heavily-accented Seljurk with many loan words and idioms from Old Serosan. It is an unpleasant language to Anglish ears, filled with hissing, glottal stops, and harsh gutturals that nearly tear one's throat out. I was not looking forward to speaking it for any length of time, and as luck would have it (and as I'd hoped), I didn't have to. No sooner had I set foot on the pier than a cry went up from the natives on the shore, and one young man leaped to his feet and stood waiting for me.

"*Hakim effendi,*" he cried, eyes bright under his once-snowy head cloth, "*Alil Aziz!* You have returned!" Much to the sailors' surprise, he spoke a variety of Anglish.

"That I have, Cadbury, that I have. I trust your village has prospered since we last were here?"

"Indeed it has, *Hakim Effendi.* I am now a father, with two fine sons. And is the Carbuncle here as well?" I indicated that he was, and Cadbury smiled broadly. "Come!" he said. "You must do honor to my poor dwelling." I gestured for Philpott to leave the *Spaniel* and join us, and Cadbury took my arm and led me down the path to the village.

Readers of my earlier publications will no doubt remember Cadbury as fondly as I do. We had picked him up, a young Phillipian gutter rat, as a translator on our previous expedition to Seros. Originally hired for a few days, he had accompanied us for the rest of our journey, from the mouths of the Aram to this nameless village on the shore of the Lake of Saco. I learned most of my Serosan from him during that trip, including a number of expressions I later came to regret. As his name was quite difficult for us to pronounce, we had taken to calling him Cadbury, after one of the porters at the University.

I had had great hopes of finding him in the village; when we left after our short trip to the top of the plateau, he had stayed behind, being quite taken with one of the local girls. From his greeting, I gathered that his wooing had been successful.

As we walked, I asked, "How long did it take to win Fatima for yourself?"

His eyes flashed, as he replied, "Not long, *Hakim Effendi*, not long. It took longer to win over her father. I had to guide many more groups up and down the river before I could pay her bride-price." He laughed. "Seventeen goats and three oxen I had to pay for Fatima's hand. But once I had gathered them, he relented, and gave them as dowry. I am a wealthy man in this village, *Hakim Effendi*, and well-respected."

"And what of Ahmed?" Ahmed had been his rival for Fatima's favors.

"He was greatly angered, *Hakim Effendi*," Cadbury replied. "But there was little he could teach a student of the streets of Phillipi. He left in shame when Fatima and I were wed."

I could well imagine. Cadbury was a strongly built young man, and had had a rough upbringing in the poorest part of the Quarter of the Seljurks. He was also as quick and silent as a snake when threatened.

The walk to Cadbury's home was a lengthy one. The Serosans do not build on the fertile land near the shore of the Aram; every inch of arable land is cultivated. The homes are found in the barren sand and rock of the desert. The cultivated band around the Lake of Saco is wider than that along the Aram itself, and the walk was correspondingly longer. Cadbury and I continued to chat idly as we walked, while Philpott followed behind in great confusion, visibly impressed with my notoriety in the remote places of the world.

At last the fields ended, and the desert began; from there, it was but a few yards to the cluster of mud-brick huts that formed the village. Few people were evident as Cadbury lead us to one of the newer, more carefully built dwellings on the western edge of the village.

"*Effendi*," he said, looking from me to Philpott, "Please honor my humble dwelling with your presence." He bowed deeply before the door. I bowed in response, and so, at my nudging, did Philpott.

"May peace rest upon this dwelling and upon all who enter it," I replied in Cadbury's own language. He motioned us in with a sweeping gesture, and we entered, removing our hats.

The interior of Cadbury's hut was divided into several rooms, of which this was the main one. It was cramped and murky, having no opening to the outside but the door, and that was blocked by a white cloth. The floor was covered by a thin but brightly colored carpet. A low table stood in the middle, and Cadbury gestured us into places around it.

"Now," he said, "we shall take refreshment." He clapped his hands, and lovely Fatima, now shrouded in long robe and veil, entered with a tray. On the tray were three small ceramic cups and a plate with pieces of unleavened bread. The tray was offered to each of us in turn, and we each took a cup and a piece of bread. Then she vanished, having said nothing at all.

Philpott, thirsty from the walk, took a big drink from the cup. He was so startled that he nearly dropped the rest.

"My goodness!" he cried. "I had thought that the followers of Aziz were forbidden to drink alcoholic beverages." I took a sip myself, savoring the dark, yeasty fluid. It was as good as I had remembered.

"Cadbury," I said, "I have been remiss in my joy at finding you here. This is my colleague and friend, Dr. Thaddeus Philpott. Perhaps you could explain to him."

"Indeed, *Hakim Effendi*," Cadbury replied. "Philpott *Hakim*," he continued, "it is true that we who worship Aziz are forbidden wine and strong drink. But this is not wine, nor string drink, but the Water of Aziz, provided for our comfort. It has been drunk in this village since before Aziz was known here."

We sipped our beer and nibbled our bread in silence for a time. When we had finished, we set down our cups, and I said, "I thank you, my friend, for the generosity of your dwelling."

This fulfilled the necessary proprieties, and Cadbury was at last free to question us. He lost no time. Rubbing his hands together, he looked at me intently. "You are on an expedition, *Hakim Effendi?*"

"Of course, Cadbury; what else would bring me to the Lake of Saco? Now that I have found you, I hope you will join us."

He frowned, and said, "Alas, my friend, my days of traveling the river are over. This is my home now. Fatima fears the pretty girls of Phillipi; she wishes no rival."

"It is not a journey down the river that I have in mind, my friend. I have come to finish what I began when last we were together."

"It is as I thought," he cried. "You are returning to Zymurgia! Yes, *Hakim Effendi*, gladly I will come."

"Capital," I said. "We will also need someone from the village who can speak with the Zymurgians, to translate for us."

"There are many such," said Cadbury, "but why seek another? I have learned to speak with the traders. I speak their tongue as well as any in the village."

"Capital," I said again. "There is one other matter, Cadbury, in which you can be of great use to us."

"Name it, my friend."

"You have seen the vessel which brought us up the river. It is our base; it contains all of our supplies and equipment."

"Indeed, *Hakim Effendi;* what of it?"

"A man may come up the river, Cadbury, to try and take it away from us. This would end all of my hopes for the expedition. Perhaps you could send word to the villages down the river."

"He shall never see Phillipi again, *Hakim Effendi!* How shall we know him?" With his bright eyes and hawk nose, Cadbury could look quite fierce; I was filled with sympathy for the ousted Ahmed.

"As to that, he shall come asking for our vessel, the *Sea-Spaniel*, and for her captain, who is named Halvorsen. But I do not wish any harm to come to him." I took Cadbury by the hand. "It is of the utmost importance, Cadbury, that no harm come to him. Do not damage a single hair of his head. Rather, send word that he is to be helped on his way."

Cadbury was understandably puzzled, as was Philpott. "Helped, Dr. Thintwhistle? I thought we wished to discourage the man."

"Helped," I said again, "and helped with great care. I wish him to arrive here, at the Lake of Saco, with no complaints regarding the attention he has received." I paused, smiling slightly. "Under no circumstances should he hold his helpers responsible for the accidental loss of his personal belongings. He must have no one to blame but himself."

Cadbury looked at me, and then began to laugh. "It shall be as you say, *Hakim Effendi*, just as you say. We shall not damage a hair of his head, and he will have only himself to blame for the loss of his belongings."

Philpott, still puzzled, turned to question me, but had no opportunity. Cadbury clapped twice, and Fatima returned, and he spoke softly to her. "Now," he said, "you must see my sons." Fine strapping boys they were, of two and one years of age, respectively, and we discussed no more business. Finally we rose to go. Cadbury accompanied us to the lake, and then took his leave, promising to send the messages to the neighboring villages, and also to return that evening.

"Why, what's going to happen this evening?" asked Philpott.

"Now that we are here," I said, "we must be about our business. Tonight our expedition team will have our first council of war. I suggest you get some rest in the meantime, as you'll get precious little for the foreseeable future."

We paused at the top of the gangplank. "Oh," I said, "and would you inform Hodgins and Carbuncle? We will meet at seven o'clock in the lounge." With that, I took my own advice and sought the company of Bruno on the sundeck.

CHAPTER 12

ᐳᐧᐸ

A council of war

W E GATHERED in the lounge promptly at seven o'clock: myself, Carbuncle, Philpott, Hodgins, Cadbury, and Captain Halvorsen. After introductions were made and Cadbury and Carbuncle finished greeting each other, we pulled the chairs into a circle and sat down. The steward circulated with bottles of sherry and suchlike.

"The agenda for the night is twofold," I began after sampling my sherry. "First, we must plan the events of the next few days. As that is a straightforward matter, it shouldn't take too long. Next, I would like to review what we know about Zymurgia, both from historical sources and from our own experience." I smiled at the gathered company. "That shouldn't take too long, either, I fear." Carbuncle grinned at that; Philpott and Hodgins just looked earnest.

"But first, our plans," I continued. "Tomorrow, we must do a survey of the line of the plateau. It's an easy job, but it will get us moving, and also it will be much easier to do from down here than it would be from the top of the plateau."

Philpott broke in. "But didn't you do the same survey on your previous trip?"

"Precisely, Thaddeus, precisely. One of my pet theories is that Zymurgia is getting progressively more remote as time goes by. It will be interesting to see how this survey compares with the previous one. Though, in all fairness, we had no Hansen's geometer last time."

"I take it, then," said Carbuncle, "that you'll be wanting me to come along and operate it?"

"But surely, Thomas, you have more important things to do here?" As I feared, he did not.

"I think I can spare the time, Leon." He smirked evilly at me. "A stitch in time saves nine, they say."

I looked at him coldly, but did not respond to his insinuation. "Very well then, yes, I'd like you to come along, Thomas. And also you, Thaddeus, and you, Hodgins. That should be sufficient." Cadbury was looking disappointed. I hastened to reassure him.

"Cadbury, once we have finished our preliminary survey work, we will want to make our first trip to the top of the plateau. You know what that means in terms of donkeys, supplies, and so forth; can you see to making the arrangements?"

"Perhaps you will not wish to work so hard," he said, sitting forward in his chair. Perhaps I looked as puzzled as I was, for he continued immediately, "How long will you be at the surveying? Three days? Four days?"

"Five days; or perhaps four, weather permitting," I replied. "We will be making two trips, one to the east and one to the west, to map the plateau's line in both directions."

"The next trader is expected in six days," said Cadbury, "though it may be seven. Who can say? If you will wait, we can ride to the top of the plateau with the trader, and have a native guide immediately."

"Capital, Cadbury, capital. That's what we'll do. We're ahead of schedule thanks to our mad rush up the river, so even if it is eight days we will still be all right. Will we need our own donkeys?"

Cadbury's eyes crinkled as he smiled broadly, but all he said was, "No, my friend, no donkeys."

I turned my attention to Captain Halvorsen. "Captain, we will need the ship's boat in the morning to travel to the east shore of the lake. I'd like to have the boat ready first thing in the morning."

"Easily done," said the Captain. "I'll detail Jackson and Perkins to row you over. You won't object to their returning to the ship until it's time to pick you up?" We quickly arranged that the boat would return for us at the end of the second day, and that we would flash a mirror across the lake if we needed to be picked up earlier.

"Well, that concludes the planning portion of the meeting," I said, waving to the steward for a refill. "Now for a little Zymurgian history. Hodgins, I believe you've finished the translations I asked for?" He nodded, stiffly, sitting bolt upright in his seat, a sheaf of paper in his hand. "Capital. Please summarize their contents for us." His eyes widened, and if anything he sat up straighter.

He did not look happy, but Hodgins is an Anglish seaman, so he rallied quickly.

"Yes, sir." He shuffled pages for a moment, as if deciding where to start.

"Start with the earliest ones, Hodgins, if you please, and work your way forward."

He nodded, and began. "The first mention is by Miletidus the Troasene, who lived in the 22nd century BU. Um, he writes of a drink called the Water of the Gods which is served at the court of the king of Seros. He doesn't call it beer, but he does say that it comes from a land far to the south."

"It seems odd, doesn't it," said Carbuncle. "Didn't the Troasenes know about beer?"

"They certainly did," said Philpott. "I've seldom heard of a culture that didn't. It's almost an invariant."

"It hardly matters either way," I said. "Old Miletidus based his writings on traveller's tales; I'm not sure he ever left Troas. He certainly never tasted the Water of the Gods, and I doubt his source had either. Also, remember that Seros may still have been largely fabulous at that time." I sipped my sherry, as Hodgins continued.

"Ah, the next mention," he said, "is in the *Serosan Campaign* of Isotragoras of Chalcedon, which was written late in the 18th century BU in Phillipi. This Isotragoras fellow was an advisor of Phillip the Great's and was with him during the conquest of Seros. The Water of the Gods was still being drunk by the king of Seros and his court at that time, and the soldiers who captured the palace identified it quite definitely as beer. They left little enough, but apparently Phillip got a taste of it, and continued importing it. According to Isotragoras, he contemplated a Zymurgian campaign, but nothing came of it. Isotragoras also says that the Water of the Gods came from a country many week's journey to the south and high in the mountains. He called the place Zumosia."

I nodded at him to continue.

"There are a few mentions during the next century or so," Hodgins went on, "but they don't amount to much. The next important document is the *Memoirs* of the Paloman general Clodius Serosicus. He conquered the last remnants of Phillip's dynasty

and turned Seros into a huge farm for the benefit of the Paloman Empire, except that I guess it wasn't really an empire yet."
Hodgins snorted and looked up. "Bit of a killjoy was old Clodius.
He disapproved of Zymurgian beer on moral grounds. He refers to
it as the Water of the God, *aqua dei*, but he knew it was beer all
right. He didn't approve of the beer they served in Paloma either.
Let's see," he said, trying to find his spot again. "Clodius was appointed proconsul of Seros, and he did two important things: he
stopped importing beer to Phillipi, and he arranged to have Seros
fairly well mapped."

"For that day and age, certainly," I agreed. Carbuncle
chuckled.

"He's the first source I've read that gives the name Zymurgia
to the land to the south of Seros," Hodgins went on. "He tried to
suppress the beer trade, but later gave it up as a bad job. Apparently he contemplated invading Zymurgia to stop it at the source,
but after he learned of the plateau and the cliffs he gave that
up, too."

"I seem to recall that his is the last source that speaks of the
Zymurgian traders traveling freely about Seros…is that right?" I
asked. Hodgins thought for a few moments, then nodded.

"Yes, I think it is. Many traders were imprisoned or killed,
and I suppose the remainder got tired of it all."

"Ah. Go on, please," I said.

"Well, the next source is the Paloman historian Musebius,
who travelled through Seros at the height of the Paloman Empire.
He found the *aqua dei* all over Seros, drunk by all manner of
people; apparently the trade had picked up considerably by then,
but most of the traders were Serosan. He ascribed healing powers
to the *aqua dei*."

"Ironic, that," I said. "Tradition has it that he sent for some
aqua dei in his last illness; apparently it spoiled in transit, and he
died of it." Philpott looked slightly appalled, but Hodgins snickered appreciatively.

"Well," he continued, "then the Seljurks swept through
around the 7th century BU and took over the whole place."

"Not the Seljurks," said Philpott.

"Followers of Aziz, then," said Hodgins. "Azizim rulers have
come and gone since then, but they've mostly suppressed the

trade even more harshly than old Clodius, on religious grounds. There are scattered mentions of Zymurgia over the next thousand years, as the source of a clandestine trade in forbidden liquor. The next important mention is in the writings of a Lyrican explorer, Giacomo Cabrini. He was the first Arrastian since the Palomans to say much about Seros, and the first to see this lake we're floating on since Clodius did his survey. He came to Seros a little over a hundred and fifty years ago, and made it all the way up the Aram to right here. He'd had so many troubles on the way, and was so upset by the sight of the massive cliffs that he lost heart. He spent some time with the local villagers, and then went home. He doesn't say anything about *aqua dei* or Zymurgia, but he does mention that the locals gave him some truly excellent beer, and that he was surprised to find such a thing in a village of the Azizim."

Hodgins straightened his pile of papers, and sat back. "And that's about it," he said. "There's been a lot written about Seros since, but not many people have made it this far south. I guess they keep getting stuck at the various monuments and things in the north."

Carbuncle chuckled again. "That's more or less what happened to Leon and I on our last trip. That writ-server in Cuprios has probably done us a real service."

"Now, Thomas," I said, "you know we never intended to visit Zymurgia on our last trip. We were just trying to get away from the visitors."

"That's true, indeed that's true. Bad as mosquitoes they were. Now, Leon, tell them about our trip," said Carbuncle.

I leaned back in my chair, waving at Baxter for a refill. I twirled my glass by its stem for a few moments as I gathered my thoughts.

"What I remember most," I said, "about our previous trip to Zymurgia is the donkeys. We hired a team of donkeys from the villagers here, and rode them to the top of the plateau. At least, we rode them where we didn't have to walk. It's a long, steep, windy, poorly maintained path, and frankly I'm not looking forward to that part of the trip."

"Do not worry," said Cadbury, "you will not have such trouble this time."

I looked at him skeptically. His brown face was solemn, but his bright eyes were laughing at me.

"Should this be true, Cadbury, I will be eternally grateful." He half-bowed in his seat, inclining his head. "At any rate, the trips up and down the cliff were as uneventful as they were painfully tedious. When we got to the top of the plateau—"

"You could hardly stand, as I recall, Leon," Carbuncle broke in.

"When we got to the top of the plateau—"

"And then you could hardly stand to be seated!" Carbuncle's broad face was suffused with laughter as he drained his glass of sherry and gestured for a refill. Cadbury joined him—in the laughter, not the sherry. I refused to be drawn.

"When we got to the top of the plateau—" I paused, and looked at my colleagues. Carbuncle had his face buried in one hand, stifling giggles, and waved me along with the other. I resumed, "our first job was to find a native guide. Either the villagers didn't suggest hiring one of the traders, or there wasn't one due, I don't recall, but we didn't have a Zymurgian guide with us."

Carbuncle had recovered by this time. "That's really what held us up," he told the others. "We had no guide, and the only Zymurgian we managed to grab didn't speak Serosan."

"That's when we found out how odd the Zymurgian language is," I said. Philpott sat up straight. "None of the old writings mention the language at all; they just say that the Zymurgians were foreigners. I'd assumed all along that the Zymurgians were of the same race as the Serosans, speaking a variant of the same language, but I was greatly mistaken. It's entirely different, and unrelated to any language with which I am familiar. I'm quite impressed, Cadbury, that you've managed to pick it up."

"Leon," said Philpott, "do you suppose I could stay here while you go off surveying? I'd like to work with Cadbury on an Anglish-Zymurgian dictionary."

"Doesn't that seem a tad ambitious, Thaddeus? You've not yet learned any other language than Anglish."

"One must start somewhere," he said, earnestly. "And besides, it could be useful." Useful to his career, I thought to myself.

"Very well, Thad. Carbuncle and Hodgins and I should manage all right between us."

"So what happened next, sir?" asked Hodgins.

"What was that, Hodgins?"

"With the one Zymurgian you managed to grab, sir."

"Oh, yes. Him. We couldn't understand a word of his language, and he couldn't understand a word of ours, but he was quite friendly none-the-less. He lead us to a kind of hut at the edge of a field of grain, just under the trees, you know, and gave us quite a nice meal, didn't he, Thomas."

"He did, Leon, he did," said Carbuncle. "As I recall, there was some kind of meat stew, and a jug of something that nearly took my scalp clean off when I drank it."

"Yes, some kind of grain spirits, I believe," I said. "It was quite potent," I said, rubbing my own scalp at the memory. Cadbury, who had of course had had none, was looking painfully smug.

"No beer?" asked Hodgins, surprised.

"Yes," said Philpott, "I'm surprised as well. I don't completely understand the Law of Consensus yet, but after beer has appeared in all of the stories for thousands of years, I'd certainly expect there to be beer."

"No beer," I said. "I don't know why that should be, but this trip I hope to find out. The important thing to remember is that the stories don't tell the whole story. All we really know is that Zymurgia has exported beer for thousands of years. What place beer has in their culture, we have no idea." I drained my glass. "Is there any more sherry, Baxter?"

"No, sir, there is not. Unless you would like me to open another bottle."

I mentally tallied the number of bottles remaining, and shook my head. "No, thank you, Baxter. Well, gentlemen, I declare this meeting closed. I shall see you all at an ungodly hour tomorrow morning. Good night." And with that, I walked carefully to my cabin for as many hours of the dreamless as I could get before morning.

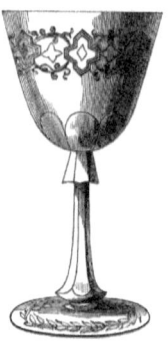

CHAPTER 13

∻

Preliminary surveys. ₰ An unwelcome visitor.

THE NEXT few days were uneventful. Carbuncle, Bruno, Hodgins, and I gathered early the next morning with geometer, transit compass, and notebooks, and Jackson and Perkins rowed us across the lake as planned. A pale green sun had appeared on the eastern horizon and was shooting rapidly towards the zenith, and the lake's ripples and wavelets shone like fine jade in its light. Hodgins and I took our ease in the stern, while Carbuncle sat in the bow, looking for fish. He later claimed that he had seen several giant trout, three or four feet in length, and who's to say he didn't? The lack of his fishing gear was a great pain to him, but we reminded him he could have a go in a few days, while we waited for the trader to arrive.

Disembarking was a chore, as the reed beds were many yards thick on the east side of the lake, and as there was no village on that side there was no carefully tended landing place. We struggled through, taking better care of the equipment than of ourselves, and getting not a few cuts in the process. I directed the men to clear an easier path before returning to the *Spaniel*.

Once we were safely ashore, we took our first sightings. This kind of surveying is straightforward if tedious; the hard part is determining your position to begin with, and Carbuncle and the geometer made short work of that. We soon fell into a routine: walk a mile or so; fix our position and write it down; take sightings on the prominent features of the plateau's edge, and write them down as well. Each sighting included the azimuth and elevation of the feature; given two such sightings from two well-known positions, and you can easily determine the position of any landmark in sight. This, at least, was the routine for everyone but Bruno, who travelled at least two miles for every one of ours. We carried on in this way for the whole of the day, traveling some fifteen miles and making only a brief stop for lunch.

When the green sun vanished on the horizon we called it a day. We were well beyond the green banks of the Aram by that

time, and it was cool at night, and very dry. There was little conversation as we settled down for the night.

A fine yellow sun, perhaps a little larger than average, awoke
us with its bright rays the next morning. Of necessity we had carried little but our equipment, water, and a little food, so breaking
camp was a simple matter. We ate much of the remaining food,
drank some of our remaining water (Bruno drank out of Hodgins'
hat), and started walking.

The hike back to the lake was a quicker matter altogether.
We had taken all the needful sightings the previous day, and
so could enjoy ourselves. The desert has a grandeur never seen
in foggy Angland, and the juxtaposition of the dunes and wadis
against the stark grey cliffs fringed at the top with greenery was
both exotic and riveting. At length, food gone, water exhausted,
we reached the shore of the lake. We had but to wait a few minutes
before the boat arrived, and we returned, happy and refreshed by
the lake water, to the *Spaniel*.

The trip to the west was much the same, and I see no point
in describing it. Surveying is an essential part of exploration, but
it is tedious and unexciting. The reader may assume that we fixed
our position and took sightings as often as we could during our
stay in Zymurgia; I will not mention it again unless it affects my
story. It is sufficient to say that we traveled west for a day, pausing
only for lunch and to pull Carbuncle out of a pit (the geometer
nearly ran off in fright); we slept, awoke, and returned to the ship
to discover that much more interesting things had been going on
in our absence.

I am indebted to both Philpott and Cadbury for their descrip-
tions of many of the events I will now relate.

Your average writ-server is a low man, cunning but not clever, quick but seldom clean. Motivated solely by the hope of gain,
he achieves his goals more by drudgery than by foresight. Frederick Fox was (and is) another breed of animal altogether. He
had indeed been waiting for us in Phillipi, checking every ship
that entered the harbor. When the mate of a rusty little scow told
him that the *Sea-Spaniel* had left Cuprios several days before he
knew we had slipped past in the night, and he knew we could only
have one destination. An intrepid man, he set out in immediate
pursuit. He went as far south as Baxur with a group of Lyrican

travelers; from there he hired a fisherman and his son to take him as far south as they would.

He was actually sailing south with them when we passed at speed; because we had come from Cuprios under sail, we were several days late by his reckoning, and until that moment had been behind him. He had happened to be looking down river, and compelled the man and his son to take the boat as close to the *Spaniel* as possible. I believe, indeed, that he beat the man away from the tiller, and guided the frail craft directly toward us. In the event, it was to no avail. Our relative speed was too high, and the shock of our passing swamped the small boat.

The fisherman had had enough by this time: he was days away from his home, and this lunatic of an Anglishman had nearly caused the wreck of his boat, his only source of livelihood. He put Mr. Fox ashore when he had finished bailing and headed north. Mr. Fox put his pack on his back, and trudged south.

It cannot have been a pleasant journey. The banks of the Aram are heavily cultivated and irrigated, making for treacherous footing at the best of times. The natives habitually travel inland, past the cultivated strip, but Mr. Fox could not afford to be out of sight of the river. Nor, though he had abundant water, was he well supplied with food. Hospitality is sacred in Seros, and any villager would have given him a morsel or two for the asking; but the villages, like the roads, were too far inland. He walked in the mud, he fell in the mud, and I rather expect he slept in the mud as well.

His trek continued until he came to a village's landing stage, upon which reclined a number of the village men, smoking and laughing. It was an odd time of day for them to be there, rather than in the fields, but Mr. Fox was too tired and hungry to notice. They greeted him like an old friend, and insisted on taking him to their village—after a vigorous dunking in the river to cleanse him of the worst of the mud. Mr. Fox protested, but they assured him that the "White Ship" had already passed; that his best course was to come with them, eat and sleep, and take the road to the Lake of Saco in the morning. Surely he would find the White Ship moored in the Lake of Saco.

Unable to resist, Mr. Fox gave in, and gratefully gave his knapsack into the hands of his rescuers. They brought him to their village, and took him to the home of the mayor (for so they call the most prominent villager), where he was received with gentle hands, with clean clothes, with cooling drinks, with nourishing food. His old clothes, and his knapsack, were taken away to be cleaned.

It is not to be wondered at that Mr. Fox slept well and long, though he did awake briefly in the night. He quickly identified the noise as an angry dog fight, judged it none of his concern, and returned to sleep. Alas for Mr. Fox! The village dogs were none of his concern...but they were fighting over the provisions the good villagers had placed in his knapsack, as it sat drying on a rock near the center of the village.

When he arose in the morning, the mayor and the chief men of the village joined him for breakfast, and then the mayor told him of his loss, bringing out the ruined knapsack. All of its contents had been torn to bits, though fortunately his cleaned suit of clothes had been spared. The villagers were devastated, and would do their best to replace his belongings—further, they would escort him to the Lake of Saco, that he would meet with no other troubles.

Mr. Fox was, naturally, quite distressed over his ruined belongings, though he cheered up slightly when his clothes were returned to him. He was soon ready to travel, and three of the village men (and no small number of the village dogs) escorted him up the river road.

I am greatly sorry that I was not present when Mr. Fox reached the lake and found the *Spaniel*. It was a moment with all of the passion of high drama, and all of the comedy of low farce. Picture Mr. Fox, bruised, footsore, coming in sight of his goal after weeks of travel. Picture him skulking in the reed beds, dirtying his clothes and person, cutting his hands and face, until he saw a man in a white coat with gold braid leave the ship in company with a few others. Picture him pulling a folded piece of parchment from his breast pocket, and appearing before the captain, writ in hand. Picture the horror and distress on the good captain's face, as Mr. Fox said, no doubt in rolling if somewhat breathless tones, "Captain Halvorsen, I serve this writ upon you, and request and require that, upon the order of the His Majesty's Chancery Court of Pelham, you immediately put the ship *Sea-*

Spaniel, and all its contents, into my governance on behalf of the creditors of Earl Clarence of Luton."

As a servant of His Majesty, as are all Anglishmen everywhere, Captain Halvorsen had no option but to take the proffered writ, and unfold it slowly, and read it. Imagine all of creation hushed after Mr. Fox's speech, the silence broken only by the sound of the parchment being unfolded. Picture the grim scowl on Captain Halvorsen's face as he did so.

Picture the dismay on Mr. Fox's face when the captain slowly turned the parchment over and over, trying to make sense of the long black streaks that were all that remained of the fine round hand of the Chancery Court Clerk. I have it under excellent authority that Mr. Fox was not best pleased. His eyes grew wide; he snatched the parchment from the captain, and turned it over and over; he took a deep breath, and said, "Captain Halvorsen, might I trouble you for stiff drink before I go?"

I myself was rather chagrined when Philpott related the story; it should have occurred to me that the man would keep the writ on his person rather than in his baggage. I silently gave thanks for the wisdom or kindness that lead the villagers to take Mr. Fox's clothes and give them a thorough washing. But that is by the way. Captain Halvorsen had realized, as I had known he would, that Mr. Fox could not be allowed to roam about loose. Although the viper's fang had been pulled, as it were, he was still capable of bringing others down on us, or of acquiring another writ. Accordingly, the captain had escorted Mr. Fox back to the *Sea-Spaniel*, given him a stiff drink (for the captain was a kind man), and asked him for his parole.

"I could see that Fox was a gentleman, though one fallen on hard times," the captain said. We had gathered in the lounge as usual, and given the events of the day the captain had joined us. "He quite understood the situation; gave his parole immediately, in return for passage home to Angland."

"Hmph," snorted Carbuncle. "And why wouldn't he? It's better accommodation here on the *Spaniel* than he's had in a while, isn't it?"

"If he thought that, he was greatly mistaken," I said. "Parole or not, I'll be more comfortable to have him where I can see him. He'll be coming up the cliff with the rest of us."

"But will that be safe?" asked Philpott. "There are more people to keep an eye on him here."

"Safe enough," I replied. "We only know one safe way down the plateau, with the *Sea-Spaniel* and crew at the bottom. He's welcome to try other methods; if he can fly, which I doubt."

I fear I was not completely candid with my colleagues in this exchange. I had other reasons for wanting Mr. Frederick Fox to join us in Zymurgia. Carbuncle may have noticed my unwonted reticence, but if so he had wisely remained silent.

CHAPTER 14

⌒

Carbuncle goes fishing. ❧ *A conversation with Mr. Fox.*
The trader approaches.

A S THE trader wasn't expected for another day or so, the 29th
of Melee was decreed by universal acclamation to be a day
of rest. Though an angler by avocation, Carbuncle did not disdain deep water fishing; he commandeered the ship's boat, and
with Bruno for company rowed out into the middle of the lake. I
settled into my accustomed deck chair on the lakewards side of
the *Spaniel*, and settled down to watch. I judged that I had the
better part—fishing is mostly sitting quietly in one place, and I
had no need to row anywhere to do that. Moreover, I was much
less likely to spill my beer (Cadbury had had a keg sent over for
us). I am unsure what the others did that day; I rather expect
that Philpott was still troubling Cadbury with his dictionary, and
I think Hodgins took advantage of Bruno's absence to get some
sleep. Fox kept to the cabin he had been assigned.

At two or so in the afternoon I was awakened from a refreshing nap by a storm of barking coming from the lake. At first I
thought Carbuncle had caught some new species of fish, a dogfish
perhaps, but was soon reassured to see Bruno standing in the bow
of the boat, muzzle nearly down in the water. Carbuncle was in
the stern, trying to master his fishing pole, which was bent nearly
double. It was hard to see what happened next, but Bruno moved
aft, and Carbuncle moved forward, and as neither had eyes for
the other they collided. In the ensuing confusion the boat turned
over. I heard ribald laughter from the deck below me, and gathered that I was not the only observer. I watched in great concern
until I saw the heads of Bruno and Carbuncle rise out of the water.

Bruno elected to have no more to do with boats, and swam
rapidly to the ship. By the time Carbuncle had righted the boat
and paddled painfully in, Bruno was warm and dry and reclining
at my feet. Carbuncle, by contrast, was damp and despondent.

"You'll never believe it, Leon," he said. "It was the largest
trout I've ever had on my hook."

"Really?" I replied. "Just how big was he? Big enough to swamp the boat, evidently."

Carbuncle waved that aside. "That was just clumsiness. The fish cut under the bow of the boat. I went forward to bring the line around the bow, and that bloody beast there ran under my feet. I'd have had him if not for that." He sat, dripping, on the next deck chair, and called for some beer. "Three feet if it was an inch, Leon. And like as not I'll never have another chance at it."

"Only three feet, Thomas? Not four? Or five?" I winked at him, and he scowled at me.

"That's right, Leon, kick me when I'm down. And sore; that bloody barge floats gunwale under when it's swamped. But I see it's no use arguing. I knew you'd not believe me."

"Believe you? How could I believe you, Thomas, when you come to me with absurd stories about yard-long trout? I'll have you know that it measured at least forty inches."

"Forty inches?" He scowled at me in surprise. "What are you saying, exactly?"

"While you were dealing with the boat, Bruno here was dealing with the fish. He brought it to shore with him." I smiled broadly at Carbuncle's flabbergasted expression.

"Bruno? That bloody beast caught my fish?" Plainly, Carbuncle wasn't sure whether to be pleased or offended. Pleasure won out. "Well, lad," he said to Bruno, "I'm glad I brought you with me." He stopped, suddenly, and looked at me.

"Now, where is it?"

"If you'd like to see it whole, you'd best run along to the galley. I believe the cook is going to prepare it for dinner. You needn't hurry," I shouted at his retreating back, "I made him promise not to touch it until you had seen it!"

And so it was that we dined, and well, on trout fillets; and Bruno had a place of honor at the Captain's table. He comported himself with dignity, chewing his fillet neatly and grinning at us all as he waited for seconds.

Shortly after I retired to my cabin that night there was a knock on the door. I had been expecting the visit, and shouted "Come in!", but I didn't move. I remained slouched in my chair, my feet up on the bunk, with Carnarvon's *Antiquities* open on my lap. The situation of the cabin was such that the door was behind me, but I knew perfectly well who it was.

"Hello, Frederick," I said, "I knew you'd remember your manners sooner or later." There was suddenly an air of hurt indignation in the room.

"That's very hard, Dr. Thintwhistle, after all I've tried to do for you."

"For me, Frederick?" I exclaimed, half turning around in the chair to see him. "It is for my sake that you've been skulking about, pursuing us the full length of Seros under an assumed name?" He started to open his mouth, raising on hand a little, but I wasn't through. "And, I might add, carrying a writ which would have ended the expedition altogether. Heaven spare me from your enmity. Oh, do come and sit down on the bed where I see you."

Somewhat hesitantly, head hung low (it was a low ceiling, and Frederick is a tall man), my former student came fully into the cabin, shutting the door carefully behind him. He folded himself carefully onto the bed.

"Hello, Dr. Thintwhistle."

"Hello, Frederick. So nice to see you."

"Perhaps I had best explain," he said. I looked at him brightly, raising my eyebrows.

"You are evidently aware," he began slowly, "that the Earl of Luton is bankrupt."

"Rumors only," I said quickly. "It has not been brought officially to our attention."

"No," he said, closing his eyes and taking a deep breath. He let it out slowly, and continued. "Were you also aware that Luton's chief creditor is the Mercantile Bank of Pelham and Bundyal?"

"Your father's bank?" He nodded.

"What are you telling me, Frederick? That your father, Sir Fosbury Forsythe, sent you out as his personal hatchet man? Doesn't he know that he has already injured me more than was necessary?" And he had. Frederick had been one of my most promising students, until his father demanded that he leave the University and join the family firm. That had been several years before.

The air of hurt indignation had returned. Frederick looked at me with sad puppy eyes.

"It wasn't like that, Dr. Thintwhistle. I heard about Luton's bankruptcy and the plans to seize his yacht. I knew what that would mean to your expedition." His eyes pleaded with me, but I did not relent. I merely waited for him to continue. "It's quite a large sum of money, Dr. Thintwhistle. The sale of the *Sea-Spaniel* won't begin to cover it, but it's a big enough piece that the firm could not ignore it." He hesitated long enough to draw and release another deep breath, and then looked me straight in the eye. "I know what writ-servers are, Dr. Thintwhistle. I thought that it would be less painful all around if I took care of it myself."

I allowed myself to soften slightly. "On the theory, I take it, that one should always shoot one's dog oneself?"

"If you like, yes. I'm sorry."

"So am I, Frederick, so am I. It's a lonely place we're in; any number of accidents could happen to a man who didn't know the terrain or the people. But I'm afraid I can't condone accidents to a former student," I said regretfully.

The blood drained from Frederick's face. "Dr. Thintwhistle, surely you're not serious!"

"No," I said, "more's the pity. It would be so much simpler. But," I said, "fortunately the point is moot. Your writ is destroyed, and therefore my expedition is safe."

He leaned forward a trifle. "I don't suppose I can persuade you to bring the *Sea-Spaniel* back to Pelham even without a writ?"

"Of course I'll bring the *Sea-Spaniel* back to Pelham. But not now, not until I'm done with it. Your father and his bank will just have to settle for that."

"I thought as much," he said. "Well, then. The captain has confined me to the ship. I'd very much like to get back to Pelham, if I may."

"You may not." I said firmly. "We'll need you to help us run the gauntlet safely on our return to Angland." He nodded slowly, but said nothing. "And besides, no thanks to your father, I've finally got you out of Angland and into the field, where you belong. When we go up the cliff to Zymurgia, you'll be coming along."

"I will," he said. It was not quite a question.

"Oh, yes," I said, "You will. Now, you'd best run along; I'll talk with you again tomorrow."

Frederick rose to go; I stopped him as he got to the door.

"Oh, and Frederick?"

"Yes, Dr. Thintwhistle?"

"Why the assumed name?"

"My father insisted, Dr. Thintwhistle. He didn't want me to drag the name of Forsythe through the mud. You won't tell anyone, will you?"

"Not unless it suits me, Frederick, not unless it suits me. Good night!"

After he left I browsed through Carnarvon for a while longer, and was soon ready for sleep.

The next day dawned bright and orange, and some hours later I was awakened by the steward's knock.

"It is the native, sir," he said, his inflection indicating all of his unspoken disdain for people who wore robes and head cloths. "He insists on speaking to you."

"I'm surprised at you, Baxter," I said. "Cadbury is an old friend, and a full member of our expedition. I'll thank you to remember that." I waved away Baxter's stammered apology, and told him to send Cadbury to my cabin posthaste. I dressed quickly as I waited for him to arrive.

"Good morning, *Hakim Effendi*," he said as he entered my cabin. He was resplendent in a snowy white robe—not the slightly tattered robe he usually wore, but clearly his best, and a light blue head cloth. That surprised me considerably; it indicated that he would be speaking for the village as a whole.

"Good morning, Cadbury," I said as I laced up my boots. I always have trouble getting the laces tight enough. "What's the occasion?"

His eyes danced. "The trader approaches, my friend. Come see."

CHAPTER 15

ᴗːᴗ

The trader arrives.

MOMENTS LATER I was at the rail, gazing over the reeds and fields to the trailhead at the base of the cliff, looking for the telltale cloud of dust. No trader in bulky goods like beer travels without beasts of burden, and the signs of their coming are clear from great distances. To my surprise I saw nothing. I looked at Cadbury carefully, searching his laughing face. "Where?" I finally said. "Surely he hasn't reached the village already?"

"You look in the wrong place, *effendi*. Look to the left: beside the waterfall."

It took me several minutes to realize what I was seeing. At last I went up to the bridge, and begged the use of the captain's spyglass. A few moments further study clarified it beyond all doubt— fortunately, for at that time the captain snatched the spyglass back from me to see for himself.

A kind of wooden platform was being lowered from the top of the cliff by means of a cable. Several figures were plainly to be seen atop the platform, which had an odd, lumpy look to the edges.

"But they are lowering it into the lake," I said in surprise.

"What else, *effendi?*" asked Cadbury. "How easier to get the kegs to market than by floating them down the river?" Cadbury was greatly pleased with himself.

"And how easier to get to the top of the cliff than by riding up with the trader on that contraption…is that the game, Cadbury?" He merely bowed and grinned.

"Ride up in that?" asked Captain Halvorsen. "I'd hate to even set foot on it. It's all kegs!"

And so it was. By noon, and without catastrophe, the ungainly contraption had been lowered into the water at the cliff's edge. Two of the figures on board were paddling it towards the stretch of shore kept clear of reeds by the villagers; a third sat at his ease on a raised platform in the middle of the raft. I assumed he was the one in charge. The paddlers seemed most surprised and entranced by the *Sea-Spaniel*, waving and gesturing at it and each other, and evidently laughing a great deal; we could hear their hoots and guffaws echo dimly from the cliffs. The trader remained silent and still, except for occasional dire glances at the others.

"Come," said Cadbury at last. "We must be ready when the trader arrives. I must ask you, my friend, not to speak with him until after the feast. No trading will be done until tomorrow morning."

Before the makeshift barge reached the halfway point, the bank was occupied by (apparently) the entire population of the village, a rowdy group of sailors, and three Anglish academics.

I cut Baxter out of the crowd—not a difficult task, as he was trying his best not to appear a part of it. "Baxter, I imagine you'll be trying to get a few kegs for the ship?"

"The captain sent me out to see what I could do, sir."

"I understand no trading will be done until tomorrow; the fellow has to be properly welcomed first. Apparently it would be a great breach of etiquette for us to raise the topic early. Pass the word among the men, will you?"

"The men will be most disappointed, sir," cautioned the steward.

"As am I, Baxter. But if this man can spare me a ride up the cliff trail on a donkey, I for one am willing to wait 24 hours for my beer."

"Very good, sir." I didn't watch him go, having eyes only for the spectacle on the lake, but from the groans behind me, I gathered Baxter was carrying out my orders.

All in all, the barge was an impressive sight. Close to I realized that it was not a raft of loaded kegs, to be disassembled when it reached market, as I had originally thought. It rode too high in the water for that. Large kegs were the basis of it, but it had a well-laid deck and a low rail around three sides. Four stout eyebolts rose from the corners to receive the hoisting cables. Although showing the scars of long use, the exposed surfaces were clean, and bright with paint. These signs of careful maintenance cheered me considerably as I contemplated the journey before me.

The platform upon which the trader was sitting proved to be made up of a square array of smaller kegs, and I gathered that these were the cargo. It was a small load, of between twenty-five and thirty-six kegs.

The trader rose to his feet as the barge glided to the water's edge. He and his helpers were as impressive as their conveyance. Much darker than their Serosan neighbors, they were strongly built, with short, very black hair. The two oarsmen wore short skirts of unbleached linen, and little else. The trader wore the same, with the addition of a cape and hat of some kind of tawny fur. I call it a cape for lack of any more precise term; it covered his shoulders but ended, I would judge, above his shoulder blades. It was held in place by a short chain that passed over his collarbones. A pendant of some kind of shiny metal hung from the center point of the chain. The hat was a squat cylinder perched on the top of his head.

Cadbury had left my side some time before; he was standing at the water's edge, exactly opposite the Zymurgian trader. Both looked remarkably solemn, given the occasion. I noticed Philpott beside me, studying the scene with a kind of hunger.

As well he might, for it was entirely unlike anything I had expected. The two men stood looking at each other for several minutes, as the crowd grew completely silent. I heard one sailor say "What's—" quite loudly, but his crewmates stifled him immediately.

Cadbury finally broke the seeming deadlock by bowing very low, almost to the ground. Rising, he shouted something in a language I presumed to be Zymurgian; it seemed to be a greeting of some kind. Then he bowed again.

The trader responded by stepping forward and raising his arms, as if to give the gathered villagers a blessing. He intoned several phrases in a sonorous, rolling chant, dipping his hands at the end of each. His speech was quite impressive, but seemed well-rehearsed, even perfunctory. When he had finished, he stepped back and crossed his arms.

Cadbury bowed once more, and chanted a reply in the same language. Finally he bowed again, and moved to one side, turning so that he faced the path from the shore to the village. As he turned, he waved one arm from the barge to the village, clearly indicating that the trader was welcome. He remained in this position until the trader barked a response and stamped his foot three times on the deck.

At that moment the tableau dissolved. The oarsmen jumped in the water and splashed to the shore, where they were helped out by many eager hands. The trader, grinning widely, jumped over the last few feet of water, and was steadied in his landing by Cadbury and his friends. There was much slapping of backs and much embracing. Apparently the trader and his men were popular visitors.

Philpott stirred at my elbow. "I wonder if the Ophir knows about this," he murmured, eyes wide. "This is simply amazing."

"What are you talking about? The trade in beer? Of course he does. We talked about it with him on our last expedition."

He shook his head slowly, still studying the scene carefully. "No, Leon. Not the beer. The beer is just a detail."

I turned to face him, frowning. "What do you mean, Thad?" I got no answer. At that moment there was a shout, and the whole crowd of people began moving down the road to the village, Cadbury and the trader at their head. The barge was left quite untended. I turned to look for Captain Halvorsen.

"What do you make of this, Dr. Thintwhistle?" he asked as I approached.

"It's fascinating, Captain, that's what I think." I nodded, and then continued, "Captain, I notice that the beer is unguarded. I foresee great difficulty for the expedition if any of it should disappear during the night."

He nodded, no stranger to the sailor's love of alcohol.

"Trading will begin tomorrow," I said. "I am sure we will be able to procure some at that time. In the meantime…I understand that there is to be a feast in the village tonight, to celebrate the trader's arrival. If your men were to bring a suitable addition, I am sure they would be welcome."

"I'm sure the cook can put something together," said the captain. "And the beer will be perfectly safe. The *Spaniel* isn't one of His Majesty's ships, you know." He grinned. "Every man on board knows that I can replace him in less time than it takes to get drunk." We parted, then, and I followed the crowd down to the village, hoping for a word with Cadbury.

By the time I arrived, Cadbury and the trader had vanished. One of Cadbury's friends saw me looking about, and sauntered over.

"You are too late, *Hakim Effendi*," he said in Serosan. "The honored trader is taking refreshment with the elders of the village, and will not come out until the feast begins. Cadbury and Thaddeus *Effendi* are with him." He pronounced the names "Kahdboori" and "Thahdayoos". "Had you arrived earlier, you might have joined them."

"Tell me, my friend," I replied in the same language. "You have met the crew of our ship. Might they be permitted to attend the feast? They are bored with the ship sitting at anchor every day, and they are eager to come." This, I fear, was a piece of unmitigated blackmail. Hospitality is sacred in these villages, and I had left the man no choice.

"Of course, *Hakim Effendi,* your men may come." He frowned at me slightly.

"Such hospitality deserves recompense before God," I answered with a smile. "My men will bring with them many Anglish delicacies; none will go hungry." He brightened immediately, and I took my leave, well satisfied.

When I reached the shore, I was at first angered to see someone clambering about on the barge; then I reflected that I had not seen my good friend Thomas Carbuncle for some time. Indeed, he had stayed behind to examine the barge and its accoutrements, few as they were. He straightened up as I approached, and walked back to the *Spaniel* with me.

"No phantasms, Leon. No phantasms at all," he said, shaking his head. "It's an odd thing."

"Why, Thomas? It's just a barge, after all, so it wouldn't have ur-sails. And the phantail is a fairly new development."

"Oh, yes, true enough. But there are none of the little conveniences, either. No lights, for example."

"There are places in Angland that don't yet have phanlights, Thomas," I said. "I still don't see what's so odd."

We had reached the top of the gangplank by this time, and paused there. We leaned on the rail and looked at the belt of the green fields and the desert beyond.

"Well, it's the construction of the barge, Leon. How the boards were shaped and smoothed, and how the kegs were made. So far as I can tell, the makers used no phantasms whatsoever." He stared off into the distance as he said this. I raised my eyebrows, but said nothing. "My experience with such things is limited, and I'd be the first to admit it," he said, "but I think it was all done with mechanical tools of some kind."

I turned my back on the view and leaned, resting my elbows on the top of the rail. "And your conclusion?" I asked.

He turned his head, and asked, "Leon, have you ever heard of a culture with no grasp of phantastics? No phantasms at all?"

I shook my head. "Never," I said. "They might be limited to lighting fires, or heating food, but they always have something."

"That's right," he said. "Neither have I. And since building things of wood is such a common activity, they usually develop phantastic tools for it. I don't see any sign of them here."

"How can you tell?" I asked.

"When you shape wood with an ether-plane, for example, it polishes the surface. The fibers almost melt together, and the grain gets a little blurry. The wood used in that barge is just plain cut wood. It's been competently worked, but the difference is unmistakable."

"Hum, hum, hum," I said. "A culture based on mechanics rather than phantastics...is that what you're suggesting, Thomas?"

"It seems unlikely when you put it like that," he said. "Still, I'll be very interested to see the inside of yon trader's home."

With that we parted, Thomas to his workroom, and I to my deckchair, to nap in preparation for the feast. I judged that it would be a long evening.

CHAPTER 16

༈

A Serosan feast. ࿇ The trading proceeds.
We refrain from damaging Dr. Philpott.

THE FEAST began shortly before sunset, and lasted well into the night. I arrived early, hoping for a chance to talk with Cadbury or Philpott, but to no avail; as I was warned, they came not forth until the feast began. And even then, I had no chance to approach, as they were escorted to positions of honor on either side of the Zymurgian trader. By Serosan protocol, I could not approach them; they would call for me if they wanted me. I resigned myself to disappointment, and settled down with Carbuncle to enjoy the feast.

The feast was held in the open air, by the light of three large bonfires. The open square in the center of the village was covered with rugs and cushions, that all might take their ease without soiling their finest robes. Low tables were arranged in an open circle, and other nearby tables were covered with platters and bowls. As it was a general celebration, there was no question of being served; everyone served themselves, except for Cadbury, Philpott, and the trader, who were served by the trader's oarsmen.

The food was remarkably good. We enjoyed a large portion of roast goat, and a kind of steamed wheat with raisins, among other treats. For drink, we had fruit juices and sweet coffee; no wine or spirits, of course, and more surprisingly, no beer. In addition, I had...but I get ahead of myself.

The crew of the *Sea-Spaniel* arrived shortly after the feast began, bearing Anglish delicacies as advertised. The men had enthusiastically followed Carbuncle's example, and caught several more of the enormous trout; one monster was fully five feet long. The ship's cook had somehow found or acquired a great quantity of potatoes. I cannot smell hot oil without remembering that evening. The galley frier was only so large, and so for at least an hour there was a steady stream of Anglish merchant sailors walking to and from the ship, each carrying a steaming basket of Anglish fish and chips.

The oarsmen appropriated the first basket for the guests of honor, naturally, and then the second and third baskets as well, as the initial offering was received with delight. Eventually I caught Hodgins' eye as he carried in his second (or third?) basket. The fish was as good as it was novel. Fish and chips is common in England, of course, but it's usually northern cod, which has a distinctly different flavor.

Eventually the flow of sailors dried up, and everyone began to eat and drink in earnest as the entertainment began. The tables were arranged in an open circle, with the diners seated on cushions around the outside of the circle. The inside was well lit by the bonfires and a number of carefully placed torches, and here stood the talebearer and his players. Story-telling is considered a great art in every land influenced by the Azizim, and talebearers are respected men. The stories, told dramatically by the talebearer with sound effects and incidental music provided by his players, were mostly of Seljurk origin. They abounded in magic fountains, enchanted bowers, and hidden gardens, and resonated oddly with the desert so near at hand. There was only one tale of Serosan extraction, that of Toth and the Wealthy Madman.

When the last tale was complete, it was time for dancing. The players moved to the edge of the circle, and struck up a spirited tune. A dozen men gathered together, and executed a complicated dance. It was something like a northern reel, but followed a circular rather than a square pattern. There was much kicking and swaying, with grunts at pivotal moments, and at times the entire ring whirled so quickly that I expected them to fly apart.

The sailors were not to be outdone. One had brought a fife, and another a fiddle, and soon the village men were learning how to dance hornpipes. That lead to other dances, and then to songs like Whiskey Jenny and The Handsome Cabin Boy—and worse. I was grateful that most of the villagers were innocent of any Anglish, and didn't realize what they were singing. Cadbury understood the songs well enough, though, and was translating them for the trader with great relish and occasional clarification from Philpott. Occasionally he turned and leered at me. I groaned, but Carbuncle just chuckled merrily.

It all wound to an end earlier than I had expected, and Carbuncle and I were just leaving, when we received a summons from the head table. We approached cautiously with eyes lowered, as is suitable, and when I lifted them I was relieved to see the trader beaming at me.

"Hakim," he said in heavily accented Serosan, "my friend Thed tells me that it is in my power to do you a great service. Gladly will I do it, for the friendship I have for him. Go now; we will speak after the trading."

Dismissed, we bowed, and retired, and returned to the ship. "'My friend Thed,' eh," I said to Carbuncle as we ambled along.

"At least young Thad hasn't completely forgotten the rest of us," replied Carbuncle.

I had no answer to that, and there was silence until Carbuncle said, "Leon, are you quite sure about bringing this Fox fellow along with us?" This is one of Carbuncle's most endearing traits: he only asks dangerous questions when no one else is about.

"His name's not Fox," I replied. "Do you remember, a few years ago, I was caterwauling for weeks about a promising student who left the University to go into banking?"

"Frederick Fox?"

"Frederick Forsythe. His father's bank is the old Earl's largest creditor."

Carbuncle chewed on this as we neared the lake shore, and eased to a halt just out of earshot of the ship. "Isn't that just one more reason to leave him behind?"

"I'd rather have him where we can see him. We'll have great trouble getting any finds we make off of the *Spaniel* when we get to Pelham if the ship is seized at the dock. Heavens, we'd have trouble just keeping our journals. Young Frederick, as a representative of the Mercantile Bank of Pelham and Bundyal, should be able to keep the hounds off of our back." Carbuncle nodded. "And besides…" I said.

"You want to force the lad into doing some fieldwork." Carbuncle snorted. "It won't work, Leon. If he had the spark you claim for him, he'd not have left. But I wish you good luck."

The trading began not too early the next morning, though earlier, I reckoned, than it would have had the trader's wares been served the night before. There is that to be said for Azizim customs: one seldom feels ruined on the morning after. On the contrary— once awakened by the hullabaloo and hubbub on the lake shore, I felt eager, energetic, and surprisingly hungry. Of necessity I put my hunger aside, dressed quickly, and went out.

The barge had been firmly grounded, and on the bank to one side, carpets had been spread over a patch about forty feet by thirty. The trader held court in the center of the carpeted region. It is a grandiose phrase, "held court", but the only one which will do. He was wearing his hat and capelet, and was sitting cross-legged on a cushion. His two men stood beside and slightly behind him.

It was not what I had expected. There was no haggling, nor even any discussion. Villagers came forward one at a time, and stood before the throne. Each carried an offering of some kind: a goatskin without blemish, a sack of grain or dried raisins, a fine garment, and so on. The trader nodded at each, and waved to one side or the other; the supplicant took his offering and left it on the carpet in the indicated spot. Then, dismissed, the villager would betake himself to the barge, remove a keg, and carry it off to the village.

As I watched in fascination, the prodigal returned unnoticed.

"Good morning, Leon. Fascinating, isn't it?" Philpott's face was open, eager as usual, and focussed on the scene before him.

"Yes," I said mildly, stifling my desire to call him to account for his actions of the last twenty-four hours. He had a doctorate, after all, and was a colleague rather than a servant. "I've not seen anything quite like it. There's no bargaining; they bring something, and then take a keg."

"Ahhh," said Philpott. "And sometimes more than one. That fellow there is carting off his third, but he only brought one sack of meal."

"Curiouser and curiouser. Though the trader seems to be doing well out of it."

"Mukden," said Philpott.

"I beg your pardon?"

"Mukden," repeated Philpott. "That's the trader's name. The servants are Foudek and Parnas. Only they aren't really servants."

"Aren't they?"

"Mukden's brothers. I gather it was his turn to wear the regalia and theirs to do the brute work."

"You've been busy," I reflected.

"It was necessary," he said. "After that welcoming we saw, I couldn't sleep for the questions buzzing in my head. Won't the Ophir be surprised?"

"Surprised about what?" I asked, feeling I had been here before.

"Wait," he said, "you'll want to see this. I had a talk with the steward and Captain Halvorsen this morning."

The crew of the *Spaniel* issued forth, dressed in their best, and came in single file for their audience with His Majesty. Each bore some gift, ranging from their second best shirts to bottles of Lyrican perfume. Each was accepted, though Mukden (for so I might as well call him) did wish to examine several of them more closely. Baxter himself carried a case of sherry and, wonder of wonders, one of Captain Halvorsen's uniform coats. Mukden admired it greatly, and I believe he'd have tried it on immediately had it not been for his fur capelet.

Eventually the flow of supplicants came to a halt. Surprisingly, there were still a few of the kegs on the barge.

"Why do you suppose no one's taking the last of the kegs?" I asked, thinking out loud.

"Cadbury tells me that the beer doesn't keep indefinitely, so they try not to take more than they can reasonably drink. And I don't suppose the sailors realize that they can take more than one barrel. I didn't tell them, because I didn't know, and the Captain said he'd punish most severely anyone who traded more than once."

"A moment ago, you were saying…" I began, but this time I stopped myself, unable to believe my eyes. The oarsmen, Foudek and Parnas, had returned to the barge, opened the bung on the remaining kegs, and were blithely emptying them into the lake.

"Well now," said Carbuncle as he strolled up to us, "Now we know why the fish get so big here." I looked at him sourly; Philpott reacted not at all, but remained focussed on the action. It was over in a few minutes.

"My goodness," he said slowly. "My…goodness." He continued to stare at the barge, apparently lost in thought, until I slapped him on the back.

"Now, Philpott," I said, "What were you saying about the Ophir?"

"The Ophir?" He blinked at me, glasses reflecting the yellow sunlight. "Oh, the Ophir. Yes, won't he be surprised?"

"About what, Philpott?" I asked with laudable patience.

"About this village." He looked brightly at me.

"Yes," I said slowly, "About this village, yes?"

"Well, wouldn't you be?" he asked, seriously.

"Be what?"

"Surprised, of course."

I just looked at him expectantly, and ignored Carbuncle's muffled snickers.

"To find out that one of his villages is a Zymurgian dependency, I mean." He blinked some more.

I looked at Carbuncle. I looked at Philpott. I looked at Mukden, but he didn't notice. I turned and looked across the fields at the village. I scratched my head. I put my left hand under my right elbow, and rested my mouth on my right hand, and studied Philpott over my knuckles. It may be that I blinked slowly, from time to time. Finally Carbuncle said, "Are you sure of this, Philpott?"

"Are you sure you surveyed the line of the cliff correctly?"

"Most certainly," I replied stiffly.

"Ethnomonotony is my field, Thomas," he said seriously. "Of course I'm sure."

"Perhaps we'd best continue this discussion in the lounge," said Carbuncle.

As we walked back to the gangplank, I noticed several enormous fish frolicking in the water near the barge.

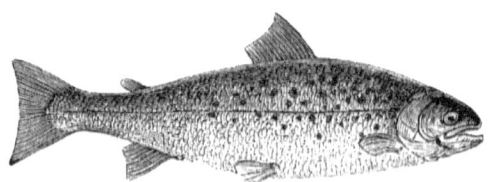

CHAPTER 17

The results of Dr. Philpott's research. ❧ We prepare for departure.

I AM NOT often at a loss for words, and the memory of it is painful to me. By the time we were settled in our chairs in the lounge, however, I felt sufficiently recovered to call for refreshment. As it was too early in the day for sherry, Baxter was soon at hand with tall glasses of Zymurgian beer. Sipping the excellent brew, I waved at Carbuncle to get on with it. Allow me to draw a curtain over the next few minutes; it is sufficient for me to state that that worthy man Carbuncle finally succeeded in convincing Philpott that we had no idea what he was speaking of. With gentle words and the persistence of a Pelham fishmonger, Carbuncle reminded him that we had not been privy to his conversations with Cadbury and Mukden, and persuaded him to start at the beginning.

Philpott pondered, pursing his lips. "The beginning...well, Thomas, I very much wanted to come to Zymurgia, and so I paid a call on you and Leon in your rooms. You can't have forgotten so quickly."

"Thad, let's assume we all have a fairly good grasp of events up until yesterday noon, when the barge arrived," said Carbuncle.

"Do we?" Philpott looked quizzically at Carbuncle. "I'm not at all sure that we do. I've hardly started analyzing my notes from Lyricum Town yet."

"For the sake of discussion, let's assume we do." Carbuncle paused, looking brightly at Philpott. "Now, just tell us what's happened since yesterday noon."

"Well," said Philpott. "The first thing that caught my attention, of course, was the ceremony when the trader arrived. I could not understand the words precisely, but I knew it was no common greeting."

"Traders of all kinds are often given a warm welcome by remote villages like this one," I said. "They bring news, entertainment, valued goods." I was objecting for form's sake, as I began to see where Philpott was headed.

"Yes," he nodded, "but this was more like a subject greeting a king. Mukden standing there, looking so stern in his regalia, and waiting to be formally greeted; Cadbury bowing so low, and speaking so submissively. I knew then that something was up. Cadbury is a good fellow, but he's as proud as any man here."

Carbuncle nodded. "He's right there, Leon. Remember that time in Phillipi, when he broke Lord Woolsey's arm?"

"Cadbury broke the arm of a peer of the realm?" Philpott was plainly shocked.

"The damn fool had tried to thrash Cadbury with his cane for not bowing and scraping," said Carbuncle.

"And anyway," I said, "Woolsey was only a viscount."

"A damn fool of a viscount," said Carbuncle. "His father was paying him to stay out of Angland, as I recall. But do go on, young Thad."

Well, then there was the feast," said Philpott. "A trader's visit might be sufficient cause for a feast, and they might even invite the trader, but I doubt they'd make him guest of honor."

Carbuncle and I nodded thoughtfully, but kept silence.

"Finally, there was the ceremony we just saw."

"The trading, you mean?" asked Carbuncle.

"Trading? I didn't see any trading," said Philpott. "What I saw were villagers bringing tribute to the envoy of a ruling nation."

"But they were trading," I said. "None of them took any beer until they had paid for it in some way."

"That's the second oddest thing about the whole proceedings," said Philpott. He slouched in his chair and stared at his feet, which were stretched out in front of him. "I really don't see where the beer fits in. Cadbury wouldn't let me question Mukden about it."

"And what was the first oddest thing, young Thad?" asked Carbuncle.

Philpott chewed on his lip as he continued to stare at his shoes. "It's so obvious, Thomas," he said, looking up. "Mukden is clearly an envoy of Zymurgia to this village. This village has clearly given him extraordinary honors; the Ophir himself wouldn't have been treated any better. For all practical purposes, these people are Zymurgian subjects." He rubbed his nose, frowning. "And yet, neither Cadbury nor Mukden seems to realize it."

"What do you mean, Thaddeus?" I asked. "How can Mukden be an envoy, and not know it?"

"You saw how stiff and formal Mukden was in public, Leon. But in Cadbury's house he was as easy and merry as his two brothers. I asked him to translate the welcoming ceremony for me, and he couldn't."

"Mukden didn't understand it either?" I sat up straight in my chair, signaling Baxter to refresh my glass.

"He and Cadbury explained to me that that is simply how it's always been done. Every detail, from Mukden's silly little hat to the way the offerings are brought, is just as it has been done several times a year for as long as anyone can remember." It clearly piqued Philpott that it didn't all make perfect sense. "Cadbury told me that the villagers don't dare change anything, for fear that the traders won't return. Why the Zymurgians keep it up, I don't know."

"That tells us one thing, at least," I said, somewhat flippantly, I'm afraid. "The Zymurgians are as tradition-bound as the Serosans."

Philpott brightened at that. "Yes, you're right, Leon, they are. I had not thought of that, being concerned with the other enigma. An excellent observation."

Carbuncle smiled at the expression on my face, and leaned forward. "Did Mukden tell you anything about himself, young Thad?"

"A little," replied Philpott. "I gather that he and his brothers live in a village near the edge of the plateau, not far from where the hoist is. His family has been trading beer—he calls it 'dispersing the waters of Basenis', Leon—they've been trading beer with Seros for generations."

"Do they brew the beer in his village, Thad?"

"I don't know, Leon. I couldn't ask, so all I know is the little Mukden let drop. I don't think so, though." Philpott stared at his shoes for a while longer. "I hesitate to even say this, Leon, because I've got no real evidence to back it up. But Mukden seems to treat the goods he got in exchange for the beer as so much gravy. He'll gladly take them back with him, but it almost seems as if getting rid of the kegs of beer were his primary concern."

"That would explain why no guard was kept on the barge," Carbuncle noted. "And why they dumped the contents of the last few kegs overboard."

Silence reigned supreme in the lounge for several minutes, as we all pondered this.

"I see two mysteries," I said at last. Philpott and Carbuncle looked at me expectantly. "First, there is the beer, the 'Water of Basenis'. There is some significance to it that we clearly do not understand. I'll warrant that the villagers don't broach a single keg until Mukden is well on his way."

"That's very true," said Philpott. "Cadbury told me so."

"I'd like to know why they bother making it, if they won't drink it," said Carbuncle.

"Second," I went on, "there is Mukden arriving like the conquering king. None of the historical sources refer to the Zymurgians as anything but traders, and shrewd traders at that. Cadbury might be willing to swallow his pride in anticipation of swallowing his beer, but I'd guess the ancient kings of Seros weren't so open-minded."

I took a deep breath, and swallowed my own pride. "Thank you, Thaddeus, excellent work. We're twice as far in the dark as we were yesterday morning, so we must be making excellent progress."

"You're welcome, Leon."

"Yes." I turned to other business. "I gather from our brief exchange at the feast that Mukden is willing to help us to the top of the plateau?" Philpott nodded. "Will there be any problem hauling all of us up at once?"

"None at all," said Philpott. "So long as he doesn't have to man the windlass himself, Mukden said he doesn't care how many loads have to be hauled up the cliff. And he said that his people will be so happy with the goods he is bringing back, they won't mind either. But he winked as he said it."

"What about transport once we reach the top?"

"I don't know, Leon. We didn't ask about that."

"Very well. And when is he leaving?"

"Tomorrow. He'll dine with the village elders and Cadbury tonight, and get an early start in the morning."

"Very good. Well, then, gentlemen," I said breezily, "we've got a lot to get together for tomorrow morning, and I believe that luncheon is first on the list. Let's get to it!"

Despite my breeziness, there was in fact quite a lot to do. Carbuncle went to see to our camping gear, our instruments, and his toolkit. I needed to have a word with each member of our exploration party, especially Cadbury, who was still in the village. I thought of sending Philpott to look for him, but immediately rejected the idea; I'd likely not see either of them until the next morning. In the end I had the steward roust out Hodgins for me, asked Hodgins to go to the village and roust out Cadbury for me, and went to pay a call on my ex-student.

Young Frederick had had a regrettably dull time over the previous days. Despite the captain's words about "parole", he didn't trust the young man and had confined him to the ship. Indeed, Frederick had spent the feast and the subsequent trading confined to his cabin. He had only just been allowed out when I found him standing near the bow, his hands clasped behind his back, staring at the falls across the lake. Their muted roar was everywhere; there is no true silence near Lake Saco.

"A sublime sight, Fox, don't you agree?" I asked as I joined him at the rail. "Imagine what it shall look like from above."

He turned to face me. "You're determined that I shall go with you, then?" His tone was dispassionate; it wasn't really a question.

I continued to take in the view. "Oh, yes, Frederick, most determined. I say, can you see that small spur of rock sticking out of the falls, about halfway down? I honestly think there is a tree on it."

"I'm surprised you trust me enough to allow me to come."

"Allow you to come, Frederick? Do you think this is a treat I'm handing out?" I looked at him, mock-surprise on my face.

"I rather expect you think so, Professor." His mouth quirked, but it wasn't really a smile.

"I suppose I do at that, Frederick," I said, turning to face him for the first time. "We shall be leaving tomorrow. I trust you will have your gear together?"

"It's little enough, Professor."

"Very good, Frederick, very good. I shall see you in the
morning, then." I turned to leave, took a step, and then said,
"Oh, Frederick?"

"Yes, Professor?" He had turned back to face the falls again.

"I suggest you not try to swim to shore tonight. Those monstrous trout are still fairly active in the vicinity, and I understand
that one of them nearly had Jackson's hand off." I smiled briefly,
then, and continued on my way.

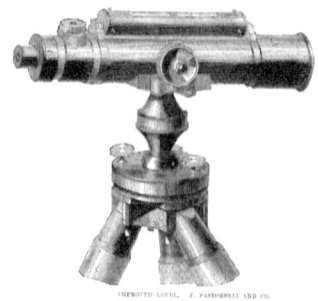

IMPROVED LEVEL.   F. PASTORELLI AND CO.

CHAPTER 18

A view from a height. ❧ *The exploration party.* ❧ *We ascend the cliff.*

I SHALL REMEMBER that 1st of Ragout with dread as long as ever I shall live.

It is thought by the simple that if one were to ascend to the top of a sufficiently high tower, equipped with a sufficiently powerful telescope, that one would be able to see the entire world. This is, of course, absurd, and any child with an ounce of sense can see why. If the world really does stretch infinitely far in all directions, and there is no reason to believe that it does not, any tower of finite height is but a minuscule bump. At a sufficient distance from the tower, even a low range of hills would hide many details beyond. Foreshortening would have muddled all detail long before that.

Somewhat more lofty objections are made, late at night, by the sophomores at Glastonbury. "Well, now", one would ask, "if you did, just for the sake of argument, ascend a high enough tower to see beyond the edge of the Known World, what would you see there? Nothing! It's unknown, innit!" "But would it be blank? Or would it become Known as you watched?" Someone else would point out that the Lands of Fable lie beyond the Known World; it wouldn't be blank, just uncertain. Eventually someone would drag out that horrid old chestnut, "If a country is inhabited, but nobody observes it, does it have a culture?" Yes, I am afraid I remember those days very well.

The real answer to the question of the tower is a dull and dreary one: if you were to ascend to the top of a sufficiently high tower, equipped with a sufficiently powerful telescope, and were to cast your gaze out over the wide world, what you would mostly see is a considerable quantity of weather. Air is lovely stuff, but in large quantities it's really not as transparent as all that. This is a fact easily checked by any visitor to the mountain streams and lakes of High Bastille. Mere geometry suggests that a Bastillian with a powerful telescope should be able to observe the hangings

in front of Newbury Prison in Pelham. Experience reveals that
one cannot, though the Lord knows I tried hard enough.

All this is by way of explaining that, though no stranger to
high places, I was utterly unprepared for the ordeal of ascending
three thousand feet of sheer cliff through air of a clarity beyond
crystalline in a rickety wooden cage swaying back and forth at the
end of a worn-looking rope made by people too dim to recognize
good beer.

It was a great pity, as I had quite been looking forward to the
experience. I was especially keen to see the terrain to the east
and west, but it was no use; the cliffs above Lake Saco form a
southward-pointing V-shape, with the waterfalls at the bottom of
the V; the encircling cliffs blocked our view in those directions.
Constrained as it was, though, it was still a view we had missed
on our previous visit. The donkey path begins some miles from
Cadbury's village, and ascends, switchback upon switchback, up
a narrow canyon leading back into the cliff. In our brief stay, we
had never come near to the cliff's edge, or seen Seros from above.

In other circumstances—more stable circumstances—it
would have been a lovely view. Seros is rather flat, and the eye
could easily trace the Aram Valley from Lake Saco all the way
north (so says Carbuncle) to the Aram delta and the city of Phillipi, with the Sea of Dogs a bright blue ribbon just beyond. The
sky was unusual in its clarity that day; true, there is little mist
or clouds in Serosan skies, but there is usually a fair quantity of
dust. That day was hot but still. No air moved, and dust was raised
only by the movements of men and their beasts of burden. Perhaps with the proverbial telescope I would have been able to see
the shores of Arrastia. I, or rather, Carbuncle. When the swaying
began I sat abruptly down on the floor and closed my eyes. Faithful Bruno rested his head in my lap, and we sat together that way
for the duration.

The day began pleasantly enough. We had got our team and
gear prepared the day before; indeed, much of our gear was already on the way. After conferring with Cadbury, who in turn conferred with Mukden, it was judged the wisest thing if we should
provide our own transport once we reached the top of the plateau.
Accordingly, Cadbury had sent the bulk of our belongings up the
trail on donkey back, in the keeping of his two nephews. These

young men were not much younger than Cadbury himself, being the twin sons of his wife's eldest brother, and I am afraid that I cannot record their names. By the time they were brought to my attention, Carbuncle had already christened them Norfolk and Suffolk, and Norfolk and Suffolk they remained for the duration of our stay. Indeed, they may still be using their nicknames, for aught I know—it is certain that I never heard Cadbury addressed by his neighbors as anything but "Khedboori". Norfolk and Suffolk had started off the previous afternoon, and would likely beat us to the top. Mukden's brother Parnas accompanied them, to guide them, and to introduce them to his countrymen.

For the sake of posterity, I suppose I should, with all due solemnity, record the names of the members of the exploration party: myself, Dr. Leon Thintwhistle; Prof. Thomas Carbuncle; Dr. Thaddeus Philpott; our Serosan guide and friend, Cadbury; Merchant Seamen William L. Hodgins; our reluctant guest Frederick Fox, nee Forsythe; Norfolk and Suffolk; to say nothing of our dog Bruno. We rose at dawn (a bright yellow sun), gathered our necessities together, quickly broke our fasts, and trooped down to the shoreline, to wait for Mukden and his brother Foudek. The previous evening they had been entertained once more by the village, though on a considerably less lavish scale, and once more proved the superiority of Azizim customs by not only arriving on time but in cheerful humor.

"Hail, my friends," cried Mukden in his accented Serosan. "It is time! Let us embark!" As we boarded, Mukden paid special attention to Bruno, who was chasing small birds among the reeds. "That is an amazing animal," he said to me. "We have no dogs so large in our land. It is a pity; my people think me a teller of large stories, and they will never believe in such a large black dog unless they see it for themselves."

"Easily done," I said, "as he's going with us." Mukden looked at me blankly, and then with consternation, as I whistled sharply and shouted in Anglish. "Bruno! Here, boy!" The dismay was replaced by surprise as Bruno looked up at the whistle, and then came bounding through the water and along the shore at my shout. The surprise did not decrease as Bruno paused to shake himself dry, leaped on to the barge, and settled himself at my feet. Mukden stared at me for another moment, and then turned to order our departure.

We all settled ourselves down where we would not be in the way, and Foudek and Mukden placed the long oars into their locks. Several of Cadbury's friends pushed the barge from the shore, and we began the long, slow trip to the base of the cliffs. Along the way, Mukden explained that we would not be able to ride up on the barge itself, as hoisting it back up was much harder than lowering it down to the lake. The barge would go first, and then the goods, and finally we would go.

Presently we arrived at a rocky ledge extending out into the lake, where Foudek made the barge fast to a wooden post. Standing on the ledge was the aforementioned rickety wooden box, about ten feet square, with windows on three sides and a door on the fourth. A heavy rope cable was attached to a ring on the top by means of a metal hook. Lying several yards away was a harness of the same heavy rope, with more hooks and another ring in the center.

At Mukden's request, we all turned to, moving goods from the barge to the ledge. When the barge was empty, Mukden and Foudek carefully attached the harness to the ring bolts on the barge's deck. The cable was detached from the roof of the box and hooked to the harness, after which the barge was unmoored.

I saw no obvious signal to the watchers on the cliff so high above, but no sooner had Foudek cast the barge adrift than the cable tightened, the harness groaned, and the barge started to rise slowly but smoothly into the sky. As it rose, and as we stiffened our necks watching it, the Zymurgians began loading goods into the box, taking care not to fill it above the level of the windows.

Eventually the cable descended again, and the box made several trips by itself until it was our turn. It easily held the eight of us, and Bruno. We entered, fastened the door carefully, and were soon being hoisted into the sky, with the results I have already related. It was nearly dark when we reached the top. The box was pulled in over the edge of the cliff by some means I could not discern in the gloom, and settled to the ground with a bump. There were shouts, and laughter, and eager hands helping us out of the box.

At last we had returned to Zymurgia.

CHAPTER 19

᠊ᢛ᠂ᢌ

The village of Tomar and its environs. ᠊ᢛ A jolly cook.
Bruno and the dogs of Tomar.

AT LAST we had returned to Zymurgia.
No doubt there are those in my audience who feared the
day would never come; who feel, perhaps, that I have lingered too
long in such diverse spots as Lyricum Town, Cuprios, and Seros.
Alas, that is the nature of a scientific expedition. One spends
months of valuable time in transit, with all of the adventures and
annoyances that entails, so that one can spend a pitifully short
time in the region of interest. And then one turns around and
goes home again. (You can go home again, you know. I've done it
dozens of times.)

Were this a scholarly work on the mythogeography of Zymurgia, I confess, the tale of our journey thither would have been
contained in one or two cogent paragraphs. It is intended for a
more general audience, however, an audience for whom the Dolce
Vita of Lyricum Town is nigh as exotic as the far-off lands of fable.
Those of my readers who would prefer a drier, more staid work
may apply to Dean Nuftison of Glastonbury University; I gather
he has a similar preference, which may one day be satisfied.

Before continuing with my narrative, I should like to describe the region in which we found ourselves for the next several weeks. Parnas had indeed preceded us, and though tired
and saddle-sore had arranged a warm reception. Several dozen of
Parnas' friends and relations were there to greet us, in addition
to those who operated the hoist. After we stepped out of the box,
which was perhaps more sturdy and well-built than I have implied, we were clasped unto the bosom of the crowd and made exceedingly welcome. The barge lay nearby, and Mukden climbed
onto its deck and made a short speech. I couldn't understand him,
of course, but it was plain that he was describing the trading voyage, and then introducing each of us by name. I waited eagerly to
see how he would manage to say "Thintwhistle", and was a little
let down when he didn't.

After that we were escorted down the road to the nearby village, of which I will say more anon. It was nearly full dark; my memories of that evening consist mostly of disjointed images of happy, laughing people bustling down the road in the torchlight. We were bustled down the road with them, and bustled into the village, and finally bustled into a house which had been prepared for us, whereupon the villagers wished us good night. Philpott was eager to talk, but, fatigued from our ordeal and expecting an early morning, the rest of us bustled right into bed. Finding no one to talk to, Philpott bustled about a bit, and then went to bed himself, for which the rest of us were thankful.

Myself, I went to bed feeling that the expedition had finally, really and truly begun. It was not so much that we had finally reached Zymurgia. Rather, it was because of the sleeping arrangements. Nothing is so truly characteristic of life on an expedition as the almost total loss of privacy. When we run out of sherry for our evening toasts, I merely sigh. When the insects become more numerous than the local people, and often of nearly as large a size, I merely check my boots for visitors before putting them on. As each amenity of life fades away, I begin to feel as though an expedition is in the offing. But it is the loss of privacy that is the touchstone. We had been sleeping one to a cabin on the *Spaniel*, except of course for Hodgins and Bruno; here we were sleeping on cots or hammocks, three or four to a room, and I was lulled into sleep by the familiar, congenial sound of Carbuncle, snoring. As I drifted off, secure in my cot, I knew that after many weeks we had arrived.

Mukden's village rejoices in the name of Tomar, which Philpott assures me is a corruption of an old Zymurgian word for "gateway". It is situated in a valley some two or three miles from the hoist, some ten miles from the upper end of the donkey trail, and some two miles west of the Aram gorge, and is called that presumably because it is the gateway to the lands to the north. The land between Tomar and the edge of the plateau is heavily wooded, providing a break against the winds which scour the cliff's edge; to the south are pastures and cultivated fields.

Tomar is a good-sized place, having something between one and two thousand inhabitants, and so might be called a town. I call it a village, because that is how it felt to me—not a village

like Cadbury's in Seros, but like a village in the Anglish countryside of my youth. The streets are narrow, but paved with cobbles.
The houses, which are generally one or two stories in height, have
thatched roofs and exposed wooden beams; the interstices are
filled with woven mats rather than plaster, but otherwise the re-
semblance was remarkable. The eaves extend far out past the
walls to provide relief from the summer sun, and the windows are
not glazed; linen curtains are used when modesty requires. The
climate is also reminiscent of Angland: warmer the year round—
it seldom snows in Tomar—but as damp. Zymurgia is a land of
sudden showers, puffy clouds, and occasional dazzling sunshine.

Most of the inhabitants are farmers, who work the nearby
fields. The rest are artisans and tradespeople: cobblers, coopers,
tailors, bakers, and so forth. All of the trades one would expect to
find in a small but vigorous and healthy town were represented,
though the goods for sale might look rather odd to Arrastian eyes.
We were surprised to discover that there was no brewery in Tomar.

The main street runs in a crescent from the north end of the
valley to the south, with buildings and side streets on both sides.
The village square is roughly at the midpoint of the crescent; it
measures approximately one hundred feet on each side, and is
cobbled like the streets. One quarter of the square is dominated
by a pool, about fifteen feet across, with its own thatched roof supported by two posts. It is Tomar's main supply of drinking water.

Our house was not on the square, nor on the main street, but
on a side street not far from either one. It had two stories, with
several sleeping rooms on the second floor and a common room on
the first, and was, Mukden assured us, at our disposal for as long
as we needed. It was a hostel used by important visitors to Tomar,
and none were expected for several months.

But all of this became clear over time. Our first action on
rising the next morning was to eat breakfast; the house was provided, we discovered, with a cook, a thin but jolly woman of inde-
terminate age named Abayla. More than a cook; she was, in fact,
the keeper of the hostel, and had a room of her own on the first
floor. Philpott tried to speak with her in his halting Zymurgian,
which is how we learned she was jolly. Abayla laughed silently,
but with her whole body: she threw her head back, a broad smile
on her dark face, and shook, wrapping her arms around her ribs

as though they would burst if she didn't hold them in. Finally she took pity on him, and indirectly on the rest of us, for we were consumed with embarrassment on his behalf—or at least I and Hodgins were. I believe Cadbury and Carbuncle were rather amused, and Philpott could never be troubled to be embarrassed on his own behalf.

Abayla took him by the shoulders and guided him to a seat at the long refectory table in the common room; when he tried to speak again, she placed a long, thin finger over his lips as she slipped a platter of food in front of him. We never found out whether Abayla understood anything Philpott was saying, as she never in our entire stay spoke to us; she simply smiled and fed us well and frequently.

Breakfast was a simple affair. There was some kind of porridge with a sweet, nutty flavor, as well as oranges and plums. For drink we had a choice of water or fruit juice. Mukden came and joined us as we were discussing our plans. I was interested to note that he had changed his manner of dress. He had, of course, put aside the fur hat and capelet of his trader's regalia, but he had also put aside the short linen skirt in favor of knee-length linen breeches, a flowing blouse or tunic of the same material, and leather sandals.

"Good morning, my friends," he said. "How do I find you this day? Is the hostel to your liking?"

"It will do very well, Mukden," I replied. "We are grateful to have the use of it."

He beamed at us. "Good," he said. "Good." Then he frowned slightly, and scratched his cheek just under his left eye, and shifted in his seat. "My friends, I have brought you here because my friend Thed asked it of me. Now I must ask a thing of you."

"Certainly," I said, "anything we can do."

"It is difficult to ask this, for guests are not to be questioned, but we have never seen such people as you. The Masters of Tomar have asked to see you today. You need not see them…but if you do not I must bid you return to the Lands Below." Mukden, who I had hitherto thought irrepressible, said these last words slowly, grudgingly, and sadly, as though prepared to see us rise in a huff and storm out of his town and out of his country. Philpott stared at him, eyes wide, Carbuncle and Fox said nothing, and Cadbury and Hodgins just went on eating.

"But of course," I said. "You who have met us and befriended us, you know we mean no harm. But what assurance do your countrymen have? Gladly we will see the Masters of Tomar." Carbuncle nodded, and Philpott began to look eager. Mukden relapsed into his happy, buoyant self.

"Now," I asked, "who are the Masters of Tomar, and when would they like to see us?"

"The Masters are those who are responsible for the well-being of Tomar," Mukden replied. "I have been asked to bring you as soon as may be. Today is a festival day, and there is much to do."

"Is the festival because you have returned from your journey?" asked Philpott, his eyeglasses glinting in the light of a blue morning.

"That is so," Mukden replied, smiling. "After each such journey, we celebrate the dispersal of the waters of Basenis."

At that point Abayla came to clear the table, and we judged it wise to be elsewhere. "Lead on, good Mukden," I said. "Take us to the Masters. Hodgins, Fox, perhaps it would be best if you stayed here for now." As we left the hostel, I whistled for Bruno to join us.

Our first excursion into the daylight streets of Tomar was a memorable one. I have compared Tomar with an English village, and rightly so, but that was not my first impression. My first impression was one of dogs. The street in front of the hostel was full of them. All were small, as Mukden had said, not more than fourteen or sixteen inches in height, with wiry frames. They were all of a type, short-haired, white with black or brown markings, and with long, pointed snouts and pointed ears that stood up straight from their heads.

Every one of them was utterly intent on Bruno's every move. They stood in a ragged semicircle around the door of the hostel, bristling and not quite snarling. Mukden was clearly taken aback, so I quickly understood that this was no usual assemblage. And indeed it was not: the forty or so dogs present represented nearly the entire canine population of Tomar.

Mukden was at a loss; we could not move from the doorway without stepping into the crowd of dogs. I do not know how long the stalemate would have lasted, as I lost my patience. "We have an appointment," I said. "I do not propose to be held back by a pack of puppies." Commanding Bruno to heel I stepped into the street, pulling Mukden with me, and the dogs perforce gave way. The snarls were more audible now, and as we walked down the street to the town square we remained at the center of a mass of ears, tails, and muddy paws. Bruno, noble dog that he was, ignored his Zymurgian cousins, and paced placidly at my side, acting for all the world as if this were a Sunday promenade on board the *Sea-Spaniel*.

The square, when we reached it, was crowded with townsfolk preparing for the festivities. Banks of elevated seats were being constructed, and a speaking platform, and rows of trestle tables occupied one full quarter. Mukden pointed out a large building across the square, one of the few stone buildings in Tomar. "The Hall of the Masters," he said. "They await us there."

We made quite an interesting sight, I am sure, six outlandishly clad foreigners with their big black dog proceeding quietly through the square, the calm eye of a storm of furry chaos. The Zymurgian dogs were running circles around us now, barking and snarling. The townspeople stopped what they were doing and watched, but to my surprise none of them attempted to calm the dogs or call them away.

I don't know how long these circumstances would have lasted, or whether the short-haired little fiends would have attended our audience with the Masters of Tomar, for as we approached the center of the square one of the barking horrors gathered its courage and nipped Bruno's tail. In a flash, in a twinkling of an eye, Bruno had turned himself about and sunk his teeth in the scruff of his attacker's neck. He shook the smaller dog, three sharp jerks from side to side, releasing the body on the third pass. The creature flew several yards to land in a motionless heap on the cobbles; its neck was clearly broken.

The other dogs, still barking, had backed away from Bruno; several were sniffing at their fallen comrade, tails between their legs. For his part, Bruno was growling low in his throat, and looking from side to side as if choosing his next victim.

With a start I realized that this could not go on. I said sternly, "Bruno, heel!" Without a backwards glance the noble beast resumed his place at my side, and we continued on our way. The remaining dogs scattered before us.

I looked back as we reached the Hall of the Masters. The dogs had dispersed, except for the lonely form in the middle of the square. The people of Tomar watched us silently as we entered the Hall, and then went back to their chores.

CHAPTER 20

ᴗᴖ

The non-universality of social mores.
Bruno and the Masters of Tomar. ᴖ We petition the Masters.

AS A seasoned traveler, I know that it is a pernicious, indeed a potentially deadly mistake to judge a place by the standards of one's home country. In Pelham high society it is the done thing when visiting an acquaintance to put one's calling card on the butler's silver tray, and to wait patiently whilst the acquaintance decides to be, or not to be, at home. Should the decision be in the negative, one must go about one's business without fuss or furor. It is considered extremely ill-bred to claim that the acquaintance is in, even when it is undeniably true; and of course bribing or otherwise attempting to suborn the butler is simply unthinkable. To be "not at home" from time to time is one of the little blessings that eases us through life. Yet in such a familiar place as Lyricum Town the simple custom has a sinister air.

Just as in Pelham, the Lyrican ritual of the calling card has its appointed steps and measures, and its own meaning. A Lyrican gentleman will always state his name and business to the majordomo of the house, unless his business is a matter touching upon his honor. Such matters are not to be discussed with servants. Thus, to silently proffer one's calling card in Lyricum Town is to request satisfaction, a challenge as unmistakeable as a slap of the hand in a public place. There are many acceptable responses. One might invite the caller in, and offer him your hospitality, and endeavor to show him that his honor is unstained. Alternatively, one might send out a card with the names and addresses of one's seconds. To be "not at home" in the Anglish sense, to fail to acknowledge the visitor in any way, is in such a case to refuse to give proper satisfaction, to decline the honor of a duel, and hence to declare oneself both in the wrong and a coward. In Lyricum Town, this is a deadly fate. Men will sneer. Ladies will turn their faces away. Small children will snigger at one's passing. Should the craven accept his responsibilities, and send his seconds to his challenger, all of course will be forgiven, at least until the duel settles the matter permanently. Otherwise, the offending individual is likely to be found adrift in the Bay of Biscotti one fine morning. One cannot refuse satisfaction forever, but one can die in dishonor.

You may think this an unlikely story, and yet it has been known to happen. I once knew an Anglish curate named Arthur Frampton, a poor fellow as obsessed with Lyrican opera as he was ravaged by hay-fever. He inadvertently sneezed during a performance of Libretto's *Canneloni,* in the opening moments of the opera's best-loved aria. He compounded his transgression by sneezing three more times and using his handkerchief noisily before the aria was complete. It was not his fault, poor fellow; it was the flower he had fixed in his buttonhole that was his undoing.

Alas, the opera singer's lover was in the audience that day, and took Frampton's sneezes as a sign of opprobrium and disdain. And well he might, for the singer's performance was memorable chiefly for its squeaks, gasps, and agonizing pauses. The offended gentleman, a man named Vittorio, came to Frampton's lodgings late that evening, and presented his card to the majordomo, intent on an apology or a meeting. An apology would have been accepted; Vittorio was not an unreasonable man. Had he peen permitted in, he would have seen the curate's streaming eyes and flushed complexion, and would have begged the curate's pardon immediately. The majordomo, a Lyrican himself, begged Frampton to reconsider. But Frampton, who had gone to bed with a hot water bottle and a pot of hot tea with lemon, would not be moved. He was "not at home," and so the majordomo reported. Vittorio was confirmed in his suspicions, of course, and took the steps that honor demanded. Poor Arthur Frampton never sneezed through another aria. He was free at last of his hay-fever; but perhaps he would have judged the price to be too dear.

It is, of course, impossible to travel in far-off lands without the occasional misunderstanding; but I have found that stout Anglish forthrightness combined with a willingness to talk to and learn from almost anyone will carry one through. So long as one is aware of the possibility of being misunderstood, and makes the necessary allowances, such problems are seldom fatal. At least, not yet.

There is, however, a related but more pernicious error, and that is to assume that the customs and mores of a country are like those of its neighbors. It is straightforward to remember that one is not at home; every detail of one's surroundings shout it out. It is less easy to discriminate between the contents of two homes side-by-side in a strange neighborhood, when one is, figuratively speaking, standing on the pavement looking through the front doors.

Mukden lead us into the Hall of the Masters, and went to announce our arrival to some servants who were standing there. I ignored them, taking in the details of the large room: tile floor, large windows, carved and painted wooden ceiling. I had just told Bruno to go lie down when Mukden introduced the servants as the Masters of Tomar. Fortunately I was facing away from them, or I fear my face would have given me away.

It is true that women are greatly protected among the Azizim, whether of Seros or of other countries. During our entire stay in Cadbury's village, the only woman we saw was Cadbury's wife, and then only because we had been guests in his home. Though I was well aware that Zymurgia was different in culture and religion than Seros, somehow I was expecting the same pattern. I can only plead distraction caused by the onslaught of Zymurgian mongrels we had just withstood…but I was quite unprepared to discover that two of the four Masters of Tomar were women, one of them young and strikingly beautiful. I was quite speechless, for the second time in less than a week.

The Masters of Tomar were dressed much like Mukden, which no doubt contributed to my mistake. Two were men, and two were women; two were old and two were young. Their garments were embroidered here and there with yellow thread, and the women's in particular were cut close to the body, leaving no doubt as to their sex. I turned to face them fully, concerned that my error was written on my face. I need not have worried, as for the moment they were paying me no attention. All four were staring at Bruno, who had obediently trotted over and lay sprawled in the corner, head up, ears and eyes alert. He was panting, and looking around the room.

The older woman asked Mukden something in Zymurgian; he spoke for some time, and from his gestures and glances out of the window, I gathered that he was speaking about the dog fight in the square. After a few questions from the others, Mukden went out, glancing at me, and came back with another villager. As the Masters questioned the newcomer, Mukden came to my side.

"They are asking about the dog fight, and this dog," he said, jerking his head toward Bruno's corner. "They heard the dog fight, of course, but those are common, and they paid it no heed." At that point the newcomer was dismissed, and the Masters called for Mukden.

The pretty young woman was leaning forward. She spoke to Mukden; at her words, the other Masters looked somewhat shocked. The younger man caught her arm, but she shook it off, and repeated her command. Mukden said to me, "Asha says she has been told that this dog obeys your commands. She saw it lie down when you entered, apparently at your direction, but she has seen many dogs lie down where they are not wanted. She wishes you to command the dog to do something unusual." I looked at Asha and the other masters; she looked eager and challenging at one and the same time. The others looked tense, but said nothing further.

"Very well," I said. I turned to Bruno, and continued, "Bruno, come!" Bruno rose from the floor, padded over, and sat down precisely in front of me. "Good boy," I said, patting him on the head. Next I pointed at Asha. If she wanted a demonstration, I would oblige. "Now, Bruno, greet Asha!" Bruno stood up, and looked from me to the woman. "Yes, Bruno, greet Asha!"

For the next several seconds, the only sound in the room was Bruno's claws ticking on the tile floor. The Masters watched in stunned silence as Bruno padded over to the young woman, sat carefully down, barked, and extended one paw to shake hands. Asha stared at Bruno, wide-eyed. He looked up at her, and pawed at the air slightly, crinkling his ears. Slowly she went down on one knee, and took his paw. She shook it gravely, and then released it. Bruno put his paw down and wagged his tail furiously.

The others had been watching this exchange with great interest. As Asha slowly rose to her feet, the young man leaned over to examine Bruno more closely, and then recoiled. He shouted at us, eyes flashing, and then simmered while Mukden translated for us.

"Nabili demands to know how you dare put a collar on one of the Pups of Basenis." The words came grudgingly out of Mukden's mouth, and he was beginning to perspire.

I looked at him in some perplexity, and then realized that it was true: none of the dogs we had seen outside had been wearing collars.

"Tell Nabili it is the dog's own wish," I said. Mukden translated, and the consternation on the Masters' faces changed to anger. The older man barked out a few choice syllables.

"They say that that is nonsense," said Mukden.

"It isn't, of course," I replied, "and I will prove it." Bruno was still sitting obediently in front of Asha. "Bruno, come!" I said. He trotted over and sat quietly. I bent over him, and unfastened his black leather collar, as the outraged Masters looked on in satisfaction. Their smug expressions vanished when I said, "Bruno, go lie down." Bruno stood, sniffing at the pocket where I had placed the collar, and trotted back over to the corner. His head was down, and his tail was between his legs, and when he reached the corner he whined. It was a soft whine, nearly a whimper. Occasionally he glanced in my direction as though to see if I was properly moved. The Masters of Tomar looked on in amazement.

Finally I relented. I took the collar out of my pocket, and said, "Bruno, come!" In two leaps he was sitting at my feet, his tail fanning the floor and his neck outstretched to receive the collar. When he had it on again, he shook all over, yawned, and lay down at my feet. "It is the dog's own wish," I repeated, crossing my arms. I was, I am afraid, beginning to get somewhat impatient, and I heard my companions muttering between themselves.

The Masters conferred quietly for a few minutes, and then moved as a group to one end of the room. As they seated themselves on four matching wooden stools, Mukden said, "The masters wish to pass over the matter of the dog, for now. They wish to be introduced to the members of your party."

I named each of us with as much elegance and refinement as I was capable of. "I am Dr. Leon Thintwhistle of Glastonbury University," I said, and bowed, "and these are my colleagues, Thomas Carbuncle, and Dr. Thaddeus Philpott." I gestured toward each as I spoke. "And this is our friend and guide, Cadbury." Cadbury bowed when I spoke his name, touching heart, mouth, and forehead in the manner of the Azizim.

Mukden translated my speech as best he could, and then listened as the Masters spoke briefly. "Asha and Nabili you know. The others are Simuny and Firenz," he said, gesturing at the old woman and man in turn.

It is a tedious thing to accurately render a translated conversation of this kind, and as tedious to read as it is to write. From this point on, I will only mention the translation if it is relevant to my tale.

"We are an hospitable people," said Firenz, "and it would pain us to deny you our hospitality." He looked away.

"Nevertheless," said Simuny, raising a droopy eyebrow, "it may yet be necessary."

"It is a terrible thing to question a guest, but the well-being of Tomar is in our charge," said Firenz apologetically.

"Why have you come to the Land Above, and what do you want?" asked Asha. She, at least, showed no trace of regret.

"We have come to meet your people, and to travel about your country, to measure it and to learn its ways," I replied.

"Are you then spies?" asked young Nabili. He was an intense young chap, I must say. "Do you prepare the way for an army? Be warned! Great Basenis looks after his pack." Asha looked sideways at him, and rolled her eyes slightly. I am perhaps mistaken, but I believe she bit her tongue as well.

"You are protected no less by the great cliff that separates your country from the lands to the north," I pointed out. "You control the hoist, and the donkey path could be held by a handful of men. Indeed, the path could easily be destroyed. Even were my people interested in conquest, your land is too remote, too difficult of entry." I shrugged.

"If you are not spies," asked Simuny, her eyes glistening, "then what are you?"

I began to speak, but Philpott interrupted me. "We are scholars," he said. Mukden could find no Zymurgian equivalent to "scholar," and Philpott was forced to try again. "We seek knowledge for its own sake," he said at last. "When we return home, we will write our new knowledge down so that it may be shared with others. Thus, the sum of human knowledge ever increases." At that, it was my turn to roll my eyes at Carbuncle. He snorted softly.

"What would you learn?" asked Asha.

"My friends would like to travel about your land, following the roads and the river, to see what may be seen. For my part, I would like to stay here in Tomar for a time. I would like to talk to your people about their lives. I would like to talk with you," said Philpott, and he looked deeply into Asha's eyes. She easily withstood his gaze for several seconds, and one end of her mouth curled up sardonically, but she said nothing. It occurred to me then, for the first time, that "Young Thaddeus" really was rather a young fellow; and barring the tweeds and the spectacles was perhaps not unattractive to women. I wondered if he knew that, and was making use of it. My thoughts continued in this vein for several minutes, as the Masters conferred among themselves. At last, they all stood, and Firenz spoke.

"We must discuss this matter further, but there is no time now. Mukden will take you back to the hostel, where you must remain until we call for you again." It was a clear dismissal, but Philpott spoke up in his poor Zymurgian. The Masters looked at him, considering, and Firenz spoke again. "Very well. You may observe the festival tonight, but you may not participate in it. One will come for you when it is time." He clapped his hands, and the audience was over.

The dead dog was gone when we re-entered the town square. As we crossed it several of the town dogs slunk quietly past, casting sidelong glances at Bruno, but there were no further incidents. Shortly thereafter we were seated once again around the long table in the hostel's common room, there to make whatever sense we could of the morning's events.

CHAPTER 21

⌣⁖⌢

The pups of Basenis.
The vital importance of sophistication in theology.
The conundrum of Frederick Fox.

CHIEF AMONG the scholarly virtues, the cornerstone of academia, is that of giving credit where credit is due. Thus do scholars build, brick by patient brick, publication by painful publication, citation by irrelevant citation, the edifice of knowledge that is our inheritance as learned men of Arrastia. The cardinal sin in the groves of Academe is to take credit for work that is not one's own—and get caught at it. Oddly, the converse—giving credit for one's work to someone else, generally someone in authority—has no such stigma. But that is by the way. Since reaching the gaudy pinnacle of Grenville Chair of Mythogeography at Glastonbury University, I have scorned to flatter; and I have always scorned to plagiarize, or otherwise take credit for another man's accomplishments. Thus it was, when we regained the hostel, that my first words were to our man Hodgins, who was playing Patience on the refectory table. Fox was watching him quietly.

"Well, Hodgins, I'm not sure but what you've landed us all in the soup. Or saved the expedition, I shan't know which until someone explains to me what just happened." I sat down at the long table, and signaled to Abayla for some refreshment.

Hodgins scratched the back of his neck with a playing card as he thought about this. "I beg your pardon, Dr. Thintwhistle?"

"It's that Bruno," said Carbuncle, "the wee puppy that's just come in and curled himself up at your feet. The Zymurgians don't know what to make of him." Quickly and concisely, he sketched out the highlights of our visit with the Masters of Tomar.

"Yes," I said. "And I couldn't have had Bruno perform all of those foolish antics if you hadn't trained him so well."

"He practically trained himself," said Hodgins. "But I'm sorry if it caused any problems."

"No, never worry about that," I said, sipping at the mug of unfermented juice Abayla had placed before me. I looked at it in dismay. "They seem so civilized," I muttered, shaking my head. "It was worth it to see their faces when Bruno begged to have his collar put back on. Thomas might disagree, but I think it's the high point of the expedition to date."

"The question is," Carbuncle asked, "why were they so fascinated by Bruno? A party of strange men the likes of which they've never seen show up on the doorstep, and they're baying over a great fish-stealing hound." Bruno shifted under the table. "Not that you aren't a grand dog, Bruno."

"We already knew," said Philpott, pushing his glasses back up his nose, "that Basenis is one of their major deities; perhaps their major deity."

"Never mind that you're changing the subject, Thad, how do you arrive at that conclusion?" I asked.

"The Water of Basenis, Leon. As far back as we have records, the Zymurgians have referred to their beer as the Water of Basenis. You can't think that a single individual named Basenis has been alive for so many centuries."

"Humph," I said. "Ask the Lord Mayor of Pelham. For that matter, ask at Eton's department store; they've been around almost as long as the Lord Mayor."

"I got these playing cards at Eton's," said Hodgins. "They've got pictures of Anglish landmarks on them."

Philpott frowned. "That's true, Leon. I suppose Basenis could be a place, or even a folk hero...but wait a moment. That's right. Master Nabili referred to Bruno as one of the 'Pups of Basenis'."

"There's the Tower of Pelham, and Lancaster Cathedral..."

"And your point would be?" I asked, swigging some more fruit juice.

"and Pelham Pond all full of shipping, and Mondrian's Wall..."

"It seems clear that Basenis must be personified as a canine of some kind, Leon."

"I've seen stranger things in Bundyal," said Hodgins, looking into the distance. "Why I saw an idol with three—"

"Let's stick to the subject, Hodgins," I said. "Philpott, what leads you to that conclusion?"

"Well, the dogs, chiefly. They run wild throughout the village, and fight or play as they please. And yet they aren't starving—they are much better fed than any stray dogs I've seen in Angland. But they aren't pets, either. No one here attempts to control them; I think several of the Masters were shocked by the very idea."

We all nodded, or least I did; that tallied with my own observations.

"And then, of course," Philpott continued, "Master Nabili referred to Bruno, and by extension to other dogs, as one of the 'Pups of Basenis'. Now, Bruno is manifestly no puppy, yet Nabili said 'Pups' rather than 'Dogs'. It seems most likely that he was using 'Pups' as we would say 'children', that is, Bruno is one of the children of Basenis."

"That would explain most of their reactions, Leon," said Carbuncle. "If your dog is semi-divine, you don't ask him to fetch your slippers. You let him go about his business, and feed him when he's hungry. If he wants to fight, you let him."

"Basenis the Dog God, eh?" I pondered that for several long breaths. "I've been to the Bundi Nations as well, and I'll wager I've seen stranger things there than Hodgins. Basenis the Dog God is tame by comparison."

"And then we came in with our own tame dog in a collar and made him do tricks," said Carbuncle.

"It would certainly explain the tension in the room," I said. "They were expecting lightning bolts and earthquakes, Great Basenis' wrath poured out on one who dared to discipline a dog." I turned toward Hodgins, and said, "With help from others, of course, Hodgins. If I'm to be blasted in my tracks, I certainly hope you'll have the decency to keep me company."

"I'll do my best, I'm sure," said Hodgins, who was dealing out another hand of Patience.

I raised an eyebrow at Philpott. "Any other thoughts?"

"Well, Leon, it all depends how sophisticated they are. Theologically, I mean." I waved him on, as I drained the mug. "If they aren't very sophisticated, they'll assume that we must have Basenis' blessing."

"Must we?" asked Carbuncle.

"Oh, yes. Because we couldn't possibly control such a good-sized dog as Bruno without help from Basenis. In that case, they will probably give us every honor."

"That's if they are unsophisticated?" I asked. Philpott nodded seriously. "What if they are sophisticated?"

"Oh, that's much simpler," he said. "If they are sophisticated, theologically speaking, they'll consider that Basenis hasn't struck us down for our sins. And then, after they've considered enough..."

"Yes?" I said. Even Hodgins had put down his cards.

"Well, they'll probably decide that Basenis is leaving our punishment up to them. So they'll probably kill us." Philpott stood up, stretched, and continued, "I shall go upstairs and work on my notes."

I followed him with my eyes as he walked around the table and over to the stairs, practically turning myself all the way around on the bench.

"Philpott?"

"Yes, Leon?" He paused with one foot on the stair.

"We're imprisoned in this hostel, awaiting the pleasure of people who may well decide to roast us for impiety."

"Yes, Leon?"

"Are you really going to go work on your notes at a time like this?"

"Oh, yes, Leon. The Zymurgians apparently have a culture stretching back thousands of years. I'd hate to die with my notes in disarray." And off he went, up the stairs.

The careful reader may have been wondering why Fox and Cadbury had not participated in this conversation. Cadbury's absence is easily explained; when we entered, he hied himself to the stables behind the hostel, where Norfolk and Suffolk were caring for our donkeys. Fox, on the other hand, had been sitting across the table from Hodgins for the duration.

Indeed, Fox's behavior was rather beginning to perplex me. He had been one of my brightest pupils. Not eager, not a flatterer, but when asked for an answer, he invariably gave the right one. After only a few semesters, he had a grasp of mythogeography that, I am ashamed to say, excelled that of many of my colleagues. In his exams, he immediately cut to the heart of whatever topic was assigned, handled it with depth and insight, and finally sewed it all up in a neat conclusion, leaving the patient not at all the worse for the experience.

During the course of a long teaching career, a professor will have many students—indeed, many each year—who can master the material that is given them. If the professor is lucky, some one or two will not only master the material, but will build on it, extending the edifice of knowledge I alluded to earlier. Frederick showed signs of being one of these. And then came the news that his elder brother, the heir to the Mercantile Bank of Pelham and Bundyal, had perished in a boating accident on the river Thyme near the town of Burton-on-Water, and his father called him to work in the family firm. I had been so confident that he would defy his father, and remain in University, eventually taking Academic Orders and joining the faculty. Instead, he quietly packed his things and left. I didn't know he was gone for a full week.

I had, I confess, dragged him along to Zymurgia in hopes of awakening his interest anew. It showed little signs of working. Since my last conversation with him, the night after the trading, Fox had said little, and done less. He had joined us on the barge the previous morning willingly enough, but had retained a stolid silence throughout the horrific ascent. He had said nothing at breakfast, though he willingly did anything we asked of him; he did not seem reluctant so much as detached.

I was put in mind of any number of students I had seen while I was still junior enough to teach the first-year course in mytho-geography. It was and is a required course, and there have always been many students from other disciplines who regard it as a waste of time. I recognized in them the same blank expression I now feared I saw on Frederick's face: the mark of one who is determined to bear what must be borne, while paying it as little attention as possible. Had so few years spent banking done this to my prodigy? It did not bode well.

I pondered this for the length of another mug of fruit juice, and came to a conclusion. "Thomas, Hodgins, Fox," I said. "Shall we have a hand or two of whist, to pass the time?"

"Now, Leon," scoffed Carbuncle. "You'd be after playing whist at a time like this, instead of getting your notes in order?" But he took the deck of cards from Hodgins and began to shuffle.

Fox enjoyed a remarkable run of luck or skill during the many hands of whist we played that afternoon; I suppose I must concede that a career in banking has its uses. But he said nothing beyond the commonplace pleasantries of the card table, nor were my attempts to draw him out successful. He played quietly, shuffling with dexterity when called upon, rarely looking up from the table, never laughing or joking. How had so few years changed him so much?

Or had he always been so self-contained? I remembered him smiling more, laughing more, but not, somehow, saying more. Had the eagerness I remembered been real, or just my own hopes projected on a carefully maintained facade of congeniality? I was no longer so certain. And yet I remained convinced of his talents. I began to worry that I had erred in bringing him to Zymurgia.

The reader may wonder why I simply didn't ask him outright. Why not confront him with my suspicions, why not take him aside and question him privately? This course of action was not far from my mind at any time during that tedious afternoon, and yet I restrained myself. I had two reasons, either of which was sufficient cause for me to hold my tongue.

The members of an expedition, like the officers of a naval vessel, form a small community. Joined by a shared interest, they are thrown together under stressful conditions for a period of many months, with little opportunity for privacy, and no means of avoiding one another. Under such conditions friendships may grow and become inseverable; alternatively, small annoyances, mannerisms, peccadilloes may grow to monstrous proportions. Minor quarrels can quite literally become murderous. And it is never wise to quarrel with someone on whose skill and good will your life may depend.

I have already related the story of Ambrose Elliot, the expedition leader who was eaten in the South Seas. It frankly amazes me that the man survived to be eaten, that he didn't meet his demise on some earlier expedition, for he had the knack of alienating anyone in any way subordinate to him, as well as many who were not. Accidents are easy to arrange in strange lands. That he did not have one I can only attribute, much to my surprise, to the basic decency of the Anglish academic.

But be all that as it may, I did not wish to begin a potentially lengthy sojourn in Zymurgia by antagonizing one of my companions. And that is all I should succeed in doing by questioning Fox directly. What could I accuse him of beyond a certain coldness of demeanor? And, moreover, a perfectly justified coldness, given that I had brought him rather against his will.

It was a pretty quandary I found myself in, and I still hadn't found my way out of it when Mukden arrived to escort us to the festival.

CHAPTER 22

⌣∶∾

Still no beer. ?❧ A Zymurgian festival. ?❧ An auction.
Philpott's unconsidered opinion.

LEAVING NORFOLK and Suffolk to keep an eye on our things, we followed Mukden down the street and into the square. It was not until he led us up to the second floor of a large house which fronted on the square that I realized the extent of the Zymurgian devotion to hospitality.

"The Masters of Tomar have decreed that you may observe our festival, but that you may not take part," he said. "Therefore, I have brought you here, to my family home. Food and drink will be brought to you, and from here you may see all that there is to see. You must not leave this house until the festival ends. I will return at that time, to take you back to the hostel."

From what I could see, it would be no hardship to stay where we were. The room had two wide windows overlooking the square, and six chairs had been placed before them. An elegant table of some reddish native wood already supported cups and an earthenware jug.

"By Prudentius!" I exclaimed after sampling its contents. "This isn't fruit juice."

"Beer?" asked Carbuncle.

"No," I said, taking another cautious sip. "Carbuncle, do you remember that friendly fellow we met on our first visit?" Carbuncle's eyebrows shot up. "I think this was distilled by his brother." As the others hastened to fill their glasses, I took a seat by the lefthand window, and set mine on the sill. I resolved to nurse it slowly. The upcoming revels might be of great interest, and I wished to keep my wits about me.

At present, there was not much to see. Mukden's house stood near the midpoint of the north side of the square, thus affording us an excellent view. The southeast quadrant was dominated by the fountain, as it had been earlier in the day. The southwest quadrant held rows of trestle tables, soon to be loaded with food and drink; the unmistakable scent of roasting meat drifted across the square and into our aerie. I sipped my drink, and began to hope that dinner would not be long in arriving.

The northern half of the square was empty, save for shadows that grew steadily longer as the pale blue sun decreased in the west. A platform, about ten yards long by three wide, had been set up at the western end, in front of the Hall of the Masters, thus putting it to our left. It was neatly but not expensively made of wood, and I imagine it was knocked down and stored in a closet when not in use. Behind it was a backdrop of white fabric, possibly some received during the recent trading. Torches, unlit in the late afternoon sun, stood ready at the two front corners, and indeed all around the square.

Carbuncle and Philpott soon came and took the seats to my right and my left.

"I wonder just what it is that they are celebrating," said Philpott as he sat down, mug in hand.

"I suppose they are rejoicing that Mukden and his brothers have returned safely," I said.

"If this is a theologically sophisticated culture, you may well be right, Leon."

"And if it is unsophisticated?" asked Carbuncle.

"Then I would expect the celebration to have a religious nature. It might be motivated by Mukden's success, but if so I would expect a strong element of thanksgiving to the deity." Philpott leaned forward in his seat and rested his elbows on the window sill, looking about eagerly for signs of thanksgiving. Or so I surmise.

Presently the torches were lit, and the Tomarens began to gather in the square. Some began to set out platters and trays of food on the tables; the remainder gathered in front of the torchlit platform. Soon the square was nearly full of white-clad figures. Occasionally a dog would enter the square from some street or alley, wander about, perhaps drink from the fountain, and wander away again. I took another sip, feeling the strong liquor begin to go my head. I was on the verge of going downstairs to look for some victuals when the backdrop was pushed aside, and four figures appeared on the platform. They were difficult to see in the torch light, but it was not hard to guess who they were.

One of them—I believe it was Firenz, the old man—came to the front of the platform. He waited there as the crowd became still, and finally, over the sound of a dog lapping at the fountain, he spoke.

"What did he say?" I whispered to Philpott.

"I'm not sure, but I think he mentioned the Water of Basenis," Philpott replied in quite a normal voice. I started, and looked down at the crowd below, but no one seemed to be paying us any attention. When I looked up again, three men were standing before the platform. One of them shouted out a short phrase, and there was pandemonium.

Every man, woman, and child in the square erupted in a frenzy of shouting and hooting. The three men stood before the platform with their arms upraised in triumph, and then were engulfed by the crowd. Still shouting, the Tomarens embraced each of the men in turn, a tide flowing up to the platform and then to the heavily loaded tables of food. In far shorter a time than seemed likely the whole assemblage was feasting, sitting on the ground or perched on the rim of the fountain. The three men sat with the Masters on the platform, and food was brought to them.

And, not a moment too soon, to us as well. I heard the footsteps on the stairs and rejoiced, for the scene before me was swaying inconstantly to and fro. Shortly thereafter, the table in our aerie was laden with roast meat, a selection of fruits, and, a miracle, a kind of cheese! We lost no time in filling our platters and returning to our seats.

"I do believe that those three men are Mukden and his brothers," I said. Philpott nodded vigorously, as if to say that I had stated the obvious. Carbuncle just grunted in agreement.

The feasting lasted for about an hour, after which the crowd assembled once again in front of the platform. The Masters moved to one side, leaving the stage to Mukden, Foudek, and Parnas. Mukden shouted out something in a jovial tone of voice, and the crowd twittered as they settled onto the ground. Then, after all were seated, a man I didn't recognize carried a large sack on to the platform. Mukden gestured at it as he spoke, apparently describing it, and then looked expectantly at the crowd. A fellow stood up just below us, and called something back. Mukden replied, and looked about the crowd. No one else stood up, and finally he nodded at the fellow and waved at the sack. The fellow came forward, stepping deftly through the seated figures, and carried the sack off.

Next, Mukden's assistant came forth with a fine embroidered robe, and a wild surmise began to grow within my breast. I watched in fascination as Mukden described it to the crowd. Several people stood up immediately, and began calling out to him. Mukden listened intently, pointing first to one and then to another as the calling continued. Eventually one of the callers sat down, to be followed shortly by another, until finally only one was standing. Mukden nodded to the fellow, and waited patiently as the man came forward to collect the robe. When he resumed his place, I noticed that the woman next to him clutched possessively at it.

"They're auctioning off the things Mukden and his brothers brought back," said Carbuncle in some surprise.

"I'd wager that's how Mukden's family earns their living. They take beer to Seros, and auction off the goods they get in return," I said. "I wonder how much the beer costs them, and how far it has to come."

We watched in silence as the items were carried out and knocked down one by one. By far the most popular item was Captain Halvorsen's uniform coat, which finally went to a rotund, prosperous looking fellow. I noted with amusement that the case of wine never appeared; was it withheld by the Masters, or by Mukden and his brothers? Or had it already been drunk?

When the auction was over, the Masters returned to the platform. One of them (from the silvery tones it must have been Asha) spoke for a few moments, and then gestured at Mukden, who spoke for a longer period of time. "He's telling about his trip," said Philpott, "I can tell that much." A hush fell over the crowd as Mukden spoke; no one moved or spoke until, with a sweeping gesture, Mukden directed their attention to us in our window. All turned to look our way, and I gulped.

"Logically," said Philpott, "this is when they should tear us to pieces. If they are going to." Carbuncle and I scowled at him, but he didn't notice, being far too intent on the spectacle before him.

Then the moment passed, and Mukden wrapped up his story. The Masters chanted a few words, holding their hands over their heads, and then left the platform. The crowd, far from attacking us, went about their business, leaving a few to clean up. The festival was over.

No one spoke for several moments. Philpott was still staring out at the square, and Carbuncle was looking into the depths of his mug. Eventually he drained it, and stood up.

"Well, young Thad," he said, "what is your considered opinion of the proceedings?"

"Why, I haven't had time to consider them, Thomas," replied Philpott, half rising from his seat, and turning to look at Carbuncle. "I won't have any definite conclusions for some time."

"Perhaps Philpott *Effendi* could share his unconsidered opinion?" Cadbury had risen from his place before the other window. He had, I feared from his tone, been drinking. He's not supposed to, of course, but among Arrastians he tends to forget himself.

"Yes, Thad," said Hodgins, also rising. "Are they going to kill us tomorrow?" Hodgins, now, I knew he'd been drinking.

Philpott pondered this last question for rather longer than I thought it deserved, and then answered, quite seriously, "I won't know until I see the Masters again."

"Really?" I said. "If they are going to kill us, you'll see the fire in their eyes?"

"Or perhaps the axes in their hands?" said Carbuncle.

He looked at us both in puzzlement. "What?"

I rolled my eyes. "When you see the Masters again, you'll know whether they are going to kill us."

He nodded. "Yes."

"How?"

"They'll tell us, of course. Weren't you listening to Mukden's translation, Leon? They are going to make up their minds, and then let us know."

The conversation might have deteriorated into personalities at this point; it had been a long, trying day. Before I could respond, though, we heard footsteps on the stairs, and then Mukden entered.

"The Masters will see you tomorrow morning," he said gravely. "I shall come to take you to them."

"Have you any idea what they will say?" asked Carbuncle.

"The Masters will see you tomorrow morning," he repeated. "Now I must take you back to the hostel."

CHAPTER 23

ᴗːᴥ

We are not torn to pieces. ᴥ A dog fight. ᴥ The Masters compromise.

THE FIRST of Ragout had been horrific; the second of Ragout had been tedious and alarming by turns. The third of the month, in contrast, was a fine day. Despite our fears of being torn asunder by an angry if sophisticated mob, the excellent food and drink of the night before had conspired in favor of slumber, and we had retired immediately upon return to the hostel. When we descended to the common room after a refreshing, though sonorous, night, Abayla was ready with a tureen of porridge and platters of fruit.

Breakfast was a merry meal. A yellow sun was shining brightly outside the common room window, and several dogs were sprawled on the cobbles, basking in the sun and obstructing the few passersby. Most glanced curiously at us, but none stared, or even broke their stride. Nor did they seem hostile. For our part, we had managed to put aside our fears. I did not intend to allow us to be killed; either we would be allowed to stay, or we would be required to go. The latter would be a disappointment, but on the other hand required no particular planning, so we naturally dismissed it.

Carbuncle finished a second bowl of porridge, and accepted a mug of fruit juice from Abayla.

"Assuming they let us stay, Leon, what shall we do first?"

I put down my spoon.

"My first concern is mapping the immediate vicinity. In the long run, of course, I'll be looking for the effects of the Law of Consensus on the terrain, and I can't do that without a proper baseline. I'll need Fox and Hodgins to come with me, at least. I expect one of the locals will want to tag along, and unless they speak Serosan I'll need Cadbury as well. I suppose, Thomas, that you'll be wanting to examine the hoist? I'm sure Mukden would be delighted to show you around."

"I believe I'll accompany you, Leon."

"Oh, really, Thomas, that's not at all necessary."

"Indeed it is. Or were you going to operate the geometer yourself?"

"Thomas, I'm really quite capable—"

"Of scaring the wee beastie to death, Leon. No, I'll be coming with you, never fear. Have you any objection to starting at the hoist? It's true that I'd like to examine the works."

As Carbuncle was in all likelihood right about my skills, I gracefully acquiesced.

"Very well, Thomas, we'll have it your way. The hoist is the proper starting point in any event, as I was in no shape to take measurements the day before last." My companions wisely did not comment. "Now, Thaddeus, I expect you'll want to stay here in town."

Philpott looked up from his notes; he had a pencil in his right hand and a spoon in his left. As he was not naturally ambidextrous, I fear he had spilled a certain amount of porridge on the pages and down his front.

"I beg your pardon, Leon?"

"I expect you'll want to stay here in town while Thomas and I are off mapping."

Philpott nodded vigorously.

"Oh, yes, Leon. At some point I'll want to visit some outlying villages or farms, if there are any, but it makes most sense to start where the most people are. I'm hoping that one of the Masters will be willing to show me about."

"Won't that give you a slanted view of the place?" asked Carbuncle. "Will the people you talk to behave normally with one of their rulers present?"

Philpott smiled at him fondly.

"Of course they won't, Thomas. I'll need to go see them all again later. But it will give me an excellent insight into the Masters and their position in the town."

"Will you need Cadbury to translate?" I asked.

"It would be helpful, Leon. My Zymurgian is still rather poor, and I would prefer to avoid confusion. If I have Cadbury along, I can be certain that he, at least, understands what I wish to say."

Just then, Mukden passed by the window, and entered the common room by the street door.

"Good morning, my friends. I have come to take you to the Masters." His dark face gave nothing away, and my fears were renewed. It was all very well to say that I wouldn't permit us to be put to death; I was not at all sure how to enforce my decree. I could only hope that our status as guests would earn us a running start.

"Very well, we are ready," I said. "Thomas, Thad, shall we go?" We rose from our seats at the table, Philpott carefully straightening his sheaf of notes and tucking them in his pocket. "Bruno, heel," I commanded as we followed Mukden into the street. I wasn't sure it was wise to bring the dog, but it might be just as foolish not to. Besides, the noble beast deserved an outing.

I had forgotten the two dogs basking outside. They sprang to their feet when Bruno appeared, as though they had been waiting for him. They showed none of the truculence of the day before, but approached Bruno slowly, heads down, tails wagging just a little. Bruno outwardly ignored them, keeping to his station at my left side as we walked a few paces toward the square, but I could tell he was eager to be let go. At length I decided that if there was to be trouble it were best to have it over with, and released him.

"All right, Bruno." At the words of release, Bruno bounded away, pouncing on the larger of the two Zymurgian dogs. He rolled over, with one dog on top and the other nipping at his tail, and then over again, and pounced on the smaller dog. All three were barking merrily, and soon three other dogs came from three different directions and the thing became a general melee. It was by no means five little white dogs against one large black one; so far as I could tell, Bruno and the first two had joined forces.

Eventually Mukden's sense of duty overcame his curiosity and he gestured for us to continue. I called Bruno to heel, and he looked at me woefully. He was lying on his side, with three dogs on top of him, one under his left front paw, and the fifth dog's right hind leg in his mouth. I merely stared at him. Sighing, he released the dogs, shook off the three others like a whale breaking through an ice pack, and resumed his place at my side. The five Zymurgian dogs tagged along behind as we continued on our way, and several others joined us as we crossed the square to the Hall of the Masters. Mukden opened the door for us, and as we entered I once again commanded Bruno to go lie down. Surprisingly, the eight or nine smaller dogs followed us in, and went and lay down in the corner beside him. There was much panting, and as the Zymurgian dogs were effectively strays, I am afraid the pile of canines was exceedingly rank in that enclosed space.

The Masters were standing before their stools; studying their faces, I saw that they were nonplussed by this new development, for which I could not blame them. Yet, I thought their dismay was tinged with a certain amount of relief.

We stood comfortably at ease as Mukden announced us, and listened attentively as Asha spoke and Mukden translated.

"Asha asks whether you could persuade the dogs to go elsewhere," he said. It was a reasonable request. I released Bruno, and gestured at the open door. Bruno wasted no time, the other dogs followed suit, and a good riddance it was. Barking, yelping, and the occasional whine formed the aural backdrop for the remainder of the meeting, but the air was substantially clearer.

The Masters seated themselves, and we three took up our positions before them. Asha spoke again.

"We have conferred at length. Because Mukden brought you to Tomar, you are our guests. Firenz reminds us that guests are sacred, and must not be ill-treated." The older man bowed. "Yet we do not trust you. We have traded with the people of the Lands Below forever, yet we have never seen folk like you. Simuny doubts your motives, and fears that you precede an army." The older woman bowed, an ironic smile on her lips. "Nabili is angered that you have restrained one of the Pups of Basenis." Nabili nodded quickly, his lips tight and his eyes cold. "It seems to the rest of us that Great Basenis is not unduly disturbed." Here, she gestured to the window and the square beyond. Nabili's lips tightened further, but he held his tongue. Asha continued.

"We are the Masters of Tomar, and the well-being of Tomar is in our charge. Because you are our guests, you are made free of the town and its surroundings." Mukden began to smile happily as he translated this. "Because we do not trust you, one of us must accompany you in all you do." His smile did not slip. "Because Mukden presented us with this dilemma without warning, he must forfeit his share of his recent journey to the people of Tomar. The Masters have spoken." Mukden turned from us to the Masters in surprise; this last bit had apparently been unexpected.

They looked back at him, nodding, and I believe Asha raised one eyebrow quizzically, as if inviting him to comment. He took a deep breath, and sagged back into his previous position.

"The Masters of Tomar are most generous," I replied. "Indeed, though we would not wish to inconvenience you, your presence with us is exactly what we most desire." Simuny looked skeptical, and Nabili clearly didn't believe a word, but neither voiced their reservations.

Next followed a lengthy discussion on logistics: when, where, and whom. When the fog cleared, we had agreed on the following terms: we would remain in the hostel each night. Each day, two of the Masters would be available for escort duty, thus allowing us to divide our forces in half, as we had intended. Mukden would also accompany one team or the other, as translator. The festival being over, the Masters had no more pressing duties than seeing to their troublesome guests, so as the day was young we set off at once.

CHAPTER 24

⌣⁘⌢

A day's surveying. ❧ *Nut cakes and napkins.* ❧ *Carbuncle is perplexed.*

THE YELLOW sun was past the zenith before we were done with the hoist and its environs. Fixing its position—my chief concern—was accomplished in a matter of minutes. Taking sightings of prominent landmarks took even less time; the hoist stands in a man-made clearing in the forest that lines the rim of the plateau. The view south was blocked by the trees, and the view north was of territory already perfectly well mapped. Even if Seros had been less well-known, the air was hazy and shimmered with the heat coming off of the desert; any measurements would have been suspect. And so, while Carbuncle poked and prodded and nosed about in the works, Hodgins in tow, the rest of us sat in the shade and threw sticks for Bruno and drank chilled fruit juice. (Carbuncle had managed to perfect his wine chiller during the passage from Cuprios.) In the meantime, of course, we had run out of wine to chill. No matter. Carbuncle had preserved several empty bottles, into which we decanted fruit juice or other potables as necessary. It was a pleasure to see the surprise on Fox's face when I handed him a frosty glass. Indeed, it was a pleasure to see anything at all there.

"My word," he exclaimed, "What is this?"

"It is the juice of the gonowah berry," I said. "Or so Mukden tells me. Oh, you mean the chiller? It's an invention of Carbuncle's."

Fox fell to studying it, while I conversed in Serosan with our guides. Cadbury was in town with Philpott, but Mukden's Serosan was quite good, as, surprisingly, was Firenz'. I congratulated him on his grasp of a tongue he would seldom have reason to speak.

"Ahh," the old man said, "It is not so surprising. Have I not made many journeys to the Lands Below?"

"He is my uncle," said Mukden, "and the head of my family. The eldest of the Hinkayas is always one of the Masters of Tomar."

That explained Firenz' apologetic air and his stress on hospitality during our recent inquisition. It also explained why he had volunteered to come traipsing over half of creation with us... it reminded him of his youth. I was about to ask him to tell me of his travels when he spoke again.

"What is your friend looking for?"

"He wants to see how the hoist works."

"It is a simple thing. Why does it take him so long?"

"Perhaps because he seeks something complicated."

It took me a few tries get that idea across to the old man, but once he had it he laughed until he choked. We plied him with fruit juice until he was calm again, though still chuckling.

"A thing that happened in my youth," he said, "Shall I tell you?"

I nodded my agreement, and he began. There was a certain amount of of confusion and explanation, and of backing and filling, which I cannot possibly convey, so I will tell the story as I finally understood it.

"I am of the Hinkaya," he said. "I have lived in the grand house of the Hinkaya on the square all of my life. It was a fine house when I was a child, as it is now, and filled with every good thing. One day my mother had baked nut cakes, and gave me one to eat. She wrapped it in a napkin, so that I would not burn my hands. Oh, it was a fine hot nut cake, with a piece of birga nut sticking out of one side. I took a big bite, and burned my mouth, and then my mother sent me out to play.

"A little while later she caught me passing through the kitchen. She scolded me for stealing another nut cake, and called me a greedy child, but I showed her that it was the same cake, with the same birga nut sticking out of one side, and the same big bite in it. And then I showed her that no nut cakes were missing. Oh, she apologized to me, and then sent me back outside.

"Ah, I was a great trial to her that day. She could not keep me out of the kitchen! Whenever she turned around, I was there, with my napkin and my nut cake. She was sure I was stealing nut cakes, but as often as she looked she saw that it was the same cake, with the same birga nut sticking out of one side, and the same big bite in it. Finally she forbade me to come back into the house until dark. She was sure I was making mischief in the kitchen, though she could not see what it was."

By this time, Firenz' lean black face was nearly round with suppressed merriment, as was Mukden's; he had clearly heard the story before. Some response seemed called for.

"And were you?" I asked.

"Oh, of course, my friend, of course. I was not stealing nut cakes, oh no. My mother would have caught me in a moment. But my brothers and I, we were making sailboats to sail in the fountain, and we needed sails. I was stealing napkins!"

This time I joined in the old man's laughter, and when I had done Fox was looking at me quizzically. I related the story to him in Anglish, as best I could.

"Why ever was he stealing napkins?" asked Fox before I reached the end of the story. I reflected for a moment on the awful power of banking to mold and transform its practitioners, giving them a keen eye to see through every situation, while evidently stifling their wit altogether.

"Never mind, Frederick," I sighed. "I suppose it doesn't matter very much." I rose to my feet, tired of waiting. "I'll just go and see what's taking Carbuncle so long, shall I?" Mukden joined me.

"What seems to be the trouble," I called out as we approached him. It was hot under the afternoon glare of the yellow sun, and Carbuncle had taken off his coat and rolled up his sleeves. He was standing, staring at the hoist and its mechanisms as if in a daze. He seemed quite puzzled. Hodgins was sitting nearby on a massive spool of rope, Carbuncle's coat beside him; he just looked tired.

"What seems to be the trouble, Thomas," I repeated.

He ran one hand through his hair, and scratched the back of his head. From appearances, he'd been doing that frequently.

"I'm just trying to figure out how it works, Leon." I looked the device over. Now I was puzzled.

"It seems perfectly plain to me, Thomas," I said. "That pillar over there, with all the bars sticking out of it, is some kind of windlass. They get a bunch of people to hold on to the bars and walk round and round. You can see where the cable is wrapped many times around the pillar, up there? They walk round and round, and that winds up the cable, which then gets coiled up on those spools over there. I guess they do that by hand." I paused, and studied it a bit more. "And that crane-thing with the counterweight on the end is mounted on some kind of swivel; I'd guess they turn it by having a group of people push or pull on that bar over there."

Carbuncle looked at me blankly as I related my guesses to Mukden in Serosan. He nodded and pointed out one or two particular refinements, which I passed along to my friend the phantasticist.

"So where," I repeated, "is the difficulty? I hate to think of what would happen if someone let go of their bar while they were hoisting—in fact, I rather think I'll go back down on donkeyback, and let the rafts fall where they may. But I don't see anything terribly complicated about it."

"So it appears, Leon, but I don't see how any number of people can manage to lift such heavy weights. There must be some kind of phantasm helping out, but I simply cannot find it." He stared at the thing in frustration.

"Hmm," I said. "I rather guess that that's what all those pulleys are for, Thomas." He shook his head.

"Why are you so surprised, Thomas? You're the one who told me you found no sign of any phantasm on the raft, and no sign that any phantasm had been used in building the thing."

"I know you're right, Leon." Carbuncle sighed, and ran his hand through his hair again. "I was hoping I was wrong. I thought that if they had no small phantasms, perhaps they would at least have one or two big ones. But it seems that they are innocent of even elementary phantastics." I could understand his disappointment. Behind the everyday bustle of messing around with the expedition's phantasms (maintaining is his word) lurked his real ambition: to find some new phantasm, such as had never been known before. Such a find would be academically satisfying, and potentially lucrative. Alas, it began to seem unlikely.

"Buck up, Thomas," I said. "The season is relatively young, and we have lots of ground to cover. Something might turn up yet. Now, we've spent enough time here. I want to survey the road from here to the donkey trail before dark."

While we were taking our ease and sipping fruit juice, Philpott was wandering from one end of Tomar to the other in the company of Cadbury and the lovely Asha. So we discovered when we returned to the hostel at the end of the day.

It had been a productive day, despite our lengthy sojourn at the hoist-head. We had surveyed the road between Tomar and the hoist, and, on donkeyback, the road from Tomar to the donkey trail which zigzagged down the cliffs to Seros below. The two roads met in a fork just north of Tomar itself, and joined to become the main street through the town. As the rest of the land between Tomar and the plateau's edge was heavily forested, we had therefore in a single day surveyed most of the open land north of Tomar. I do not say that we saw everything there was to see, by any means. The road from the donkey trail to Tomar is fully ten miles long, and there are occasional trails running to one side or the other. It was in a hut along one such—I have no recollection which—that Carbuncle and I were entertained on our first visit.

There was one particular trail that intrigued me. It started at the fork in the roads just outside of Tomar, and ran due north into the woods. The other trails were narrow but well-tended; this one was wide, almost as wide as the roads. It was also much overgrown, not just with shrubs and bushes but also with saplings and a few good-sized trees. It spoke of something once important but now forgotten or abandoned. We had no time to explore it that day, or I would have followed it to its end. It could not be very far; the plateau's edge was only a few miles to the north. Lacking the time, however, I eased my curiosity by inquiring of my guides.

Mukden looked down the overgrown way, and shrugged.

"It is an old road. No one goes there now."

"But it must have lead somewhere once upon a time. Where did it go?"

"The hoist was not always where it is now. When it was moved, the old road fell into disrepair," said Firenz. "Nothing is left there, my friend. Soon the road itself will be swallowed by the forest."

That was certainly true; it had been half-swallowed already.

On the walk back to Tomar I related Firenz' story of the nut cakes to Carbuncle and Hodgins, who laughed appreciatively. I did not discuss the context in which it was told. Carbuncle is a sensitive soul, and he had been sadly disappointed that day.

When we returned to the hostel, Philpott was already seated at the refectory table, sipping fruit juice and working on his notes.

"Ah, Philpott, just the man I wanted to see," I said, sitting down across from him. He looked up at me blankly, pen in hand, eyes owlish behind his spectacles. Then he seemed to snap into focus, and put down his pen.

"Oh, hello, Leon. Did you have a productive day?"

"Indeed we did, and I've a story I want to share with you." I related Firenz' tale for the third time that day, and I fancy it was the smoothest telling so far. Philpott listened attentively, nodding from time to time. He didn't look at me, but rather into the space over my left shoulder, as though he were silently comparing the tale with same slowly moving canvas behind me. When I related that Firenz' mother had forbade him to enter the kitchen, sure as she was that he was up to no good, he pursed his lips and raised his eyebrows, and nodded again.

"I take it Firenz was stealing the napkins for some reason?"

"Yes, to make sails for some toy boats," I said, not very graciously. It was the second time I had had the punch-line cut off by my listener. Philpott just nodded.

"Yes, Leon, a fascinating tale. I'm glad you passed it along to me. There was a time, you know, when no academic who valued his reputation would have anything at all to do with such folk tales. Now, however, we know that such stories are a window onto a culture's collective soul. This is a particular fine one, and I must write it down before I forget the salient details. I don't suppose you could relate it again?"

And so I went through the story a fourth time, unsure whether to be pleased or otherwise. As I spoke he seized his pen and made many rapid scrawls.

"Thank you, Leon, I believe that will do."

"You are welcome, Thad." I poured myself a glass of fruit juice, unfermented and un-chilled, but sweet and wet. Just then, Abayla served dinner, and any further discussion of the day's events was postponed as we did it justice.

CHAPTER 25

⌣⁚⌇

A little gossip. ॐ A promenade. ॐ "Aybahsmaht!"

AFTER DINNER, Philpott refused to give details about his day, beyond the statement that Asha had shown him and Cadbury all around the town.

"You see, Leon, I must write down my observations while they are still fresh. If I were discuss them now, I should not be able to refrain from reflecting upon them. I fear they would be quite compromised." Suiting deed to word, he bent back over his notes and continued to write rapidly.

Carbuncle and I were quite unable to change his mind, and I fear I was growing angry when I observed Cadbury signaling to me from down the table. I glanced at him, and he winked quite deliberately in response. I raised my eyebrows questioningly. He jerked his head at Philpott, and raised his eyes to the ceiling. Then he smiled broadly at me. I nodded back.

"Thad," I said, "I'm sure we all have the greatest possible respect for your observations, and I quite see the importance of getting them down on paper as soon as possible. However..." He raised his eyes to look at me without actually raising his head.

"Yes, Leon?"

"Wouldn't it be less distracting for you to work upstairs, as you did last night?" He nodded his head slightly.

"Indeed it would, Leon, but I'm afraid the light is very bad. Also, there is no table. I shall be fine right here." And he lowered his eyes to the page, and resumed his scribbling.

I grimaced at Cadbury. I was eager to hear what he had to say, but clearly we couldn't discuss it in front of Philpott. I examined my options.

I could, of course, suggest that Cadbury, Carbuncle and I adjourn upstairs, but I discarded that as too obvious, especially if Fox and Hodgins joined us. Also, if there were no tables upstairs, there were also no chairs, and no cups, and no Abayla to keep them filled. I was not about to let Philpott drive us from the most comfortable room in the hostel.

I glanced at Abayla, rubbing my chin. Would she be willing to find a table and a better lamp for the second floor? Possibly… but so far she had shown no inclination to heed any request which did not involve the pleasures of the table. And anyway, it might just tempt Philpott into working late at night, when the rest of us were trying to sleep. Reluctantly I discarded that idea as well.

I glanced at Cadbury (exasperated, frowning at Philpott), and at Carbuncle (who shrugged). I pondered my only other alternative for a few moments, examining its flaws, but decided I had no other recourse.

"It's a fine evening," I said, looking pointedly out the window. "Carbuncle, perhaps you'd care to join me for a promenade in the town square?" Cadbury brightened at once, and Carbuncle looked thoughtful. Philpott sat straight up.

"Are you sure that would be wise, Leon?" he exclaimed, his brow furrowed. "I am fairly sure that the Masters do not wish us to travel about on our own."

"I think you're judging their wishes too harshly, Thad," I said, with a certainty I did not feel. Carbuncle leaned back in his chair, looking like a spectator at a sporting match. "Indeed, they asked to accompany us while we pursued our investigations, but I mean to do no investigating tonight. I mean only to take the evening air for a time, and then return here."

Philpott still looked worried.

"They seemed quite clear on the subject, Leon."

"Now, now, Thaddeus," I said. "I am sure they wouldn't wish to deprive us of our evening constitutional. I am sure that if we inquired, they would gladly give us leave, but as you see we have no way of inquiring."

"But to assume their consent, Leon, strikes me as dangerous. And should they approach you during your walk, you cannot even explain your intentions to them!" By this time Philpott had put down his pen, and was staring at me in consternation.

"That is easily fixed," I said. "We shall have Cadbury accompany us, and he will translate should it become necessary."

"You are determined in this, Leon?"

"Quite so, Thaddeus."

"Very well." Philpott sighed, and began gathering his notes together into a neat pile.

"What ever are you doing, Thad?" I could see Carbuncle hiding a broad grin. Cadbury's eyes had widened considerably.

"I am coming with you, of course, Leon. I cannot let you and Carbuncle go into danger by yourself. If you are determined to go, I shall attend you." Cadbury closed his eyes and put his hand over his face; Carbuncle was racked with silent guffaws. Fox, as usual, was impassive. For my part, I saw no graceful way to extricate myself from either the walk or Philpott's presence on it.

"Very well," I sighed. "Would anyone else care to join us? Fox? Hodgins?" Fox silently shook his head; Hodgins, I saw, had fallen asleep with his head on his arms. I looked under the table. "Bruno?" Bruno raised his head from his paws, and wagged his tail slightly, then laid his head down again. That, at least, was not surprising. Like any dog on a ramble in the country, he had covered at least five times us much ground as the rest of us.

I got up from my seat. "Shall we go?" I said, with a cheerfulness I did not feel. I was, in fact, feeling rather a fool as we stepped into the street. Because of a childish schoolboy's love of gossip, I was quite possibly endangering the success of the expedition, and to no profit. I could not discuss Philpott's adventures with Cadbury while Philpott himself was present, it simply wouldn't do. It would be indiscreet. Nor could I back down gracefully. My ludicrous display obliged me to visit the town square, with or without Philpott. I could, of course, order him to stay behind, but his sense of duty would force him to come anyway; I would merely be causing needless friction.

So distracted was I by these thoughts that we were fully into the square before I realized that Philpott's presence or absence was at worst immaterial, at best an unmixed blessing. With a sinking heart I discovered that my plans for an evening constitutional in the square were not unique. The square was brightly lit by the torches around its perimeter, and at least half of the village's population were in it. A regular promenade was in progress, with about half of the crowd drifting slowly in the clockwise direction, and the other half drifting just as slowly in the counterclockwise direction. There were knots and eddies of conversation here and there where folk had met friends or relatives, and laughter, and shouted greetings and catcalls as well. It was a fascinating sight, but clearly no place for any kind of private or intimate discussion.

I glanced at my companions, and then shrugged. We had come for a promenade in the square, and a promenade we had found; we might as well join it. I threw back my shoulders, shot my cuffs, and started to drift. Carbuncle, Cadbury and Philpott perforce began to drift after me.

It is not to be thought that our arrival passed without notice. Indeed, we were objects of great interest from the moment we entered the square, and though no one was so rude as to stare or to discuss us openly within our earshot, I could see many flashing glances and hear a distant whispering among the townspeople. I smiled at everyone we passed, bowing slightly to the Tomaren ladies. They for their part were quite bold, making eye contact as easily as though I were a brother, or perhaps an old uncle. This should not surprise me, I thought, reflecting upon the lovely Asha.

As we drifted along, the distant whispering began to acquire form; it seemed to me that I was hearing a single word, endlessly repeated, first on one side, then on that side, indeed from every corner of the square. I could not quite make it out; it was something like *"aybahsmaht"*. I was on the verge of asking Philpott and Cadbury if they could hear it, and if so if they knew what it meant, when my foolishness received its reward. I should have expected that our presence would be noted by the Masters of Tomar, and had I wished for a maximum of unpleasantness I would have chosen no other of the four than the one who now blocked our path: young, zealous Nabili.

Nabili was not well pleased to find us abroad in the evening. He had said nothing yet, but his expression was plain to read: righteous anger mixed with a certain repressed joy. We were not supposed to be out, and he was glad to be the one to chastise us. Perhaps I was reading more into an angry visage than was actually there, but I do not think so. It had been evident in our meetings with the four Masters that Nabili did not like us and wished to be well quit of us. It hardly seemed fair to me; we had done nothing to attract his ill-will.

When confronted by irrational malice, a commodity by no means in short supply in the University, I find that there is only one truly satisfactory response: unstinting good humor. And so, seeing Nabili glowering darkly in our path, I smiled broadly. I bowed, hand to my heart, and rising I greeted him warmly.

"What ho, Nabili old fellow," I said. "A pleasant evening, I must say." And I beamed at him as Cadbury tried to translate my words. Not that young Nabili listened to him.

"Aybahsmaht," he said harshly, and spat on the cobbles.

"Such lovely weather," I said. "Is it always like this, this time of year?"

By this time the four of us were standing shoulder to shoulder. Philpott and Cadbury were on my right and left, with Carbuncle just beyond Cadbury. Nabili spat out a few more words, which I could not make out at all.

"Just a moment, old thing, do you mind? I need a translation," I said, and leaned over to Cadbury. "What did he say?"

"He asks why you did not stay in the hostel, as you promised," Cadbury whispered back.

"Why, we promised not to explore without an escort," I said to Nabili. "At present, we are not exploring; we are simply enjoying the fine weather. Surely there is no harm in that?" And I beamed at him some more as Cadbury translated. We were now at the heart of our own eddy in the flow of the promenade, indeed, a veritable maelstrom of people. I think most of the crowd had gathered around to see what would befall us. I bent to hear Cadbury translate Nabili's response, when a silvery voice interrupted.

It was Asha, of course. I did not understand her words, save for the single monosyllable "Thed", but the warmth of her expression and her voice were unmistakable. She was clearly glad to see us—or to see "Thed", at any rate, for she came up to him and took his arm as she continued to speak.

"She is telling Nabili that we are here at her invitation," whispered Cadbury to me.

"Are we?" I whispered back.

"No," he replied. "But now you have seen with your own eyes everything I would have told you in private." By this I presumed he meant Asha's friendliness toward Philpott.

It is an odd thing, really. Philpott is the quintessential scholar, the don's don if you will. His studies are of more import to him than his next meal, or indeed of several meals beyond that. He has little experience of the world, and is often taken by surprise, noble Bruno being the example in chief. His speech is somewhat stilted, his concerns alien to most people, his appearance pleas-

ant though not excessively handsome, his soul rather detached
from the day to day.

And yet, people like him, and he them. Wherever we went,
he was soon acquainted with everyone, high and low. Back on the
Spaniel he was on first name terms with his pal Bill Hodgins and
his chum Richard Halvorsen. In Lyricum, Hodgins had nearly
caused a riot by questioning the greatness of the great Rotini; I'll
be bound that Philpott, with the same questions and attitudes,
would have had them buying him drinks. I do not understand
it, nor am I sure that he is entirely aware of it, and perhaps that
unselfconsciousness is part of his charm. At the moment I was
simply glad that it was functioning as usual.

It took Asha just a few moments to mollify—or at least over-
rule—young Nabili, after which we began to drift again, with
Asha still on Philpott's arm. After several minutes Nabili was
comfortably far behind, and Asha began to speak seriously to
us. She had never intended for us to be strictly confined to the
hostel, yet it was foolish, Cadbury translated, for us to come to the
square unescorted. Cadbury explained that we had had no means
of requesting an escort, and had therefore presumed on their hospitality. It was a shrewd statement; Asha immediately promised
to wait on us each evening, so that we could join the promenade
with a proper escort. After that she became more cheerful, and
we made several pleasant rounds of the square before she lead us
back to the hostel.

Perhaps Cadbury put a slight emphasis on the word proper
in his translation, or perhaps the emphasis was present in Asha's
actual speech. I do not know...but watching her chatter away
by Philpott's side, I began to wonder whether propriety was her
greatest concern.

CHAPTER 26

⌇⁙⌇

The expedition proceeds. ⁊ Giggles and gooney balls.
Dinner with Roshnoy the grain balancer.

A S IT turned out, my rash, childish, I will even say foolhardy, insistence on venturing into the square unescorted bore the most delectable fruit, and the next weeks went swimmingly well. Each day Carbuncle and I went surveying in the countryside, and each day Philpott went ethnomonotonizing in the town, and each evening we dined well and then joined the promenade in the square. By the second week's end we had surveyed all of the principle roads and fields in the vicinity, and many of the smaller ones as well. At the time we had no idea what progress Philpott was making, as he persisted in his refusal to speak of it.

Good times often make poor tales, yet there is much to tell of those two weeks. We had been given to believe that each of the four Masters of Tomar would be escorting us in our daily rounds— that is, that the duty would rotate among them so that each would spend time with us. In the event, that did not happen. Firenz and Mukden were our invariable companions on our surveying trips, just as Asha escorted Philpott and Cadbury about the town. In the evenings, it was always (but for one notable occasion) Asha who came to collect us, though Firenz frequently joined us later. We saw little of Simuny or Nabili, or rather we spoke seldom with Nabili, for he was a constant presence if we were abroad in the town. He never came near, but his eye was often upon us.

For my part I was pleased with the arrangement. Firenz was a delightful old soul, and his knowledge of Serosan both eased conversation and lessened the strain on Mukden's translating skills. It was therefore from idle curiosity that I questioned him about it. He answered readily enough.

"Asha has her own reasons for remaining in town," he said, casting a wry look sidelong at me; we were on donkeyback, riding down a dusty road south of the town. I nodded, and he nodded, and then he continued. "Simuny is as old as I," he said, "but not as strong as she was. She could not manage all of this tramping and traipsing about the countryside. It is hard enough for me! I have not slept so well in many years."

"And glad I am for your company, my friend," I said. "But if it is hard for you, could not young Nabili take your place from time to time?"

Firenz leaned over to the left, and spat on the ground. "That for young Nabili," he grunted. And no more would he say.

I must say that I was surprised to find that his feelings about Nabili so closely matched my own, though I silently questioned his answer about Simuny. She had not seemed notably frail the few times we had met.

As a side effect of our nightly promenades, we began to meet more of the Tomaren people. This was due in no small part to Carbuncle's increasing disappointment and frustration with the state of Zymurgian phantastics, if indeed I may even use such a positive term for such an apparently non-existent thing. There were no phantasms anywhere we went. Granted, we were out in the country most of the day, where phantasms might reasonably be scarce, but there were none in the public areas of the village, nor any in the hostel. It's possible that Philpott might have encountered some in his travels about the town, but such was his concern for Carbuncle that I believe he would have overcome his unnatural reticence and mentioned them; always assuming, of course, that he noticed their existence.

As I have said, Carbuncle is a man who must be tinkering, and our geometer and other instruments required only so much tuning when used daily. Finding no native Zymurgian phantasms to tinker with, it was perforce necessary for him to make his own. Time and materials were both in short supply, of course, and so his creations were small and simple: things that whirled on the ground, or flew through the air, or turned colors while playing a tune. Toys, in other words. Each morning he packed a small box with materials and oddments and his current projects, and during our rest breaks or on our ever-lengthening rides a-donkeyback he would take them out and tinker with them, crooning at them softly. By day's end he'd have another little thingumbob. It was all magic to me, of course.

Firenz and Mukden were much taken with his creations (as, indeed, was I), but not half so much as the Zymurgian children.

Each evening Carbuncle would bring a toy or two to show off to the people we met in the square; before many days had passed there was always a crowd of small dark figures waiting for him in the square, ready to drag him off in a flurry of shouts and giggles.

I believe the most popular creation was a gooney ball. The children had never seen one before, naturally, and weren't sure what to make of it. It didn't seem to move or fly or change color like Carbuncle's other toys; it was just a red ball, about a foot in diameter. Carbuncle put it on the ground and gave it a kick, and naturally enough the youngsters went swarming after. A fine game had just developed, the ball shooting all around the square, when Carbuncle cupped his hands around his mouth and shouted, "Gooney!". The complexion of the game changed instantly, as any Anglish lad would have expected. Before they had been kicking the ball merrily to and fro; now it was still moving merrily to and fro, but not one of them could so much as connect a toe with it. There were several minutes of spreading consternation, at the end of which a circle of horrified children stood and stared at the errant red ball. One or another would jump into the middle of the circle, trying to grab the ball, but the ball simply would not be caught, remaining always at least one foot away from the pursuer's outstretched hands or feet, until one particularly sharp young girl managed to work it into a corner.

"Gooney!" said the ball as she laid her hands upon it, and the poor girl jumped back, lost her balance, and might have come to harm if her friends had not come to her aid. She approached it again, reaching our her hands gingerly, but the ball neither spoke nor attempted to get away.

"All right, Thomas," I said to Carbuncle, who was chortling merrily. "Don't you think you had better go explain it to them?"

"No need, Leon, no need," he replied, wiping his eyes. "Look."

And it was true. The girl had carried the ball back into the middle of the square, put it down, and hollered "Gooney!" at the top of her voice. The ball jumped a little, and resumed its evasive activities, to the utter delight of the assembled youngsters, and not a few of their parents. Play resumed, rules were devised, and the next night additional torches were brought in, the better to light the center of the square for the children's play. Gooney ball remained a popular pastime for the duration of our stay in Tomar.

Several evenings later we were approached by the rotund gentleman who had bought Captain Halvorsen's uniform coat at the auction. He was a broad and beaming fellow, with curly white hair, bad yellow teeth, and a ready supply of laughter. Asha introduced him to us as Tomar's grain balancer, and translated his request that we be his honored guests for dinner the following day. It was by no means clear to us what a grain balancer's duties entailed, though he looked remarkably well-fed; consequently we accepted with alacrity, at which he beamed even more widely than before. Then he called out, "Gooney!", clapped Carbuncle on the shoulder, and laughing, moved on through the crowd. I don't suppose he realized what he done to the gooney ball game going on a few yards away, but I detected some high-pitched muttering until the children got things squared away again.

The following day we returned to the hostel after our day's work, and got cleaned and dressed as best we could; and then Asha and Firenz came to escort us to dinner.

The grain balancer, whose name was Roshnoy, lived in a fine big house directly across the square from that of the Hinkaya, Mukden's family. Roshnoy himself met us at the door, and escorted us up a flight of steps and into an upper room where a long table was set. The company consisted of Roshnoy and his wife, Asha, Firenz, and Mukden, and all of our company save for Norfolk and Suffolk.

The food and drink were excellent, being similar to that which we had had the night of the festival. I said us much to our host, who smiled. Mukden translated his response with a grin of his own.

"He says is sorry not to have more greatly excelled the table of the Hinkaya; he shall have to try harder."

"And why is that, friend Mukden?"

"The Hinkaya and the Vastids have ever been rivals in Tomar. My great-grandfather would never have entered a Vastid house, nor been welcome in one."

"The Vastids, then, are an important family in Tomar?"

"Indeed. Just as the Hinkaya are responsible for dispersing the waters of Basenis, the Vastids are responsible for balancing the grain."

"And do they also count one of the Masters of Tomar in their number?"

Mukden grunted. "Nabili," he said shortly. I would have asked him more, but at that time my host's voice reminded me of my rudeness in monopolizing the translator.

Though the food was good, the conversation was necessarily rather stilted. Politeness dictated that we converse with Roshnoy, for which we needed Mukden's services as translator; politeness further decreed that we not talk over much among ourselves. The dinner was thus a rather constrained affair. At a loss for topics of conversation, I asked after Roshnoy's position. After much confusion and discussion, it became clear.

The economy of Tomar, like that of any other agricultural town, is based on farm produce. Many different crops were grown in the vicinity, but the dominant crop was the grain, similar to wheat, which we had eaten as porridge every morning since our arrival. The Vastid family were the managers of the town granary. I thought for a moment that Roshnoy's title implied that he was responsible for weighing out the measures of grain in some way, but I was mistaken; "balancer" is an exact translation, but "accountant" or even "banker" would be a better one. The Zymurgians have no coinage; wealth is held as shares in the contents of the grainery. When a farmer brings his harvest to the grainery, he receives so many grainery shares. He must have shoes, clothing, and tools; for these things he transfers grainery shares to the ranchers, bakers, tailors, and so forth. Roshnoy's principle responsibility was keeping track of the shares owned by each member of the community.

"But surely you know all this!" he exclaimed (via Mukden). "Thed asked all of these questions of me many days ago." I shot a glance at Philpott, who had the grace to look embarrassed, and replied, "Firsthand knowledge is always to be preferred."

Not surprisingly, Fox had played a reasonably large part in the discussion. Now he asked a question which I daresay would never have occurred to me.

"Your system works very well for transactions among the citizens of Tomar; but what of trade with other towns?" Mukden translated the question, and Roshnoy, pleased with such a clever audience, began to expound on Basenis knows what. Before he had gotten very far, and before Mukden had translated any of his speech, Asha announced that it was late, that the promenade was beginning, and that it was time to go. Roshnoy looked hurt, but nodded at another word from Asha, and ponderously stood up, thanking us all for our presence. We thanked him in turn, and silently filed out into the square.

Naturally I braced Cadbury as soon as I could. We linked arms, and strolled along, pretending to watch the children at play.

"What was his nibs saying when Asha interrupted him?"

"He said not much, *Hakim Effendi.* He mentioned a tithe, and the dispersal of the waters of Basenis."

"Tomar pays this tithe to some other town?"

"It seems not, my friend. Tomar does not pay this tithe, though other towns do."

"Do the other towns pay this tithe to Tomar?"

"I do not know, *Hakim.*"

And with that I had to be satisfied, though I wondered what Philpott could have added to it, Philpott with the lovely Asha ever by his side.

CHAPTER 27

ᴗᵜᴗ

*Philpott's abstraction. ᐛ An interview with Mistress Simuny.
The love of Philpott's life.*

ONE AFTERNOON Carbuncle and I returned from our rounds to find Philpott madly pacing the floor of the common room...if the term "madly" may be used to describe a slow, methodical wafting from wall to window and window back to wall. His chin was supported on his right palm, and his right palm was supported by his left hand, his eyes were cast down and his hair was cast up, and his forehead was cast in lines of worry.

"Philpott, what's wrong?" I cried, or some other such words; his only response was to hold up one hand toward me, palm out, for a few moments. It was only a few moments, because then he changed directions. This is a universal sign in academia, understood in institutions of higher learning throughout Arrastia; it means, "Do not distract me." Sometimes there are subtexts, such as "I am about to achieve a breakthrough!" or "I am having enough difficulty already!" or even, in some circles, "I am thinking Great Thoughts; kindly do not allow your sophomoric presence to sully me on my way to Enlightenment." In Philpott's case it was clearly the second of the three.

As it happens, this was the memorable evening when Asha did not come to escort us to the square. After dinner—a meal Philpott took in a very few precise quick bites, before resuming his pacing—Firenz and Simuny appeared at the door as our evening's escort. I was rather surprised, and considered Philpott's unease with renewed interest.

The two masters offered no explanation for Asha's absence, but merely invited us to join them in the square. Carbuncle and I arose immediately, while Philpott merely raised his hand once more, and continued pacing. It seemed to me that Simuny regarded his antics with a certain satisfaction.

Simuny was still rather a mystery to me. In our few encounters I had observed her willingness to state unpleasant truths, and had a certain admiration for her forthrightness on those oc-

casions, but I was not at all sure that I liked her. It was therefore
something of a shock when she took my arm as we reached the
square, and held me back as the others drifted off into the crowd
with Firenz. She looked at me coldly, studying my face, and then
jerked her head (and my arm) toward the Master's Hall. I went
willingly enough, though I was not at all sure how we were to
communicate with each other.

We entered the Master's Hall not through the large doors that
lead into the reception room, but through a smaller door some
ways down the main street. Simuny lead me up a flight of stairs,
and down a corridor to a covered balcony toward the back of the
building. Had it been daylight, we would have had an exception-
ally good view of the forest north of Tomar; instead the stars were
bright in the sky, their cold unwinking lights contrasting oddly
with the few wavering, flickering lamps and torches I could see in
the houses to the north.

There was a small table, and two chairs placed near it; on
the table was a candle, and a pitcher, and two small cups. As
we entered a third person appeared out of the shadows and held
one of the chairs for Simuny; she waved me into the other. The
third person filled the two cups from the pitcher—the scent alone
told me what it was—and retired into the shadows. Simuny raised
her cup, looking over it into my eyes, and said, *"Deir Basenis
neras ka somus, Aybahsmaht."* Before I could respond, I heard
the unknown servant say, in Serosan, "The jaws of Basenis close
never upon you, *Aybahsmaht.*" I was startled, as it was Mukden's
voice. Simuny never looked from my face, nor seemed to have
heard Mukden.

One does not survive a life in academia without acquiring
a certain cunning. If one cannot play the game without knowing the rules, one has chosen the wrong vocation. I raised my
cup, smelling the heady liquor within, and said, "Nor upon you,
oh Mistress of Tomar." Mukden repeated my words in his own
tongue, and Simuny, smiling faintly, threw back her drink like a
sailor in the lowest tavern in Lyricum Town. I did the same, and
we put down our glasses at the same moment. The rules were becoming clearer. Mukden's role was that of translator, only, and an
invisible translator at that. I was here to talk with Simuny, quietly,
unofficially, and alone, and Mukden was simply not present.

As so often before, it is tedious to render the process of translation; and indeed, Simuny had so managed things that I became less aware of Mukden's presence as our conversation proceeded. Thus, I will write as though we were speaking directly to each other, as we for all practical purposes were.

"Do you know who I am, *Aybahsmaht?*"

I looked politely at her, head slightly tilted; it seemed a rhetorical question. "You are a Master of Tomar," I replied slowly. "The well-being of Tomar is your responsibility."

"Yet if the Masters share a single goal, they do not speak with one voice," she said. "Perhaps you have noticed."

I nodded. "Firenz," I said, "speaks with the voice of welcome and friendship, whereas Nabili does not."

"Young Nabili is the voice of the past." She grunted. "There are none so protective of things past as those who have not lived with them." She stared at the candle's flame. "And you, *Aybahsmaht?* With what voice do you speak?"

"With the voice of reason, I hope, Mistress. I am a scholar." Mukden stumbled over the word scholar; I am not sure he ever quite understood what it meant.

"The voice of reason, *Aybahsmaht?* Perhaps we can indeed speak profitably to one another."

"I should like nothing better, Mistress." She grunted again, and gestured at the shadows. Mukden came forward, his features yet indistinct in the flickering light, and refilled our glasses.

"Asha," she began slowly, not looking directly at me, "is the voice of the future. You have seen. She is one who will risk much, perhaps all, on a single throw, the better to learn what the future holds. She is a seeker after new things, not a guardian of the old." Simuny looked up. "It is ever thus, with the Masters of Tomar. A voice of welcome, a voice of the past, a voice of the future."

"And what is your voice, Mistress?"

She chuckled ironically, "The voice of reason, as you said. The voice of clear-seeing. I once greeted tomorrow as eagerly as Asha; now I am wiser." She straightened in her seat. "But not all wise, *Aybahsmaht*. Tell me, if you will. With what voice does Thed Philpott speak?"

I sipped my drink as I formulated a reply. Clearly we had gotten to the meat of the conversation. It was deadly serious, yet a ghost of laughter danced in my throat. It was like a scene from some dreary, earnest modern novel, in which the young girl's guardian inquires after the intentions of the young man. Is he a rake? A gambler? A cad? Is he trifling with her affections? Or is he a man of means who will marry her honorably?

I saw at once that it was useless to prevaricate; Simuny held all of the cards, if Asha had confided in her, whereas I still knew little or nothing about Philpott's activities of the past weeks.

"Mistress," I replied, "my friend Thaddeus is a scholar, a lover, yes, but a lover of knowledge. He studies people in all times and all places, and attempts to find the patterns that bind them together, whoever they be." I cast about, trying to work out how to describe the obsession of the true scholar. "His studies are his first love, his joy, his reason for existence." I finished my drink, waved for another.

Simuny studied me, as though trying to discern the patterns that bound me together.

"Is it so?" she said, finally. It was not a question, but rather a statement of disbelief.

"Mistress, I believe you have the advantage of me. I have been out in your countryside for many hours each day, while Philpott is with Asha. I have no knowledge of what passes between them during that time, as Thaddeus will not speak of it. They have seemed friendly as we promenade in the square; that is all I know. Perhaps Thaddeus is fascinated by young Asha, but I fear as a source of knowledge, only. But perhaps Asha has confided in you? Perhaps you know more than I?"

Simuny laughed, a harsh cackle, and laughed again. "Perhaps it is so, indeed. Oh, the presumption of youth, *Aybahsmaht*, the presumption of youth. Asha has not confided in me, would not, but my eyes can see and my ears hear. I know that Asha spoke harshly to your young man this day, from outraged modesty, as I thought. But perhaps it was outraged vanity."

"It may be so, mistress. I have seen nothing to indicate otherwise."

"Very well, *Aybahsmaht*. I thank you for your observations." Then, addressing Mukden directly for the first time, she said, "Kindly escort him back to his friends."

I rose, bowed, and followed Mukden from the balcony and down into the street. "Asha is her daughter," he said suddenly. "Simuny was the voice of the future once. Someday Asha will be the voice of clear-seeing. She must make her own mistakes, or she will lack the wisdom she will need to see clearly."

"And what were Simuny's mistakes?" I asked without thinking.

"I have never dared to ask."

I had no notion of how to respond to this admission, and so pondered it as we walked side-by-side through the thinning crowd to the corner where Carbuncle stood with Firenz, surrounded by children.

"Mukden," I said, stopping short. "Will you tell me something?" He stopped also, waiting for the question. *"Aybahsmaht,"* I said. "I have been hearing this for days now. You did not translate it when Simuny used it. What is its meaning?"

He looked at me ruefully, and then shrugged. "It means, 'He whom the Dog obeys', my friend. Now I must go."

By this time it was far too late to consider the implications of my new title; and besides, it was time for a serious confrontation with Philpott. I stepped forward, and ruthlessly extricated Carbuncle from the swarm of admirers. Cries of "Gooneybah! Gooneybah!" followed us from the square.

Philpott had mercifully ceased his pacing, and was seated at the refectory table, when we returned, head in his hands. Most astonishingly, there was no sheaf of notes covering the dark wood like dirty snow. There was, however, a large mug by his right hand, and by the smell it had not contained fruit juice. I had seldom seen Philpott the worse for drink, and immediately thought of his days on Cuprios, carousing with the sailors in the bars near the harbor. For one long moment, I seriously considered the absurd possibility that he had been out carousing while we were gone. Then he lifted his head and looked vaguely in my direction. When he spoke, his voice was hollow, but unslurred.

"I've been blind, Leon." He had that far-off look in his eye. Oh, ho, I thought to myself. Evidently Asha's outburst had done some good.

"I should say so," I said, assuming an avuncular manner, as I took a place across the table from him.

"And a fool," he said, still looking into the distance.

"That's not an unusual reaction," I said, thinking of the girls I had known in my youth. Carbuncle snickered as he sat down beside me.

"All these weeks, and I never realized...." His hand blindly reached out for the cup, and lifted it to his lips. When he put it down he cradled it with both hands. He looked over at me.

"If only you had brought it to my attention, Leon. But how could you? You weren't here, and I wouldn't discuss it."

"Still, it was obvious enough for all that, Thad," I said, gently.

"Obvious! There are no churches in this town, Leon! No churches, no chapels, no temples, not a one. Do you know what that means?"

I rather thought it meant that he was getting ahead of things. Surely he wasn't considering marriage?

"Well, you could hardly expect to find Mother Church in a place like this," I temporized. My head was starting to pound, as it usually did when I talked with Philpott late in the evening.

"It must be outside of town, Leon." He stared at me, his need written plainly in his eyes. "It must be, Leon. Have you seen it, Leon? A church or a temple? Anything like that?"

"Don't you think you're getting a little ahead of yourself, Thad?"

"Ahead of myself? What do you mean, Leon? I've been looking for it for two weeks!" Two weeks? Oh, dear, had love struck him that badly?

"Well, but it won't do, Thad, it simply won't do. What kind of a future would you have? What about your career?"

"Future, Leon? How could it harm my career?" Thad was looking very puzzled. There are none so blind, I thought to myself.

"I'm sorry, Thad, she's a very nice girl, but you really mustn't. It wouldn't be fair to her or to you."

Thad was looking straight at me, really giving me his attention for the first time all evening—or all week.

"Leon? What are you talking about?" It was my turn to look puzzled.

"Why, your love for Asha, of course. And hers for you."

"My love for Asha! And hers for me? Leon! Whatever do you mean?"

"It's been obvious, Thad, as I said. Of course, after that bold declaration of yours when we first met her, it's hardly surprising. You're a good-looking young fellow, after all. And then, of course, you've been squiring her about the town all day, and about the square all evening. What else is a young girl to think?" Or an old don, I might have added. Philpott looked stricken.

"Oh, Leon. Is that what she thought?"

"I fear it may be so, Thad."

He was still looking at me, but I think he was no longer seeing me. Carbuncle arose, and snagged a pitcher from the sideboard, and refilled Philpott's mug. He left the pitcher on the table.

"Drink up, young Thad, for I think you're in need of it," he said. "Now I'm for bed. Good night."

I got myself a mug, and sat with Philpott for some time, neither of us speaking. When at last I rose and weaved my way upstairs, he was still at the table, still staring into space.

CHAPTER 28

✌ ∴

The story of Hillip and Asha. ❧ Nabili's secret.
Carbuncle's great discovery.

O N THE following day, the 17th of Ragout, Carbuncle found
what he had been longing for.

Firenz and Mukden came for us at the usual time; Asha did
not come for Philpott, which was just as well, as Philpott did not
come to breakfast. He had sat up, drinking, later than I had, and
had started earlier, and was, as they say, "not fit". We left him
in his cot, with Cadbury and Fox to see to his needs, and went
out. Cadbury remained as a matter of course; he had grown quite
devoted to Philpott. We had more or less assumed that Fox would
join us, but he begged fatigue, saying that a banker's life had not
prepared him for this constant tramping about. I assented, though
I raised an eyebrow at Carbuncle. Young Frederick had shown
no difficulty in keeping up with us for the past two weeks, not to
speak of his journey up the Aram to Lake Saco.

For the first time since our arrival we were at a loose end. We
had explored the immediate surroundings, except in the vicinity
of the river; we had so far ignored the river as we expected to follow it south when we moved our base camp to another locale. We
had not yet discussed these plans with our hosts, however, and it
seemed likely that we might yet be some days in Tomar straightening up after Philpott. That could not be done with Philpott in
a state and with Asha evidently disinclined to be forgiving. All
in all, I went out that morning motivated more by a strong desire
not to be in the hostel than by any interest in my chosen field,
and when Carbuncle suggested we pay another visit to the hoist I
gladly agreed. At worst it would be a pleasant walk, and at best
perhaps my friend would discover something new.

As it was but a few miles, and we needed no particular gear,
we left all but one donkey behind. Carbuncle, Firenz, Mukden
and I walked companionably along; Hodgins brought up the rear,
leading the donkey on whose back Abayla had packed another
of her excellent lunches; Bruno ran back and forth, ahead and

behind, in his usual mad rush. As we sauntered along, Firenz told us a story of his family.

"Many, many generations ago," he said, "my ancestor Hillip travelled far and wide in the world below, dispersing the waters of Basenis. It was much harder then than it is now, for there were many more barrels, and each was dispersed by hand. We did not understand, then, the power of the great river Aram, which touches every land. My nephews are now gone for but a few days; when I was young, I was away for little longer. But Hillip, my ancestor, would remain below the cliff for week upon week, returning home only four times a year when the new waters were ready."

One may readily imagine that Carbuncle and I listened with enthusiasm. Warned by Cadbury while yet "in the world below", we had refrained from asking direct questions about the waters of Basenis, and little information had been forthcoming. I did not know at that time what Philpott might have learned on the topic, but I suspected that it was little enough.

"Now Hillip loved a girl of the Vastid, for at that time, as now, the Vastid and the Hinkaya were at peace. He courted her each time he was at home, and brought her rare gifts from the world below. Each visit he asked her to be his bride, and each time she accepted his gifts and declined his proposal, making some pretty excuse. In truth, she liked him well enough, and his stories of far-off lands, and in his absence spurned all other suitors. Oh, there were many young men who wished to marry her, for her name was Asha, and she was indeed as beautiful as the Asha you know." Here the old man kissed his fingers with a loud smack. "She would have none but Hillip, and yet she would not have Hillip either. This went on and on, and each homecoming became more painful for Hillip. He yearned to see his love, and dreaded her refusal. His gifts become more costly, and her refusals more pretty, until finally my poor ancestor was in a confusion! At last he went to her and demanded an explanation. 'You will not marry me, and give me joy; yet you will not marry anyone else and end my suffering,' he said. 'Why is this? My heart is yours... what must I do to make it acceptable to you?' 'Your great and gallant heart is perfectly acceptable to me,' she told him, 'but it is here seldom enough. Why should I share it with those you meet on your travels?'

"Now this was an unkind thing of Asha to say to Hillip, for he had always been most faithful to her. Had he been otherwise, he could not have afforded the many fine things he had brought home for her, and he said so. 'Yes,' she said, 'but a living, breathing man is a finer thing still.' At last he agreed to give over his sacred duties if she would marry him, though he must make several more journeys before his younger brothers would be ready to take them on in full. And she agreed, and they were wed that very day, and there was great rejoicing."

We reached the hoist just as Firenz reached this point in the narrative, and Carbuncle desired him to wait, and to resume the story after he had completed his investigations. Accordingly, we chose a flat rock with a pleasant view of "the world below", spread a cloth, and sat down to an early lunch of bread, cold meat, cheese, fruit, and chilled fruit juice, while Carbuncle stormed about in the vicinity of the hoist looking for some small phantasm he could make friends with. At last he rejoined us, despondent, and sat down to eat.

"Still nothing?" I asked.

"Still nothing." He smiled wryly, just a flash, and then went on. "I feel like a drunkard looking about the house for a bottle of spirits after the taverns have closed. 'I know there used to be a flask in this cupboard, because I put it there myself. It wasn't there when I looked a few minutes ago, but perhaps I missed seeing it.' Well, the cupboard is still bare."

We gave him time to eat his fill, and then began to saunter back down the road, leaving Hodgins to pack the donkey and follow along after. Firenz needed little encouragement to continue his story.

"Out of love for his new wife, Hillip put off his next departure as long as he could. He was the head of the Hinkaya, and so the running of the household in his absence would be in Asha's charge; he wanted her to be well-established before he left. Oh, they were happy together, and then the day came when he must leave. There was no hoist then, and so his last duty before leaving was to see that each donkey was carefully laden, that there were enough supplies for himself and his men, and that each man had a donkey to ride. His men had made many trips with him before, and knew their work well, and so he was amazed to find an extra donkey in the baggage train, and an extra donkey with saddle and bridle. He went to his younger brother, who had the ordering of the donkeys, and demanded an explanation. His brother, my many-times great uncle, pointed back at the saddled donkey, upon whose back was now seated the lovely Asha.

"'What are you doing?' he asked her, though indeed it was a silly question, for of course she was going with him. 'I married you for all time, not just for four times a year,' she said. 'But only the Hinkaya may take the water of Basenis to the world below,' he said. And she smiled at him, and said 'So am I not the Mistress of the Hinkaya? You were ready enough to leave me in charge.'

"My ancestor Hillip was no fool, and he knew when he was beaten. Indeed she went with him, the first woman of our people to take part in the dispersing of the waters. And she went not once, only; whenever Hillip went below and returned again, his wife Asha returned with him. And in between they had many fine children."

I have not yet said much about Zymurgian weather, as it had not much affected our work. It often rained in the early afternoon, and it was our habit to seek whatever shelter there was and sit it out. It never lasted long, and the moisture always brought that pleasant, earthy smell up out of the ground. As it happens, the daily shower began just as Firenz was finishing his story; we heard the last few words under a stand of trees by the side of the road, just short of the fork where our road met the road to town and the road to the donkey trail. We settled on a fallen log under the trees, and watched the rain stream slowly down. Bruno settled into the litter at my feet, head on his paws, and watched with us. We made a companionable little group, the more so as Carbuncle had filled a hip flask with the native liquor and proceeded to share it around, "against the chill."

And then, just as the rain started to lift, Bruno raised his head and pricked up his ears. He seemed to be staring at the mouth of the abandoned road we had noticed during our first day's surveying. I laid a calming hand on his head, and looked to see what I could see. As I watched, a figure in Tomaren white entered the junction—from the abandoned road.

"And who could that be?" I said aloud. "I thought no one went there anymore." Firenz looked up, saw the figure, and froze.

"It is Nabili—where did he come from?"

"From the abandoned road. You know, the one you said lead to an older hoist site."

"My friends, we must go," Firenz said quickly, rising. "Come."

"But what of our man Hodgins?" For he had not yet caught up; I imagined him a half-mile off, exhorting the donkey to greater speed.

Firenz stood silent for a moment, hand on chin. "Yes. Wait for him. Then you must find your own way back to town, I fear, for Mukden must come also. My duty calls me." And before we quite had time to react, Firenz and Mukden had hurried down the road in pursuit of Firenz' colleague, Nabili. I looked at Carbuncle in some surprise.

"What just happened, Thomas?"

"I think perhaps our friend Nabili was seen doing something he oughtn't."

I nodded slowly. "Shall we go see what it was, Thomas?"

"Now, now, Leon. If Thaddeus were here, no doubt he'd tell you that you would be abusing Firenz' trust in you if you did."

"And your point would be, oh Gooneybah?"

"Oh, it's not my point, Leon, I won't claim it. But what of Hodgins?"

I was casting about, trying to determine how to leave him a message, when man and donkey came into view. Bruno rose delicately to his full height, stretched thoroughly, and trotted down to meet them. Carbuncle and I rose also as man and beasts drew up to where we were sitting. I offered the flask to Hodgins, who was looking rather sour. He took a nip and handed it back.

"Thank you, Professor. Where're old Muck-and-Firey?"

"They had some business to attend to, and so do we," I said. "Tie that donkey to a tree or something, and then follow me."

And so we walked to the end of the abandoned road, and then on down it. The first twenty yards or so were wild with small shrubs and larger bushes, and it was only by following the marks of Nabili's passage that we were able to find our way. From that point, just barely out of sight of the main road to Tomar, a narrow but carefully tended path stretched off to the north.

Someone—Nabili, most likely—came here fairly often, Firenz' words notwithstanding.

I am not adventurous by nature, though I have acquired a small taste for adventure. Truly, I would have been happy spending the season in Lyricum Town, listening to Rotini's music. Had I been Hillip's beloved wife, I likely would have stayed home. Occasionally, however, the thrill of discovery is awakened within my bosom. On this day it was spiced with a feeling of trespass, such as I had not felt since my clandestine trips to the larder in my school days. We Were Not Supposed To Be Here. I was enjoying myself thoroughly, I must say. The rain had gone, the sun was shining, the sky (what we could see of it) was blue, the air was sweet, the birds were singing, my dog was bounding to and fro.... all in all it was as pleasant a tramp in the woods as any I have ever taken. I was grateful to the hand that had cleared the way, however, for we could not have gone three steps off of the path without becoming hopelessly entangled.

After a mile or so, our way was blocked by a wall of reddish stone perhaps five or six yards high and of unknown extent. So heavily vegetated was the wall that we could only dimly discern its presence under the mat of vines and leaves. Its origin, whether natural or artificial, was anyone's guess.

"There must be more to it than this," I said. "Nabili would not have come this far just to turn around again."

We commenced pulling at the mat of vines, and soon were rewarded by a far-off glimpse of daylight. The vines concealed a narrow tunnel which went right through the barrier; we were seeing the light at the end, at least ten yards off. I looked at Carbuncle, and he at me, and, shrugging, we pushed our way through the vines. There was much less vegetation in the tunnel, and the regular pattern barely evident on the sides in the dim light put the matter beyond doubt; the wall was man-made, and not of stone but of some kind of rectangular brick. We hurried through, and found ourselves in a square courtyard perhaps one hundred feet on a side, and surrounded on three sides by massive walls like the one through which we had just entered. Whoever had tended the path had not had time or effort to spare to maintain the courtyard as well. The center, though originally paved with stone, was now a green field, with occasional columns and sinkholes. It was also home to a fine community of cottontail rabbits, at which Bruno rejoiced greatly. A worn path continued from where we stood to the far side, which was occupied, as my more astute readers will have guessed, by Philpott's missing temple.

It could not be anything else, out here in the woods by itself. It was a tall building, of the same reddish brick as the walls, though not nearly as overgrown; the walls seemed to have protected it from the worst of the vegetation. The architecture was ponderous, rather than uplifting, staid rather than ornate; one can do only so much with brick. Steps led up to the facade, which was lined with brick pillars on other side of a wide doorway. The pillars seemed to extend through the roof, creating a matching row of stubby turrets. Through the doorway, which had no door nor any sign of one, we could see daylight. As one we moved forward and into the temple.

It was as simple inside as out...the same utilitarian style, the same lack of ornamentation. It was a big barn of a building, one cavernous, echoing space. The floor was sparsely covered with leaf-litter, due not only to the open portal. The whole northern end of the temple was open. The northern wall was no more than four feet high, and beyond was nothing but sky; the temple was built right up against the cliff. Most dramatically, the center of the room was dominated by a massive statue of a dog, easily ten feet high at the shoulder. The explicitly male figure was standing on all fours, tail raised high over its back, and facing out toward "the world below." It was the same reddish color as the walls and floor, apparently being made out of bricks that had been shaped in some way. The leaf litter had been swept from around it, leaving it at the center of a circle of clean, bare brick. Between its forepaws was a small pile of flowers, leaves, and other vegetable matter.

"Score one for Philpott," I said to Carbuncle. "Looks rather like Bruno, doesn't it. Except for the color. And the size, of course." And indeed it did; the unknown artisan had surely not taken the small Zymurgian dogs we had seen in Tomar as his model. "I wonder why there aren't more dogs like this around now?"

As I pondered, Carbuncle examined the statue. "Leon, come see." When I approached, he said, "Feel this," indicating the leg of the statue. I did so, and was quite surprised. The material was not the red brick I had thought it to be. It felt smooth but not cold, quite unlike any ceramic I had ever felt. There was just the slightest hint of a grain, both to the touch, and, as I looked more closely, to the eye.

"Carbuncle, this feels like some kind of wood," I said. "I've never seen wood with grain so fine." I went and examined the short wall to the north. It was indeed made of the same material: wooden bricks about a foot long, and perhaps four inches wide and three high. I tried to pull one loose, but it held fast. I shook my head. "It doesn't make sense, Carbuncle. Why would they cut a tree into bricks? And why would all of the bricks be exactly the same size and color?"

"It's not that kind of wood, Leon," cried Carbuncle, who was beaming. "This is wood-like, but it's clearly not wood. It was manufactured in some way."

"Manufactured? We haven't seen any signs of that in the village."

"No matter," said Carbuncle. "These bricks were manufactured by some kind of phantasm. They are too smooth and too uniform to have been made in any other way." He took a deep breath, the breath of a man who has been vindicated. "And think of the amount of vegetation out there, Leon. This temple has been here for centuries. Do you see any sign of decay?" Indeed, I could not. "There's a phantasm out there somewhere, Leon," said Carbuncle, "and I mean to find it."

If this were one of those overly thrilling novels which are so popular these days, we would, upon leaving the temple, have found ourselves surrounded by a mob of angry natives, armed with poison-tipped arrows. The chapter would end with me muttering "Keep a stiff upper lip," to Carbuncle and then striding boldly forward to try to bluff my way out. The remainder of the narrative would depend, of course, on whether I succeeded.

As a serious explorer who deplores all such ridiculous narrative contrivances, I am therefore glad to say that there was no angry mob to greet us in the courtyard when we finally left the temple and collected Bruno, nor were we shot at as we walked back down the path. Real life isn't like that, I thought, as we crept through the last maze of bush and shrub to the main road.

And there they were. "Keep a stiff upper lip," I muttered to Carbuncle.

CHAPTER 29

⌣ ⌣

We are not torn to pieces, again.

THERE WAS a distinct shortage of arrows. That was my first thought during the long moment that we stood and stared at each other, and my second was like unto it. There was also a distinct shortage of shouts, yells, accusations, and so forth. I could not even detect a low muttering hum, like the growl of a beast about to strike. I had no more time for reflection just then, but I have replayed the scene in my mind many times since, and what strikes me most is the posture and facial expressions of the members of the crowd. They were slouching, less ready to leap than to collapse. They did not hold their heads high in righteous indignation. They wore, not righteous scowls, but sullen frowns. They looked, if I may use the expression, hang-dog. The four Masters of Tomar were at the forefront, and there, at least, there was a variety of expression. Firenz looked chastened, Simuny somewhat cynically amused, Asha warily excited. Nabili alone scowled, his dark face darkened still further with hatred and humiliation.

But, as I have indicated, these reflections came later. I was attempting to formulate in my mind the bold, passionate speech by which I would save our lives when Carbuncle strode boldly forward (I might even say eagerly), and said, "I say, could you tell me where the bricks came from?"

The Tomarens stared at him. We stared at him. He smiled, looking from face to face in hopes of an answer. Though I could not see, as he was facing away from me, I am sure his mustache was twitching.

"They don't speak Anglish, Thomas," I said, helplessly. He turned at the waist to look at me.

"Good heavens, you're right, Leon!" And he continued in Arabic, "Mukden! I see you back there, boy, come out." And without waiting for Mukden's response, he dove into the crowd and grabbed the young man. The townsfolk backed away, leaving the two men in the open.

"The bricks, Mukden! Where did the bricks come from?"

Mukden was clearly unsure how to answer. His eyes were wide, and though he his lips moved he said nothing as he looked at Carbuncle's hand, which gripped his upper arm tightly, and then at Carbuncle's face.

"Oh, I'm sorry, Mukden, do forgive me," said my colleague, releasing his grip on Mukden's arm and patting it gently. "Now, the bricks. You know the bricks? Where did they come from?"

"He doesn't know the bricks," said Firenz, stepping forward. "He has never seen them." He sounded puzzled.

"But you have, have you? So where—"

Simuny's voice cracked like a whip. Mukden moved away from Carbuncle, and drew himself upright, as she spoke again, more softly.

"You have seen the temple," he translated.

"Yes, we have—" I started to say, trying to regain control, but I don't know that anyone but Bruno noticed. He looked up from his place at my side, and panted.

"Yes, we have seen the temple, of course we have seen the temple, how else would we know about the bricks?" cried Carbuncle. "Now, will you please—" but Simuny was speaking again.

"Were you not angered?" translated Mukden. The crowd had drawn together; the people were leaning forward, eyes moving rapidly from Carbuncle to Mukden and back.

"Angered?" Now Carbuncle sounded puzzled. "On the contrary, I haven't been so happy in weeks." He looked around, and seemed to notice the size of the crowd for the first time. "Dear me, what seems to be the trouble?"

If trouble there was, it seemed to evaporate with Mukden's translation of Carbuncle's words. There was indeed a collective sigh, and the people seemed to grow taller as they straightened up in relief. There were smiles, and shouts, and men slapping each other on the back, and all manner of tension left the air— except for friend Nabili, who looked murderous. Firenz and Asha were openly grinning at each other, and even Simuny looked not displeased.

The torrent of relief dwindled to a trickle as Simuny's voice rang out again, loud and then soft, as before.

"Simuny says you had best come back to town," said Mukden, taking first Carbuncle and then myself by the shoulders, his smile writ broadly on his face. "She says there is much to discuss."

CHAPTER 30

⌣∶∾

The wrath of Basenis. ⇜ Basenis and the Aybahsmaht.

I FREELY ADMIT that this present volume is intended not for my colleagues in the field of mythogeography, but rather for the general reader. That is, it is what scholars disparagingly call a popular work. It is my earnest desire that it will be so in fact as well as in name, yet there are limits to the narrative artifices I am willing to use to that end. I am not above adopting a thrilling manner, or withholding a fact until its revelation is dramatically most effective. I will happily build suspense over our fate in various tight situations, though it must be obvious to the reader that the existence of this book is predicated upon our survival. And yet, I am subject to a constraint not felt by the authors of fictional works, a constraint forced upon me by the rigors of Academia, not the least of which is our good Dean Nuftison: I must tell the story as it happened. There will be those who doubt my sincerity in making this assertion. I beg their pardon, but I assert it again, and I offer this for proof: were I writing a work of fiction, would my heroes have escaped the wrath of a mob of angry natives by prating about bricks, of all things? I should say not. The brawny academics might have subdued the tribe's champions in single combat, perhaps, or slaughtered the entire crew with a penknife after blinding them with the contents of a bottle of ink, or even overawed them by a noble oration. But bricks, forsooth? It is not to be thought of. It makes no sense. It is unsatisfying.

And if it is unsatisfying to the reader, it was equally so to me. As Carbuncle, Hodgins, and I sauntered back to Tomar, surrounded by a crowd of elated Tomarens and lead by the Masters of Tomar, I was in a state of extreme puzzlement. A life in academia has bestowed upon me a certain understanding of how people behave, but little understanding of why. The Tomarens clearly had not wanted us to see the temple; yet now that we had, they were happy. Nabili clearly had known about the temple; yet he wasn't supposed to go there.

"This makes no sense," I said at last, venting my frustration upon Carbuncle. "It makes no sense at all."

"I care not," he replied, "just so long as I find out where those bricks were made." I congratulated him on a pragmatic, if unhelpful, attitude.

The crowd began to disperse when we reached the first houses, as individuals moved off to share the good news (which was? I still didn't know) with their friends and neighbors. At length we reached the Hall of the Masters, and entered the reception room. Simuny barked a few orders, and soon we were each provided with a stool and a glass of spirits. The masters had their own stools, of course; evidently they proposed to speak with us as equals. Nor did the surprises end there—as Nabili moved to seat himself on his stool, Simuny barked again, and Nabili jumped as though stung. He swung around, glaring at the old woman, who gazed dispassionately back. She spoke a few quiet words; Nabili's angry response nearly overwhelmed the quieter responses of Asha and Firenz. He glared at them, too, and then turned back to meet Simuny's implacable stare.

It was a long, tense moment. Then Nabili spit on the ground at Simuny's feet and, turning in place, strode towards the door. Hodgins was forced to jump out of his way, or he would have been knocked down. Simuny's voice caught Nabili at the door. As she spoke, she fingered the yellow embroidery that hemmed her garment. Nabili scowled at her, and was gone.

Smiling now, Simuny gestured us to our seats, facing the masters on their stools. Mukden took up his position against the wall, halfway in between us, ready to interpret. I took advantage of this short pause to ask the first question.

"If it would not be offensive to the Lady Asha, might a messenger be sent to our friend Thaddeus Philpott? I believe that our discussions would interest him greatly."

Through Mukden, Asha herself answered. "Why should Thed's presence offend me?"

I exchanged glances with Simuny before answering. "I was given to understand that you and he had quarreled yesterday."

"And so we did," Asha replied. "But today, everything has changed, as you shall see. I have no objection to Thed's presence." And suiting deed to word, she summoned and dispatched a servant to fetch Philpott. We sat quietly, sipping from our glasses, until the servant returned, Philpott, Fox, and Cadbury in tow. The servants hastily put out three more stools, and handed each a glass. Philpott looked troubled, Fox bored, and Cadbury, as always, amused. As our friends were seating themselves, I pressed my advantage.

"And now," I said, "perhaps you could explain the meaning of our exchange out at the crossroads, for I confess I do not understand it at all."

"All in good time, *Aybahsmaht*," replied Simuny. Although we required Mukden's services at the time, I will as usual dispense with them here. "Why did you come to our land?"

I raised my eyebrows. "As I have said before, we came to study your land, and for no other reason."

"So you have said. And why did you bring that beast with you?" Simuny was pointing at Bruno, who was sprawled on the floor by my side.

"He's my dog. He goes where I go. In my country they say that an Anglishman's best friend is his dog."

"Yes, things are different in your country, so you say. Great Basenis is unknown in your Angland?"

"Utterly, honored Simuny," I said.

"Just so. It is because of that beast that you are here now. When Mukden and his brothers first brought you to Tomar, we were angry. We did not wish you to be here. Hospitality forbade that we mistreat you in any way, and so our plan was to return you to the lands below immediately. Your beast forced us to reconsider."

She looked meaningfully at Firenz, who continued the explanation. He spoke in Serosan, which Mukden translated into the Zymurgian tongue.

"Nabili argued that giving commands to one of the Pups of Basenis showed deadly presumption, which would surely be repaid with holy wrath. He said we must dispose of you quickly, lest Basenis' anger fall on our Town." The old man paused, frowning. "Oh, he was a sly one. He cared more for the insult to Great Basenis than for any threat to Tomar." At this last statement, Philpott sat up, and began to pay proper attention.

"I argued," continued Firenz, "that only one anointed by Great Basenis could so command one of his pups. We know Basenis' wrath from of old; it is swift when he is slighted. Such a man must not be balked, lest Basenis' anger fall on us." His mouth quirked slightly to the left. "Nabili was not pleased by my argument." Idly, I reached down and scratched behind Bruno's ears.

"Asha," he continued, and here Asha leaned forward, "agreed with Nabili that commanding a dog was surely an affront to Great Basenis. If Great Basenis did not avenge the slight, then surely that meant that Great Basenis had no power over you. Perhaps, she said, Basenis ignored you because you came from a distant land. Or perhaps you were more powerful than Basenis. Nabili countered this argument. Surely no one is more powerful than Great Basenis, who has ruled over our land since time began? And surely the waters of Basenis have been dispersed to every country? Surely every land is subject to Great Basenis? But so far from strengthening his own case," laughed Firenz, "he thereby strengthened mine. And so therefore we let you stay, though we kept you under close watch."

"I see," I said. "You were unsure of our status, and therefore gave us the benefit of the doubt, as we say in Angland."

"Yes, my friends," said the old man. "That is it."

"But then, if you thought us possibly the anointed of Basenis, why did you seek to prevent us finding the temple?" No sooner had I finished my sentence than Philpott had whirled in his seat.

"Temple, Leon? Where—"

"Later, Thad, later," I whispered back.

"But—"

"Later!"

"Why, because of the neglect," said Firenz, a little surprised. "If you were messengers from Great Basenis, how could we let you see the state into which his temple has fallen? Surely you would call down Basenis' wrath upon us."

"You are no longer worried about this, I take it," said Carbuncle.

"No, my friends, we are not." He smiled broadly at us, as did Asha. Simuny merely grimaced. "You have seen the temple, and its state did not distress you. Surely you are not servants of Great Basenis!"

Philpott leaned forward, and asked, "But if you were worried about Basenis' wrath, why did you neglect the temple?"

Firenz looked sheepish, as who would not? "We have quarreled with Great Basenis, Thed. So far we have avoided his wrath. But Basenis is no longer worshipped in Tomar, nor in any town or village in the land, saving only the holy city, Basenis Basor. We worship him not, and yet we must serve him, lest he send his wrath upon us. It is forbidden to go to the temple, or to bring offerings to Basenis." I thought then of the pile of flowers and green leaves between the statue's paws. So young Nabili was something of a renegade!

"In many lands," said Philpott, "service to one's god lies mainly in the bringing of offerings. How do you serve him, if you do not worship him?"

"Why, we disperse his waters. For this we are exempt from the tithe that all other towns must pay to the Keepers in Basenis Basor."

"And what form does the tithe take?"

"Grain and cured meats for the Keepers, and clippings for Basenis in his temple."

"Clippings?" I asked, surprised.

"Yes, chaff, and leaves and twigs, and other plant matter."

"What ever for?"

"To feed Great Basenis in his temple."

"Great Basenis eats leaves?" I exclaimed. Carbuncle was beginning to nod very slowly. "Leaves? Surely there are trees enough near Basenis Basor to give Basenis all of the leaves he wants. You pay your tithe in leaves?"

"Not we," said Firenz, "but the other towns, yes. Great Basenis requires it. His hunger is great, and Basenis Basor lies in a barren plain."

One should never ask a question if one does not wish to know the answer. There are, indeed, many things I would be happier not knowing about; the making of sausage, for instance, and the workings of His Majesty's government. Yet there are some questions that will not lie still, and that must be asked. It is like having a rash: scratching is painful, and yet one cannot help scratching.

"And the waters of Basenis, that you disperse instead of paying the tithe—where do they come from?" Firenz looked at me strangely; clearly the answer was obvious. I had feared so.

"From Basenis Basor, my friend. Where else? From Great Basenis in his temple in Basenis Basor. They are his waters."

I thought it best to change the subject.

"How did Basenis lose your devotion?"

"Not in my time, nor in my grandfather's time, but in his grandfather's time, the tithe was larger, and the quantity of waters to disperse greater. It was a great weight on our people, the need to feed Basenis and disperse his waters properly. There was a drought in those days, and while it lasted nothing grew. The trees were without leaf, and the fields without grain. Our cattle grew thin, and we grew thin too. There was little to send to Basenis Basor. The Keepers and Great Basenis went hungry." At this, Firenz paused, and he and the others bowed their heads, not in reverence, I thought, but in remembrance. "Great Basenis came forth from his temple in search of food, and found none, for the land was bare. Then was his wrath visited upon the folk of the towns, who had worshipped him and served him since time began. Basenis roamed the land, devouring all in his path. Entire villages were consumed, from the thatch on the roofs to the foundations; many of our people died. At last he was satisfied, and returned to his temple." Firenz raised his head, and straightened, and looked me in the eye. "Do you wonder that Basenis lost our devotion? Is not the land in his keeping? We served him, and he gave us death and destruction. When the rain returned, we resumed the tithe, but never as much as the Keepers demanded. Each generation has decreased it, and each generation has had less water to disperse. Would that we could end the tithe altogether!"

Carbuncle had been fidgeting beside me for some minutes, and could contain himself no longer.

"The bricks, Firenz! The temple we saw was made of bricks. Did they come from Basenis Basor as well?"

"Yes. As the waters are his waters, so the bricks are his bricks. The city of Basenis Basor is built of his bricks, and each year it grows larger. The temple here was built in ages past when the bricks were more abundant; they have decreased with the tithe as well. None leave Basenis Basor now."

"It is an interesting tale you tell, Firenz, but it happened a long time ago. I find it hard to believe," I said. "Are you sure it is true?"

"When I was boy, there was a town named Tyridi. Its people served the Keepers, traveling to Basenis Basor each morning and returning home each evening. As each generation had done, the towns decreased the tithe. It was too much, and Basenis came forth." There was a hush upon the room, and Firenz smiled bleakly. "Tyridi was destroyed. My father was there, seeing to the waters. He perished."

All of this time, Cadbury had been providing a running translation, in English, to Philpott, Fox, and Hodgins. Now there came a question from an unlikely source.

"You had told us nothing of this until today," said Frederick Fox. "Why are you telling us now? What do you want of us?" Cadbury translated his words, and I seconded them in Serosan.

"Yes, what do you want of us?"

"Today," said Firenz, "we learned that you are not servants of Basenis. We can decrease the tithe no further without arousing Basenis' wrath upon us. You, *Aybahsmaht*, are he whom the dog obeys. Perhaps, with your help, we can free ourselves from our slavery. This is the hope that Asha shared with us on your arrival."

CHAPTER 31

ᴖᴗ

Politics and practicality.

"WELL, THIS is a fine kennel of fish," I said as we entered the hostel.

"Kettle," said Philpott, ever vigilant.

"Kettle?" asked Cadbury, who hadn't heard the expression before.

"Kettle?" asked Carbuncle, who hadn't been paying close attention.

"Of fish," said Hodgins, helpfully.

"Of fish?" asked Cadbury.

"Oh, of fish." said Carbuncle.

Fox said nothing.

"Kennel of fish I said, and kennel of fish I meant," I said as we sat down around the refectory table.

"Kennel?" asked Cadbury.

"It's a place you keep dogs," said Hodgins, helpfully.

"Dogs and fish?" asked Cadbury.

"It's a figure of speech," said Hodgins. "It means being in a pickle."

"In a pickle?" asked Cadbury.

"It means we are in trouble, Cadbury," said Carbuncle.

"Oh," said Cadbury. "What kind of trouble?"

"Political trouble," said Carbuncle.

Fox said nothing.

"Are we going to help them?" asked Philpott.

"That's the trouble," I said. "We can't."

"Why not?" asked Hodgins. "The folks here are good people. Why can't we help them?"

"To begin with, their request is based on a false premise. They assume that Great Basenis has no power over us, given that he hasn't struck us down, and that we might have power over Great Basenis, given our power over Bruno, here."

Bruno woofed.

"Perhaps we do," said Cadbury.

"Not likely," said Carbuncle. "If Basenis were a genuine deity, which as a member of the established church I cannot admit, it might perhaps be true. It is much more likely, though, that the beastie is some kind of phantasm."

"A phantasm!" cried Philpott. "Do you really think so?"

"I do. At the temple—"

"Yes, yes, the temple, Thomas, tell me about the temple!"

There was nothing for it but to describe our excursion to the temple in detail for Philpott, Fox, and Cadbury, and we did so. I will not repeat it here.

"And so," continued Carbuncle, "I knew that the bricks were produced by a phantasm. Today, Firenz told us of a wrathful idol that is fed 'clippings', and produces, as it were, beer and bricks. The implication was quite clear: the beer and bricks are not produced in the capital near Basenis' temple; they are produced by Basenis himself."

"I begin to see why the folks here don't drink the brew themselves," said Hodgins. Well, he's a sailor, isn't he?

"Be that as it may," said Carbuncle. "What we've got so far is a sophisticated industrial phantasm, made in the shape of a giant dog, which is capable of converting plant clippings into a valuable beverage and building material. Perhaps the form of the phantasm is rather unpalatable, but that's a detail."

Fox was paying close attention, I noted, though he remained silent.

"What about Basenis' wrath when hungry?" I asked. Carbuncle shrugged.

"We have many phantasms which require some kind of fuel or fodder; the phantail on the *Sea-Spaniel*, for example. One could conceivably design one that foraged for itself when necessary, but it would be complicated, and of little value. We'd really rather the *Spaniel* didn't take off on its own when it got hungry. Apparently Basenis' creator thought it was worth the effort."

"Why would one do that?" asked Fox.

"Perhaps the processes embodied in the phantasm are easy to sustain but difficult to start. If the *Spaniel's* phantail runs out of fodder, it simply stops working. Give it more fodder, and it starts

again. Basenis might be different. I'd guess Basenis' creator wanted to ensure that his creation would never run out of fuel."

"So when Basenis terrorizes the countryside, it's not the deity carefully chastising the unfaithful, it's just a phantasm consuming fodder without discrimination?" I asked.

"Precisely. And that's why we can't help the Tomarens,
Hodgins. Basenis is clearly carefully designed not to go hungry,
and it might be impossible to defeat that design. And further, if
we did succeed we might never be able to find out how it works."

Fox raised his eyebrows.

"An excellent analysis, Thomas, but that's not why we can't
help the Tomarens," I said.

"It's not?" asked Hodgins.

"It's not?" asked Carbuncle.

"It's not?" asked Philpott.

Fox said nothing.

"No. The reason we can't help the Tomarens is that we are
representatives of His Majesty's Government."

"We are?" asked Philpott, and "You are?" asked Fox, more
or less simultaneously.

"We are," I said.

"We are, indeed," said Carbuncle. "I had forgotten."

"Do you remember, Thaddeus, before we left Pelham, that we
received a warrant from the crown, authorizing the expedition?"

"Why, no, I don't."

"We did. It's standard procedure for expeditions carried out
under the auspices of the Royal Mythogeographic Society."

"What are the implications of having this warrant, Leon?"

"It says that we (that is, you, Thomas, and I), are conducting
the expedition at the King's command, and are therefore not to be
trifled with. It's one reason we got such good service at the naval
yard on Cuprios."

Fox turned pale.

"You mean," he said, "that my errand was futile from the
beginning. Had I caught you with a valid writ, you'd have waved
the warrant in my face and sent me on my way."

"Alas, hardly that," I said. "The *Sea-Spaniel* is legally just
a hired merchant vessel, and therefore not protected by the warrant. Furthermore, it belongs to the Earl of Luton, and thus was

hired essentially for free. We've no funds to hire a replacement, and so its seizure would have been catastrophic.

"But that's beside the point. The point is, courtesy of that warrant, we represent His Majesty here in Zymurgia. There was a time when the king encouraged political adventuring by people in our position; the Bundi Nations were built that way. But those days are past. The King's government would have harsh words for us, and perhaps yet harsher deeds, if we were to foment rebellion here in Zymurgia."

"Rebellion?" cried Philpott. "What are you speaking of, Leon?"

"You're the ethnomonotonist, Philpott, as you have occasionally reminded me. The Zymurgians evidently have a two-tiered society, with these 'Keepers' at the top and the people of the towns at the bottom. What place will there be for the Keepers if the townsfolk succeed in killing Basenis? It looks like rebellion to me, and we can't have any part in it."

"On the other hand, Leon, we must get a good look at that phantasm," said Carbuncle. I noticed Fox nod slightly at this, though I am not sure he was aware that he did it. "I don't think the Tomarens will let us travel south if we don't go along with their plans."

"I suppose we must pretend to go along, and see what happens," I said.

"What, you mean deceive them?" asked Philpott. "I am shocked and distressed that you would suggest such a thing, Leon. They are our hosts. Deceit should have no place in our dealings with them."

"As it has had no place in their dealings with us, Thad? But we needn't lie. We can tell them honestly that we have no idea how to solve their problem, but that we are willing to go have a look," I said. "If after having a look we have no advice to offer, we can hardly be blamed for that."

The argument continued for some time after that, Carbuncle maintaining that we must travel to Basenis Basor and see the phantasm in its temple, and Philpott maintaining that as Anglish gentlemen we must avoid deceit in all its forms, and would do better to decline to help the Tomarens and leave their country at once. They hadn't resolved their differences when the rest of us retired for the evening, but it didn't matter. South we would go.

The next few days were furiously busy, and not just with preparations for the journey. Nabili, we discovered, had lost his position; that had been the meaning of the brief drama we had witnessed in the Hall of the Masters. Denial of Basenis was considered unwise, but overt worship was utterly forbidden, as was visiting the old temple. For a master of the town to do so was to be a traitor to the people under his care. So, as we saw, Nabili was publicly rebuked and stripped of his office, and left the Hall of the Masters in a bit of a huff. Nabili's seat traditionally went to a Vastid, so we had been told, and so we were surprised when Mukden was installed in Nabili's place the next day. He was chosen in part, I think because he was our friend and the other masters hoped to secure our good will, but more because he had proven himself both capable and discreet. Not even Roshnoy the grain balancer, Nabili's relative, seriously disapproved. It was explained to me later that Mukden would certainly have taken his uncle's seat when Firenz could no longer carry out his duties; when Firenz stepped down, another Vastid would be brought in.

The installation of a new Master was of course an important occasion, and that necessitated another festival, which necessitated another day of rest. We enjoyed Mukden's feast rather more than the previous one as we were allowed to take part. I am certain that I did none of the things that Carbuncle has since claimed that I did. As I am endeavoring to write only the truth, I shall not discuss the matter further. It is sufficient to say that our preparations were made in due course, if perhaps more slowly than would be usual.

Fig. 1.

CHAPTER 32

ᴥᴥ

Forward to Basenis Basor. ᴥ Asha and Philpott. ᴥ An unexpected guest.

WE SET out early in the morning of the 21st of Ragout, bathed in the golden light of a fine orange sun. We would be proceeding south along the main road towards the capitol, visiting several other towns along the way. So much, I thought to myself, for charting the course of the Aram river; perhaps we would manage it when we came north again. The party included a number of Tomarens, led by Asha and Mukden, plus the entire expedition team, from Philpott, Carbuncle and myself down to the donkeys and their handlers, Norfolk and Suffolk. It would be a lengthy journey, as Basenis Basor was evidently several hundred miles away. I say "evidently," as none of our guides had ever been there. This distressed me. We were riding into what might be a quite uncomfortable situation, and I wished to hear all I could about Basenis Basor and its inhabitants before we got there. Consequently, I plied our guides with questions.

I asked questions of Asha and Mukden as we rode down the road between fields of grain and stands of trees. I asked questions of the man who prepared the evening meal when we stopped for the night. I asked questions at the campfire in the evening. By the third day, I couldn't think of anything else to ask, which was just as well because none of the Tomarens wanted to talk to me anymore.

The difference between first-hand knowledge and hearsay is the stuff legends are made of. Most of my questions centered on Basenis Basor and its inhabitants, the Keepers. As none of the Tomarens who were with us had actually been there, the information was all second and third-hand, and some of those hands had been dead for decades. I naturally assumed that a certain amount of exaggeration had crept in, and adjusted my thinking accordingly. I later discovered that the stories I heard on the trail, far from being fanciful or overstated, did not go far enough.

Here is the picture I managed to put together. Basenis Basor was a city of straight avenues and large buildings, all made of the same bricks that had so excited Carbuncle. The Temple of Basenis itself stood in the center of the city, and the avenues radiated out from it in all directions. Was it much like the temple we had seen north of Tomar? No, it was much grander. The avenues were also paved with brick. Little grew there, although there were wells, and cisterns for catching the rain. It stood in the center of Zymurgia, in the center of a barren plain. Perhaps the plain had once been grassy; perhaps there had once been trees in Basenis Basor; but if so Great Basenis had devoured them.

The only inhabitants of Basenis Basor, other than Great Basenis himself, were the Keepers. They were a people wholly dedicated to the service of Great Basenis. The Keepers fed Basenis, and removed the waters and the bricks, though the barrels into which the waters were placed were provided by the towns of Zymurgia as part of the tithe. The Keepers never left Basenis Basor, which they alone had built. The new bricks were used to extend the city, or enlarge existing buildings. The Keepers were wholly dependent on the towns for their food and other necessities. Somewhat to my surprise, they were neither reviled nor molested by the Tomarens. In England, where the clergy are largely supported by a tithe on their flock, it is fashionable in some circles to accuse them of being wolves in shepherd's clothing. Here, I suppose, it was clearly necessary that someone have the job of attending to Basenis' monstrous appetite. In any event, the Keepers were almost a race apart. A Keeper might occasionally emigrate to one of the towns, but townspeople never became Keepers; or perhaps they had, once upon a time, but it never happened anymore.

I have referred to Basenis Basor as the "capitol"; perhaps "holy city" would be a better term, for the Keepers in no sense ruled or reigned over the towns. All they required was the quarterly tithe, and enlightened self-interest guaranteed that the towns would continue to provide it. I asked at one point whether the Keepers were not subject to Basenis' wrath just as the townspeople were, and it was explained that they were not. Basenis would not eat his own bricks, and so long as the Keepers stayed inside their brick houses they were safe enough from being devoured—provided they did not starve in the mean-time.

So much for Basenis Basor. We would see what we would see; the present problem was getting there. And with such delightful company, lovely weather, and beautiful countryside, it was hard not to imagine that we were on holiday. The holiday atmosphere was enhanced by the high spirits of—but I get ahead of my tale.

Those of my readers who are inclined to romance will no doubt feel, with some justification, that I have left young Philpott hanging. Several chapters ago I left him sitting at the table in our hostel in the wee hours of the morning with a succession of drinks inside him. He had just discovered that he had been, as it were, trifling with a lady's affection, something no gentleman will ever do. Philpott is so much the gentleman that it had never occurred to him that his voracious desire for knowledge might be misconstrued. It is now time to fill in the details, as best I can. I am indebted to Cadbury for much of what I will now present.

To tell the story properly, I must return to the beginning of the month, and the first day of our investigations. Carbuncle and I had gone out surveying, accompanied by Firenz and Mukden; Philpott and Cadbury had started exploring the town, accompanied by Asha. Up until that day, Philpott had had little hesitation in sharing his observations and conclusions with us. Indeed, he had been almost too forthcoming on some occasions. Yet after his first day with Asha, a veil of silence fell. He claimed he did not wish to discuss his observations until they were complete. This was not entirely unprecedented. He reserved judgement for a couple of days when Mukden and his brothers first arrived in Seros, for example, and so while I was inordinately curious I was not concerned. But as the initial days of silence stretched into one week, and then two, I began to worry. This culminated in my private interview with Simuny, the revelations about Philpott and Asha, and Philpott's night of heavy drinking.

Whatever I may have thought at the time, it is clear that Philpott's reluctance to speak had little to do with the lovely Asha. The very idea of a romantic entanglement had shocked him utterly. No, Philpott had spent the past weeks in a state of genuine puzzlement, a victim of his own expectations. At the beginning of our stay, he had suggested to us that the Zymurgians were theo-

logically either sophisticated or unsophisticated. Their reaction
to Bruno and their failure to put us to death had lead him to believe that they were theologically unsophisticated, i.e., supersti-
tious, credulous, and easily deceived by a little smoke and a few
mirrors. Consequently, while inquiring into every aspect of life
in Tomar, he had primarily been searching for signs of Basenis-
worship. The lack of a prominent temple had been a sore blow
to him, but he rallied. Perhaps Basenism, for so he thought of it,
was a mystery religion, a faith whose liturgies were performed in
private, and only open to the initiated. Rather than a temple, perhaps he should be looking for a crypt. It seemed unlikely, given
the many references to Basenis which we had already heard, but
it could not be ruled out.

The missing temple had been obvious by the end of the first
day. Consequently, he had spent the next two weeks combing the
town, eyes wide open, asking questions of everyone from Roshnoy
the grain balancer down to farmers met by chance in the street.
He entered every business, every shop, every home where he could
procure a welcome for himself. He never asked openly where and
how Basenis was worshipped—if Basenism was a mystery religion, that would likely cut off the flow of information completely.
He asked about everything else under the suns. He steered the
conversation to spiritual matters as subtly as he could, but to no
avail. After two weeks, he had heard nothing and seen nothing to
indicate where and how Basenis was worshipped in Tomar.

The difficulty in searching for something hidden is that the
only proof of its existence is finding it. If it is difficult to find it,
it is still more difficult—indeed, nearly impossible—to conclude
that therefore it does not exist. One can only go on looking, or
give up in disgust. Young Thaddeus, alas, is not a quitter, or he
might have considered alternative hypotheses. He presumed that
the Tomarens were theologically unsophisticated, and therefore
required a place of worship, and that therefore if he dug deeply
enough he would hear of it. He did not consider that they might
be unsophisticated but also disaffected; while so common in our
present age, disaffection had no part in Philpott's noble (if pedan-
tic) character.

Throughout this period, Asha was ever at his side, guiding
him, introducing him, answering his questions, and steering him

from place to place. At last, frustrated after weeks of fruitless searching, he judged he had nothing to lose by a frontal assault. Consequently, he asked Asha where and how Basenis was worshipped in Tomar.

As we have seen, this was not a topic Asha was prepared to discuss, and she declined to answer. Philpott pressed her, and she continued to demur. His questions and his intensity persuaded her that perhaps she had been wrong; perhaps we were emissaries of Great Basenis; perhaps Philpott would be angered by the Tomaren lack of devotion. He remonstrated with her, and she, in extremis, picked a quarrel with him. She escorted him frostily back to the hostel and abandoned him there, and that's where I found him after my discussion with Simuny.

If Philpott was a victim of his preconceptions, Simuny and I were no less so. A young man and and a young woman thrown constantly together; the man handsome, virile, exotic; the woman beautiful, intelligent, adventurous; how could love, however ill-advised, fail to blossom between them? If they quarreled, how it could it be other than a lover's tiff? So Simuny and I, in our age and condescension, and yes, in our taste for romance, so Simuny and I had concluded.

We were greatly mistaken, and we each should have known better. Consider Philpott: handsome, yes, virile, yes, exotic (to a Zymurgian), yes; aware of anything beyond his studies, no. Anything and everything is a topic of study to Philpott; he sees the world through glasses of parchment and black ink. And of glass, too, of course. I was speaking metaphorically. Consider Asha, as Simuny should have: beautiful yes, adventurous yes, but above all intelligent and charged with Tomar's welfare; a starry-eyed innocent, no. Her daily task was not only to escort Philpott about and assist with his inquiries, but also to prevent him from learning anything he ought not. She must be constantly on guard, while remaining outwardly charming and helpful. Another woman might have been seduced away from her duty—I say "might", for Philpott would have given no encouragement in the matter—but not Asha. Simuny's suspicions and apprehensions were as absurd as my own.

And yet our conclusions seemed plausible, indeed, plausible enough for Simuny to summon me, and plausible enough even then for me to confront young Thaddeus with them.

I feel rather embarrassed about the whole affair, I must say. Had I kept my mouth shut I would have spared myself a considerable quantity of annoyance.

So matters stood on the morning of the day Carbuncle and I found the abandoned temple. Asha had not come for Philpott that morning, as my readers will recall; she judged the best way of preventing further questions was to maintain a haughty and injured silence. She was indeed fond of him, rather as one might be fond of some strange and exotic animal; hence her pleasure that afternoon and her willingness to send for him. She no longer had any need to avoid him, and so no longer needed to maintain her angry pose. So much for Asha. But what of Philpott?

It had been brought to his attention, so he thought, that he had been trifling with the affections of a young woman. Nothing had been farther from his mind, of course, but once the idea had been raised he could not dismiss it. Had Asha formed some kind of attachment? She had spoken no word of it if so, but then a wellbred lady would not. He considered her behavior, her constant presence, the way she took his arm during the nightly promenades. He considered the way he had pressed her for information, and the way she had responded. He knew he was blind to some things; he looked up to me (more's the pity) as an authority on life in the wide world. He was forced to conclude that his attentions had been misunderstood, and that the young lady had formed a sincere attachment for him.

This was very bad. Philpott is the very model of the Glastonbury don: absent-minded, more fully married to his work than he could be to any woman, doomed to a life of scholarship and increasing eccentricity; rather like Carbuncle and myself in other words. Marriage formed no part of his plans; nor, as a younger son of the Earl of Luton, could he expect to marry just where he pleased if it did. Oh, he would be granted some latitude—but marrying a dusky native of some far off, nearly fabulous land was simply not on, no matter how beautiful, no matter how charming, no matter how much he wanted to.

Did he want to? He didn't think so. In any event, he must break the news to Asha as gently as he could. He hated the very idea, but a gentleman could do no less. This was the primary reason Philpott opposed the journey to Basenis Basor, and maintained that we should leave the country immediately. Having discharged his responsibilities, he wished to be elsewhere as soon as possible.

The days preceding the start of our journey were furiously busy, as I have already indicated, and Philpott had no opportunity for a private conversation with Asha, though they met frequently. The need for secrecy being abolished, her usual buoyant spirits were fully restored, and she never failed to greet him with fondness and delight. What could he think? What could the rest of us think, for that matter? The error of our judgement had by no means yet been brought home to us. It seemed a typical romantic ploy: an angry quarrel followed by sunshine and daisies, all intended to keep the prospective suitor on his toes and off his balance.

So matters stood on the day we left Tomar. So far from leaving Zymurgia and Asha forever, he was was doomed to spend the next several weeks, at a minimum, in daily proximity to her. Never let it be said that young Thaddeus is a coward! He judged, and rightly in my estimation, that he must speak to Asha immediately. Better to disillusion her at once; things would be unpleasant for a day or so, but she would recover; she was no naive, sheltered miss. He was already guilty of misleading her; he did not propose to maintain the charade for one moment longer than necessary.

I have been engaging in a most unconscionable practice during the last paragraphs; I have been pretending to know the thoughts of others, as and when they thought them. Nevertheless, I maintain that the story I have just presented is essentially true; it is based on numerous conversations I had with the principles over the succeeding weeks. It would have been far too tedious to present them in full. I shall now resume a more normal narration of events.

We spent the first day of the journey, as I have previously indicated, riding along the main road through fields of grain and occasional stands of trees. Some appeared wild; others had the look of cultivated windbreaks. I spent the day riding in the company of Mukden and Asha, plying them with questions. Philpott

moved about, but was generally one of the group, listening carefully to the questions and answers, and making a note now and
then; his poor donkey was quite splattered with ink by the end
of the day. He asked few questions himself, and indeed seemed
somewhat preoccupied.

As the orange sun was vanishing in the east, we came to
a clearing by the side of the road. Mukden informed me that it
was one of the regular stops used by the men who conveyed the
waters of Basenis north to Tomar. It was a pleasant place to camp,
and as we stayed in a similar place each night of our journey I
will describe it in some detail. There was abundant dry ground
under the spreading trees, so we need not fear the nightly rains;
there was a cistern of rain water sufficient for all our needs; there
was excellent forage for the animals in the surrounding meadows.
There was a large fire ring, around which to gather in the evening,
and several smaller fireplaces, suitable for cooking, and a suf-
ficiency of firewood. We used what we needed; each morning, as
we were breaking camp, several of the Tomarens gathered more.

As we were making camp that evening, I noticed that Philpott
was keeping an eye on Asha. Aha, I thought. Eventually she was
alone, seated on a rug outside of her tent. It was in fact our tent;
as the only woman in the company, we had thought it necessary to
guarantee her privacy, and she had gracefully accepted our generosity. She was working on something; mending a garment that
had become torn during the day's journey, perhaps. I am unsure.
I was not surprised to see Philpott put down his things, and walk
over and greet her. The rug on which she sat was ample for two,
or even more, to sit down, and at her gesture he sat down beside
her and began to speak earnestly to her. I reflected to myself that
it was fortunate that he had taken the time to learn the language,
for it would be most inconvenient to pursue his amours through
Cadbury—a fine fellow, but perhaps not the ideal go-between.
I could not hear what he said (and would not have listened if I
could, I assure you), but the look on his face was the very picture
of the Young Anglish Gentleman Doing His Duty. I was rather
surprised; it seemed an odd way to approach the girl one loved.

I was considerably more surprised by Asha's reaction. She
laughed, merrily and with delight; her laughter filled the clearing. Philpott no longer looked dutiful. He looked at her carefully

as he spoke to her, and in response she laughed again, and then responded more quietly. He began to look, of all things, relieved! She spoke to him again, and he gestured in my direction; I averted my eyes hurriedly as they both turned to look at me. I therefore did not see it, but Carbuncle, who by now was watching the show avidly, assures me that the gaze she cast upon me was both amused and thoughtful. Philpott and Asha chatted for a few more moments, and then he arose, a smile on his face and a spring in his step, and went about his business.

I trust that the nature of their conversation is as clear to my readers as it was mysterious to me.

That night I found a snake in my bed. It gave me a few bad moments, but on the whole it was an inoffensive snake, a dark brown in color. I carried it gently into the meadow and set it free. Snakes are often attracted to human body warmth on cold nights in the wild, and although it was not particularly chilly I did not find its presence remarkable.

CHAPTER 33

ٮ؞

A few hands of whist. ? *Toad in the hole. ?* *A matter of taste.*

AFTER THE practical details of breaking camp were attended to, the second day of the journey was much like the first. I spent the day pestering the Zymurgians with my questions, and they began starting to avoid me. Philpott spent much of the day riding nearby, listening to the questions and answers; he seemed more at ease than he had the day before. More relaxed when Asha was nearby as well; at least once I saw them riding side by side, talking merrily. Apparently their discussion of the evening before had cleared the air in some way. I didn't mention the snake to anyone; finding wildlife in one's bed is an unremarkable phenomenon in the wild, and the topic never arose.

By the end of the day we were well into the wilderness. Zymurgia is a large, sparsely inhabited country, and most of the inhabitants are gathered into the townships which dot the landscape like currants in a scone made by a particularly stingy baker. The road was well-maintained, though, and the trees, while tall and broad, were set far enough apart to give the woods through which we rode a park-like air. The leaves were green, and the light filtered through them was green as well; it was like traveling through an emerald.

We reached our second camp after an easy day's ride, men on donkeys traveling faster than carts loaded with barrels of beer. I asked Mukden whether we should travel on towards the next camp along, but he rejected the idea. One stage was easy, but two would take too long. He might attempt it in an emergency, but not otherwise. I did not argue with him; I was glad for the rest, not yet having been broken to the saddle as it were. Still, it made for a long evening. Sitting around the campfire chatting is pleasant enough, but I had an inkling that I might find our hosts disinclined to chat with me.

I had reckoned without Hodgins, who had his own ideas about how to pass the time on the trail. Once camp was properly made, he dragged some rocks together near the fire, put a box lid across them, and pulled out his deck of cards. He had an attentive audience before he had finished shuffling, and soon Carbuncle, Fox, and I had sat down to a game of whist with him. Cadbury, Philpott, Asha, and Mukden sat nearby; the two Zymurgians paid particular attention, having never seen playing cards before. We played several hands, and then Carbuncle and I resigned our seats in favor of Asha and Mukden. While Hodgins explained the rules to them, Carbuncle dug out a wine bottle filled with Zymurgian spirits and passed it around. As novices, our friends made their share of foolish mistakes and had their share of beginner's luck, and if any large predators were inclined to investigate the camp I am sure the raucous laughter persuaded them to go elsewhere. The party broke up, late and happy, and we stumbled to our beds.

The following morning I found a toad in my left boot. I never put on my boots without looking inside first, even when at home in England; it is simply second nature after so many nights on the trail. I am glad I checked them as usual—had I attempted to draw on the boot without looking, I might have injured the poor creature. It seemed an odd place for a toad to go to ground, especially as the boot had been standing upright, but I had seen stranger happenings in strange lands, and didn't ponder it for long. I did comment on the quantity and diversity of the wildlife at breakfast, as I recall, citing the snake and the toad as examples, and if Asha smiled and Philpott chuckled, well, there was nothing so odd about that.

If my readers think that I was being more than usually slow, I can only beg them to consider the circumstances. I am no longer so young as I once was, and a day in the saddle is tiring even to those who are used to it. On top of that we were stopping every half-an-hour or so to fix our position and take bearings to any landmarks we could see. And so far, nothing so very odd—from my point of view—had yet occurred. In the wild one encounters wildlife; and if the wildlife is sufficiently abundant, some finite fraction is likely to find its way into one's belongings. It is only natural.

On the third day I ceased asking questions, in a desperate bid to become more socially acceptable, and once more we played cards late into the evening. I woke once, briefly, feeling as though someone had perhaps touched me or shaken me in some way. I sat up in my bedding, there under the trees, and looked around; the camp was still, and shaking my head, I quickly lay down and was soon asleep once more. Some time later I was dreaming that I was trapped in a Seljurkian bath, and that the sadistic attendant was sitting on my chest and scrubbing at me with a course, heavy towel. Eventually I become so uncomfortable that I woke up, only to find that my dream was largely true. Some large black creature was engaged in licking every inch of my exposed bedding from my nose down to my toes. It had one heavy paw planted firmly on my chest.

I froze, of course, and let the creature have its way with me. It is easy to freeze when a large black creature of unknown species has a paw on your chest to keep you from moving. I suppose one wants to avoid attracting attention to oneself, foolish though that sounds. I lay there for what seemed like hours, breathing as softly as I could and trying not to move a muscle, even when it shifted its paw and its claws dug in a trifle. Dull claws, I must say, more like a dog's than a cat's, though this creature was clearly rather larger than Bruno. Where was Bruno? I asked myself. Why was Bruno allowing this large importunate creature to taste my bedding so intimately?

In due course it removed its paw, and began snuffling about my toes. Rejecting them, which I thought showed good taste, it moved up to my face; I nearly choked as its warm, moist muzzle passed over me. The aroma of its breath, slightly sweet, was nearly overpowering. Apparently it didn't think much of my face, either, for it gave my blanket one or two final licks, and waddled off, scuffling through the leaf mould. It vanished from sight long before the noise of its passage died away. When I was sure it had left, I sat up to take inventory. My blanket was rather soggy, and a bit sticky, and my heart was pounding, but otherwise I was little the worse for my experience. I lay back down, and began to ponder.

Why had whatever it was wanted to taste my bedding so thoroughly? Why my bedding, and not Carbuncle's? For that matter, why hadn't my visitor been frightened off by Carbuncle's snoring? He slept not ten feet away. And where was Bruno? He had slept at my feet the previous night, but there was no sign of him.

Even an old fool can see through a brick wall in time, as my father used to say. A snake in my bed; a toad in my boot; a large animal of unknown provenance giving me (and me alone) a head-to-toe tongue bath; and these on three successive nights. Clearly someone was being clever. That touch I had felt; clearly someone had put something on me to attract the animal, just as they had put the toad in my boot and the snake in my bed. Humph, I said to myself. Perhaps I had been a little too eager with my questions, but this was hardly called for. I knew how to deal with this sort of practical joke, though, and this sort of practical joker. Smiling, I turned over and went back to sleep. I would have my revenge in the morning.

I arose at the usual time, just in time for breakfast, and dressed rapidly. My blankets were still a little clammy, but I rolled them up carefully, shaking them first to remove the bits of leaf and gravel from the underside. I packed the rest of my things quickly, sealing my bag. On my way to breakfast I walked casually around the camp. Peeking out of the top of Philpott's bag I noticed a box of salt. There was no reason why it shouldn't have been there; every expedition carries plenty of salt. Not only is it a preservative, but camp food can be rather dull without it. On the other hand, there was no particular reason why it should be at the top, rather than the bottom; the Zymurgian cook had his own stock of salt and other spices, and used them to good effect. Glancing about to see that I was unobserved, I picked up the box and shook it gently; it was only about half full. That was distinctly odd, as we hadn't done any of our own cooking since the day we left Pelham. I growled deep in my throat as I returned the box to its place; things were becoming clearer.

Having completed my investigations, I went and got my bowl of porridge. I smiled broadly at the cook, and greeted him cheerfully. He smiled back. I smiled at my colleagues. I smiled at my Zymurgian friends. I asked how everyone had slept, and allowed how I had slept very well indeed. I made no mention of the thing that had accosted me in the night, and I watched everyone's expressions very carefully. I noticed that Bruno was lying by Hodgin's feet. Hodgins, perhaps? Cadbury seemed to be smirking, but then that was habitual. Carbuncle merely greeted me warmly, as did Philpott and Asha. Had it been Philpott?

Everyone seemed cheerful, and glad to see me; I didn't notice any one particular person who seemed more interested in my night's sleep than the others. Had I been mistaken? Had I dreamed it? I thought of my clammy blankets, and the toad, and the snake, and thought not. It would be necessary to raise the stakes a trifle. I put down my tin cup of juice.

"I say, Carbuncle, that toad I found yesterday reminded me of something."

"And that would be, Leon?" said Carbuncle, not looking up from his bowl.

"Do you remember the time in Anselms? When a wild boar ran through our tent in the middle of the night?" I was looking at Carbuncle, mostly, but I tried to keep a corner of an eye on the others.

Carbuncle laughed and put down his bowl.

"I suppose it's accurate to say that the beastie ran through our tent, Leon, but a little misleading, wouldn't you say?"

"What happened?" asked Hodgins.

"Evidently," I said, "we had pitched our tent across an animal run. It was a dark night, and a dark green tent. It was warm, so we had the tent flap folded back."

"About halfway toward morning," continued Carbuncle, "we were awakened by a drumming noise. It was loud to begin with, and getting steadily louder. We had just pegged the sounds as hoofbeats when something ran straight into our tent, went right between us, and the next moment the tent was gone. The something had bowled into the back of the tent, which was sealed shut, you know, and had taken the tent with it, stakes and all."

"And then," I said, "there was a horrible crashing noise and some angry squealing."

"Muffled squealing, Leon, muffled squealing."

"Muffled squealing indeed, Thomas," I agreed. "The creature, which was thoroughly tangled in the remains of our tent, had fallen into a nearby gully, and was thrashing about wildly."

"What did you do, Leon?" asked Philpott.

"We killed it. Ate very well for several days, we did," said Carbuncle. "Bit of a sad thing, of course, but wild boars are too dangerous to trifle with. And it had broken a leg as well."

I kept a close eye on my companions as we related the old story. Did Philpott and Asha share a knowing glance? I thought they did. Did Cadbury smirk a little more broadly? Was that a fit of coughing on Hodgins' part, or was he stifling laughter? It was time to escalate once more.

On the previous night, someone had seen fit to turn me into a human salt lick. I'd go straight for the jugular.

"Could someone please pass me the salt?" I asked mildly.

Hodgins stared at me, and started coughing again.

"Did you say a little more salt, Leon?" asked Carbuncle, dead pan.

"Why, no, Thomas. I didn't."

"Oh, I thought you did."

Philpott was pursing his lips, trying to hide a grin. Asha said something to him that I didn't catch, and her grin was too big to hide. Mukden started to laugh out loud.

"What did she say, Cadbury?" I demanded. His eyes were beginning to bulge slightly.

"She said, 'What did he do with all of the salt we gave him last night?', *Hakim Effendi.*"

"Perhaps a neighbor borrowed it?" asked Mukden.

This was too much for Hodgins, who blurted out a muffled "Excuse me!" and vanished behind the trees. I could hear him falling all over himself with laughter.

"A fine crew you are," I said, becoming angry. "I could have been eaten alive last night. I suppose I should be grateful that the creature's meal was properly seasoned. Frankly, I'm surprised you you didn't just spit me and roast me first."

"Take it easy, old chap," said Carbuncle. "You were in no danger at all."

"No danger? Let's season you tonight, then, shall we? Perhaps you'll change your mind when a huge beast is leaning on your chest!" This brought forth another round of laughter.

"It was nothing but a squamunk," said Philpott. "They're harmless vegetarians. They just like salt."

"A squamunk, eh? And just how big is a squamunk?" I asked.

Mukden held a hand about a foot above the ground. "About so high," he said.

"They're evidently a kind of rodent," said Philpott. "There's a colony over in the meadow."

"So high?" I asked, holding my own hand about a foot above the ground. They nodded. "So high? And yet somehow it managed to keep me pinned to the ground with one paw?" More laughter. Somehow, I felt, they weren't taking me seriously, and I finished my porridge and my fruit juice in a sullen silence. I had the last laugh, though, between moments of feeling ill, because just then the bear came shuffling back into the camp, preceded by a horrified Hodgins. Everyone shrieked, and it was truly gratifying and a blessing to my ears.

CHAPTER 34

⊷∶∾

The danger of jumping to conclusions. ∂● Trees of mystery.
The bottle of Waterloughs'.

THE BEAR did not trouble us with its presence for long. It had smelled breakfast cooking, I suppose, and thought there was a chance for a bite to eat. The cook ignored the compliment, and began to bang a metal spoon against a cast iron pot as loudly as he could. The bear sat down and watched him, scratching one ear with a forepaw. Bruno began to bark, straining at Hodgins' strong hand on his collar. Taking the hint, the rest of us began to shout and wail as loudly as we could, except for Philpott, who merely said "Oh, dear," over and over again. The bear looked around at all of us, sitting up and looking for all the world like a Bundi idol, until it quite suddenly tired of the noise and sloped off into the woods. When it was safely gone, a profound silence settled upon the group; then, by tacit agreement, everyone rose and began to break camp, the more quickly to put our ursine friend some distance behind us.

I didn't move; I remained sitting where I had been when the bear appeared, tin cup in hand, empty bowl at my feet. After all, it hadn't liked my taste the previous night; what cause had I for worry? But I mustn't lie: in truth, I felt vindicated and ill all at once, and was none too sure of keeping my feet if I stood up. I thought it best to remain where I was until the shaking went away.

As soon as his gear was packed, Philpott came over and sat down on the log by my side.

"I say, Leon, I'm terribly sorry."

"So it's you I must thank for my unexpected guest?"

"Yes, Leon." He hung his head.

"And the toad?"

"And the toad."

"And the snake?"

"No, I don't much like snakes. Asha did that one herself."

"Asha?" I looked at him in some surprise. "Were my questions that irritating?"

"Oh, no, Leon," said Philpott, scratching the back of his neck. "No, it had nothing to do with that. It was because of what you told me the other night."

"What I told you? What did I tell you?" Let my readers remember that it was still early in the morning.

"That Asha was in love with me, and that I had given her every reason to think that I reciprocated her affections."

"She isn't?" This was news to me.

"No," said Philpott, "and she never was. I spoke to her about it after we stopped the first night." He proceeded to tell me some of the events of the past weeks; as I have already related them once, I shall pass over them quickly now.

"But why did she put a snake in my bed?"

"To teach you a lesson, she said, to keep you from jumping to conclusions." Philpott gulped as he said this.

"I'll have you know that I never jump to conclusions, Thad, not ever. And I think it is only fair that you tell Asha that Simuny reached the same ones." I smiled to myself as I saw Philpott file that tidbit away. Why should I suffer alone?

"All right," I went on, "so much for the snake. What prompted the toad?"

"Well, we got so little reaction with the snake," he said. I noted carefully his use of the word "we". "Asha said we needed to try again, and insisted that it was my turn. She had one of the men catch the toad, and I put it into your boot. I had to stand the boot up so the toad couldn't get out."

"Tell me, Thad, how many of our company knew about this?"

"By that time?" He thought for a moment. "All but one, I'd say." So everyone had been in on it. Humph, I thought to myself.

"And the bear?" I asked.

"We didn't expect the bear, Leon, I'm terribly sorry about the bear. The toad didn't get any reaction either, so Asha said we needed to try again. Mukden pointed out that squamunks live in this area, and that they love salt." He put his face in his hands for a moment. "I can only surmise that bears love squamunks and salt both."

"Just see to it that it doesn't happen again," I said. In truth, I was pleased rather than otherwise. It meant that I wasn't likely to find anything in my bed that night; it also meant that my concerns for Philpott's future happiness were groundless.

Later that day, as we were following the road through the dense woods that cover that part of Zymurgia, Carbuncle brought his donkey next to mine.

"How old would you say these trees are, Leon?"

"I don't know. Centuries, perhaps. More for the largest," I said.

"I would agree. So why are they still here?"

"What do you mean?" I asked my friend.

"We know that Basenis has visited his wrath down upon the country many times in the last hundred years or so, rampaging about, and eating everything in sight. We know that entire towns have been destroyed. Why towns? Why not these stands of trees? He eats tree clippings normally; there are plenty of unclipped clippings here, and and the towns are far and few between."

"The mostly likely explanation is that Basenis sought out the towns on purpose," I said. "Do you suppose that there might be something to the 'Wrath of Basenis' after all?" Carbuncle snorted.

"It must have been attracted by something that exists in the towns, and nowhere else," he replied. "The only alternative is that Basenis was being vindictive, which I can't believe. It's just a phantasm, after all."

"A vindictive phantasm?" I said. "I meet them frequently. What's so odd about that?"

"Now then, Leon, don't be projecting your own shortcomings onto beasties that have never done you any harm." He frowned at me severely.

"No harm, Thomas? What about the time—"

"I know all about it, Leon, and I stick by my statement. You're just clumsy with them, that's all." Without another word, he persuaded his donkey to surge ahead, moving it up several ranks in the procession.

We played whist again that night, as usual. Mukden and Asha were becoming quite good at it, which was causing tempers to fray a trifle; and after several nights of whist it was becoming rather boring. After several desultory rounds, Carbuncle sprang up from his place by Mukden's side.

"Carry on," he said, "I'll be right back." And he jogged off toward the spot where his things were. He reappeared almost immediately, a bag in his hand, and resumed his place. "Game's getting a little dull, it seems to me. Perhaps we can make it a little more interesting."

"It is already interesting," said Asha, in heavily-accented Anglish. I was astounded. I hadn't realized that she was learning it. Philpott leaned over to her and explained quietly that Carbuncle was suggesting a wager of some kind.

"What stakes are you thinking of?" I asked. "We don't have any money."

"Only this," he said. "I've been saving it." And he opened the bag and pulled out, wonder of wonders, a flask of Waterloughs' single malt whisky. Hodgins swore softly to himself, and I felt my eyes brighten just looking at it. Carbuncle set it gently in the middle of the table. "For the winner," he said. "Though he might have to share a wee dram with the rest of us."

"Good heavens, Thomas, how did you manage to save such a thing as that until this late in the trip? I thought all of our Anglish spirits had been drunk long since."

"Oh, I had stashed it with some of my equipment, I don't quite remember why. I ran across it while I was repacking everything I wanted to take South."

Interest in the game revived quickly after that. Hodgins' playing cards were dirty, but the play itself was scintillating; the game seemed to have moved to a whole new level. I won't bore my readers with a trick-by-trick narrative, as such things are insufferably tedious, and in any event I don't like to brag. Suffice it that when the points were counted I was the victor.

Carbuncle picked up the bottle of amber liquid, and studied its label for a moment. Then he handed it to me.

"There you go, Leon."

I caressed it lovingly. I still have that bottle of Waterloughs' that I won with some playing cards from Eton's; it is before me now as I write. I can still remember the crackle of the fire, and the stars shining down on us, and the look on everyone's face as I put the flask, unopened, into my hip pocket and said, "Thank you, Thomas." Oh, it was a blessed moment, watching politeness and outrage waging war in their eyes. When I saw that politeness was beginning to lose, I relented.

"Am I going to find anything unpleasant in my bed tonight?"

"No, Leon," said Philpott, and Asha shook her head.

"Ah. Good. Now, is anything unpleasant going to find me in my bed tonight?"

Philpott and Asha shook their heads.

"Better. Well, would anyone care for a nightcap?" I asked, and there were general nods as I pulled the flask from my pocket. I still have the flask, but in the morning the whisky was no more than a memory.

CHAPTER 35

Confrontations in Bandeku. ∂◆ Ascending the tiger.

O N THE 25th of Ragout, the expedition reached the Zymurgian town of Bandeku, that being the first town south of Tomar
which lies directly on the main road. For the past two days we
had been traveling through the wilderness, a much forested landscape of small hills and smaller valleys where our line-of-sight
extended only to the next bend in the road. It was thus with a
great shock of pleasure that we came down through the trees and
saw a wide, fertile valley spreading out below us. The road runs
in a straight line due south through the fields and orchards that
cover the Valley of Bandekukana like the squares of the proverbial patchwork quilt. Many miles away the land rises again into
a range of forested green hills. At the base of these hills, though
invisible to us as yet, another highway runs east and west; just
beyond the crossroads, on the lower slopes, stands the town of
Bandeku. Like Tomar, it is a farming community; as a crossroads,
it is a larger town than Tomar, with all that that implies.

Because of its situation on the hillside, we caught sight of
Bandeku many hours before we arrived. The construction of
Bandeku is much like that of Tomar—the same exposed beams
and thatched roofs, so reminiscent of our own Anglish countryside. After several days on the road, the town seemed to beckon
in welcome over the fields of grain. It seemed a likely place to get
good food, good drink, a comfortable bed and a good breakfast in
the morning, with lots of hot water for bathing. As we drew near
the view was blocked by the trees of the orchards through which
we rode, until quite suddenly we came out of the trees and found
ourselves in the town.

Casual travelers are rare in Zymurgia. Wagon trains of beer
travel north from Basenis Basor to Tomar four times a year, gathering up the tithe on their way back south; other wagon trains
transport grain and other foodstuffs from town to town after the
harvest. Other than this trade, which is minimal by Anglish stan-

dards, few people are seen on the roads. Indeed, we met no one, traveling north or south, between Tomar and Bandeku. In such a country, the arrival of travelers is always an event of great moment in the life of a town. The arrival of unusual and unexpected travelers is a thing of surpassing wonder, an event to be cherished, a story to be told and retold to successive generations of children. The people proclaim a day of jubilation and dance in the streets; they roast the fatted calf, and serve it with the local wines and spirits. This is the theory, at any rate. To say that I was disappointed by our initial reception in Bandeku is to understate the degree of my emotion by several orders of magnitude.

To begin with, the northern reaches of the town appeared to be deserted. We saw only one young man, and he did not seem glad of our presence. He stepped out of a house into the street some fifty feet ahead of us, and began walking away; when we hailed him he turned and stared at us, eyes wide, and then raced off toward the center of town without speaking.

"Is this normal?" I heard Carbuncle inquire of Mukden.

"No, it is too quiet. I have been here many times before, and have never seen the streets so empty."

"Perhaps they are holding a festival today," Philpott suggested.

"It may be so," said Mukden. "But I have never known the people to run away from visitors."

Lacking any better plan, we continued into town. We would have done so even if we had been mobbed by eager townsfolk. As Masters of Tomar, Asha and Mukden's first responsibility was to present themselves before their opposite numbers in Bandeku's Hall of the Masters. The towns of Zymurgia, though bound together by trade, the tithe, and the Dispersal of the Waters, are essentially autonomous and fiercely independent. Each is governed by its leading families, in the persons of its masters. It is rare for a town's masters to leave their town for any reason, and their reception by the masters of other towns is uncertain. No town, so far as I know, has ever attempted to dominate its neighbors; indeed, the distance between towns makes it unlikely that any such attempt would succeed. Nevertheless, a traveling master is an object of suspicion. Under the circumstances, Asha and Mukden could do no other than seek out Bandeku's masters straightaway, lest their natural caution be roused.

We had not proceeded far into the town when we heard a low rumble ahead of us, and then beheld a mass of people walking slowly towards us. They were lead by two men and two women who proved to be, unsurprisingly, the Masters of Bandeku. Wishing to give no offense, we stopped directly after they appeared, and waited for them to approach. They stopped about ten yards away, and looked at us with grim, closed faces.

I judged that Mukden would be too busy to translate, and betook myself to Cadbury's side, where I was soon joined by Carbuncle. As usual, I will dispense with the tedious details of translation.

One of the Bandekun masters, the younger man, spoke first.

"Who are you, and why have you come to Bandeku?" His tone implied that we should not have come, and that we might come to agree with that assessment. Mukden stepped forward, and spoke.

"Has Bandeku fallen so low that hospitality to old friends is forgotten? I am Mukden of the Hinkaya of Tomar, and I say I have never met with such a reception in any town of the Land Above."

The Masters of Bandeku studied him dispassionately; there was an embarrassed stir in the crowd, and a man came forward and spoke to them. The speaker nodded, and turned back to us again.

"Very well. Mukden the Disperser of Waters is indeed known in Bandeku. But who are his companions?"

"I am no longer a Disperser of Waters. Asha of the Carinu of Tomar and I are Masters of Tomar. We acknowledge that we have no mastery in this place, and we respect the mastery of the Masters of Bandeku." At this, the Bandekun masters inclined their heads politely. "Our companions are people of Tomar, and several travelers from the Lands Below."

"So we have been told," said another master, the older woman. "Is this Tomaren hospitality? To bring the wrath of Great Basenis down upon us?"

"On the contrary," said Asha, somehow concealing the surprise I am sure we all felt. "They bring with them the power to quench Basenis' wrath for ever."

It was like turning a key in a lock; I could almost hear the click as the tension climbed to a higher level. Feeling surprisingly reckless I called Bruno to my side and stepped forward myself.

"Bruno, speak!" Bruno barked cheerfully. I could tell I had the full attention of the Bandekuns.

"Bruno, greet the man," I said, indicating the original speaker. Bruno bounded forward toward the man, whose eyes bulged as the black dog sat at his feet and extended a paw, panting. Bruno pawed at the air a few times, but the man made no effort to take his paw. Finally he put it down, and looked around at me.

"Bruno," I said, "play dead."

I fancy I could feel the sigh go up as Bruno lay down and rolled on his back, legs in the air. Finally, at my signal, he got up and trotted back to my side. There was silence for several minutes; the Bandekun masters clearly did not know what to make of Bruno's display. At last Asha spoke again.

"Either these men are servants of Basenis, or Basenis has no power over them. This you have seen with your own eyes. I say that Basenis has no power over them. I say as well that I have travelled far today, and do not wish to debate theology in the street. What of Bandekun hospitality?"

Matters improved somewhat after that. The Bandekun masters shouted a few orders, and in less than a quarter of an hour we found ourselves installed in a hostel much like the one we had occupied in Tomar, though rather larger. We were told that we were to be given time to rest and refresh ourselves, and then we must appear before the masters. A guide would be sent to us at the appointed time.

"They were expecting us," I said, when we were alone. "How can that be?"

"Nabili," spat Mukden, who was livid. He had managed to hold his temper during the confrontation in the street, but it had been a close thing. Asha nodded.

"I did not see him at all in the days before we left Tomar. I assumed he was licking his wounds in private. Instead, he must have come south."

I nodded, for I had noted his absence myself, and been grateful for it.

"Should we expect difficulties here?" I asked.

"I had not thought so. Now I do not know."

As further speculation was clearly fruitless, we busied ourselves with eating and drinking and washing off the dirt of the road, and awaited our summons.

I should like to give a complete report on our meeting with the Masters of Bandeku, but I cannot, as I was not invited. Indeed, when the messenger came to escort Mukden and Asha to the Hall of the Masters, "the wizards from the Lands Below" were explicitly directed to remain behind. Mukden was furious and apologized profusely to me, but I, though disappointed, refused to take issue with our exclusion. After all, one must maintain appearances.

"Who knows what Nabili has told them?" I said. "The welfare of Bandeku is in their hands, is it not? They must do as they see fit."

This observation brought Mukden to a standstill; unused to the requirements of his new office, he had not seen it in that light.

"A poor thing it is," he said, much chagrined, "when a wizard from the Lands Below must remind me of my duty!" Asha and Philpott exchanged smirks and a chuckle or two at his expense, after which the messenger reminded us all that the Masters of Bandeku were waiting. He lead Asha and Mukden into the street. The rest of us perforce sat and stewed.

The casual reader may be excused for thinking that I have lingered over long on our days of travel from Tomar to Bandeku— that I have written too much of the minor incidents of the road, rather than getting on with the story. It is true that I remember those days with great fondness, which has perhaps lead me to expand upon them inordinately, but they were also the last days for some time when I felt I was in any way in control of things. Once we reached Bandeku we mounted the proverbial tiger, and it was many days before we were able to dismount; and by then the damage was done.

Asha and Mukden did not return until late in the evening, by which time we were nearly past caring. Hodgins had played innumerable games of patience, no one having the energy for whist; the rest of us, aside from the brief, bright interval in which we dined, having sunk into a dispirited, tedious funk. Nor were Asha and Mukden in good spirits when they returned; the conference had begun badly and the atmosphere had improved only slightly as the evening wore on. The problem was simple. The Bandekuns were greatly in favor of muzzling old Basenis for good and all; they simply doubted our ability to do so. Bandeku, by virtue of its greater proximity to Basenis Basor, had had the wrath of Basenis visited upon it with rather more regularity than Tomar, and its inhabitants were disinclined to arouse that wrath needlessly. That the "wizards from the Lands Below" had escaped Basenis' wrath to date was unpersuasive; perhaps Basenis was using us to test the Bandekuns, and merely waited for their acquiescence.

"What did Nabili say to them?" I asked. Mukden began to fume, and Asha answered for him.

"He told them that the Masters and folk of Tomar had been enchanted by wizards from the Lands Below. Under the enchantment, we would seek to so enrage Basenis that all of the towns of the Land Above would be laid waste. Then, the wizards would slay Basenis and take the Land Above for themselves."

Carbuncle snorted. "Nabili is no fool, we must give him that."

"Is Nabili still here?" I asked.

"No," said Mukden, who had finally calmed himself. "He was here yesterday and left early this morning; he went to warn other towns."

"I don't suppose he told the Bandekuns that he had lost his mastery in Tomar?" Mukden laughed at the idea.

"He is no fool. He never admitted having been a master."

"What did the Bandekuns say when you told them?" asked Philpott. This turned out to be the key question of the evening, for Asha and Mukden had not, in fact, enlightened the Bandekuns about Nabili's antecedents.

"Would you have the Bandekuns think we cannot manage our town?" spat Asha. "A man like Nabili should never have been given Mastery. It is a shame Tomar will feel for generations. Do you wish us to cry our shame to the world?"

"If it will persuade the Masters here to discount Nabili's statements, yes, I do. Won't they be as angry at his actions as you were? And once they are angry with Nabili, you should have a much easier time."

And so it proved. The next morning Asha and Mukden laid Nabili's whole story in front of the Masters of Bandeku, begging forgiveness for having withheld it previously, and pleading shame as the cause. As I had foreseen, active Basenis worship was as unpopular in Bandeku as in Tomar; further, the Masters fully understood our friends' reluctance to speak of these things. They were left with but one question: could we do it? Could we slay Basenis, or at least render him harmless? Asha and Mukden assured them that we could.

"You said what?" I cried.

"We gave them our word as Masters of Tomar," replied Mukden solemnly.

CHAPTER 36

⌣⁚∾

The Holy City. ⁊◞ *The muster of Zymurgia.* ⁊◞ *Camping on the outskirts.*

NEARLY A month later, on the 22nd of Sobriquet, we crested a pass and had our first glimpse of the Holy City in the Barren Plain. The sun was orange that day, and its light shining through the late afternoon haze and the dust of our passage cast a brown glow over the plain below us. Though "plain" seemed a singularly poor name for such a broken, lumpy, barren surface as we saw before us. It stretched off to the southeast, mile after mile of low hills, gullies, and broken ground, with no vegetation. Far off in the distance, one mound rose head and shoulders above the rest. The road ran before us into the midst of the chaos, after which I could not trace its further progress.

"Very nice," I said to Mukden, who was riding beside me. "Where is the city?"

"We are here; the city lies before you."

Cutting off an angry retort, I took a closer look. What I had taken as desolate barren hills in the haze and the poor light were in fact hundreds—thousands, rather—of buildings. Though softened and rounded by distance, I knew, as if I had touched them, that every building in that awful city was made of brown bricks.

"Then that larger structure, there..." I gestured hesitantly.

"It is the Temple of Basenis, my friend."

I was struck dumb. Never had I seen, never had I conceived of a city of such immensity. Later, having taken the opportunity to survey the limits of the Barren Plain, I determined that Basenis Basor covered no less than four hundred square miles. Four hundred square miles of built and paved land, with never a tree, never a weed, never an open spot save the plaza surrounding the Temple of Basenis in the center of the city.

It had been a busy month. Once given Asha and Mukden's word, the Masters of Bandeku lost no time. Runners were sent to the villages to the south, to counter Nabili's lies and prepare for our arrival; other runners were sent east and west to the villages in those regions. The Bandekuns did not intend to march on the Holy City with a few dozen men; they intended a general rising. If the curse of Basenis could be removed from their lives, the Keepers would not be allowed to interfere. The combined forces would sweep them away, and the wizards would be allowed to work their magic in peace. Philpott became rather concerned at the prospect of violence, as did I.

"They are going to slaughter the Keepers?" he burst out as Mukden explained the plan to us. "Leon, Thomas, we must not condone this. We must head North at once!"

This discussion took place several days after we had arrived in Bandeku; during that time we had not been allowed to leave the hostel for any reason. We were well-fed, and every care was taken, but we were denied all freedom of movement. In Tomar we had been welcomed as guests, and therefore the Tomarens had felt compelled to treat us warmly; the Masters of Bandeku had no such compunctions. We had not been welcomed into the city; we had not been presented to the Masters; and indeed I did not speak directly to them, then or ever. The Bandekuns were willing to use us for their own ends, but were unwilling to be too close should Basenis elect to take his much-delayed vengeance upon us. Thus, we were held at arms' length from the time we entered the hostel until—but I get ahead of myself. Of our party, only Asha and Mukden were privy to the planning meetings and strategy sessions; the rest of us languished in captivity, waiting impatiently for the next modicum of news.

"Go north!" Hodgins snorted. "Do you really think we would make it out of town?"

"Nevertheless," began Philpott, heatedly, "it is our duty as Anglishmen—"

"Be at peace, Thed," interrupted Asha. "There will be no slaughter. The Keepers are few; our force will be many. There will be no need for battle." And with that Philpott had to be content.

"For myself, I am much more concerned with what we shall do when we arrive in the Holy City," I declared with nasty look at Asha and Mukden. I was still angry with the pair of them for promising our aid to the Bandekuns, for the reader will recall that we had only promised to "take a look." The accused hung their heads slightly.

"It was necessary," said Asha. "We could not return to To-mar in disgrace."

"It wouldn't be so infernally distressing, my good woman, if we had the least idea of how to do it!" I fear my disgust and anger showed on my face, for she recoiled; but then Carbuncle spoke up cheerfully enough.

"Be at peace, Leon," he said. "Don't torment our friends unnecessarily."

I rounded on him with wild surmise.

"You've figured it out?"

"I have a solution in mind, yes. It's terribly inelegant, not at all the sort of work I would wish to be remembered for, but I believe it will serve." To do him credit, Carbuncle didn't appear the slightest bit smug or self-satisfied.

We waited.

"Well?" I said.

"Yes," said Philpott, "What is it, Thomas?" We all looked at him in expectation. I felt butterflies of relief roaming the insides of my abdomen.

"I'd rather not say, until I've seen the beastie itself. There may be some factor I'm neglecting to consider."

"Thomas!" I glared at him in mute appeal.

"Sorry, old fellow. And anyway, if I told you our Bandekun hosts might find out, and then they might decide they no longer need us. I won't give over my chance at the only phantasm in the whole bloody land just to satisfy your curiosity." And with that I had to be content, though it galled me. Nevertheless, I was comforted to know that Carbuncle had a plan. It was clear that we must offend either the Foreign Office in Angland by meddling with Zymurgian politics, or our Zymurgian hosts by failing to do so; in the event the Zymurgians were much closer.

Over the next several days we had little to do but sit at the upstairs windows of the hostel and watch troops of Zymurgians arrive from the neighboring towns. Mukden and Asha were with us for most of that time; now that the plans had been made, it was clear that Bandeku was in charge, and had little use for the Mas-ters of Tomar. They were called upon only when the Bandekuns had questions to ask us, for they would not talk to us directly.

We left Bandeku on the 7th of Sobriquet. It was a comical sight; several hundred Zymurgians marched south, followed after an interval by our little troop, all mounted on our donkeys, followed after another interval by several hundred more Zymurgians. This was the pattern all of the way to the Holy City. They would not let us ride in front, though it was a nuisance to keep reining in the donkeys, for fear of losing us; they would not let us ride in the rear, for fear of us leaving; even on the road they did not wish to be too close to us. And so we journeyed along, an army ahead of us, an army behind us, and ourselves in the middle. I will say this, they gave us the best accommodations at night, for we camped at the way stations as we had on the way to Bandeku, while the armies bivouacked by the side of the road.

We passed through two more towns on our way south, Lisera and Basenilat; at each we were bustled into the hostel, bag and baggage, and left to stew for a day or so as the Bandekuns wrangled with the local masters. Our wants were attended to, scrupulously; our wishes were just as scrupulously ignored. In the morning would come the rap on the hostel door, and off we would go again, so much human cargo. After each stop the columns of troops stretched farther before us and behind; by the time we reached the Barren Plain on the 22nd, we were traveling with not less than three-thousand Zymurgians. As it was thought that there were not more than five or six hundred Keepers, Asha's projection of a bloodless takeover seemed ever more likely.

The city did not occupy the entire plain; there was a narrow band a few hundred yards in width between the base of the hills and the first buildings. We rode the last stretch of dirt road in silence, awe struck; as we crossed the invisible line separating city from plain we felt paving beneath the hooves of our donkeys, and I bent over to see. The road was quite overlain with dust and grime, but beneath I could see the regular pattern of bricks.

Basenis Basor being the size it was, there was clearly no question of marching on the Temple of Basenis before morning. Messengers went down the line of troops assigning us nearby buildings to camp in. Yes, to camp in. I have called Basenis Basor a city; but it was a city of ghosts. It was no thriving metropolis; the largest part of it was deserted, dirty, and unkempt. The brick structures had weathered as little as the temple near Tomar, but all was overlain with a thick layer of dust. I felt a chill as I considered the vanished millions who must have once lived, worked, and played in this place.

The building to which we were assigned was some slight distance into the city, perhaps a quarter of a mile or so from the main boulevard. It was pleasant enough, under the dust; it was a low building of only one story, with a pilastered facade and a balustraded deck on the roof. Due to the dust inside, we left the interior to the donkeys and took the roof for ourselves, pitching camp just as we had so often in the open country. Rain water was available from a cistern, which was fortunate as all of the exits were guarded. The Bandekun masters, still firmly in control, were taking no chances with the foreign wizards.

There had been little to say around the camp fire in the preceding days; we had all gotten dull and tired from constant travel. How that was changed our first evening in the Holy City! None of us had gazed upon its majestic expanse unmoved, and conversation flourished. I speculated on the vanished peoples who had once thronged the city, and conjectured what it must have been like in rapturous detail.

"I'm sorry, Leon," interjected Philpott. "I fear you must be mistaken."

"I beg your pardon?" I said, politely enough.

"I don't believe this house has ever been lived in. I don't believe it was intended to be lived in. There is no kitchen, to begin with."

"He's right, Leon," said Carbuncle. "I'd expect to see an oven of some kind, or at least a fireplace."

"Perhaps they built a fire in the center of the floor," I said.

"There's no sign of it; I'd expect to see soot on the ceiling at the very least."

"Well, perhaps it was a shop of some kind, or a meeting place."

Philpott wagged his head a trifle. "I suppose it could be, Leon. But where is the furniture? If anyone had lived here, or kept a business here, I'd expect to see some sign of it. When a population shrinks, the survivors don't tend to take all of their ancestors' things with them; where would they put them?"

At this point Mukden came up to the fire; he had been dis-cussing some small matter with the Bandekun masters. We put the question to him.

"Thed is right," he said. "No one has ever lived here. The Keepers are given bricks by Great Basenis; they believe they must build with them. Once upon a time bricks were brought to Tomar and other places, and temples built, but the Keepers do not like to leave the Holy City. Even at their greatest extent, the Keepers have always lived in the quarters surrouding the Temple. Some few of these houses have been used as camps by travelers to Basenis Basor, as we are doing; most have been undisturbed since the day the Keepers finished constructing them."

"How fast is the city expanding?" asked Carbuncle.

"It reached its present size long ago. Basenis brings forth many fewer bricks now than in past times; the Keepers use them to expand and enlarge the temple and the buildings near it. Some of them have walls many feet thick by now."

So I was reluctantly compelled to abandon my vision of a city of ghosts, for it was less lively even than that. A necropolis is at least filled with the once-living; Basenis Basor was a city of the never-born. I shuddered despite the warmth of the fire, watching the firelight flicker on the facades of the buildings around us, buildings alive for the first time with human touch, and human voice, and human warmth.

CHAPTER 37

⌁⁖⌁

Rumors of battle. ❧ The wizard's demands.
The architecture of Basenis Basor.

THE FOLLOWING morning we were awakened by the sound of shouts and many feet. The houses on all sides had been stripped of the only occupants they had ever known; the Zymurgian forces were marching on the heart of the Holy City. We had not been consulted, nor were we officially informed, but the inference was unavoidable. Only our guards and ourselves remained at the edge of the city.

There was an uneasy silence at breakfast. Asha and Mukden had assured us that there was to be no violence, but Asha and Mukden were confined with the rest of us. Would the Keepers choose to fight? If so, I failed to see how bloodshed could be avoided. Eventually they would return for us and escort us to the Temple; what would we see? Blood in the streets? Rooms of maimed and dying men? I shook off the scenes of carnage that crept upon me like a vision. The Zymurgians were not violent people, of that we could be sure. And yet, was the alternative better? I pictured masses of frightened men, women and children rounded up like cattle, and herded into small, insanitary chambers. I thought of the Foreign Office, and of my Royal Warrant, and groaned. Like as not I'd never be allowed to leave Angland again. Hundreds of men and women, starving, thirsty....

"Oh, dear," said Philpott, who was staring into space. I shook off my dark broodings, and focussed my attention upon him. "Oh, dear."

"What is it, young Thad?" Trust Carbuncle, I thought.

"Thomas, you don't suppose....they won't forget to keep Basenis well fed, will they?"

Now there was an unpleasant thought. Basenis stepping down from his place, howling, whining with hunger, loping through the streets of his city....Basenis, in his divine wrath, consuming the cream of Zymurgian manhood....

"I shouldn't think they would be so foolhardy, Thad. Still, if we hear barking I suppose we should go downstairs."

Carbuncle's calm voice was like a splash of cold water. Of course. While the rest of us were stewing and fretting over the the wrath of Basenis the God, Carbuncle was contemplating Basenis the beer-and-brick-making phantasm. Silently I cursed myself for having lost my scholarly objectivity. Then the possible fates of Basenis' Keepers rose again in my heart, and I cursed myself again.

It was a most unpleasant day. Carbuncle remained calm, quiet, and aloof, and I judged it best to leave him with his thoughts. For my part I was restless, pacing back and forth along the balustrade that encompassed the roof deck and pausing at intervals to stare at the temple in the distance, a brown hummock on the horizon. Philpott and Asha sat quietly talking in a corner; Hodgins, Cadbury, Fox and Mukden played innumerable games of whist. The monotony was broken only by lunch and dinner; the conversation at either meal was conducted largely in monosyllables. After dinner, tired of pacing, tired of waiting, worn out with worry (the curse of an active imagination) I settled down with my back to the balustrade and cradled my head in my hands. There was nothing to be done; the Keepers were dead or imprisoned, and I was imprisoned, and there was nothing to be done. I sat there for what seemed like (and almost certain was) hours on end, and was about to retire gratefully to bed when there was a stir in the chambers below. The donkeys were snorting and stamping, and then Norfolk (or Suffolk) stuck his head up out of the stairwell and called for Mukden. With an effort I remained in my seat; I knew from experience that I was not wanted, and that the messenger would not speak to Mukden in my presence. Shortly thereafter Mukden reappeared and called us all together. I nearly stumbled on rising; my muscles were stiff and sore.

Quickly and concisely, Mukden gave us the news. The city had been taken without bloodshed. The Keepers were fewer than expected, and had been rounded up quickly and without struggle. When at last they had been made to understand what was happening to them, they raised a great outcry, not on their own behalf but on behalf of their god. Basenis must be fed, Basenis must be constantly attended and cared for. Let them remain in captivity, so long as they could minister to Basenis. The Bandekuns, as I have observed before, were no fools, nor were the other Zymurgians who had joined with them. The plea was granted, and a small, rotating group of Keepers were allowed to carry out their duties. Under guard, of course; for the first time in memory, perhaps for the first time ever, non-Keepers were allowed into the Holy of Holies, the sanctum of Great Basenis himself. I shuddered, thinking of the terrible sanctum of Basenis' gullet, and the numbers of non-Keepers Basenis had consumed in his wrath.

The following day we would be escorted to the temple to work our magic.

"What," said Carbuncle, "Do they think it is that simple? They waltz us up to the temple, we mutter a few choice incantations, and all is well?"

"I don't know, Thomas," I said. "Is it that simple? You haven't told us, as I'm sure you'll recall." Carbuncle snorted, but otherwise ignored me.

"Mukden," he said, "when they come for us tomorrow I want you to explain to whomever is appropriate that the magic will likely take some weeks. Lord, man, the beastie has been waiting for thousands of years, give or take a day, it can surely wait another month. I need time to study it."

"You spoke before of an inelegant solution," I reminded him.

"So I did, and as I said before I am not yet ready to unveil it. I'm sorry, Leon, but it could be disastrous to our plans. Or to mine, at least." Carbuncle paused a moment, and then turned back to Mukden.

"Tell them that I will need a large room in which to work, preferably in the Temple itself, but not directly in the presence of Basenis. Also, I presume there is some store of as-yet-unused bricks; tell them to find it, but not to do anything with them. No, I don't need to see any; I've seen lots, thank you, and I am sure I can wangle a few more from Basenis himself." Mukden looked a trifle shocked at that last remark. "Finally, our party will need lodging somewhere in the immediate vicinity of the Temple."

"I will tell them, my friend. They may not listen; because of our failure with Nabili, Asha and I are not highly regarded."

"If they do not listen and obey," said Carbuncle, "then they have wasted their time, as we won't do a stitch for them. Tell them that if you must."

Our escort came for us in the morning, as we had been told, and waited impatiently as we finished our breakfast and broke camp. We were lead through the maze of streets to the boulevard, and so on down to the Temple district.

I may as well take this opportunity to record my first impressions of Basenis Basor. The boulevard ran in a straight line from the north edge of the city to the temple, and continued on the far side to the south edge. It and its east-west companion were the only proper streets. The rest of the city was a mass of individual buildings of all shapes and kinds, and of wildly varying sizes. No two buildings butted up against each other; rather, each was surrounded by a lane or alley of paved ground three to four yards in width. Thus, once away from the boulevards one could not walk in anything like a straight line for longer than the side of a single building. One could only try to meander around this edifice and beside that one, and so progress by stages in the desired direction.

The buildings changed as we drew closer to the Temple. I hesitate to say that the architectural style changed, for it was enormously variegated throughout the city. One saw low, bench-like buildings such as the one in which we had camped cheek-by-jowl with pyramids, towers, triumphal arches, massive oblong blocks of many stories, and other, less easily characterized constructions. Yet at the outskirts of Basenis Basor the buildings had a uniform simplicity. If they had pilasters, the pilasters were squared off and unornamented. If a roof or terrace had a balustrade, the uprights were mere stacks of single bricks, with a double stack at intervals of ten or twenty feet.

By the time we reached the halfway point, that pleasing if stark simplicity was gone, and ornamentation ran riot. I was reminded of the statue of Basenis in the temple near Tomar, with its carefully shaped and carved bricks. Similar work had been done here. Where before a wall might be lined with square pilasters, here the pilasters were larger, carefully rounded, and surrounded by many narrow pillars. Walls that would have been flat and featureless a few miles back became heavily carved. Towers that would have extended nobly into the air were covered with gingerbread and spires. I observed the trend with interest, and amused myself with speculating on the reasons behind it. Then I realized that the buildings were the same; the ornamentation had clearly been added at a later time, as the same simple lines were visible beneath it. I imagined a wave of ornamentation starting at the center and washing out, and finally spending itself before the extreme limits of the city had been reached. When we stopped for lunch, I was able to verify that the ornamentation was on the outside only. Clearly Philpott and Mukden were right; the buildings of Basenis Basor were works of devotion only, terribly over-decorated, but showing great care and love on the part of their makers. I wondered what delights awaited further in.

In the event, I was disappointed. The outer ring of buildings had been built to use up bricks simply, quickly, and efficiently; in the middle ring the builders had invested considerable effort (too much, in my view) to make them beautiful; in the inner ring the ornamentation was overlain by yet a third wave of construction, and here the effort, all too clearly, had been to consume bricks as quickly and as close to the Temple as possible. The buildings looked confined, overweight, like a man wearing too many sweaters. Where noble pillar-flanked entryways had once stood, one saw a facade of solid brick with one man-sized opening. Balustrades were filled in, and topped with row after row of additional brick. Windows were but slits. The lanes between the houses shrank to two to three yards from three to four, and the average height had increased. We began to feel as though we walked in the bottom of a canyon, heading ever deeper into the mountains. Before us, drawing ever nearer, at the end of the boulevard was the vast bulk of the Temple of Basenis.

In my mind I had been expecting, illogically enough, something like the Tomaren temple: a courtyard, and past that a hall open to the north. Basenis, ten feet high at the shoulder, would stand in the center of the hall, and his Keepers would rush back and forth, constantly feeding him and carrying away his products. The reality was staggering.

The Temple of Basenis rose like a mountain from the center of a great plaza, the only open space we had seen all day. It was at least two-hundred yards from the line of houses to the tem-

ple wall. The temple might once have been ornamented like the
buildings in the middle ring, but now it was more an amorphous
mass of brick rising steeply up from the plaza, here rising in crags
and obelisks, there flattening into terraces, and everywhere dot-
ted with windows. There were many doors at the base as well.

The temple's most notable feature was a broad staircase of
brick leading to a vast opening about halfway up the side. As
we approached, I soon realized that it was a staircase for giants;
the steps were easily five feet high and as many feet deep. The
opening to which they led was too high to see into, and also was
in shadow, but I readily guessed that Great Basenis stood within.

We were met at the base of the stair by representatives of
Bandeku and the other villages. I do not know what Mukden said
to them, but they bore their disappointment calmly enough. We
were taken to a place where we were given food and drink, and
then to a large dwelling which fronted on the plaza some distance
from the boulevard. I use the word "dwelling" with precision, as
it had clearly been inhabited in recent memory. We were assured
that the previous occupants were well and were being taken good
care of, guards were posted at the exits, and then we were left for
the night. Tomorrow Carbuncle's research would start. Tomorrow
we would set eyes on Great Basenis.

CHAPTER 38

་༔་

The wrath of Basenis. ?• Nabili's fate. ?• The fruits of research.

IT IS several hours before dawn. The Plaza of the Temple of Great Basenis is deserted, and the Temple looms in the darkness. There is a flash of movement between two houses, a lighter spot in the dimness, and then a figure creeps into the square. It is gaunt, and it staggers slightly as it crosses the open space. It looks around itself carefully, keeping nearly still, and then scuttles many yards before stopping and looking again. It is in rags. It carries a sack clutched to its breast.

After many brief halts it reaches the base of the gigantic stairway that leads to Basenis' den in the heart of the Temple. The top of the first step is level with the figure's head. The doorways to either side promise an easier ascent to Basenis' lair, but much greater risk of detection; the figure ignores them. It throws the sack onto the step, and puts its hands on the edge. After a weary time, the figure pulls itself up, getting first one knee and then its entire body onto the step. It lays there, panting, clutching the sack. And then it rises, and throws the sack onto the second step.

Dawn finds it crouched, nearly exhausted, on the next to last step. One more effort, and only a low parapet will separate it from its goal. There is not much time; already the footsteps of the Keepers can be heard within. It is time for Great Basenis to greet the dawn and be presented with the morning's offerings. The figure struggles up the last step, and grabs its sack. After a long time it creeps to the parapet and peers over. Its heart nearly stops as Basenis howls.

Great Basenis stands twenty yards away on a floor of polished stone. The image in the Tomaren temple is but a dim reflection of His glory. Great Basenis, jet black, towers over the Keepers who walk slowly past Him. Each Keeper carries a basket of leaves and twigs and straw, and empties it quickly into a manger of brick which stands before the god. Basenis' blind, staring eyes do not move as His massive head descends and removes a mouthful from the manger. His head rises as His great jaws grind the fodder to bits; the figure can hear the crunch and the rasp. Then, after a time, His head descends again, slowly and inevitably.

The hall is richly carved and decorated, but the figure has eyes only for the god. Basenis straddles a pool cut in the stone of the floor; the pool collects the *Aqua Dei*, the Water of God, and channels carry the divine fluid away to other chambers. A heap of brown bricks litters the floor behind Basenis; as the Keepers leave they stop and fill their baskets with as many bricks as they can carry.

The figure watches, and bides its time. The line of Keepers is coming to an end. Basenis is on a near-starvation diet, for there is but little food. The figure opens the mouth of its sack and removes the contents. When the last Keeper is refilling his basket, the figure rises, and steps over the parapet. It lurches quickly across the yards of brick and then the yards of stone, its hands filled with brown leaves and withered flowers. It climbs into the nearly empty manger, hands held high over its head, face lifted up in worship, an ecstatic smile on its lips. Basenis' head slowly descends, and His jaws close on the figure. As the Keepers watch in horror, the head rises and the jaws grind on and on....

A shout of terror—my own—split the night as I sat bolt upright on my cot. It had been five days since we had arrived in the Holy City. Thanks to Nabili, it had been two days since I had been able to sleep without nightmares. I do not know how Nabili entered that hall where mighty Basenis broods; his ordeal on the massive stair is the product of my over-eager imagination. The rest of his fate is unquestioned. He had certainly approached Basenis, leaves and flowers in hand, and climbed into the manger as I have described. I was grateful, sitting there on my cot, to reflect that the god had not, in fact, devoured his worshipper. That would have been too much to bear. Not that Nabili had survived his foolishness, not by any means. The mighty jaws had closed over him and raised him high—and then, with a flip of the neck, Basenis cast him aside. He struck the wall of the chamber with great force, and was killed instantly. I remembered vividly the sight of his crumpled body lying at the base of the wall, with dead flowers scattered round and about.

Apparently Nabili had arrived in Basenis Basor several days before we had. After the Bandekuns had sent out their messengers he began to find every door closed to him in town and village. I don't know whether the Holy City had been his ultimate goal all along, though I consider it likely. In any event, he had sought out the Keepers, and tried to warn them of the evil wizards from the Lands Below. He had begged to enter the service of Basenis with them. They responded to his overtures with disdain and contempt, as a few moments of thought would have predicted, and cast him out. He had hovered about the outskirts of the settled area in the days since, growing ever thinner; there is little food in Basenis Basor, and no Keeper would aid him. At last, desperate, he had sought the help of his god, and his offering was rejected. Carbuncle and I were in Carbuncle's workroom in the Temple, but a short distance from Basenis' den, when we heard the tumult and came and saw Nabili's body. He had proved to be my enemy, yet I would not have wished that end upon him. Nevertheless it was fitting: he died as he had lived, in misguided devotion.

Paradoxically, Nabili's death was of great benefit to us, for it convinced the Bandekuns that Basenis' wrath was unlikely to be roused against them. Nabili had trespassed and had not been devoured, but merely cast aside; his subsequent demise was seen as incidental, an indication of divine unconcern with Nabili's fate. And surely if Basenis was angry, others would have been taken and Nabili, his worshipper, spared? Not that the expedition was just a Bandekun show any longer. On our arrival in the Holy City, messages had been sent to the towns to the south and east and west, calling on them to send their representatives to Basenis Basor. These envoys were trailing into the city day by day, and the Zymurgian force was now led by some kind of inter-town council. I am unclear on the details, as I was not a member, nor was I generally invited to take part in the council's deliberations. The important thing is that while the council still regarded us with suspicion, they were no longer frightened by our presence. Moreover, having seen the eagerness and industry with which Carbuncle threw himself into his work, they were the less worried that we might skip off, leaving Basenis unmuzzled. This new-found confidence manifested itself in greater freedom for the rest of us, freedom which I immediately used to survey the city as best I could. Carbuncle was dead set against my using the Hansen's geometer without his help, and as his time was fully occupied we were compelled to make do with older methods. I prevailed upon my friend to take one reading, that being the location of our hostel, and with that as our benchmark we did well enough.

It is well that I was able to fill my time with surveying, as it was a long, tedious period we spent in the Holy City. Carbuncle was the only one with much to do, and though he often kept Hodgins or Cadbury or Mukden or all three on the go, finding things out and fetching and carrying, time hung quite heavily on our hands. The only diversion was the evening meal, when Carbuncle would share with us the discoveries of the day.

He began his investigations, to my surprise, not with Basenis himself, but with his bricks. He explained that it was possibly to determine quite a lot about a manufacturing phantasm by examining its products. We accepted his explanation at the time, little knowing what else he had in mind. And indeed, there were several puzzling aspects to Basenis' bricks. First, how had previous generations of Keepers managed to carve them? Hodgins had tried, in the inimitable tradition of travelers everywhere, to carve his initials into the wall of the house in which we stayed our first night in the Holy City, and had been entirely unable so much as to make a scratch. Second, how did they bind them together? In all the city there was no trace of mortar; in any given building the bricks looked as though they had simply been stacked in place. And yet they were immovable; all of our efforts had failed to dislodge even a single one. There proved to be but one answer to these two questions.

Carbuncle brought home several unused bricks and put them on the table after the meal was cleared away. (I should say in passing that the Zymurgians took excellent care of us, even while treating us somewhat as pariahs; the food was of necessity plain, but they did not stint on the quantity or on the service.)

"I've found out how they managed to carve these creatures," he announced. "Observe!" And he took up a carving knife, an ivory-handled affair that had come all the way from Eton's department store by cart, ship, and donkeyback, and examined its edge keenly. We watched with breathless anticipation, looking from the knife to the brick and and back again. He tested the edge with his thumb. Then, taking a whetstone from his pocket, he proceeded to sharpen it carefully. After several minutes he was satisfied, and put the whetstone back in his pocket. Eyes twinkling, he looked around at us. "Would you mind terribly giving me a hand, Leon?" he asked. I hastened to assure him that I would not. "Very good. Would you take this carving knife and put it away? We won't be needing it tonight, but that blunt edge was distressing me." Somewhat nonplussed, I did as he asked, and hurried back to the table. When I returned, he picked up a butter knife, also from Eton's, and dangled it between two fingers about three feet over one of the bricks. "Are you ready?" he asked. We hastened to assure him that we were. "Very well," he said, and dropped the butter knife. The force of the drop drove the dull blade at least an inch into the brick.

"The bricks are really quite soft before they've been cured," he said. "They carve them first, and then set them in place. Once they have been cured, they are as we have seen them."

"And how do they cure them?" asked Fox, who had been watching with great interest.

"The same way they stick them together. Shall I show you?"

"Oh, indeed," said Fox, to be echoed by the rest of us.

"Very well. Leon, could you fetch me a glass of water?"

I fear I grumbled rather loudly as I fetched it. Carbuncle will cater to his sense of drama at times like these, and I have learned that it doesn't pay to balk him.

"Here's your drink," I said gruffly as I handed the earthenware mug to him. "Now can we get on with this?"

"Oh, the water isn't for me, Leon. It's for the bricks." He took two of the bricks, removing the butter knife from one of them, and placed them side by side in front of him. Then, holding the mug carefully, he poured a few tablespoons of water on the top of each, rubbing it around with a finger. When the water was distributed evenly, he picked up one of the bricks, turned it over so that the wet side was on the bottom, and placed it on the other brick. He squared them up neatly, poured more water over the pair of them, turned the pair over, and poured the last of the water on the underside. "There you go," he said. "What Basenis has joined together, no man shall put asunder. When they dry, which won't be long given the air here, they will be fully cured. More than that, they will be permanently attached."

"Really," said Hodgins. "Hand them over here, will you? And one of the uncured ones, too." Taking the butter knife, he tried to dent the wet surface of the bricks, and failed. Then he turned to the uncured brick, which by comparison offered little or no resistance. Using the butter knife, he had soon whittled a little statue of Basenis himself. I had another mug of water ready, unasked, and how some of my colleagues would laugh to see me fetching water for a common seaman! Trimming another block into a base for the statuette was the matter of but a few more minutes; then Hodgins carefully moistened the statuette's paws and the top of the base, and set the one on the other. Then he carefully emptied the rest of the water over the pair, making sure that every surface got wet, and set the statue and its base down on the table.

"Very good, Hodgins, very good indeed," said Carbuncle, examining the statuette carefully. "Do you mind if I pick it up?" Hodgins perforce gave his assent, and Carbuncle studied it carefully. "Now watch," he said. And before Hodgins had time to react, Carbuncle hurled the statuette against the wall with all of his might. So far from shattering, it bounced off the wall and ricocheted into Carbuncle's left shin with a loud thump. Hodgins dove for his creation, swearing mightily, and recovered it from under the table. It was, of course, unharmed, though I could not say the same for Carbuncle's shin.

"What did you go and do that for?" said Hodgins, looking the statuette over for any signs of damage.

"To demonstrate," said Carbuncle, between gasps, "the material's great...durability." He had sat down abruptly and was holding his shin with both hands. "Once it's set...and cured.... there's no...shifting it."

Once he had regained his composure, Carbuncle laid out for us his plan of attack.

"The first point, of course, is whether or not the wee beastie can be shut off," he began.

"You said you had a way of doing that," I said. "Are you as mistaken about that as you are about its size? It must be at least twenty-five feet high at the shoulder."

"I have a way of destroying the beastie, which is not the same thing. Once destroyed, it is gone forever." He looked at me from under raised brows. "That would be a great loss. If I can shut it off, though, I can probably turn it on again later. If so, we can satisfy our hosts, and preserve the beastie for study."

"Do you think it likely?" asked Fox, leaning forward.

"Not at all likely. Its builders went to great efforts to make sure it would never go hungry, which implies that if it ever stopped doing what it does it would be difficult or impossible to start it again. Still, I might be mistaken."

Fox pursed his lips, and waved at Carbuncle to go on.

"Next, if it can't be shut off, can it at least be stopped in a non-destructive way? I might at least be able to study it, even if it no longer works." We all nodded.

"Finally," Carbuncle said, "can I duplicate it."

"Duplicate it!" exclaimed Hodgins. "Isn't one of the creatures enough? Wouldn't two of them get hungry twice as fast?"

"Oh, I don't mean on the same scale. Can I build a smaller phantasm that does the same thing Basenis does? If I can build one, I can build another, and it won't matter what happens to our canine friend. Just think about having your own little Basenis about the house. Beer on tap all year long, for price of yard clippings, hey?" Carbuncle's eyes were sparkling. "And think of the commercial possibilities!"

I glanced at Fox. It was clear that he was doing just that.

"Of course," Carbuncle mused, "keeping it fed might be a chore; can't have it roaming the neighborhood devouring curates and small children, can we? Perhaps it could be made to hunt mice...."

"And what is the likelihood of duplicating the phantasm?" Fox again.

"Oh, very likely, very likely. What one phantast can build, another can duplicate; or at least I can. I should be quite sanguine, if I thought I could have whatever time I need."

"And what if our hosts don't give you enough time?"

"I suppose I'll have to tell them how to destroy Basenis anyway."

CHAPTER 39

ᴗᴗ

The council grows impatient. ❧ Muzzling an idol.
Of warrants and wine-chillers.

IN THE event, Carbuncle had three weeks before the council grew restless. We passed the time in various ways. I did my surveying, as I have already related; Philpott was much with Asha and Mukden; Fox, to my surprise, spent considerable time talking with our guards, using Cadbury as an intermediary. The guards soon voted the two of them capital fellows, and chatted merrily with them while casting stony glances at the rest of us. Hodgins, of course, was busy with Carbuncle in the Temple.

By the 12th of Aughtnever, Carbuncle had progressed considerably. He had discovered no means of shutting Basenis off gracefully, nor indeed any means of stopping Basenis short of the destructive method he still refused to discuss with us. Indeed, he had cut off that line of research altogether, and was concentrating his efforts on duplicating Basenis' capabilities.

"I'm quite close to completing the little pup," he said. We were seated at the dining table, having just finished yet another plain meal. "Except for one little detail," he was adding, when one of our guards hailed Mukden.

"The council," he said, simply, and was off. He returned in a surprisingly short time. "You are summoned," he said to Carbuncle and I. "I told them that only you could answer their questions." He grinned at Philpott. "I told them that I would not dare to speak for such powerful wizards in this matter."

"They want to know what's taking so long, eh?" I asked.

"Indeed, my friend. You are the famous wizards from the Lands Below."

"Just Carbuncle and I?"

Mukden pondered that. "They did not say."

"Fine, that's fine. We'll all go." His face showed concern. "I'm sure everyone here is as tired of these four walls as I am. It's about time they should condescend to speak to us." With a shrug, then, Mukden lead us from the room.

The council met in a fine big house on the east side of the temple plaza, comfortably out of sight of the stair leading to Basenis' den. As we walked I asked Carbuncle what he intended to say.

"I'll tell them how to stop Basenis forever, of course. It's too bad, but there it is." Fox was walking on Carbuncle's other side; I noticed that he was chewing his lower lip. Several times he looked about to speak, but we reached the council chambers before he made up his mind to it.

"Council chambers" is a rather grandiose term, I fear. One pictures the Hall of the Legates in Lyricum Town, or perhaps Vulgar House in Pelham: dark wood, rich tapestries, the whole brightly lit by chandeliers and lamps in wall sconces; the councillors wearing fine satins and velvets, and gold chains of office. The council chamber in Basenis Basor was simply a large room with a high ceiling, filled with a diverse collection of chairs, tables, and Zymurgians. Some few had the golden embroidery of mastery; the rest were clad simply in white. There was no ceremony. We were led before the group, and one of their number, a rotund master, stood up and spoke shortly.

"Basenis still feeds. Why is this?" translated Mukden.

"Because you have not prevented him," replied Carbuncle. When his words were translated, a susurrus of indignant commentary filled the room. The speaker was forced to rap on a table several times to restore order.

"Explain yourself. Do you wish to anger Basenis? Do you wish more of our homes and folk to be devoured? When Basenis hungers, people die."

"Yet you have the power to starve Basenis, while yet preserving your homes."

The councillors stared at him. The speaker's upper lip curled, and he waved a hand at our guards, stopping in mid-gesture as Carbuncle spoke again.

"Send for bricks and fresh water."

The speaker was raising his hand again, when Carbuncle spoke in a tone he usually reserves for underclassmen. "Send for bricks and fresh water!"

The speaker rolled his eyes, and gave a few orders. Slumping into his chair, he then ignored us until those he had sent returned with a jug of water and several baskets of bricks. Carbuncle com-

mandeered a table, and pulling a knife from his pocket he quickly constructed a crude model of the temple. It came complete with
stairs and Basenis' den. All eyes were upon him as he pulled
Hodgins' carving out of his coat pocket and placed it within the
model. He had been curing the bricks carefully with water as he
placed them, so that when he was done the model was solid as
rock. The speaker looked at him quizzically.

"And so?" translated Mukden.

Carbuncle smiled. Taking the few remaining bricks, he
quickly covered over the mouth of Basenis' den leaving not the
slightest opening. He finished by pouring the last drops of water
over the model.

"What happens when Basenis grows hungry?" he asked.

The assembled company stared at him in silence, and then
at the model. I believe it was Mukden who first began to laugh;
for myself, I felt quite the fool. Of course it was obvious. The one
thing Basenis would never eat was his own bricks, nor did he ever
molest the Keepers in their brick homes. If brick was sufficient to
keep him out, surely it was enough to keep him in. "Show off," I
muttered under my breath.

After that the councillors were considerably more cheerful,
and the speaker himself unbent enough to wish us a good night as
we were lead from the room. I gathered that preparations for the
work would begin the very next day.

Fox sought me out after we had returned to our dwelling. He
looked worried.

"Professor Thintwhistle, may I ask you a few questions? Con-
cerning your Royal warrant." Eyebrows raised, I gave my assent.

"Suppose your friend succeeds in duplicating Basenis, and
brings the duplicate to market. The profits would clearly be the
fruit of this expedition. Who is entitled to the money?"

"We are, of course, as leaders of the expedition.
Carbuncle, Philpott, and myself. His Majesty wishes to encour-
age exploration."

"The three of you? What about the Earl of Luton? Didn't he
put up the funds?"

"Indeed he did, but as a gift to the University. I suppose Philpott might give the old fellow a hand, given his financial difficulties...speaking of which, why is the earl in financial difficulties?

The timing seems odd, him having just donated so much money for the expedition." I looked questioningly at young Frederick. Turn about is, after all, fair play.

"Bad luck. He was invested heavily in Bundi trading shares. The company involved—not mine, I am glad to say—lost several ships recently, and share prices plummeted. As he had borrowed heavily from our bank with the shares as collateral we felt it necessary to call the loan." He paused. "If not the earl, what about the University?"

"The University benefits by the prestige of claiming such distinguished explorers for its own, and by hope of rich bequests from the explorers' estates. No, if Carbuncle succeeds it is the three of us who will profit."

"Does that also apply to Carbuncle's wine chiller?"

"Certainly not. It is true, he produced it while in transit on the *Sea-Spaniel*, but it was all his own work; he could have done it just as well at home. Any profit he realizes from it will be his own."

Fox nodded sagely, rising to his feet. "Thank you, Dr. Thintwhistle. You have been of great service to me."

After he had left, I did a little nodding myself. No doubt he had hoped to seize Carbuncle's duplicate along with the Sea-*Spaniel* when we left Seros. I was quite disappointed in him for cherishing such a thought, and retired with a heavy heart.

When I came down to breakfast, Fox was gone. I didn't notice his absence right off, any more than one notices when a familiar piece of furniture is removed; still, one feels a strangeness, and casts about for an explanation. The furniture in our dining area was minimal, consisting of a table and several benches, all of which were present. Was someone missing? It seemed clear that someone must be, yet I could not think who it was. I was finally forced to review our journeys in my head, skipping from high point to high point, until I had the answer. Fox was gone, and Cadbury too. They weren't at the table, and I knew they weren't in the bedroom upstairs, for I had been the last to rise.

"Where," I asked the room in general, "have Fox and Cadbury gone off to?"

"We don't know for sure." Philpott broke off his conversation with Asha long enough to answer me. "They arose shortly after

I did, and went out to chat with our guards. When next I looked, they were gone."

"How long ago was that?" I asked only out of idle curiosity. I thought it unlikely that Frederick would get into serious trouble, which shows that intuition has serious flaws. Or not, depending on your point of view.

"Several hours," said Philpott.

"I apologize for not waking you, Leon," said Carbuncle. "There seemed no point. Either they are escorted, and thus beyond our control, or they are on their own, in which case I'm sure they will be returned to us shortly."

As I could not but agree, I applied myself to my porridge, and to the view outside our window. It was a fascinating sight. As I have already related, our quarters were in a building that fronted on the plaza, and faced Basenis' den, high on the side of the temple. As I watched, workmen were setting up a wooden framework over the den's opening; massive bales of fabric lay on the upper steps of Basenis' stairway.

"To keep the rain off, do you think, Thomas?" I said, gesturing across the way with my mug of fruit juice. He nodded sagely.

"It is a reasonable assumption. I suppose they must shroud each of these buildings before working on it, or the first rain would ruin all of the unused bricks."

I nodded in response, and continued to stare moodily at the temple. Some half-an-hour later I sat up straight. In addition to the large framework over the den opening, a narrower framework sprouted out on both sides. It ran horizontally to east and west, ultimately turning south around the temple at both ends.

"Thomas? It appears as if they are building their tent all of the way around the temple. Why would they do that?"

"Structural strength, mostly. Once those bricks have cured completely, you can't get new bricks to stick to them anymore. If they covered over just the opening, Basenis could push the cover away without any great difficulty. Instead, they will lay a band of brick from the cover all of the way around the temple and back to the cover again on the other side. It isn't terribly elegant, but it will work."

"Hmm. Is all that work the reason you're still here, rather than at your workshop?"

"Yes, they didn't want me underfoot. Though it really doesn't matter; my scale model is very nearly done. It just needs to be activated, and believe me, there is no hurry. I rather think our hosts would tear me to bits if I gave them another Basenis to feed." Thomas said this in a more than usually sardonic tone.

At that point our conversation was interrupted by the return of the prodigal writ-server, though indeed Frederick and Cadbury looked anything but repentant.

"Good morning, Professor Thintwhistle! A fine day, isn't it?" Fox was distressingly cheerful for such an early hour. "I bet the view is even nicer from the roof. Thaddeus, Asha, would any of you care to join me?"

I was not disposed to move, nor was Carbuncle, but the rest of our party traipsed up the stairs to the roof deck, leaving the two of us alone.

"I'm disappointed in young Frederick, Thomas," I began, and described Frederick's questions about Carbuncle's model. "I am sure he meant to seize it along with the *Spaniel* on our way home to Angland. Our warrant prevents him, fortunately, but it is still a despicable act. How I had hoped this expedition would bring out the mythogeographer in him!" Carbuncle made noncommittal noises as I expanded on my theses, being far too well-bred to say "I told you so." These pleasant ruminations were eventually disturbed by Frederick himself, who descended alone down the stairs and took a seat by the two of us.

"Professor Carbuncle, did I just hear you say that your working model is...well, working?" He looked lighthearted but quite earnest at the same time.

"In theory, only. The actual device still needs to be activated." Frederick waved that away.

"And once activated, it will produce beer and bricks in proportion to the amount of vegetable matter and water dumped into it?"

"So far as I can tell, that is so."

"In fact, if you were to construct enough of them, every house in all of Angland could have its own, isn't that right?"

"In theory, again, yes, I suppose they could."

"And provided they were well-cared for, they would never wear out?"

"The prototype hasn't, given some thousands of years."

"Excellent." Frederick looked from Carbuncle to me and back again, looking us both squarely in the eye, as he said, "Gentlemen, I have a business proposition for you."

CHAPTER 40

꒦꒷

Frederick makes us a proposition. ꝥ *"Gooneybah!"*
We leave the Land Above. ꝥ *A writ-server in Lyricum.*

"I REALIZE IT is vulgar to discuss business at the breakfast table; I beg your forgiveness." Young Frederick paused. "You are probably unaware, Professor Carbuncle, that 'Fox' is not my real name." Carbuncle raised one eyebrow. "My parents named me Frederick Forsythe." Carbuncle raised the other eyebrow. "I am also an employee of my father's company, the Mercantile Bank of Pelham and Bundyal."

"How astonishing," said Carbuncle dryly.

"I see," said Frederick, looking reproachfully at me.

"I had to tell someone, Frederick. And besides, I had spoken of you to Thomas when you were a student of mine."

"No matter. Gentlemen, under the terms of your warrants, you and Dr. Philpott are entitled to any profits made from the sale of Basenis phantasms. I would like to buy your working model. In addition, I'd like you to agree not to build any more."

"What?" I exclaimed. "How impertinent he is, Thomas. Why should we agree to any such thing?"

Carbuncle looked uncomfortable, as I could well understand. His models are his pets. "I suppose, having bought my model, you intend to pay others to duplicate it?"

"On the contrary." Fox—nay, Forsythe—smiled brightly at the two of us. "I wish to guarantee that no such phantasm ever leaves Zymurgia."

"And you'll pay us to ensure this? What ever for?" I confess, I was mystified.

At that, Forsythe put his hands flat on the table and leaned forward.

"Dr. Thintwhistle, Professor Carbuncle, you see before you the head of the newly-formed Zymurgian Trading Company. I have just come to an agreement with the Zymurgian council regarding the future dispersal of the Waters of Basenis. I intend to disperse them farther and in greater quantities than they have ever been dispersed before."

"What future dispersal? Basenis is going to be starved to death," I observed sourly.

"I think you will find that that is not to be the case. Entombed, yes; they won't take the risk of letting him run loose. Yet he is quite a large deity, and man-sized doorways are quite sufficient to provide for his wants."

Carbuncle was nodding. "So you've persuaded them to let you disperse the waters throughout all the Lands Below, is that it? What do they get in return?"

"Access to a variety of trade goods from Angland and other countries. I expect that tools and other household phantasms will be especially popular."

Carbuncle grunted in response. "So, where does my model come into it?"

"I judge that the market for the Waters of Basenis is quite large," replied Forsythe seriously. "Yet suppose each of those potential customers could produce his own beer at a cost of a few clippings? Every countryman would be a potential competitor. I can sell one man a pint of Zymurgian beer over and over, but I can sell him his own brewery only once. No, sir, I would rather see your model of Basenis properly disposed of."

"You are quite aware, are you, that my model has never been activated?" asked Carbuncle, looking Forsythe directly in the eye.

"More than that, I am content that it should remain so."

"And how do you propose to make this worth our while?" I asked. "Bear in mind that you must satisfy Philpott as well. We won't make any agreement that excludes him."

"I have already come to an agreement with Dr. Philpott. As for the two of you, I would like to make you shareholders in the new company. You would each receive five percent holdings."

"Only five percent?"

"Now, Leon, five percent seems more than fair to me," said Carbuncle. I looked at him in some surprise. "After all, we would not be involved in the day-to-day operations of the company, nor are we putting up any capital. In essence, we are being paid not to cause trouble. If the company succeeds, and how can it not with such a fine product and such an able manager, it must necessarily make us rich. I think we should accept."

"You do?" I sat back and looked at him blankly. "Frederick, what arrangements did you make with Philpott?"

"I agreed to clear his father's debts. In addition, Dr. Philpott is joining the company. He will be heading our offices in Tomar."

"Philpott is staying in Zymurgia? But why?"

"Perhaps you had better ask him that question yourself," replied Forsythe. "Now, have we a deal?" I nodded helplessly, and in a few minutes I had signed my name to a document naming me the owner of a one-twentieth share of the Zymurgian Trading Company.

After the events of that morning, there was no further need to stay in Basenis Basor. The council was eager for Frederick to return to the Lands Below and get the trade going, though not, I think, as eager as he was to begin it. By signing his name, Carbuncle had agreed not to pursue his investigations into Basenis' nature any further, and thus had no desire to remain; and I need hardly say that the rest of us had tired of the Holy City weeks earlier. Nor had the council any reason to detain us, once Carbuncle had divulged his scheme for muzzling Basenis permanently. On the contrary, they were glad to see us depart, with our donkeys and our dog and our odd, wizardly ways. Within twenty-four hours we were plodding north along the main boulevard toward the edge of the city.

To our mixed joy and sorrow, Mukden remained behind. The prestige of the Masters of Tomar, which had fallen so low over the matter of Nabili as to prevent Mukden and Asha from having any place in the new council, was greatly restored. It was young Frederick's doing; in his deal with the council he demanded that Tomar would remain the gateway to the Lands Below, and that all trade would pass through the Tomarens' hands. In all fairness, I must say that I was on the whole pleased with Frederick, however repellent I might find his grasping nature. He had treated Philpott, Carbuncle, and myself quite fairly, and had also guaranteed that Tomar, the home of his friends, would take its rightful place among the towns of Zymurgia. He might easily have accomplished his desires without considering us at all.

I never asked Philpott why he was staying in Zymurgia, as there was no need. I had gone immediately in search of him, of course, to make enquiries, but when I found him sitting on a bench on the roof, hand-in-hand with Asha, I tabled my queries indefinitely. A young man and and a young woman thrown constantly together; the man handsome, virile, exotic; the woman beautiful, intelligent, adventurous; how could love, however ill-advised, fail to blossom between them? So I had asked myself in Tomar, when indeed the seeds of love had not yet sprouted. Philpott had disavowed any tender feelings, and I had therefore assumed that no such feelings would develop. Evidently the road and our enforced sojourn in Basenis Basor had been more fertile ground for romance. As much a victim of my preconceptions as ever, I had failed to see what was happening even while observing it daily. Ah, well.

In due course we arrived in Tomar, after a journey remarkably untarnished by snakes, toads, or bears in the night. There was a festival in honor of our return, of course, two solid days of feasting in the town square punctuated by laughter and many cries of "Gooneybah! Gooneybah!" The children of Tomar, at least, would remember the wizards from the Lands Below with fondness. And then, true to my resolution, we took the donkeys on down the trail to the Lake of Saco. On the thirty-first of Aughtnever we slept in our own cabins aboard the *Sea-Spaniel* for the first time in fully three months. I confess I had approached the lake in some trepidation, for fear that another writ-server had made it so far up the river and claimed the *Spaniel*. Nor am I certain that none tried, but if writ-servers there were during our absence I never heard of it from Captain Halvorsen or his crew. Our arrival was inevitably followed by another day of feasting to celebrate Cadbury's return home.

I had few regrets in leaving the Land Above; if I had failed to chart the course of the mighty Aram to its headwaters in Zymurgia, that was merely because I had charted other parts of the country. Indeed, I am not certain whether I could have charted the river in any event; by all Zymurgian accounts, the Upper Aram is a swift, shallow, rocky stream, unsuited for any kind of river transport, and the banks of the Aram are no more easily passable, as it lies in a gorge as often as not. I had taken many measurements which might serve to illustrate the actions of the Law of Consensus; and most importantly we had travelled further into Zymurgia than perhaps any outsiders before us had ever done. It was enough to be going on with. Moreover Dean Nuftison was expecting us in time for the Winter Term. Despite our potential future wealth, Carbuncle and I had no desire to distress the good dean unduly. Taken all-in-all, it was time to go home. In the early days of the month of Upover we set forth down the mighty Aram for the open sea.

Sensitive to the possibility that writs for the *Spaniel's* seizure might still be in circulation, we bypassed Phillipi in the night. Young Frederick had promised to deal with any such that we encountered; nevertheless, we wished to keep the number of confrontations to a minimum. From Lyricum Town Frederick could send a communique to the bank headquarters in Pelham, thus ensuring that we would make a peaceful landfall in England. To Lyricum Town we proceeded with all dispatch, therefore, arriving there on the 20th of Upover. It was a delightful passage, as indeed are all sea-voyages in good weather, and it was enlivened by the presence of Philpott's bride-to-be. Like her namesake of old, Asha had stoutly refused to remain at home while her man travelled afar in the Lands Below. I do not believe Philpott made more than a token resistance; far from it, he was eager to show Asha his home country, and to introduce her to his father.

From this angle, a stopover in Lyricum was almost a necessity. Asha's usual garments, while modest and attractive, would be considered most unseemly in Pelham even if the weather permitted their use. During the days we spent in Lyricum Town, the couple were able to procure fine gowns and other garments such as fashionable Anglish ladies wear; indeed, as the fashion in Pelham always trails the fashion in Lyricum, Asha would be rather better dressed than any Anglishwoman who dared to snub her or condescend to her on account of her skin.

While waiting for the Lyrican tailors to complete their work, Asha, Philpott, and I were able to attend a performance of Rotini's masterpiece the *Gelato*, the triumphant conclusion of the *Rigatoni Cycle*. (Hodgins was allowed to join us, on his promise that he would not discuss the piece with anyone until we returned to the *Spaniel*.) Asha, I may say, was as shocked by certain members of the audience as Philpott had been. In due course the gowns were finished, and Frederick having received a positive response to his communique we made ready to leave.

A most droll scene was enacted on the quay shortly before our departure. A grimy, unshaven fellow, stinking of wine, presented himself at the gangplank and brandished a greasy bit of paper. He demanded to see Captain Halvorsen just as Frederick returned, communique in hand.

"And what is that, my good man?" inquired Frederick.

"It's a writ of seizure, and I'm seizing this here vessel."

"Are you? May I inspect it, please?" Grudgingly, the grubby fellow handed it over. "Hmm, yes, just as I thought," said Frederick, and methodically began to tear the writ into shreds.

"Here, give it back, that's illegal, is what it is, give it back!" shouted the server in a frenzy. Only the quick action of the two sailors guarding the gangplank prevented him from assaulting Frederick bodily.

"Do you know who I am?" asked Frederick.

"A lawbreaker, is what you are," muttered the server.

"In point of fact I am not. In point of fact, I represent the creditor on whose behalf the writ I am now casting to the winds was written. The creditor is now satisfied, and no longer requires seizure of this vessel, as this communique makes quite clear. Good day!" And Frederick tipped his hat, and went aboard. The server made as if to follow, but soon found himself in the water instead, courtesy of the two sailors. All in all, it was rather hard luck on the writ-server; he had somehow managed to sustain himself in Lyricum Town, not an inexpensive venue, for some months, waiting for the *Sea-Spaniel's* return, only to find that his patience had been wasted. And though he was badly in need of washing, the waters of Lyricum Harbor are not well suited to that procedure.

CHAPTER 41

A spring afternoon in Glastonbury.

SEVERAL MONTHS after our return to Angland I joined Carbuncle for afternoon tea in his university lodgings. A yellow sun was vanishing into the west, and a crackling fire exactly complemented the cold beauty of spring outside Carbuncle's windows. It had been a pleasantly relaxing interval, students and lectures to the side. Asha of Tomar was now Mrs. Philpott, after a grand ceremony in Glastonbury Cathedral; the lovers had honeymooned in Angland and then returned to Zymurgia laden down with gifts and household items. They had departed in mid-Jannissary, on the self-same *Sea-Spaniel* which the Zymurgian Trading Company had purchased from the Earl of Luton. Frederick had gone with them in his capacity as president of the new firm, eager to see the ever-wider dispersal of Basenis' waters begin as soon as possible. I induced Hodgins to leave his sea-going life and become my secretary; his upbringing and his experiences made him perfect for the job. In any event, Hodgins would not have willingly parted with Bruno, and as I had no intention of parting with Bruno myself (he is at my feet as I pen these lines) some compromise was necessary.

And so Carbuncle and I had settled back into our usual routine of lectures, study, and alternately baiting and placating Dean Nuftison, until the spring afternoon of which I write, when our minds were drawn back to Zymurgia by the unexpected arrival of several packing crates. With the porter's aid we pried the lids off and investigated, scattering sawdust on Carbuncle's Bundi rug in the process. The crates proved to contain a note from Frederick Forsythe, and several dozen bottles of Zymurgian beer. The note read as follows:

> *10 Larch 681*
> *Tomar, Zymurgia*

My dear professors Thintwhistle and Carbuncle,

  As you will see by the contents of these crates, the waters of Basenis are being dispersed in earnest. These are the very first bottles of Basen Ale to reach Angland; I send them in thanks for your teaching, and for your aid this past summer and fall. The Zymurgian Trading Company would not exist without you.

  I had hoped to deliver them in person; as I cannot I will drink your health here with Thaddeus, and hope you will drink ours in due time.

> *Sincerely,*
> *Frederick Forsythe*

Carbuncle called for clean mugs, and soon we were sampling the beer which would, no doubt, sweep the world. It was as good as I remembered. In between sips I studied the label. It featured the words "Basen Ale" over a reasonable line drawing of Great Basenis himself, absent, I noticed, the system of ponds and troughs by means of which the beer was collected. Only to be expected, I supposed.

"Rather decent of young Frederick, don't you think?" said Carbuncle.

"Indeed. Though I still admit to some disappointment. It is unbecoming of me to criticize a man who will likely make me wealthy, but I still think he would have made an excellent mythogeographer."

"Hah!" replied my friend, who had been reading the label on the back of the bottle. "Is there such a field as Applied Mythogeography, Leon?"

"Heavens, no, Thomas, what are you thinking? Mythogeography isn't phantastics, after all, how could you apply it? I mean, well, there's cartography, I suppose, but…"

"Listen, then." And he read the following words from the back of the bottle:

"For over two-thousand years, the people of Zymurgia have devoted their lives to producing the world's best tasting ale. Nothing is allowed to interfere with the brewing process, which uses only the choicest ingredients and rain water. Now they offer it to the people of the Known World. The Zymurgian Trading Company is proud to bring you Basen Ale."

"Oh, dear," I said. "You don't suppose…"

"It does seem calculated to ensure the future supply, you must admit."

I stared into the fire, sipping my beer slowly. "I wonder if it will work," I said. "So far as I know, no one has ever tried to make use of the Law of Consensus. A rather frightening thought, that."

"Yes," said Carbuncle, "but potentially lucrative. And is it really worse than what has been going on in the Bundi Nations for the last hundred years?" I nodded; the Nations were notorious for occasional outbreaks of sectarian and anti-Anglish turmoil. "With a few simple lines, Frederick may have ensured peace in Zymurgia."

I nodded, still pondering. A new thought struck me. "I say, Thomas, could you explain something to me?" My friend nodded as he took a pull at his mug. "Back in Basenis Basor—your model—why were you so willing to sell it to Frederick? It's not like you, especially as it was nearly ready for activation."

"It was completely ready for activation, Leon, and that's why I sold it." I raised my eyebrows in silent query. "I could never have brought myself to activate the beastie, Leon, that's all."

"Why ever not?"

"I suppose there is no harm in telling; perhaps if you put it in that book you're supposed to be writing, it will prevent others from wasting their time." I looked out the window, half-expecting the sun to pass behind a cloud, so dolorous were Carbuncle's tones. "Human sacrifice, Leon, that's what it would have taken."

I recoiled so strongly I nearly upset my mug. I stared at it, feeling rather queasy. "So that's why it was designed never to be shut off." Carbuncle nodded.

"That's right. I would guess that even the original phantast found the price to be unpleasantly high. But there's worse, Leon."

"What could be worse? The Keepers haven't been feeding people to Basenis, have they?"

"No, but I rather think Basenis has been feeding himself from time to time. There must be a reason why he ravaged the villages and left the forests alone."

I put my mug down, and wiped my hand on my trouser leg. "Then it wasn't famine that caused Basenis to go prowling?"

Unexpectedly, Carbuncle smiled. "Oh, I rather think it was. I suspect that when Basenis' reserves run low, he needs a little extra life force to keep going. If the Zymurgians keep Basenis as well fed as young Frederick would like, I doubt they will have any trouble. Though I confess, I would not want to be the first fellow into Basenis' den in the morning."

"I wonder what effect this news will have on sales," I said, looking at my mug sadly.

"Cheer up, Leon," Carbuncle said to me. "Once the public have got over drinking idol-urine, I don't think a little human sacrifice will discourage them much." He took another pull at his mug. After a doubtful look at mine, I took another sip. It was delicious.

ACKNOWLEDGEMENTS.

✌ ☙

O NE DAY around the turn of the century I got my first lap-
top; and then I wrote some software to produce nice looking
HTML from a simple text markup I called "extended HTML".
And then I wanted to use it for something, so I sat down, and
started writing my first novel. ("Hi, my name is Will, and I'm
a geek.") I'd been reading about great explorers and scientific
expeditions of the Victorian era, and I thought, I've never seen
a fantasy novel with quite that flavor. I came up with a name—
Through Darkest Zymurgia!—and dove in.

I wrote it a scene or two at a time, and as I wrote it I read the
scenes aloud to my wife, Jane, (which made bad phrasing stick
out like a sore thumb); and she enjoyed it, and I enjoyed it, and
much to my surprise I finished it. I handed it to an editor a friend
of mine was acquainted with, and she told me that it was good
enough to publish but that the publishers weren't buying this kind
of thing. Undaunted, I sent it off to a major science fiction pub-
lisher; it came back seven days later, unread. And at that point
I decided that the fun part was writing and let the manuscript
collect dust.

After that I wrote another novel (which is complete but un-
revised); and then another, *Vikings at Dino's;* and by that time
indie publishing had happened, and my eldest son nagged me
until I got *Vikings at Dino's* into print. And I thought, well, in for
a penny, in a for a pound, and decided to get *Through Darkest
Zymurgia* into print as well. Apparently you, Constant Reader,
liked it well enough not only to keep reading but to read these
few words as well.

Anyway, I want to acknowledge the readers and listeners who
told me the book was good: my wife Jane; Pam Adams; Ian Hamet;
Julie Davis. But even more than that I want to acknowledge the
authors whose influence I saw in this book on re-reading. Stephen
King notes somewhere that writers are like milk; they taste like
what they've been standing next to in the refrigerator. And I might

add, put in enough of them and it makes quite a smoothie. So here they are, in alphabetical order.

Douglas Adams, of course. John Barnes' *One for the Morning Glory*. George MacDonald Fraser. H. Rider Haggard, especially *King Solomon's Mines*. Sven Hedin. Peter Hopkirk's books on *The Great Game* and Central Asia. Jerome K. Jerome's *Three Men in a Boat* (to say nothing of the dog, Bruno). Owen Lattimore's *Desert Road to Turkestan*. Patrick O'Brian, for nautical flavor. Elizabeth Peters, especially her tales of Amelia Peabody Emerson in Egypt. Terry Pratchett, whose world is also flat. *Incidents of Travel in Yucatan*, by John Lloyd Stevens. Sir Francis Younghusband. And most especially the master himself, P.G. Wodehouse, who is honored twice by name: in the city of Pelham, and in the founder of Thintwhistle's school, "Woody" Grenville.

I wasn't attempting to channel any of these writers; but each of them contributed in some way to the final dish.